T0121360

FINDING Lenore

ANN EDWARDS

BALBOA.PRESS

A DIVISION OF HAY HOUSE

Copyright © 2021 Ann Edwards.

All rights reserved. No part of this book may be used or reproduced by any means, graphic, electronic, or mechanical, including photocopying, recording, taping or by any information storage retrieval system without the written permission of the author except in the case of brief quotations embodied in critical articles and reviews.

Balboa Press books may be ordered through booksellers or by contacting:

Balboa Press
A Division of Hay House
1663 Liberty Drive
Bloomington, IN 47403
www.balboapress.com
844-682-1282

Because of the dynamic nature of the Internet, any web addresses or links contained in this book may have changed since publication and may no longer be valid. The views expressed in this work are solely those of the author and do not necessarily reflect the views of the publisher, and the publisher hereby disclaims any responsibility for them.

The author of this book does not dispense medical advice or prescribe the use of any technique as a form of treatment for physical, emotional, or medical problems without the advice of a physician, either directly or indirectly. The intent of the author is only to offer information of a general nature to help you in your quest for emotional and spiritual well-being. In the event you use any of the information in this book for yourself, which is your constitutional right, the author and the publisher assume no responsibility for your actions.

Any people depicted in stock imagery provided by Getty Images are models, and such images are being used for illustrative purposes only. Certain stock imagery © Getty Images.

Print information available on the last page.

ISBN: 978-1-9822-7101-5 (sc)
ISBN: 978-1-9822-7102-2 (e)

Library of Congress Control Number: 2021913070

Balboa Press rev. date: 07/22/2021

"For Andy and Every Other Beautiful Soul Who Has Blessed Me with Their Love"

Contents

Chapter One 2
Chapter Two 18
Chapter Three 34
Chapter Four.. 50
Chapter Five... 58
Chapter Six 72
Chapter Seven 88
Chapter Eight 98
Chapter Nine 111
Chapter Ten... 121
Chapter Eleven.. 136
Chapter Twelve 147
Chapter Thirteen 159
Chapter Fourteen 171
Chapter Fifteen 186
Chapter Sixteen... 199
Chapter Seventeen..209
Chapter Eighteen 219
Chapter Nineteen..226
Chapter Twenty 235
Chapter Twenty-One 248
Chapter Twenty-Two...252
Chapter Twenty-Three...263
Chapter Twenty-Four..270
Chapter Twenty-Five...284

"An emaciated goat!" The warlock's pale grey eyes were molten silver now, his face a mask of fury. "How dare you even consider this a suitable offering to the One we serve?"

"But, I…"

"Silence!" The warlock brought the tip of his jeweled sword to the acolyte's neck, pricking the skin just enough to draw a few drops of blood. "Don't insult me with your simpering excuses!"

It would have been so easy just to slit the man's throat and be done with it.

But the full coven was needed for tonight's special ritual.

There must be thirteen.

He lowered his sword.

"Get this pathetic beast into the altar room. Now!"

Chapter One

The high-performance engine grumbled at the insult of being slammed into first gear as Diana turned sharply onto a dirt road she would have sailed right by if it hadn't been for the marker she'd been told to look for, an old whitewashed wagon wheel leaning against a sturdy oak. Dodging a few potholes, she inched her way along until she came to a neatly graveled drive that led to a small parking area behind a surprisingly modest white frame colonial. The paint was pristine, the trim a crisp burgundy, but the structure was far less imposing than she had expected it to be.

Swinging through the automatic motions of a tight k-turn, she backed her gleaming red Porsche into a narrow slot between a high rhododendron hedge and a well-traveled white Jeep Cherokee. She knew it wasn't likely that any reporters had followed her here, but years of being pursued by paparazzi had taught her the wisdom of ducking into a concealed spot wherever possible, always positioning the car for a quick getaway.

Cutting the engine, she flipped the visor down to check the mirror for any touch-ups that might be needed. Lipstick, definitely, and she quickly dabbed on a fresh coat of pale coral to replenish what her nerves had chewed away during the two-hour drive up here from Manhattan. Other than that, she was satisfied that she looked her best. No crying jag yet today, so her eye makeup hadn't smudged, and hairspray had done its job keeping her long blonde mane in place.

Unable to come up with any other delaying tactic, she grabbed her purse and climbed slowly out of the car, locking it with a quick chirp of the remote and sliding her keys into an easily accessible jacket pocket at her right hip. She had no reason to think that she'd need to run from an emergency situation while she was here, but old defensive habits died hard. With a quick glance to scope out her immediate surroundings and seeing no sign of having been followed, she set out on a slate walkway that led up toward the front of the house.

She'd only taken a few steps when she felt the all-too-familiar stirrings of a panic attack. Willing herself to stay calm, slowing her pace as much as she could without coming to a complete standstill, she began the deep breathing yoga technique that she knew was her only escape from a full-blown meltdown. As she hoped, within a few minutes her breathing began to normalize.

When she reached the crest of the incline at the end of the walkway, she paused to allow her pulse to settle. While she breathed slowly and deeply, she tried to focus her ricocheting thoughts on the serenity of the landscape that had just come into view. Vineyards and orchards dotted the hills as far as the eye could see, and the Hudson River glistened in the valley below, its majestic passage guarded by the soaring heights of the Catskill Mountains. It seemed inconceivable that the steel canyons of New York City were little more than a hundred miles away from this idyllic spot.

Well, kiddo, she thought, taking one more long, deep breath, you're as ready for prime time as you're likely to be today, so let's just get it done. She had just turned toward the stairs that led up to a covered porch, when the front door was opened by the woman she had come to see. They'd never met before, but dogged media coverage had made each of them instantly recognizable to the other.

"Welcome, Diana!" Slender and tall, lithe and limber as a dancer, the renowned psychic gave a little wave and hurried down the steps.

"Hello, Ariana!" Before their session today, a screening phone call had determined that they'd both been fully vaccinated against Covid months earlier, so Ariana didn't hesitate to extend both her hands in greeting. A chill ran through her when she grasped Diana's hands.

As Diana reluctantly pulled away from the warmth of Ariana's touch, a lifelong habit of assessing the competition had her wondering how Ariana's modest appearance could be so compelling. Her face was completely unadorned, except for the palest bronze lip gloss. Her jet black hair was piled into a loose knot atop her head, and she was casually dressed in khaki pants and a beige shirt under a bulky brown cardigan. Her brown leather clogs had clearly seen some mileage, and her only visible jewelry was a colorful strand of quartz stones that hung about her graceful neck. It all stopped being a mystery the moment she focused on the woman's eyes. They were a remarkable indigo color, dark sapphire flecked with violet. Framed by arching dark brows against fair skin, those captivating eyes simply drew you in and wouldn't let go.

"Any trouble getting here?" Ariana gestured for Diana to follow her up the steps.

"None at all. Traffic leaving the city was the usual crush, but your directions were perfect."

"Glad to hear it." Ariana had left the front door slightly ajar. She pushed it fully open now and led the way into the front hall, closing the sturdy oak door behind them and quickly keying in a code on the high-tech alarm pad near the entrance. The precaution surprised Diana. In broad daylight, in rural Columbia County, New York, in such an ordinary looking old house, it seemed almost paranoid. Moments later, when she saw the magnificent art collection that adorned the living room walls, she completely understood the precaution.

Coasting smoothly into hostess mode, Ariana invited her younger visitor to take a closer look at some of the paintings that she was so obviously admiring. She wasn't a procrastinator by nature, but she shared Diana's clear reluctance to begin their session. Every one of her formidable instincts were screaming that they were both in for a harrowing experience.

When they'd completed the circuit of the living room art collection, Ariana drew aside the draperies against the far wall and pointed to the deck just beyond the previously concealed glass doors. "That's where we'll be doing our session today." Seeing the panic in Diana's eyes, she quickly added, "It's enclosed, so we'll be warm. I promise."

Totally unconvinced, Diana nodded slowly, unable to think of a single polite thing to say, understanding now why her hostess hadn't offered to take her coat when she arrived and grateful now for its warmth. Between sickness and sleep deprivation, her body's thermostat was in freefall most of the time, as unreliable as her treacherous heartbeat.

"There's a powder room just down this hall." Ariana led the way along a short corridor off the living room. They passed what had to be the family room, its functionality defined by a huge flat-screen TV, cushy sofas, and a wall of books and what were probably board games. Just a few steps further down the hall was a small sunny yellow bathroom, its door partially open.

Ariana flicked on the light and did a quick scan of the room to make sure that the lemon-scented soap and daisy-patterned hand towels had been freshly stocked. They were flawless, just as she had expected.

"See you out on the deck, Diana." Ariana was already retracing her steps along the corridor, silently apologizing to her wonderfully thorough, efficient, and completely trustworthy housekeeper for that final check on the bathroom. Ariana knew that obsessive-compulsive disorders were typical of the Virgo personality, but she didn't like thinking of herself as being typical anything, and it both amused and annoyed her to know that she was.

A few minutes later, Diana made her way out to the deck. Ariana was putting the finishing touches on a tea tray that was set out on a pine table between two Adirondack chairs. "The tea is ready, Diana" she smiled. "Please, have a seat."

When Diana had settled herself in the nearer chair, Ariana handed her a steaming cup. "It's my own blend. Hope you like it." It was meant to soothe jittery nerves, not intrigue the palate, and she was fairly certain that Diana would loathe it.

"Smells wonderful." Good manners demanded the polite lie, and Diana smiled brightly, but the stuff actually smelled awful.

Suppressing a grin, Ariana gestured to the tea tray. "Please, help yourself. Maybe some honey?"

Diana glanced at the honey, cream, sugar, lemon and some unidentifiable pale brown squares that she guessed were both wholesome and flavor-free brownie wannabes. "No thanks. This is fine." Silk purses and sow's ears came to mind, and she didn't see any point in even attempting to make the foul-smelling concoction more palatable.

Trying to find a comfortable perch on the sharply angled contours of her chair, Diana took a tentative sip of tea and somehow managed not to wince. While Ariana added lemon and honey to her own cup, Diana took a closer look at her surroundings.

The deck was snugly tucked under what appeared to be an extension of the second story eaves. The old house seemed to wrap itself around it on three sides, but a scattering of small skylights and an outside wall of French doors kept it bright and cheery. Two of the glass doors were open now, and Diana smiled at the sight and sound of a miniature waterfall merrily splashing in the midst of a serenely beautiful rock garden, its evergreen plantings seamlessly extending into the foliage of the woods beyond.

"What a lovely spot!" said Diana, thinking how much lovelier it would be without the sharp scent of the pungent herbs that were scattered in clay pots all around the deck.

"It's a little Spartan," said Ariana. "But it's ideal for my work."

Diana ventured a deep breath and almost laughed at the instant heady sensation. Maybe all the smelly foliage wasn't so bad after all. "Certainly is peaceful out here. And the energy flow is incredible!" She was surprised to feel warm enough to shrug off her coat, but left it draped on the back of her chair just in case.

Ariana smiled and nodded her agreement as she slid smoothly back in her chair and tried not to laugh at Diana's fidgeting. "I'm afraid the chair's design is a little diabolical, Diana. It compels you to lean back into it and really relax, or suffer. No in-between." She guessed that the lowly Adirondack chair had never had a place in this young woman's pampered world.

"Okay... Here goes." Diana set her teacup down on the broad arm of her chair and slowly eased herself back until her head was resting against the hard pine slats. She just hoped that Ariana wasn't reading her thoughts at that moment. The uncushioned chair was an absolute monstrosity.

Eager for a non-threatening topic that might help her jittery guest feel more at ease, Ariana turned the discussion to Diana's sister. "I was nearly speechless when Beth called to set up our meeting. Since when did she become a believer?" Beth Wendell was a features writer for Newsworld magazine and one of the few reporters Ariana hadn't learned to fear.

"Since..." Diana shook her head and laughed gently. "Actually, since never. Even though she buys me things like this occasionally." She touched a hand to the Herkimer crystal pendant that glittered against the deep burgundy of her sweater. "Beth's still the skeptic she's always been. It absolutely makes her crazy that I'm so into anything to do with the paranormal." Diana struggled to swallow another sip of tea. It just never got any better.

A smile danced in Ariana's eyes as she recalled her first meeting with Beth. "I remember how my jaw dropped when your sister flat-out told me, not ten minutes after she arrived on my doorstep, that she thought trance-channeling was a complete sham and that anybody who actually believed in it had to be delusional."

"But the article..."

"I know," Ariana chuckled. "She promised to keep her personal bias out of the final product, and she did. Go figure. A reporter with integrity. I was stunned." Seeing Diana begin to relax, she allowed the silence to play itself out for a few moments longer, before adding, "It was good to talk with her again after such a long time."

"I'm just grateful she called, and doubly grateful that you were able to see me on such short notice. With all your books and CDs, I know how busy you must be."

Ariana inclined her head and nodded. "The real priority, of course, is my daughter, so keeping the publishers happy is always a challenge. I've pretty much had to give up all private consulting because of time constraints." She smiled at the question she saw in Diana's eyes. "Beth was very persuasive."

"My big sister to the rescue yet again," smiled Diana.

Ariana heard no hint of resentment in her tone, only love. Trying to give Diana's nerves a little more breathing room, she said, "Tell me a little about the rest of your family. Like everyone else, I admit to being shamelessly curious about the real people behind the great Gresham empire."

Diana gave a reluctant little nod. "Not much of our family left, I'm afraid. Our folks and grandparents were killed in a plane crash when we were just kids." She wondered if that awful ache would ever go away whenever she thought of them. She reached for her tea, and then thought better of it, brushing an imaginary fleck of lint off the sleeve of her beige jacket instead. At that moment, nothing would have been more welcome than a good hot cup of oolong. Or better yet, a good stiff brandy.

"Beth's just two years older than me, Ariana, but I kind of forced her into the role of surrogate mom and never let her escape it."

"What about your legal guardian?" The whole world had heard the story about the orphaned heiresses to the Gresham-Wendell fortune, but she was trying to get Diana to loosen up, and encouraging her to talk about the people she loved seemed the easiest way to do it. She could only regret her young visitor's clear aversion to her special blend of calming tea.

"My mom's sister Olivia was our legal guardian," explained Diana. "But even at the ripe old age of seven, Beth was more responsible than Aunt Liv has ever been." Ariana was pleased to see Diana smile, her eyes full of affectionate memory.

"Aunt Liv and her whole crowd followed the seasonal migratory path of the idle rich every year. They still do. Kind of like snow geese with Infinite Visas. " Ariana smiled and nodded her appreciation of the image, as Diana went on speaking.

"We tagged along with them everywhere, traipsing all over hell and gone for years. Beth just got sick of it. Soon as she was eighteen, she went away to college, then to work. 'Work' was and is the original four-letter word to my aunt."

Diana crossed one long slender leg over the other and brushed a wisp of pale blond hair back from her brow. "Me too, I guess. I really enjoyed all the mindless fun and games, so I stayed with Aunt Liv. At least that's where I was until... Until the doctors told me the bad news."

She took a deep breath, exhaling on a sigh. "We were partying in Switzerland at the time, but it didn't take me long to go running back to Beth like a homing pigeon. Dearly as I love Aunt Liv, Beth's my touchstone, really the only consistently stable element in my life. I don't know what I'd do without her."

Braving another sip of tea, she continued reminiscing about the two women who had been so important throughout her life. Ariana was pleased to see her beginning to wind down, more tranquil now, hopefully ready to move on to the deeper relaxation she would need for the psychic journey they were about to take together. When Diana was silent for a few moments, even attempting another sip of tea, Ariana decided it was time to test the waters.

"You already know what to expect here today, Diana." They had discussed the procedure by telephone just the day before. "Any questions before we start?"

Diana's cup clattered against its saucer as she quickly moved her tea to a safer place on the table beside her. "I don't think so," she said, embarrassed by the shakiness she heard in her voice. Stiffening her spine, she sat bolt upright, white-knuckled fists clenching the arms of her chair.

Seeing how frozen the waters still were, Ariana summoned megadoses of warmth and encouragement into her voice. "You know, we don't have to do this, Diana. If you're having any second thoughts at all, perhaps..."

"No. I'm fine. Really I am." Suddenly aware of her contradictory body language, Diana whipped her blond mane back over her shoulders with a pert toss of her head, uncrossed her legs, and solidly planted her feet on the ground as she unclenched her fists and eased back into her chair. Primly crossing the palm of one hand atop the back of the other, she took a deep breath and managed to relax her facial muscles into some semblance of a smile. "No second thoughts. Just some last-minute nerves, that's all. Let's do it."

Ariana nodded slowly, every instinct warning her to go no further with this session. But what reason could she possibly give for sending Diana away now? "Okay," she sighed. "Let's get on with it then."

Ariana took a long, slow breath before raising a tutorial forefinger and speaking sternly to Diana. "You absolutely must remember to breathe deeply while I'm in trance state. Channeling Philip can sometimes be exhausting, and I may need to tap into your chi, your life force, to get me through. Your breath will keep regenerating that chi, and I need to depend on it being there when I need it."

Diana was already practicing. Eyes wide, she was emulating Ariana's example and breathing slowly, deeply and evenly. Please God there would be no panic attack while Ariana was off somewhere on the astral plane.

"Good," said Ariana. "As long as you can do that and keep alert, we'll both be fine. It's not going to be a very productive session if the two of us end up in trance mode."

"Trust me," said Diana, leveling her gaze at Ariana. "There's no way I'm zoning out today." She hoped her voice sounded more confident than she felt. Fussing with her hands, she tried resting them on her thighs, then clasping them in her lap, before settling on the solid comfort of gripping the chair's armrests. "Anything else I need to know?"

Ariana felt the hope in Diana's heart, and it gave her no joy. As much as she hated having to do it, she cautioned, "Please remember that Philip is simply a very wise old spirit who has chosen, for whatever reasons, to reveal himself to me. I'm only a channel for his words, and he's not a miracle worker."

"Disclaimer duly noted," sighed Diana. She quickly glanced away, but not before Ariana saw the sheen of tears in her eyes. Diana's voice was barely above a whisper when she spoke again.

"Marita, the healer I told you about yesterday, keeps insisting that my nightmares hold the key to a cure for my illness. She calls it a 'healing nexus'." Diana swallowed hard, blinking back tears before she allowed her gaze to meet the psychic's once more. "Unfortunately, she keeps coming up empty whenever she tries to find it. That's why I'm here."

Diana clenched the armrests even harder as she leaned forward. "If there's anything, anything at all in those awful dreams that could help me, I've got to know. Time's running out on me." She gave a little cough to masque the sudden break in her voice. "Philip may just be my last chance to get some answers before it's too late."

Slowly nodding her understanding, Ariana sipped thoughtfully at her tea for a few moments. "Okay then," she said, settling her cup on the table between them and regretting the sudden tight kink at the back of her neck, always an unwelcome herald of a difficult session to come.

"Let's take a closer look at those nightmares before we go on, Diana. It often helps if we can bring the demons into the light of day. At least it's worth a try."

Seeing the young woman's hesitation, Ariana focused on sending her whatever calming energy she could spare. Forcing the appearance of relaxation, she rested her hands on her lap and smiled encouragingly. Diana had described her dreams during their phone conversation the day before, but only in the most general terms, and Ariana needed to know more about them.

Diana nodded reluctantly. She didn't want to discuss her nightmares at all, but she hadn't driven all this way to be evasive. "It's always the same, Ariana. Exact in every detail." She took a deep breath, sighing it out, trembling hands clutching the armrests of her chair.

"I'm lying naked on a stone slab somewhere in the middle of the woods. I'm outside. I'm cold. I can smell the pine trees and see the stars, but there's no moonlight. The only light at all comes from a big black candle at my feet. People in dark hooded robes are dancing all around me, chanting strange words. Suddenly, a figure looms above me chanting louder than the rest. The voice is male, and I can never remember his features, but he has the iciest gray eyes imaginable. He's holding a big jeweled sword, and I wake up just as he lunges forward to..."

"Enough!" commanded Ariana. Suppressing an involuntary shudder, she reached across the table to grasp Diana's hand. It was ice cold. And no wonder. Even the unspoken horrific details of the nightmare had just flashed through her mind's eye. "Let it go now, Diana. Just let it go."

She continued holding Diana's hand until she seemed calmer, then gave it a gentle squeeze and leaned back in her chair. There was only one other thing about the dreams that she needed to know. Then they could abandon the subject entirely. She watched Diana carefully.

"The timing could be significant, Diana. Exactly when did the dreams start?"

"Soon after I was diagnosed. I was still in St. Moritz at the time, and I went to see a psychic there, Lily Verne, someone I've been seeing off and on for years. Unfortunately, dream interpretation isn't her forte. She sent me to someone else, and I've been bouncing from one referral to another ever since."

"And no one's been able to help at all?"

Diana shook her head. "Not until Marita."

"And I presume you vetted all these psychic advisors thoroughly, yes?"

Diana nodded. "My watchdogs at Dunsford Security do their homework really well, Ariana. Everybody checked out okay. Plus, 'though I've never gone near any of the dark stuff, I've been exploring the paranormal world long enough to recognize the charlatans."

Ariana studied the lovely young woman before her. The flawless complexion, vivid blue eyes, delicate features, and shining blonde hair made her appear even younger than her years. She could well imagine what an easy mark she would be for the all the fakes and frauds eager to milk her misery for their own profit.

"Just how old were you when you started seeing psychics?" asked Ariana.

"Sixteen. My sixteenth birthday, to be precise. Aunt Liv hired a famous Brit as part of the entertainment, and I was hooked. Since I got sick, of course, it's become kind of an obsession. My sister's terrified that the brain tumor is making me crazy. I guess I am too. Sometimes my behavior's erratic as hell, even for me."

Ariana was rapidly remembering all the reasons why she had given up regular private consultations years ago. It was heart-wrenching. And the karmic responsibility of direct involvement with individual lives was always a precarious juggling act. Added to that was the problem of having to deal with the occasional high-profile client such as Diana who was a magnet for the one thing she had truly learned to loathe: publicity.

Ariana vividly recalled Diana's world. She had been part of it once as the wife of a brilliantly successful investment banker, each of them from old money, their names prominently listed on everything from the Social Register and Quest 400 to the Southampton Blue Book. His sudden death had changed everything.

The planned two-month mourning period spent with her daughter at the family's weekend retreat in the Catskills had extended into a permanent move, and primarily because of Philip. He had made his unexpected debut just two weeks after her husband's passing, causing a cataclysmic upheaval in her career, lengthening the shadows of what were already the darkest days of her life.

The transition from Dr. Alexandra Ariana Reed, legitimate mental health practitioner, to a psychic channeler known only as Ariana had been a painful one, and she had suffered more than her fair share of ridicule at the hands of the press because of it.

In the beginning, it was generally agreed that she had suffered a complete nervous breakdown after her husband's death and was projecting Philip from her subconscious as a replacement for all that she had lost. Over time, however, as Philip's predictions began validating his existence, the press began treating her with slightly less disdain, and she didn't need or want to allow the media vultures back into her well-ordered life.

Published transcriptions and CD's of her own privately channeled sessions with Philip generated healthy royalties for the college scholarship foundation she had endowed in her late husband's memory, and her ego didn't require any more than that for sustenance. She quietly did frequent pro bono work for police departments in the Northeast, and she occasionally did individual consultations, but always, as now, with reluctance. She simply hadn't been able to refuse this dying woman's plea for a meeting with Philip.

Knowing she had put off the inevitable long enough, Ariana took a last sip of tea. "Well, we've a lot to do, Diana, so we'd best get on with it." She put their cups on the tea tray and carried it to a storage unit that was recessed into the wall behind them. It had a wide ledge at waist height, perfect for a work surface, and she settled the tray there before opening the drawer beneath it to retrieve the items needed for their session.

She returned with a white beeswax candle, matches, and two small tape recorders, each of which she carefully arranged on the table between them. While lighting the candle, Ariana whispered a prayer that Diana couldn't quite hear. She then repositioned one of the tape recorders by a fraction of an inch. "I suppose you know the reason for these, Diana."

Diana nodded. "One for you, one for me, both recording simultaneously in case of mechanical malfunction." She had been through enough channeling sessions to know the drill.

Ariana extended a hand toward the recorders. "Okay with you if I turn them on now?"

"Of course."

In a clear, strong voice, Ariana began praying for protection from the darkness. "Let no positive or negative forces from without or within harm us. Let only light and love surround us. Let Michael the blessed Archangel shield us from the powers of darkness. And let his sword of light protect us throughout our journey to the other realm. Amen."

When she was finished, she took a deep breath, did a few shoulder rolls to help ease that insistent kink in her neck, then settled herself more comfortably against the back of her chair. "Before I get into alpha state, I just want to give you a little warning about Philip's slightly unorthodox presentation skills."

Diana nodded her understanding. "I've devoured every transcript, tape and CD you've ever done."

"I'm flattered. But only my private sessions with Philip have ever been released. All consultations with clients are and will always remain completely confidential I assure you."

"Glad to hear it." She felt a nervous little tic at the corner of her mouth. It totally mocked her attempt at a smile. Licking her lips, she forced her head to relax against the back of the chair.

"Just be prepared for more theatricality than you've ever heard on the published tapes. Philip loves performing for a new audience."

It occurred to Diana that Ariana could have been describing a well-loved but undisciplined child.

"Apart from the physical limitations of my own voicebox," explained Ariana, "please understand that I have absolutely no control over what he says or how he says it."

"I understand," said Diana, her fears beginning to escalate.

"You'll be fine, Diana. Philip is an entirely spiritual entity who can't hurt you in any way. Ask him whatever you like, and he'll respond with complete candor. Sometimes he's brutally frank, sometimes he goes off on a tangent and gets to be a bore, but he's always honest. That much I can promise you." Knowing how sick Diana was, Ariana couldn't help but worry about the toll this session might take on her already depleted energy reserves. "Are you sure you're up to all this?"

Not trusting her own voice, Diana bit at her lower lip and slowly nodded.

"Okay, then. Let's begin." Ariana closed her eyes and began breathing deeply.

Diana focused on keying the rhythm of her own breathing pattern to Ariana's. As the minutes passed, she continued into deeper relaxation, breathing slowly, lulled by the gentle murmur of water splashing along the garden rocks. Remembering Ariana's instructions, she was desperately struggling to resist the beckoning haze, vaguely aware that she was losing the battle, when a booming voice suddenly jolted her back to her senses with an instant adrenaline rush.

"Lenore! We meet again at last!" The normal pitch of Ariana's voice had dropped a full octave, its volume several decibels louder than it had been before.

Diana couldn't remember Philip's voice being quite so forceful on any of the audiotapes or CD's she'd heard over the years, and its almost hostile tone sent shivers of apprehension dancing along her spine. She did a quick perimeter scan, then craned her neck to peer through the glass doors leading to the living room. There was no one else in sight. Had Philip actually sensed another presence nearby? Or had he simply not known her real name?

Feeling more than a little uneasy, Diana glanced nervously over her shoulder once more, then refocused her attention on Ariana. The psychic seemed completely untroubled, as outwardly placid as she had been before, her breathing too soft to be heard, her eyes closed, her face a tranquil mask. Her earlier warning about Philip's theatrical bent suddenly flashed into Diana's mind, and she remembered to breathe deeply again, smiling at her own skittishness.

Clearly, Philip was making a grand entrance. She just wished he hadn't gotten her name wrong. Insulting, and certainly not very reassuring. What kind of reading could she hope to get if he didn't even know who she was? Willing herself to relax, Diana waited quietly for him to speak again, but the seconds continued to tick away in silence. Was he waiting for her to say something? Summoning her courage, she whispered, "Philip?" Hearing the fear in her voice, she shook her head, cleared her throat, and called to him again, this time very decisively. "Philip, are you there?"

"I am here, Lenore." The voice still had a distinct bass resonance, but it was almost soothing now, so soft that Diana had to strain to hear it. And yet her pulse had once again kicked into overdrive. Why? Trance-channeling wasn't a new experience for her. She thought she knew the whole drill. So what was going on here? And why did Philip persist in calling her 'Lenore'? If he was totally confused about her identity, this whole session would be a colossal waste.

"Philip, this is Diana Wendell speaking. Diana Gresham-Wendell. Do you know who I am?"

The response was immediate. "You are the entity who is now called Diana, but I first observed you as Lenore, and Lenore you have always been to me."

Diana nodded and smiled, relieved that he knew who she was after all. Past-life regressions with Lily were familiar territory to her, and the name 'Lenore' had never surfaced in any of their readings over the years. She could only guess that Ariana and Philip were hooked up with a more extensive astral pipeline than any of Lily's.

Curiosity trumping her nervousness, Diana said, "You mean we actually met during a previous incarnation?" She was surprised by the fragility in her voice. It sounded like that of an insatiably curious and very young child.

"No. I was never of your world. I observed your activities only because they touched upon the life of one whom I had been sent to guide."

"Really? When did all this happen?" When he offered no reply, she persisted. "When did this person you call 'Lenore' live as a physical entity on the earth plane?"

This time, the response was unhesitating. "She chose to incarnate during the darkest days of the last Great War," intoned the voice. "She entered your earth plane on the very day that mankind unleashed the destructive force of the atom upon itself."

History had never been Diana's forte, but even she knew what he meant. "Are you saying that she was born on the day Hiroshima…"

Philip interrupted with a shout. "Yes!" In a less forceful tone, he added, "With her first breath, she drew untold power from the negative energy released throughout the world on that terrible day."

Diana needed only a few seconds to do the math. "Then how can I possibly have lived as Lenore? Hiroshima was only about seventy years ago, and I'm already twenty-seven. Lenore's life and mine would have overlapped. Unless she died very young."

"She did."

"Even so, it's not very likely that her soul would have reincarnated again quickly enough to be born in me. I've read that some souls go for centuries between incarnations."

"Not yours."

"Why? Why not mine?"

"There was a need, and you returned."

She was fascinated by the notion that she might have returned to the earth plane as quickly as

Philip had indicated, but she was afraid to waste time exploring the past when there was so much she needed to know about the future.

"You know I'm dying, don't you?" Diana was glad to hear the strength and clarity in her voice. She hadn't trusted it to be so.

"Your physical body will cease to function one day. Such is the lot of all mortal entities."

"Will it be soon?"

"Soon?" He seemed genuinely perplexed.

It took her a few moments to think of a concept of time that would be meaningful to him. "Will I live long enough to have children?" Her voice was barely a whisper.

"Such is not ordained in this incarnation."

The oracle has spoken, mused Diana, her eyes misting, but she was fiercely determined not to waste precious time with tears. Philip could vanish at any moment, and they still hadn't talked about her nightmares.

"Is there anything I can do to change that destiny?" she asked in a small, almost inaudible voice.

"It would be unwise to try. You have chosen your fate to repay part of the grievous karmic debt your soul incurred as Lenore."

"What debt? What did she do?" Diana's tone was sharp with impatience. She didn't even attempt to hide her resentment at the turn the conversation had once again taken. Why was he so obsessed with this woman Lenore?

There was a long pause before Philip answered. "Lenore was a powerful witch," he said, his voice totally without inflection or emotion. "High priestess of a black coven. Many innocents were sacrificed at her altar."

The final scene from Diana's nightmare flashed before her mind's eye, but she wouldn't allow herself to embrace the karmic connection Philip was trying to establish. "You're talking of medieval horrors. How can any of that have to do with someone who was born in the nineteen forties?"

"Your dreams relive the past, but the past is ever the present, as it was once the future."

She refused to be drawn into philosophical word games that could only waste time. "Look," she sighed, "I've done past life regressions before. Many times. I've seen myself as everything from a pioneer woman in the wilds of Wyoming to a French courtesan, a Roman matron, an Egyptian slave, even a knight in the Crusades. Never, and I repeat, never, have I seen myself as a witch, and surely that would have been one of the first past lives to emerge, especially if it was as significant as you seem to think it was."

"Your subconscious has kept Lenore buried in your unconscious mind. She is there, and she has grown impatient. She is the cause of your nightmares. They will continue until you acknowledge her presence and begin to make amends for her misdeeds."

Diana was angry with his insistence that Lenore's fate, if indeed any such person had ever existed, was inextricably linked to her own. What did any of it matter anyway? She already had the answer she had come to find. With one simple phrase: 'such is not ordained in this incarnation,' he had annihilated her last hope of finding a cure, and she had little interest in anything else he might have to say.

She quietly resolved to say nothing more, hoping that he would soon grow bored with her silence and go off to whatever part of the astral plane he inhabited when he wasn't amusing himself by taunting gullible mortals. Numb with despair, she wanted to run away and hide somewhere, cry until she couldn't cry any more. But she knew she couldn't leave until Ariana awakened.

A strange sound suddenly emanated from Ariana's throat. It wasn't a laugh, not even a chuckle, but Diana sensed that it was an expression of amusement. "What's so funny?"

"Nothing. Everything. The irony of it all! Your predisposition to doubt and distrust would have served you well as Lenore, but it is entirely misplaced now. I am not your enemy! I am here to be of service to you, to help you along the karmic path you have chosen."

"So you say."

"And so you should believe. There is proof of all I have said. It rests with those who knew Lenore. A few have aligned with dark forces that continue to keep them on your earth plane. Find them and you will find your destiny."

Diana swallowed hard. "Just a little wild-goose chase to amuse me while I'm waiting around to die -- is that it, Philip?"

"Your levity insults me and mocks the laws of karma. I have shown you the true path. Do with it what you will."

It was a dismissal, and Diana thought she would have been glad to see him go, but she suddenly felt panic-stricken, as if a lifeline had just been snatched from her grasp. After all, he hadn't said that a cure was impossible, only that it wasn't ordained. But what about the power to change destiny -- wasn't that what free will was all about? What if her destiny really was somehow linked to those who knew Lenore, whoever she was? What if she could find them and somehow balance the karmic scales in time to...?

"Wait! Please don't go yet." She spoke quickly, certain that he would soon be gone. "Who are these people who knew Lenore? How can I find them?"

There was a long period of silence before Philip responded. "They are still to be found in the village where she lived and died."

"What village? Where?"

"Not far from this place. You have been there before in your present body."

"I've been to villages all over the world! Please. Can't you be a little more specific?" She felt the tears streaming down her cheeks, but she didn't even raise a hand to wipe them away. She couldn't move. She was scarcely able to breathe. It seemed an eternity before he replied.

"Look for a cemetery high on a hill overlooking a pastoral valley. Begin your search there."

She waited a moment, hoping for more, but no further information was forthcoming. "It's really not very much to go on, is it?"

"I can say no more. I have already said too much. All you need to know is within you, Lenore."

"But I'm not Lenore! When I look within, there are no answers, only questions."

"The answers are there. You have but to acknowledge them. For too long you have ignored your innate spirituality, dabbling in the psychic world like a clumsy neophyte, subconsciously fearful of repeating Lenore's terrible mistakes, but all that is over now. You will soon be passing out of the earth plane, and your higher self, your soul, has already begun preparing for the journey. Through prayer and meditation you will find the gifts and knowledge that you seek."

Diana heard the unmistakable finality in Philip's words and she wasn't surprised when, moments later, Ariana began to stir. Her lashes fluttered open, indigo eyes slowly coming into focus as her gaze settled upon Diana.

"How did it go?" she asked, her voice not quite her own yet.

"I'm not really sure." Diana gave a self-conscious little laugh as she frantically brushed tears from her face. Suddenly chilled to the bone, she pulled her coat back on and buttoned it with trembling fingers.

Ariana gave a small tired smile. "I'm guessing Philip gave you his usual overdose of food for thought." She flicked the rewind buttons on both tape recorders and gathered a few wayward silken tendrils back into the hairclip atop her head.

Diana sighed. "And then some." She stood, a determinedly bright smile on her face as she belted her coat. "It's certainly been... memorable." Reaching for the purse she'd tucked beside her on the chair, she inquired about Ariana's fee.

"You owe me nothing, Diana. Please accept my humble gift with the blessings of the universe on all that you do." She stood and touched a hand to Diana's forearm as she said a formal closing prayer for her safety and well-being. By the time she was done, the tapes were rewound. She tested them both, then, satisfied with their clarity, ejected one and handed it over to Diana.

As they said their good-byes, she could see that Diana's aura was dark with fear and confusion, but until she heard the tape of her session with Philip she didn't dare try to ease her distress. From long experience, she had learned not to trust her judgment or her instincts in the exhausted and disoriented moments following a prolonged trance.

"Perhaps we can meet again, Diana, after I've had a chance to hear what Philip had to say."

"That would be lovely. I'd like that." Diana knew that the lie would be transparent to Ariana, but she didn't really care.

When she was finally alone on the desolate country road that led from Ariana's to the main highway, she gave up trying to be brave. When she saw an ice cream shop that had been boarded up for the winter, she braked into the rutted driveway and parked in the empty lot adjacent to the ramshackle old building.

Idling was not the Porsche's forte, but she needed it running as much for warmth as for safety, so she didn't cut the engine. She quickly checked to make sure the doors were locked, then cracked both windows so she wouldn't asphyxiate herself. Pulling a wad of tissues out of her purse, she settled in for her own private pity party.

After all she'd done to set the stage, she felt ridiculous when the tears never came. What was wrong with her? She almost laughed at that one. What wasn't wrong with her? The mood swings were getting worse every day. Plus, she was probably too angry to cry.

Through Ariana, Philip had just confirmed what all her doctors had decreed. Basically, there wasn't a damn thing that could be done for her, and it was all over but the shouting. She was angry with everyone and everything, including herself. Maybe herself most of all for mindlessly partying her life away. Had she ever done a single thing that she could point to with pride?

Playing her own devil's advocate, she reminded herself that she had every right to enjoy being young, carefree and rich as Croesus. She'd never deliberately hurt anybody, well not much anyway, and she'd donated millions to charity every year. Why not have fun? What was wrong with letting the good times roll? Sure, she'd made some mistakes, but that didn't make her a bad person, did it?

She was no stranger to the seven deadly sins, and she welcomed two of them now. Anger and pride were exactly the one-two punch she needed to get her sorry butt in gear. She would admit to being a royal screw-up most of her adult life, but she damn well could and would make the best of whatever time she had left. And she suddenly knew exactly how she would do it. She'd never gone anywhere gently, and she wasn't about to start now.

Tossing the unused tissues back in her purse, she closed the windows and revved up the Porsche. Skirting the worst of the potholes in the parking lot, she turned back onto the rural country road that was the shortest route to the main highway that she needed to get home. By the time she was cruising along the scenic Taconic State Parkway, she'd come up with what she thought was a brilliant plan. The first hurdle would be convincing her sister that she wasn't totally certifiable.

There was no misunderstanding the Dark Lord's warning.

The entire coven was in grave danger.

But how could this possibly be happening?

Chapter Two

"That you, Di?"

"Better be me, huh?" Locking the door to Beth's penthouse behind her, Diana quickly reset the alarm on the hallway keypad and followed the sound of her sister's voice into the living room. Wearing her usual at-home uniform of jeans, fuzzy socks, and a baggy sweater, Beth was huddled with her laptop at one end of the plush ivory sofa opposite the fireplace. The intensity of her expression screamed that she was racing to meet a deadline for her weekly Newsworld features column and wouldn't welcome being interrupted.

The moment their eyes met, Diana could only sigh with relief when Beth immediately closed the laptop and unceremoniously shunted it off to the coffee table. Swinging her feet to the floor, she waved Diana forward. "Come sit, baby sister." She patted the cushion beside her. "Rough one, huh?" Diana's heart gave a grateful little lurch as she snuggled into the comforting warmth of Beth's arm about her shoulders.

"Yeah." Her voice was ragged with the threat of all those tears she'd been unable to shed in that deserted parking lot. She swallowed hard, breathed long and deep, then swallowed hard again. She was so tired. If she started blubbering now, she wasn't sure she'd have the energy to stop. "Tell you all about it later, Sis. First I need a drink, then a nap."

"Long day," sympathized Beth. "Let me get that drink." She gave Diana's shoulder a little squeeze before getting up and going to the built-in liquor cabinet in an alcove just off the living room. There was always a bottle of their favorite Chopin vodka in the bar's mini-freezer, and she poured each of them a double shot, no ice needed or wanted. Grabbing two coasters, she dropped them on the black lacquered coffee table as she handed Diana her drink and sat back down beside her. They clinked glasses and took a few quick anesthetizing sips of the vodka.

"You know," said Diana, her voice a little hoarse and shaky as she held her glass up to the light from the table lamp beside her, "for a beverage that's touted as being colorless, odorless and tasteless, this is so damn good that it's almost obscene." She again touched her glass to Beth's "Here's to the Poles and their incredible potatoes!" She took another few sips, then patted her sister's arm. "Relax, Beth. I haven't used any heavy-duty meds since yesterday."

The best doctors money could buy had handed her an open-ended death sentence months ago, and her life had become a living hell ever since. The horrendous waiting game was all about pain management and coping with drastic mood swings. There was no hope of a cure for her particularly insidious and inoperable brain tumor, so she could be gone in an instant, or she could linger for many months. Meanwhile, depending on how bad the pain was, she alternated between booze and drugs to deal with it. Thankfully, she'd thus far been careful not to mix them within any twenty-four-hour period. Or if she had, she'd kept it from Beth and been lucky enough not to have put herself into a coma.

Comfortable now, thanks equally to Beth, vodka and the cheery blaze in the gas fireplace, Diana shrugged out of her coat and left it where it fell on the cushion behind her. Glancing at the treasured Patek Phillipe watch that had been her last birthday present from Beth, she thought about the long evening stretching ahead of them and dreaded the thought of weeping those hours away in her room. Trying to sound nonchalant, and failing miserably, she said, "What say we go out for dinner tonight, Beth? I could be ready by six-thirty, if that works for you?"

"Works fine." Beth's daytime domestic diva Paulina was a world-class cook and she'd left a meal for them that only needed to be heated, but it was clear that chicken tarragon at home just wasn't going to cut it tonight. Lately, Diana's moods had been running amok. Sometimes there were angry outbursts over small things that normally would never have caused her a moment's unease, and she was constantly vacillating between brooding silence and bright exuberance. Last night, she'd wanted complete solitude. Tonight she apparently wanted people, bright lights, and the vibrant in-your-face energy that post-Covid New York was slowly reclaiming as its own.

They quickly agreed on drinks at the Carlyle and a way-off-Broadway show, topped with a late supper at Sardella's, Diana's favorite Italian restaurant in the Village. She wouldn't even consider Beth's suggestion that they throttle back on the night's activities a little, and she was especially excited about seeing the play.

"Lousy reviews, but Aunt Liv's ex is apparently sizzling hot!" Diana laughed. "Surprise, surprise, huh?" Their aunt was the original cougar, and the play's male lead was just one of her many former conquests. Diana had never met this particular heartthrob, and she was really looking forward to checking him out. Startling Beth, she suddenly jumped to her feet and launched into a fair imitation of a hyperkinetic Hip-Hop queen. "Yay! We are going to parteee!"

Beth managed a laugh and quick applause, but only because she wanted the manic routine to end. Happily, it did, but not before all the bumps and grinds had stolen more oxygen than Diana could comfortably spare. Color draining from her face, she bent over, rested her hands on her knees, and took several deep breaths. Beth said a quick prayer to her sister's guardian angel and didn't allow herself to breathe normally again until she saw a tinge of pink reappear high on Diana's cheekbones.

Slowly straightening her spine, Diana sighed, "That was dumb." She shook her head. "Thing is…" Biting her lower lip, resting hands on hips, she blinked back tears and took a deep breath. "Thing is, Beth… For tonight. Just for tonight. I have to pretend that I don't have a care in the world. I want normal for a change, complete with kamikaze cabs instead of armored limos and bodyguard chauffeurs. You up for it?"

"You bet!" Beth leaned forward and tugged at Diana's hand to get her to sit down. She was still looking a little rocky as she slumped back onto the sofa. Leaning her head back, she kept a fierce grip on Beth's hand until the dizziness subsided.

Long moments passed before she was finally able to broach the unthinkable, unspeakable reality that plagued their every thought, every minute of every day. In a small and scarcely audible voice, she said, "Obviously, Ariana and Philip rained on my parade big-time today, Beth." On a long sigh, she added, "But I'm okay. Really I am."

"Oh Hon, I'm so sorry." Beth wanted to hug her, hug her hard, but Diana's body language was broadcasting that she wanted no part of it, so she contented herself with continuing to hold her hand.

Knowing that she would completely lose it if Beth were to hug her right now, Diana desperately sought a distraction that would hold back the tears. When her eyes fell on the huge Caillebotte painting above the alabaster marble fireplace, she was at least able to smile. The painting had always been one of her favorites, a Paris street scene awash with vivid colors that animated the monochromatic serenity of the room's ivory tones. Just looking at it tamed her erratic heartbeat. With silent thanks to the genius of Caillebotte that had spared her from making an even bigger ass of herself, she wrenched her gaze away from it and downed the last of her drink.

"I'd better get that nap," she said, giving Beth's hand a quick squeeze as she stood. On the way to her bedroom, she was thankful for the small victory of remembering to carry her empty glass to the sink at the bar. All too often lately, she found herself forgetting the most basic courtesies, and it was terrifying.

When they arrived at the Carlyle that night, all eyes turned to view the strikingly attractive pair being led to the most desirable of secluded tables. Diana, with her pale blonde hair shining in a straight fall to her shoulders, was dressed with her usual flair for the dramatic. She wore a hot pink beaded silk dress that clung to every curve, a glittery and sexy counterpoint to her sister's conservative black wool sheath. With her auburn hair and green eyes, Beth tended to downplay color in whatever she wore. New York chic with its signature little black dresses always suited her just fine.

Even their jewelry was a vivid contrast. Diana wore pink sapphire earrings with a matching bracelet. Beth wore a single strand of pearls and pearl button earrings. She never wore important jewelry when she went out exploring in the Village, but nothing could ever convince Diana to leave her big gems at home. As she had said before they went out, "Nobody ever expects to see jewels like this outside a vault, so they just figure they're pink glass and cubits." Beth knew that Diana had been grossly underestimating both the beauty of the stones and the savvy of the general population, but it was all heavily insured, had little or no sentimental value, and Diana could readily afford to replace them, so she hadn't argued the point.

The champagne they ordered, Diana's favorite vintage of Cristal, arrived without delay. The drink and food preferences of the beautiful young Gresham heiresses were well-known to maitre d's at all the top restaurants in Manhattan, and they were always assigned the best servers available. After their waiter had filled their glasses and set out a plate of appetizers, they toasted one another and took a few moments to savor the bubbly. "Sooo good," said Diana.

"Mmmm," sighed Beth. "Wonderful." She had so many questions she wanted to ask about the session with Ariana, but she didn't dare. Diana had said that she wanted to pretend that she didn't have a care in the world tonight, and Beth could only watch and wait while her sister set the agenda.

"No questions, reporter lady?" Diana laughed, her eyes dancing. "I'm impressed, Beth. Such restraint!" She popped an olive into her mouth and took her time chewing it. Rejecting the bait, Beth smiled and quietly sipped her champagne.

Diana played it out only a little longer, taking her time about swallowing that one very small olive, and enjoying a few more sips of Cristal before telling Beth about her session with Ariana and Philip. While they polished off the last of the Cristal, Beth listened in rapt silence to her sister's skillful reshaping of her harrowing experience into a series of almost comical little vignettes. It was all a sham, of course. Diana clearly didn't want to resurrect a boatload of pain for both of them to agonize over, so Beth wasn't about to call her out on any of it. Until she dropped the bombshell.

"Come again?"

"You heard me." Diana gave her a mischievous grin. "Who knows? Maybe I'll find the right town, do something wonderful for somebody there, get a karmic reprieve, and live to be a hundred. I figure it's gotta be worth a shot."

And besides, thought Diana, it happens to be the only shot I've been given, so I'm going to take it. Even Lily said she should go for it. She'd called her old confidante and psychic advisor just before she'd taken her nap that afternoon, and Lily had been completely supportive of the idea. Predictably, Beth's reaction was the polar opposite of Lily's. Her wordsmith sister seemed to have lost all power of speech.

"Oh come on, Beth, where's your spirit of adventure? Just think of the fun we'd have visiting all those little burgs again!" She signaled the waiter for another bottle of Cristal and excused herself to go to the ladies' room. She wanted to give Beth some time to gather her thoughts before she said anything more about her plan.

Beth could scarcely breathe. Was this it? Was this the final bridge into madness? Why else would she even consider spending her last days on earth searching for someone who had probably never even existed? Please God, please let there be another explanation!

In desperation, she came up with one possible scenario that could make some sense. What if maybe, just maybe, Diana simply wanted to say a final good-bye to some of the places she loved best, but she didn't want it to sound morbid? That would be reasonable, wouldn't it? And what if she decided to turn that sad journey into a lark by camouflaging it as an insane quest for someone named Lenore? If that really was Diana's plan, and Beth prayed that it was, she could only admire the genius of it.

By the time she saw Diana weaving her unsteady way back toward their table, Beth still didn't know if she was dealing with total insanity or a clever ruse. She only knew that she would be playing along with it, whichever it was. Diana had clearly made up her mind to go and was presuming that Beth would be going along with her. Well, she was right about that. No way would her baby sister be traveling the last miles of her life's journey alone, but she wasn't about to put that thought into words, so she had to play a little hard to get. Diana would instantly know the truth if she agreed too readily.

The moment Diana had settled herself back in her seat, Beth said, "You're really serious about this, aren't you?"

"Absolutely, positively."

Beth sighed and shook her head. "Okay. Bear with me here." She edged a little closer to her sister. "I just want to make sure I've got this straight, Di." She lowered her voice to a whisper. "If I agree to go -- and at this point, let me tell you, that's a big 'if' -- the two of us would essentially be hauling our sorry asses to just about every jerkwater town you've ever visited, hoping to find some solid historical facts about a murdering bitch of a witch who very possibly never even existed. Is that about right?"

Diana laughed. "Damn straight, girl! Fun, huh?"

They were still laughing as they exited the Carlyle ten minutes later, champagne-induced giggle fits that continued to erupt during the cab ride downtown to a theater that turned out to be little more than a storefront just off Christopher Street. Exiting the cab, Diana almost collided with Jeff Stratton, one of the Dunsford Security detail assigned to protect them.

Beth and Diana had long ago given their bodyguards standing orders to keep their distance, but urban violence was a constant threat and the area was so mobbed that the security team had been forced to close ranks. It was unfortunate that some staggering drunk had blocked Jeff's way, or he would have been able to disappear into the crowd before Diana saw him.

Jeff was one of the newer agents, but Diana had no intention of cutting him any slack. "Hey, Jeff! Long as you're here, how about paying the cabbie? A hundred bucks should do it." She folded her arms and glared at him while he reached for his wallet. He could only hope that he had enough on him to cover it.

Beth had already paid the fare before leaving the cab, and she immediately positioned herself between Jeff and Diana. "It's already been taken care of, Jeff. But thanks anyway." Jeff's usual post was at the lobby entrance to the private elevator for Beth's penthouse apartment. There, he was always discreet, looking almost apologetic for bird-dogging her every movement, but field duty was obviously a whole new ballgame for him.

Diana was determined to have the last word. She was tapping her foot now, really over-reacting. "I know you guys are always somewhere within hailing distance, but I sure as hell don't want any of you in my face. Ever. Not ever! Got that?" She spun on her heels and bolted into the theater.

"Forget it, Jeff," soothed Beth. Diana didn't want anyone at Dunsford Security to know she was ill, so Beth said the only conciliatory thing she could think of that would respect that wish. "She's just having a really bad day."

As he watched Beth walk away, he couldn't imagine a kinder or more beautiful smile than the one she'd just given him. Quite a lady, he thought. He knew he'd take a bullet for her any day if he had to, but her stuck-up kid sister was a whole different enchilada.

Within minutes of the play's opening lines, Beth and Diana knew that the show would never make it uptown, despite the Adonis who had the lead. With silent apologies to Olivia, they left early and went directly to Sardella's where they ordered up a feast.

Over bruschetta, antipasto and a really fine cabernet sauvignon, Diana pushed for a final, definitive commitment from Beth. "It's not as if we'd be going all over the world, Beth. Philip said 'not far from this place,' when I pressed him on the location. Not a word about crossing an ocean to get there."

Feigning one last moment of indecision, Beth bit at her lower lip and gazed thoughtfully at an unsuspecting olive sitting on her plate. She popped it into her mouth and took her time savoring it, just as her sister had done earlier. Diana was already grinning when Beth sighed, "You win."

Diana leaped up from her chair to give her sister a bone-crunching hug. "Thank you, thank you, thank you!"

"You're welcome." Beth laughed, disentangling herself from Diana's grasp. "Now sit down and get busy." She reached into her purse for her ever-present reporter's notebook and pen, then passed both to Diana.

"What's this for?"

"Well, for starters, we'll need a list of all the stateside small towns you remember visiting."

Diana's eyes suddenly misted. "I was afraid you were just humoring me. But you're really not doing that, are you?"

"No, I'm not humoring you, Di. This could actually be a fun trip." She raised her wineglass. "So start writing and let the quest for Lenore begin!"

Sardella's elegant Tuscan décor, truly superb cuisine, and exceptional waitstaff was an open invitation to gluttony, and they happily consumed thousands of calories while they reminisced about some of the more memorable places they'd visited over the years. By the time they finished their espresso and the few bites of tartuffo that was all either of them could manage for dessert, 'The List' had expanded to more than a hundred small towns and villages.

It took two rounds of espresso before they were sure their legs would carry them to the front door. Beth had already put a call through to Jeff Stratton, so a limo was waiting for them when they left the restaurant. She hoped Diana didn't kick up a fuss about it and was relieved when she actually seemed glad to see the driver, thankfully not Jeff, opening the rear door for them as they walked to the curb.

As soon as they arrived at Beth's apartment and reset the alarm, they both kicked off their shoes, tossed their coats on a hall chair and hurried into the living room to call their Aunt Liv. Diana put the secure landline on loudspeaker so that she and Beth could give their aunt a full report on her former leading man, and Olivia was soon crowing with delight over their colorful descriptions.

"You'd better hurry if you want to catch the play, Aunt Liv." Beth and Diana were sitting on the couch, their feet resting on the coffee table. "I don't think it's going to last much longer," laughed Beth.

"Don't listen to her, Aunt Liv. The guy's pecs and package guarantee him center stage for another year at least." The peal of Olivia's laughter brought tears to Diana's eyes. "I sure do miss you, Aunt Liv."

"Me too, love. Nothing's much fun since you left. I'm about ready to pack up my tent and head back to New York."

Diana feigned a shocked voice. "And leave the divine Jean-Pierre?"

Beth decided to quit while she was ahead. "Hey you two, I'm signing off. Diana can fill me in later. Love you, Aunt Liv." Before her aunt could object, she disconnected the loudspeaker and gave the handset to Diana.

Keeping Diana's illness a secret from Olivia was so hard that she always ducked out of their group conversations as quickly as she reasonably could. Diana had insisted on being the one to break the awful news to their aunt, but she still hadn't worked up the courage to do it, so Olivia had no idea of how seriously ill her niece was. Whenever they spoke, Beth had to censor every word she said, a painful process with someone as dear to her as Olivia was, and she hated it.

Tonight there would be more subterfuge. No way could Olivia be told the real reason for the trip they would soon be taking. Without a hint of nervousness or evasion, Diana would lie convincingly about wanting to chase down some spring skiing before the season ended, but Beth didn't have a fraction of her sister's acting ability. It was simpler just to end the conversation and go to bed.

Beth intended to read until Diana came in with an update on her talk with Olivia, but her book was no match for the grueling day and all the booze. She fell asleep in the middle of a particularly dull paragraph and was jolted awake when Diana came whirling into the room. "Good news, Beth! Oops... Sorry. The light was on and I..."

"No problem." Beth elbowed her way into a sitting position. "What's the good news?"

Diana bounced onto the bed and tucked her legs under the blankets. "The good news, the great news, is that I actually managed to convince Aunt Liv not to come back to New York for at least another month. I figure that's about how long it will take us to check all of these out. Diana had torn the list of towns from Beth's notebook. She waved the pages in the air.

Beth groaned. "All of them?"

"Sure. Why not?"

Beth was fully awake now, her practical streak already kicking into overdrive. "Because we'd be traveling non-stop for weeks, that's why not!" Diana's doctors kept her well-supplied with pain-killers, everything from oxycodone to morphine, and sometimes she was totally incapacitated for days. Either Beth, her housekeeper Paulina, or a private nurse had always been around to look after her during the worst spells, but traveling would present a whole new set of challenges. Unfortunately, the stubborn set of Diana's jaw told her that she would have to find some way to manage it all on her own.

"Here, let's have a look." She took the list and did a quick scan of the pages. "Jeez, what a mess, Di. Go get a couple of legal pads and pencils from the den. Let's see if we can make some sense out of all this." As Diana left the room, Beth called out, "And change into your PJ's, for God's sake. All those beads are blinding me!"

Within minutes, Diana returned in comfortable flannel pajamas and warm socks. She gave Beth one of the two legal pads and pens she had brought with her and scooted back under the blanket. When she handed her four-page list to Beth, Beth immediately gave the top two pages back to her.

"Let's start categorizing them geographically," Beth suggested, "then we can combine our lists. Hopefully we'll be able to put together an itinerary that won't have us on red-eyes every other day."

Diana blinked. "I keep forgetting we'll be flying commercial. Damn."

Beth shook her head and laughed. "That's what you said you wanted, right?" Over dinner at Sardella's, they had discussed logistics and agreed that using a private plane from the Gresham fleet for their bizarre jaunt would raise too many flags at corporate. Olivia chaired their company's Board of Directors, and neither of them wanted her scrutinizing every detail of their itinerary.

It was five o'clock in the morning before they finished compiling their list. Diana would hopefully be free of nightmares and able to sleep as long as she needed to, but Beth had to drag herself out of bed at seven. No way could she be late for work today, not with the bad news she had to break to her boss.

Promptly at nine o'clock, Beth arrived at the office of her managing editor, Chad Martin, only to be told by his secretary that he had been called to an urgent meeting with their publisher. She caught up on some paperwork in her own office until two hours later when Chad called to say he was back at his desk and was expecting her.

She had taken great pains, literally, to look her best today. Her suede stilettos were killing her feet, but they were a perfect match for her forest green suit. The skirt just skimmed her knees, showing more leg than her norm. Her pale yellow silk blouse had a sexy little drape to the modest neckline, and she had styled her hair to fall in soft waves about her face. Playing girlie games wasn't her style, but today she knew she would need every feminine wile she could muster. After just five minutes in Chad's office, she was wondering why she had bothered with any of it, especially the damn shoes.

Settling into one of the two visitors' chairs across from his desk, Beth steeled herself for what she knew his reaction to her announcement would be. As expected, he started out with a litany of every complaint she had ever voiced to him about her sister's past behavior. She certainly couldn't fault his memory. She could only regret her own careless words that had completely blinded him to some of Diana's more redeeming qualities.

"She's been playing you for years, Beth, and I can't believe you actually let her talk you into this!" Long and lean, with the physique of the track team captain he had been in college fifteen years earlier, he paced the length of his corner office, door to windows and back again, hazel eyes blazing, the unbuttoned jacket of his gray pinstripe suit framing fisted hands that hitched at his hips. When he finally came to a halt long enough to really look her square in the eyes, she saw that he had already burned off the worst of his anger, but he was still itching for an argument that she didn't want to give him. Never breaking eye contact with him, she said nothing.

Chad folded his arms and tried to stare her down, but the set of her jaw told him to let it go. Shaking his head and heaving a huge sigh, he turned away and slowly walked to the double window overlooking Lexington Avenue. Leaning a shoulder against the dark oak window frame, he tried to will his rapidly escalating pulse into submission. If only she didn't take his breath away every time he looked at her! Several moments passed before he could trust his voice not to betray him.

"Look, Beth, I know how sick your sister is." He turned to meet her gaze, trying very hard to look at her eyes without actually looking into them. It was a subtle distinction, but one that had thus far kept him from making a total ass of himself. "If you had come in here this morning and told me you wanted time off just to be with her, I wouldn't be giving you a moment's grief. Surely you know that. But this trip -- it's lunacy!" He raked a hand through his meticulously groomed mane of thick chestnut hair, the only vanity Beth had ever detected in him.

"So you're going to punish me for being truthful, is that it? I could have lied, you know. I could have told you..."

"I know. I know." He waved away her explanation and tried to focus once more on the only distraction available to him just then, the bustle of activity on the street thirty stories below. After a few moments, he turned to face her again. "Come on," he said. "Let's get out of here." He walked toward her and took her hand as she stood. "I think we could both use some air."

Still holding her hand, reluctant to break even that small connection, he buzzed his secretary and instructed her to field all his visitors and calls for the next two hours. "I'll be at the Press Box." Slamming the receiver on its cradle, he turned to Beth. "Maybe some of this will start to make sense after a few drinks." He forced himself to release her hand a nanosecond before opening the door to the corridor.

Their favorite corner table was already occupied when they arrived at the Press Box, and being compactly wedged between other diners did nothing to improve Chad's mood. Beth waited for his bourbon to arrive before even attempting to placate him.

"We're not going to be away that long, you know."

"Oh really?" He took a quick gulp of his drink. "Seems to me it's going to take you months to run down that inane list." The thought of her being gone for several weeks was making him crazy. He knew he should back off, but he couldn't stop himself from digging the hole even deeper.

"No, it won't. It'll only take about four weeks, five at most. Diana and I stayed up half the night narrowing it down and organizing it. We fly to eight cities, drive to twenty-three towns, and we'll be home before you know it."

Chad drained his glass and signaled the waiter for a refill. "Listen to yourself. You know, of course, that this is absolutely the nuttiest idea you've ever come up with."

"It wasn't my idea!" A Junior League type at the table to their right glared at Beth. She glared right back.

"But you're condoning it, Beth, and you should have better sense."

"Look," she sighed, her patience now a slender thread, "let me run this by you one more time. Correction. Make that one last time. My sister wants to say good-bye to a few places she'll never see again, and she's using this crazy Lenore thing as a pretext. What's wrong with that? She's dying, Chad. I could lose her at any moment, and I intend to be right by her side for as long as I can be. It's that simple."

Before Chad could respond, the waiter came with his second bourbon and asked if they were ready to order. "I sure am," said Beth, smiling up at Chad. She was hoping that food might succeed where liquor was obviously failing to improve his mood.

"Nothing for me," Chad snapped. He sampled his fresh drink and pointedly avoided any eye contact with her. He knew he was beaten, and it galled him that he couldn't think of a single conciliatory thing to say. His only excuse for his bad behavior would be the truth, and that was something he could never admit to her. He was going totally ballistic just thinking about her being so far away from him for so long.

Beth had had enough. "Look, let's just forget about lunch," she said, tossing her napkin on the table, shrugging into her coat, and shouldering her purse as she pushed back her chair and stood. "I'll e-mail you the piece on missing kids as soon as it's done." The subject matter was so gut-wrenching that Beth knew she'd be hard-pressed to meet her deadline, but she damn well would. With a curt nod to the gaping Junior Leaguer and an apologetic look toward the waiter who was still standing there with pencil poised over his order pad, she stormed out of the restaurant.

Chad raced after her, but he wasn't quick enough. By the time he maneuvered his way past a tour group dawdling at the front door, Beth had already vanished into the noontime crush streaming along the sidewalk. Returning to his table, he consumed a liquid lunch, cursing his own stupidity, already missing Beth, and hating himself for needing her so much.

Since they'd met two years ago when she was first assigned to his staff, their professional relationship had trumped any prayer of having a personal one. Apart from chaste little pecks on the cheek after drinks or business dinners that often had very little to do with work, they'd never even kissed. Still, he'd somehow managed to find himself loving everything about her, except for her damn bank account. His pride could have withstood a wife with millions, but billions was a whole different ballgame. He was no fortune hunter, and no way was he ever going to have her or anybody else thinking that he was.

Rather than take her anger home to Diana, Beth decided to exorcise her black mood with a little retail therapy. Falling into step with the rushing throng, she cut cross-town to Fifth and window-shopped along the way for a bon voyage gift for her sister. She wasn't sure just what she wanted, but as soon as she saw it in a Tiffany showcase, she knew she'd found it: an intricately carved gold pin in the shape of a majestic unicorn rearing up on its hind legs and holding aloft a gleaming bluish-white crystal sphere. Diana had always been fascinated by mythical creatures, particularly unicorns, and, considering the bizarre nature of their journey, the whimsical little pin couldn't have been more appropriate.

Beth declined the miniature turquoise shopping bag that was so easily recognizable to every thief in the city. Tucking the small blue box into her purse, she set out for home, allowing the sunny sky and crisp February air to banish all melancholy thoughts of Chad. They had both over-reacted, and neither was likely to apologize. She certainly wasn't. Time enough to sort things out with him when she returned.

A few blocks from her apartment, she stopped at a deli for takeout sandwiches and coffee. It would be weeks before she and Diana saw a Manhattan deli again, and no other place in the world had pastrami like New York.

As soon as she opened the door to her apartment, the aroma of hot pastrami brought Diana to greet her at a run. "Bless you, my darling sister." She took the bag from Beth and peeked inside, inhaling deeply through a wide grin. "Divine. Absolutely divine! Let's hurry up and eat before Paulina gets back from shopping with more of that damn health food."

Beth detoured into the kitchen for some knives, forks, and two bottles of Heineken, while Diana brought the deli lunch into the den. Moments later, she joined Diana at their favorite informal eating nook, a rectangular oak table with cushioned benches set against a long window that commanded a spectacular view of the East River. Tearing open the bag, they used it as a communal placemat and immediately attacked their food, munching happily at the crusty rye and lean, spicy hot pastrami liberally spread with deli mustard. Coleslaw, German potato salad and kosher pickles made lunch into a feast.

After the first few bites, they began discussing the details of their itinerary. Diana had telephoned

Harry Cardinale, her personal travel agent, early that morning. He had a small but thriving agency on the upper East-side, and Diana used his services whenever she wanted to slip under the radar of Gresham Enterprises. She was thrilled at the prospect of leading all her watchdogs on a merry chase.

Over the years, Olivia and her nieces had regularly availed themselves of a quiet don't-ask-don't-tell kind of agreement with Paul Dunsford, the head of the security agency contracted to protect the three heiresses to the Gresham billions. As long as he personally was always kept in the loop about their little side trips, he would respect their confidence, although it was understood that he would never misinform Olivia if she demanded to know the specific whereabouts of her nieces. Beth couldn't remember a time in their adult lives when Olivia had played that particular trump card. She was simply too jealous of her own privacy not to respect theirs.

"When will the tickets be ready, Di?"

"Late this afternoon. Harry said he'd send them by messenger or bring them over himself. The usual hard copy of the itinerary will be in with the tickets, but he's also emailing one to me so I can shoot it right over to Paul. Can you imagine what will be going through his head when he sees it?" Diana smiled happily. She loved Paul dearly. They all did. He was smart, discreet, incredibly good-looking, totally professional, and so analytical that she knew he'd make himself crazy trying to figure out why they were really going to so many strange places. She was fairly certain he wouldn't be buying the story about spring skiing.

"Tell you what, Di. When Harry arrives -- and we both know he will definitely not be using a messenger -- I'll tell him you have a migraine or something. If he sees you, we'll never get rid of him in time to pack."

If Diana had ever had a fan club, Beth knew that Harry would be a charter member, not only because she was one of his best accounts, but also because he was completely besotted with her. The moment he saw Diana, it was as if his wife Vera and their five kids had never even existed.

"Good idea." Diana took a very satisfactory bite out of the kosher dill pickle she'd saved for last.

Beth smiled at her sister's innate ability to derive maximum pleasure from every moment. She had enjoyed her pastrami on rye as much as last night's gourmet meal, each, in its own way, perfection. Depending on her meds, Diana's appetite had been running the gamut from non-existent to voracious, and Beth could only be thankful for every meal that her sister was able to eat and enjoy.

The tickets arrived just after six o'clock, predictably handed over by a very hopeful looking Harry Cardinale. Middle-aged, graying, and impeccably dressed, he was sporting a pencil-thin mustache that seemed oddly comical in the lean angular face. His dark eyes were already smoldering in anticipation of seeing Diana, and his practiced smile faltered when he saw that it was Beth who had just opened the door. He'd brought a bottle of Dom Perignon to wish them a bon voyage, no doubt intending to share it with Diana.

"I know Diana will be delighted with this," said Beth, accepting the champagne from him, but not inviting him inside. "She'll be so sorry she missed you."

Beth held out her free hand for the tickets that Harry still hadn't surrendered. Under the level gaze of her green eyes, as honest and direct as Beth herself, Harry suddenly found himself thinking about buying some flowers for his wife or maybe taking her out to dinner. Maybe both, considering the generous bonus that Diana had already wired into his account. He handed the tickets to Beth, wished her a wonderful trip, asked that Diana be given his kindest regards, then scurried off to the elevator.

Beth waited until the elevator doors had closed behind him, then double locked the door leading from the hall to the apartment. After resetting the alarm, she shouted an "All clear!" to Diana.

Diana was laughing when she came into the living room "Time-wise, that has to be a record for Harry."

"Yeah. Well, he didn't have much say in the matter." Beth handed the champagne to Diana and began thumbing through their tickets as she walked back into the living room. "Everything seems to be here. Even the car rental arrangements."

"And he emailed the itinerary, as promised," said Diana. "Already sent it to Paul."

Over champagne, cheese, and crackers, Beth and Diana sat on the oversized living room sofa and carefully checked the tickets against the master list they had compiled the night before. It was an odd conglomeration of sentimental favorites and places where Diana recalled seeing rural towns overlooking pastoral valleys.

"I'm impressed," said Beth, tossing the tickets onto the coffee table. "Can't believe he did all this so quickly. Doing business with a lech obviously has its advantages."

"Lechery has nothing to do with it, Beth. Well, not much anyway. For a ten-thousand dollar bonus, Harry would…"

"Ten thousand? You have got to be kidding!"

Diana laughed. "Good looks get you just so far, kiddo." She popped the last cube of cheese into her mouth, then went into the kitchen to forage for more snacks. While she was gone, Beth retrieved the little boxed unicorn from her purse and set it on the coffee table next to the wine bottle. When Diana returned to the living room, the big bag of pretzels she was carrying nearly slipped from her hands the moment she saw the trademark blue box.

"A present from Tiffany's -- all right!" Grinning happily, she tilted her head from side to side, dropped the bag of pretzels on the coffee table, sat beside Beth, and reached for the small package. "It's not even my birthday -- this is so exciting!" She was just about to untie the white Tiffany bow, when her joyous expression abruptly froze. She looked tentatively up at Beth. "It is for me, isn't it?"

"I don't see anybody else here, do you?" Beth laughed at the pure glee in Diana's eyes as she tore off the ribbon and opened the box.

The moment she saw the little unicorn, Diana started crying. Almost reverently, she lifted the pin from its elegant satin folds. "Oh, Gran, it's so beautiful!" With trembling hands, she moved the pin closer to the lamp beside her and angled it so that the bluish-white crystal sphere could better catch the light. Suddenly, her hands fell to her lap and the little unicorn tumbled to the floor, but she didn't even seem to notice. With silent tears streaming down her face, she kept staring blankly at her empty hands as if they still held the unicorn.

Beth was numb with fear. The doctors had said it might happen this way, diminished hand-eye coordination, worsening confusion, blackouts, memory loss, then... "No!" she shouted, pushing the heavy lacquered coffee table away from the sofa and crouching before Diana, half-kneeling so that they were at eye-level, so close that she could feel her sister's breath on her cheek. Clenching Diana's hands in hers, squeezing hard on cold slender fingers that offered no resistance, Beth called her sister's name, watching closely for some sign of recognition, but there was none. She grasped Diana's shoulders and shook her, shook her hard, shouting her name even louder than before.

When Diana's voice rang out like a klaxon, Beth knew that she had never heard a lovelier sound. "What the hell are you doing, Beth? I think you just jarred a filling loose!" Wherever she had been, she was back now, evidently with no memory of having been gone at all. "What's your problem, girl?"

Beth's mind was a blank. She had no idea what to say. Until she saw a glint of gold beside her on the rug. "Ah, here it is!" She scooped up the unicorn and handed it over to Diana. "It fell. I was just bending down to pick it up when... I guess I lost my balance and kind of grabbed onto you for dear life. Sorry to be such a klutz." She didn't know whether to be relieved or even more worried when Diana didn't question her feeble explanation. Heart hammering, she watched Diana once again cradle the unicorn in her hand.

"Thank you, Beth. It's so lovely. Just perfect. Really perfect." She gently set the pin in her lap as she retrieved a tissue from her pocket and dabbed at her eyes. "I'm a regular little waterworks tonight, aren't I?"

Beth held up the empty Dom Perignon bottle. "Maybe you're allergic to any champagne that's not Cristal."

"Very funny," said Diana, "but possibly true," she laughed. "Remember the night Aunt Liv gave us each our first full glass of Cristal?"

"How could I forget?"

Beth was relieved to see Diana carefully lift the unicorn from her lap and once again hold it up to the light, without any alarming results. As she returned it to its nesting place in the Tiffany box, she began reminiscing about Beth's sixteenth birthday.

Their aunt had thrown a lavish party for her at their villa in St. Tropez. Beth had just gone to bed when a very drunk and lusty-eyed Baron Jean-Luc de Montvalle came staggering into her room, clearly determined to seduce her. Following hot on his heels was Olivia, a tiny virago, blue eyes flashing fire. Looking up at his greater height, she slapped his face and ordered him out of her niece's room. Screaming invectives, she half-dragged half-pushed him into the corridor and didn't let up until they reached the front door. Alerted by all the commotion, one of her junior staff was already holding the door open when she got there. Stifling a grin, the young attendant watched his employer literally kick the baron out of the house with a shouted vow that she would personally excise a particularly sensitive part of his anatomy if he ever even attempted to go near one of her nieces again.

The St. Tropez grapevine greatly embellished the already juicy story into a fitting tribute to the living legend that was Olivia Gresham-Lazare. She wasn't a woman given to idle threats, and her treatment of the high-and-mighty baron put the world on notice that there were serious consequences for anyone who even threatened harm to either of her cubs. Not only was he publicly humiliated, but he was quietly dropped from guest lists all over the continent.

Diana loved talking about their aunt, and Beth encouraged her to go on until she was satisfied that her sister's memory was intact. When she was sure that there wasn't a hint of the total disorientation that had occurred with the unicorn, she gave in to exhaustion and suggested they both get some sleep.

For centuries, the jeweled athame had been entrusted to each High Priest or High Priestess chosen to lead the coven.

The powerful sword was his now, and he was determined that it always would be, as long as he drew breath.

Holding the gleaming athame aloft, he entered the altar room where the coven had already gathered and begun their traditional chant in praise of the Goddess who had long ago been chosen to guide them.

His deep baritone soon dominated the fervent chorus that invited Hecate and the horned god who was her consort to join their circle.

Chapter Three

Apart from celebrity fund-raisers and waving the corporate flag at command performances for Gresham Enterprises, Diana had rarely traveled to California. Skiing was her passion, not sun and surf, and whenever she started out for the West Coast, she seldom made it beyond the glorious ski trails of the Rockies. It was a pattern that was now paying handsome dividends in her search for the town where Lenore was supposed to have lived.

Explaining her reasons for the trip to the people she loved most had been tricky. She'd told Olivia and Paul that it was a spur-of-the-moment ski trip, and she let Beth go right on thinking that her search for Lenore was only an excuse for making a sentimental journey to places she loved. Beth hadn't said as much, but Diana seldom had trouble reading her sister. Or anyone else for that matter. She had confided the entire truth in only one person: Lily Verne.

For the past six years, Lily had worked tirelessly to reprogram all the undisciplined habits Diana had acquired during almost two decades of toying with paranormal phenomena. Diana had been just seven years old when she first became aware that she could teleport objects at will. Back then, it had only been a harmless little trick to her, and she'd been genuinely confused by her nanny's horrified reaction to her first sight of a small paper clip scooting across the table toward Diana's outstretched hand. Crossing herself and praying to "Dios Mio," the woman threatened Diana with every dire punishment she could think of should she ever again attempt "the devil's work." Self-preservation had Diana giving all the requisite promises in record time, but she meant none of them. The only lesson learned that day was the importance of keeping all future telepathic experiments entirely to herself.

She began practicing secretly at night in her room, not even letting Beth know what she was doing. At that stage of their lives, Beth was such a little straight arrow that the few years separating them might as well have been a generation, and Diana couldn't trust her to keep quiet about something so far off the grid.

At first it was thrilling, as she rapidly progressed from paper clip, to pencil, to pen, but when her fledgling talent hit a sudden plateau, balking at anything heavier than one or two ounces, she quickly grew bored with it and decided to spend more time with her horses instead. She became an accomplished rider, but she abandoned all equestrian dreams when her hormones asserted themselves at thirteen. The opposite sex had suddenly become far more interesting than steeplechase events.

Leaving the care of her horses to the grooms at Olivia's stables, she'd plunged headlong into anything the New Age had to offer that would help her love life. With a level of exuberance attainable only by teenagers, she began exploring astrology, palmistry, spells, love potions, tarot cards and crystals, her telekinetic gift nothing more than a vague memory of a bizarre childhood talent. Until the night of her twenty-first birthday.

She and the man she'd been dating seriously for several weeks -- she couldn't even remember his name now -- had just returned from a party Olivia had thrown for her in Davos, Switzerland, where she was living at the time. They were snuggled up together on the sofa in the great room of her ski lodge and enjoying a cozy nightcap, when she asked him about a catty remark one of the women at the party had made.

The glib response she expected never came. Instead, he laughed a little too cheerfully and began hemming and hawing his way through a string of possible explanations for the nasty rumor that was clearly circulating among their crowd. All the alcohol he'd consumed that night was digging him into a deeper hole with every word, and it was child's play for Diana to poke and prod her way to his admission of guilt.

Pathetically vowing his undying love for her, pleading for her forgiveness, he swore that the other woman had been strictly a one-night stand. Diana repeatedly told him to leave and never come back, but he refused to go. Grabbing her shoulders, he pulled her against him and assaulted her mouth with his.

Locked in a feral embrace by two hundred pounds of solid muscle and bone, she used the only weapon available to her at that moment and bit down hard on the tongue that had just plunged into her mouth. When he screamed, she was able to jump away from him and grab her gun from the purse she had earlier tossed on the coffee table. The small .22 had been a gift from Olivia long before she was old enough to get a license for it, and she seldom went anywhere without it. Not that she'd ever actually shot anyone, but occasionally, as now, it was a great equalizer.

Aiming the business end of the small pistol at his groin, she once again demanded that he leave and never come back. He was furious, and he was drunk, but he wasn't stupid. He raced out of the apartment and headed for the elevator at a run.

Slamming the door behind him, trembling from the after-effects of all that had just happened, she put the gun back in her purse and retrieved her cell. She needed to alert Paul Dunsford to add yet another disgruntled ex to his watch list, and she was relieved when his voicemail picked up and she was able to leave a quick summary message, rather than relive all the gory details.

Her anger kept escalating as she stormed around the room screaming obscene epithets at the universe. Before she even realized what she was doing, she had picked up a prized Lalique vase from an end table and hurled it against the nearest wall. The crashing, tinkling sounds that resulted were satisfying enough to have her reaching for another treasure to destroy, when suddenly the entire room came alive with flying objects that tumbled and shattered all around her. In a panic, she fled into the bedroom, but the pandemonium followed.

Hurrying into a walk-in closet, her cell still clutched in her hand, she pulled the door behind her and wasted no time putting out an S.O.S. The closet light had gone on automatically, so even with shaking hands she had no trouble finding the speed dial for Lily Verne. Breathing a sigh of relief when Lily answered her private line, Diana quickly explained what was happening.

"Ecoutez! Listen to me!" her mentor commanded. Following Lily's precise instructions, Diana focused on breathing deeply and slowly as Lily's calm voice guided her through meditative techniques to clear her mind. Lily stayed on the phone with her for several minutes, until the mayhem beyond the door subsided into silence. Only then, after saying goodnight to Lily, had she finally allowed herself to cry.

Lily knew all about Diana's psychic dabbling as a child, and she wasn't at all shocked by what had just happened. She had worked with psychic energy fields long enough to know that a powerful gift such as Diana's could be suppressed, even for a very long time, but it would never be denied.

That terrifying incident had occurred almost six years ago and now, thanks to Lily, Diana was completely in command of a very powerful telekinetic gift, a secret known only to Lily. She used it to fetch and carry things she needed only when she was alone, and her daily meditations kept it under control, so she saw no reason to tell Beth and Olivia about it. Why worry them? They didn't need to know that her little flying trick was all grown up now.

As disturbing as her session with Ariana and Philip had been, Diana knew that she owed them a great debt of gratitude. Not only did she now have a glimmer of hope in her heart and a reason to wake up every morning, but she also hadn't been plagued by migraines or nightmares since she'd made the decision to look for Lenore.

Lily attributed her renewed lease on life to being on the right karmic path, and she hoped that was true. She'd hate to think she'd become completely delusional. Still, with every other road leading to a literal dead end, what choice did she have except to follow this one? Why not pull out all the stops trying to find someone who knew Lenore or at least had heard of her? If there really was some healing nexus in the nightmares that had plagued her for so long, she had to find it while there was still time.

There turned out to be only five places in all of California that met the criteria of being a familiar small town on high ground overlooking a pastoral valley, and Diana grinned at their distinct northerly track when she saw them plotted on her computer screen. It was a corridor instantly recognizable to any self-respecting ski-bum.

She and Beth had flown into San Francisco and picked up the white Lexus SUV rental their travel agent had reserved for them. After dinner at Tarantino's on Fisherman's Wharf, they stayed overnight at the St Regis before heading north toward Mt. Shasta and the Oregon line the next morning.

A few hours into their trip, they saw the first mileage marker for the Cascades. "Jeez, Beth," Diana laughed. "Remember the last time we were up this way?"

"How could I forget?" Beth shook her head and smiled at the memory.

"How old were we when we made that God-awful trip? Early teens?" Reminiscing was an important part of Diana's strategy to keep Beth thinking this really was a sentimental journey, but it was tough remembering things she'd never paid much attention to in the first place. Blasts from the past had never been her style.

"Let's see... I think you were twelve and I was fourteen, give or take." Beth laughed. "Zits and crushing boredom come vividly to mind."

They had been living in Paris for two years, happily ensconced with their aunt in an elegant house on the Faubourg Saint-Germain, when Olivia decided it was time for them to become reacquainted with their homeland. A well-meaning friend had told her that she might have been remiss in raising her nieces as expatriates, and Olivia had become overwhelmed with guilt. In typically exuberant fashion, she immediately arranged to drag the girls on a cultural juggernaut through the United States that summer. The Pacific Northwest had been the last stage of their itinerary, and they'd hurried through it, anxious to end the ordeal and return to the friends they had left behind in France.

"Poor Aunt Livvy. We were absolute beasts!" Diana laughed, her glee belying the words. Surprising herself, she realized that she was actually having fun skipping back along Memory Lane. "It's a wonder she didn't put us in an orphanage right then and there."

Beth glanced at the GPS, glad to see that they were making good time, while Diana tried to figure out the car's high-tech audio system. About the only thing that came in loud and clear were a few country-western stations. "Jeez, Beth. This thing has me stumped. Sorry, but it's hee-haw or nothing."

"Nothing then. Why don't you go ahead and plug into your iPod? I'll give you a nudge if I need you."

Diana didn't argue. She hadn't had time to meditate that morning, and she really needed it. Beth would have been surprised to know just how many Tibetan bowl and wind chime sounds were stored on that little electronic lifesaver. "Works for me." She pulled the iPod from her Kate Spade tote. "Sure you don't mind?"

"Absolutely not. I need to think about the angle on that feature I'm supposed to be doing for Chad. It's still not right, and it's making me crazy."

"Not surprising, given the subject. It's about missing kids, right?"

Beth nodded. "Yeah. And no matter what approach I use, it's all so horrific that balancing the piece is impossible."

"What a living hell for parents," sighed Diana. "You wonder how they survive it."

Beth nodded. "Best they can hope for is kidnap for ransom. That at least gives the kid a chance of getting back home alive."

Beth grabbed her water bottle from the well between the seats and took a few good-size gulps. Just thinking about those poor kids sucked the life out of her. "Pointless for both of us to be getting depressed, Di. Find some happy stuff on your iPod and enjoy."

Diana didn't need to be persuaded. She tucked in her earbuds. "Good luck with the brainstorming, Beth!" She knew that brainstorming, by definition, required at least two people, but her own reserves were too depleted right now to contribute anything to the process. She closed her eyes, flicked on the iPod and immediately began to relax. When she next opened her eyes, she wasn't at all surprised to see that more than an hour had passed. Her meditation sessions frequently went that long.

"Welcome back, sleepy head. Have a good nap?"

"Wonderful!" She arched her back and stretched as far as the seatbelt would allow. She tucked the iPod back into her tote and tried scanning the radio again, but still found nothing either of them would want to hear, so she started singing instead. Slightly off-key at first, she found her range and began humming a little tune that quickly morphed into a full-blown Parisian torch song. It amused her to realize that she had subconsciously chosen one of their aunt's favorites.

Listening to Diana sing, Beth's thoughts were once again focused on Olivia, and she wondered for at least the hundredth time how much longer it would take her sister to work up the courage to tell their aunt about her illness. After what had happened the other night with the little unicorn pin, Beth was terrified that time would run out on Diana before Olivia had the chance to say a final good-bye to the child of her heart. That would destroy her, and she'd never forgive Beth for allowing it to happen.

When the torch song ended with a vibrato flourish, Beth laughed. "Okay, so you've sung for your supper, and it's pit-stop time anyway. Keep an eye out for a decent place to eat."

The GPS guided them to a tourist trap just off the highway, but at least the tablecloth was clean and the overpriced food decent. It was getting dark, and Beth was really tired. She could only guess how much of a strain the trip was on her sister. "Next item on the agenda is a place to spend the night, Di. Check your cell and find us a chain, okay? I'm not in any mood to risk a Bates motel."

"You got it." Diana quickly located a Marriott about ten miles down the highway.

They checked in, had drinks at the bar to unwind a little, and took the elevator up to their two-bedroom suite on the third floor. The beds were so comfortable that Beth fell asleep as soon as her head hit the pillow. After her daily phone call to Lily, Diana did another long meditation, but it wasn't until she listened to ocean waves on her iPod that she was finally able to drift off to sleep.

Beth had put in a wake-up call for six. After breakfast at the hotel's hot buffet, they checked out, gassed up at a Chevron station near the entrance to the highway, and were on their way to the Cascades before seven.

Cutting inland from the Coast Range, Diana insisted on taking her turn at the wheel, promising to let Beth know when she'd had enough. By alternately driving and napping, they were able to cover a lot of miles in record time, but Beth didn't like the frantic pace her sister was setting. Still, as long as Diana's energy level wasn't going into a tailspin, she decided to let her control their timetable.

The GPS readouts on their cellphones and the dashboard were invaluable, but only up to a point. When satellite connections were lost in the mountains, they still needed to scavenge information at gas stations, coffee shops, and visitors' bureaus to pinpoint the exact location of every cemetery within a twenty-mile radius of their first destination, Mt. Shasta. Beth still couldn't believe their upcoming agenda, and she tried desperately to forestall it.

"I'm really beat, Di. How about we find a hotel and catch up on some sleep?"

"No way, Beth. We're not checking in anywhere until we've checked out at least one cemetery." Diana laughed. "That had to be the most bizarre statement I've ever uttered in my entire life."

A hundred miles later, in the foothills of Mr. Shasta, they finally found a graveyard that passed their topographical litmus test. It was a desolate place hugging a windswept hillside that had been mired in mud by the February thaw. A burned-out frame structure, which must once have been a church, stood vigil on the crest of the hill beside the cemetery, but there was no aura of sanctity about the place. Beth edged the Lexus onto the shoulder of the road and stopped, but she kept the engine running.

"What now, Di?" There was no gravel or paved walkway visible between the road and the cemetery, just drenched grass and rivulets of mud. "Looks like we should have brought hip boots and waders." Beth would gladly have gunned the engine and watched the mud fly as she drove off at top speed, but she knew this one had to be completely her sister's call.

Diana was having serious second thoughts. Lowering her window, she craned her neck for a better view. "With all the water running down this way, it's probably not so bad up there. What do you think, Beth?"

"I asked you first, remember?" Beth smiled encouragingly. "Your call. Just name it."

Diana took one deep breath, then another. "Wow," she said, sounding for all the world like the child she had been on that first visit to this region so many years before. "This really is exciting, isn't it?"

Beth knew that Diana actually meant 'terrifying,' but she wasn't about to comment on it. She simply continued to keep the engine purring while she pretended to rummage in her purse for a pack of gum. She wanted to give her sister all the time she needed to gather her courage.

At least a full minute passed before Diana declined the offered stick of gum and gave an intrepid little smile before opening her door. "Come on, Beth. Let's do it!" She unclipped her seatbelt, but didn't go anywhere.

Beth couldn't fault her sister for not wanting to leave the car. She didn't want to get out either. Diana's foot hovered in mid-air even after the engine had been cut and the keys securely tucked into Beth's jacket pocket. She didn't budge until Beth stepped out of the car. Only then did she abandon her seat and march bravely along the apron of grass in the direction of the cemetery. Beth shook her head and quickly set off after her.

By tacit agreement, they stayed together, ignoring the obvious savings in time and energy had they each started at opposite ends of the graveyard and worked their way toward one another. Efficiency wasn't something either of them cared about right now. A pungent herbal smell was almost overpowering, and the place was so creepy that they weren't about to go their separate ways.

"WTF, Beth. Why does this place make me want to order a pizza? Is that really oregano?" She pointed a sweeping finger at the ground cover.

"Sure is." Beth explained something she recalled from researching an article on ancient burial customs a few years earlier. "At least as far back as the Egyptians, people thought that oregano helped the soul of the dead find peace in the afterlife. This stuff was planted so long ago that it's just taken over."

They worked quickly, carefully examining each row of headstones before looping back to check out the next aisle. They had almost covered half the cemetery when they finally came upon a weathered marker with the name 'Lenore Spencer' engraved upon it.

Diana laughed nervously. "Well, Watson, what do you think?"

"I think it's probably too old a grave to be what we're looking for, don't you?" Beth was hoping she agreed. The stone had tilted into the soft ground, and the dates were completely obscured by mud. With a little effort, she was sure they could wipe off enough of the gunk to read the inscribed dates, but she wasn't eager to get that close to the object of their discussion. Diana nodded, evidently sharing her misgivings, but she didn't say a word.

For several moments, they continued to examine the headstone without inching any closer to it, each of them trying to subdue fear with reason. Suddenly the blare of a car horn on the main highway jolted them back to their senses and reminded them that other human beings were alive, well, and not very far away.

"Oh come on," said Beth. "This is silly. Let's have a look." She took the first brave step forward, and Diana followed. Foraging in pockets and purses for tissues, they began cleaning mud from the lower section of the marker until they were finally able to decipher the year of birth.

"1894," said Diana, embarrassed by the relief she heard in her own voice. She shook her head, perplexed by her own emotions. "It's so weird. For a minute, I was actually worried that we got lucky? Is that crazy, or what?"

"Well, if it is, then we've both got issues," admitted Beth. "Come on. Let's see if there are any others."

Ten minutes later, Diana's attention was diverted by a distinctly German name engraved on a marker. "You won't believe what just popped into my head." She laughed softly. "Remember that day we wandered off to explore the dungeons."

Beth shook her head and smiled. "How could I forget? I think it was the only time Aunt Livvy ever actually struck either one of us."

As they recalled that memorable day's events, Diana was amazed to discover that she remembered every detail with crystal clarity. She had been four and Beth six. They were visiting a friend of Liv's who owned the most marvelous old castle on the Rhine, and the temptation to see the forbidden dungeons had been too great. They had crept from their beds one night, taken a flashlight from the kitchen, and descended to the level below the wine cellar, their wonderful adventure coming to an abrupt end when the flashlight batteries gave out. There they were, in total darkness, unable to find their way out, huddled together in a rat-infested cell, clinging to one another for warmth and comfort throughout the long night.

In the morning, when their British nanny discovered that they weren't in their beds, she sounded the alarm and a full-scale search immediately began. Olivia was sure that they'd been kidnapped or had drowned in the Rhine, and she was desolate for the few black hours that it took to find them.

As the girls were brought up from the cellars, Liv ran to crush them to her bosom, drenching them with tears of gratitude as she crowned the tops of their small heads with her kisses. Within moments, thankfulness gave way to rage. Their nanny was unjustly but promptly sacked, and the children's slang vocabulary expanded exponentially as Liv soundly thrashed their bottoms.

"Why do you keep remembering the times we had Aunt Liv pulling her hair out?" asked Beth. "We really weren't such bad kids."

"We weren't exactly angels either."

Beth laughed. "No, but then we'd been through an awful lot, Di. We'd just lost Mom, Dad, and all the Grans. In one horrendous moment, our whole world was kicked out from under us. Aunt Liv's too." They were both quiet for several moments thinking about that awful plane crash in the Alps. Their parents and grandparents were on their way to their favorite resort in Garmisch, retired RAF Ace Grandpa Wendell at the controls of his plane when its engine failed.

"Besides," said Beth, eager to get out of the dark place their thoughts had taken them, "Aunt Liv wouldn't have known what to do with a pair of model children. She would have been bored to tears."

"Right. Dream on." Diana smiled, loving her aunt with all her heart. "What do you think would have happened to us without her, Beth?"

"Luckily we never had to find out." Beth's voice caught on the words, as she turned away from the grave marker that had catapulted Diana's thoughts back to the episode of the dungeons. "Come on, Di. Let's finish this last section and get out of here."

They found two more tombstones bearing the name of 'Lenore,' but the dates were again wrong. Their Lenore, as they had come to think of her, had been born August 6, 1945, and none of the three Lenores in the cemetery was a possible match. Beth wished Diana had thought to ask Ariana's phantom friend about Lenore's surname. It would have made everything so much simpler, but then she supposed that was precisely why her sister hadn't inquired. Diana clearly needed a pretense for going on this farewell journey to her favorite haunts, and an easy Google search would have sabotaged the entire scheme.

By the time they arrived back at their starting point, they were both thoroughly depressed. "So many forgotten souls in this desolate place," sighed Diana, her thoughts mirroring Beth's as they looked at a small grave marker that sloped into the ground at a sharp angle, its engraving completely eroded by time and the elements. "I wish we'd thought to bring some flowers, Beth." They crossed themselves and took a few quiet moments to honor those who had been buried there, crossing themselves a second time before hurrying back to their car. Beth drove off as fast as the muddy embankment would allow.

After two more non-productive days exploring desolate graveyards in the northern part of the state, they drove up to Medford, Oregon, dropped off the Lexus, and caught a flight to Sun Valley, Idaho. Beth longed to detour south and warm her winter-weary soul on a sunny beach, but Diana's pilgrimage inevitably took them to higher and colder elevations.

After Sun Valley, they stopped at the Utah resorts of Snowbird and Alta, then Jackson Hole, Wyoming, before finally going on to Colorado. Wherever they went, Diana always managed to ferret out little pockets of New Age mania. Beth was astonished, and Chad would have been horrified, at how readily she was able to find a psychic or get a card reading even in the most remote mountain towns. It seemed that those who couldn't afford go to gurus in the Himalayas were settling for the Rockies instead.

They devised a workable schedule that seldom varied: awake at six, light breakfast, then on the slopes at seven. By ten, they would be back at the lodge so Diana could rest for a few hours before lunch and an afternoon of Lenore-hunting, a process that repetition made far less traumatic for each of them. Afterward, they would have a long, leisurely dinner, then go to their rooms early so that Diana could do the meditating she had grown to rely on so much and take any medication she might need to get a decent night's sleep. Beth's routine was to order chamomile tea from room service and work on her article before reading herself to sleep.

At long last, six days before they were scheduled to return to New York, they found a likely candidate in their quest for Lenore. The cemetery was about an hour's drive from Crested Butte, Colorado, and the woman's name had been Lenore Mariczek. Born in 1945, she had died in 1963, and her last name was unusual enough to be easily traced online. The birth date was August 10th, not the August 6th they were looking for, but Diana didn't have total confidence in Philip's ability to fix Lenore's birth at a specific point in time.

As she explained to Beth, "They don't exactly have calendars on the astral plane, so it's very possible that the date was a little off. No question it was just about the time they dropped the bomb on Hiroshima -- Philip wouldn't have screwed that up -- but I think we should figure on a few days give or take, just to be on the safe side."

Beth couldn't help but feel uneasy about Diana's mindset. Tracking down Lenore might once have been only a pretext for making this trip, but it seemed to be taking on a life of its own as the days and weeks passed, and the game was starting to become a little too serious for Beth's comfort.

Under the pretext of writing a "55+ in Colorado" feature for Newsworld, Beth phoned Lenore Mariczek's parents and sighed with relief when they reluctantly agreed to an interview that same day. Diana was chomping at the bit to check them out, so Beth had needed to mobilize every weapon in her arsenal of persuasiveness to make it happen.

As soon as they saw the modest house and met the elderly couple who welcomed them into their rustic little home, Beth figured this had to be a wasted trip. She couldn't imagine any scenario that had these two unpretentious people raising a devil child. Still, she knew how deceiving looks often were and, since they'd used the Newsworld cachet to get in the door, they would definitely be going through the motions of an interview.

The Mariczeks refused to be recorded, but were marginally okay with being photographed. When they saw the pricey Nikon digital slung over Diana's shoulder, they presumed she was a photographer with the magazine, and Beth saw no reason to disabuse them of that notion. Diana had taken her trusty old Nikon with her on the trip to document some of the grave markers they'd come across, and she'd seldom been without it during their travels. Her cellphone camera was the best of its kind, but the clarity of the Nikon couldn't be beat, and it was certainly coming in handy as a convincing prop right now. She took a few quick shots of the couple before capping the lens and sitting down on the sofa next to Beth.

For the next several minutes, she enjoyed quietly observing her big sister at the top of her professional game, asking questions, jotting down some kind of shorthand in her notebook, and exhibiting so much interest and concern for the challenges faced by seniors at rarified altitudes that a real rapport quickly developed between her and the Mariczeks.

It was all going beautifully until Beth asked how they and other local residents who didn't profit from the ski trade felt about the seasonal influx of affluent tourists. Expecting a typical townie response about visitors ruining the place, she and Beth were both dumbfounded when the question brought tears to Mrs. Mariczek's eyes.

"I'm sorry, Miss Wendell," said Lenore's mother. "She was our only child, and she's been gone almost sixty years, but I still miss her every minute of every day." Beth said nothing. What could she say?

"She was only eighteen," continued Mrs. Mariczek. Pulling a lacy handkerchief from her sleeve, she dabbed at her eyes. "It was her first year away at college, and she was coming home for Christmas. Her car was run off the road by some drunken rich boy not ten miles away from here."

Her husband's gnarled hand reached out to grasp his wife's frail one, their eyes so full of misery that Beth's heart ached for them.

"I think it's fair to say that we have no reason to be grateful for the visitors who come here, Miss Wendell," said Lenore's father. A reserved man of few words, he stood and laid a protective hand on his wife's shoulder, his body language effectively telling them that they'd outstayed their welcome.

"Of course," said Beth, gathering up her notebook and purse. "How could you possibly feel any other way?" Shame and guilt washed over her for never giving a thought to how painful her poking and prodding at the past might have been for them. She had selfishly used them simply to cross off another small town from Diana's list, and even that had been a dismal failure. They'd crossed off nothing and no one today. Lenore Mariczek might be a long shot, but she was still the only reasonable possibility they'd come up with thus far. If nothing more promising developed over the next few days, Beth was sure that Diana would be doing some deep digging into the Mariczeks.

Beth stood and nodded to Lenore's parents. "Thank you so much for your time. We're both so very sorry for your terrible loss." She turned away, Diana close on her heels, as the old couple escorted them to the door. Beth couldn't get out of there fast enough. They were still snapping on their seatbelts when she pulled away from the house.

"I feel like such a sleaze," said Diana. She glanced back at the house. "Oh jeez, Beth. She's waving. She's actually standing out on the damn porch all alone and waving at us." Diana lowered her window and waved back while Beth focused on the dicey mountain road and blinked back tears.

Four days later, in a suburb of Greeley, they found their second possibility, Lenore Trotter, who had been born August 8th, 1945, and died at the age of sixteen. With the help of the town librarian, they found her obituary in the old newspaper files and learned that she had been the daughter of the town's long-deceased Methodist minister. There was nothing written about an accident or illness, and Beth had to wonder if the girl had committed suicide or accidentally overdosed on drugs as so many teens had been doing for far too long. The obit was the only lead they had, but in a town of three thousand people, it was enough.

Ten minutes beyond Greeley, they entered the small town of Denville and drove directly to the Methodist church, a well-kept and dignified old brick and frame building. As Beth parked the car, Diana said, "Nice not to have to rely on maps and magnifying glasses any more to get where you're going, huh?"

"It's fantastic! But I still wouldn't want to travel without a map. Remember when we lost the signal the other day?"

"Only for a few minutes. It was all those humongous trees."

"Maybe so, but that dingy old map we picked up earlier really came in handy until the satellites found us again." Beth cut the ignition and used the visor mirror to freshen her lipstick. Both women were slow getting out of the car. It had been a long day. Diana was rolling the stiffness out of her shoulders when she noticed Beth doing a mini-backbend.

"You too? I feel positively creaky, Beth!"

"It's the damn altitude. No complaints, squirt. This was all your idea, remember?"

"Yeah, I know." They locked the car and went to the front door of the rectory. With a hand poised over the bell, Diana asked, "Do you think we should have called ahead for an appointment?"

Beth shook her head. "It's the pastor's residence. All God's children welcome anytime, right?"

Diana rang the bell, smiling at the tinkling angelus chimes they heard from inside. Within moments, the door was opened by an attractive middle-aged woman dressed with understated chic in a grey pencil skirt and black sweater. "I'm Reverend Cudahy's wife, Mary Cudahy. How may I help you?" She was tall and well-proportioned, a modern-day Maureen O'Hara in size, colleen coloring, and lilting speech. Beth knew that all Irish weren't Catholic, but it just seemed odd that Maureen's clone would be a Methodist.

"I'm Beth Wendell, and this is my sister, Diana Wendell." No hand was offered to shake and no offense taken in this era of killer viruses. "Sorry to intrude, but we were hoping you might be able to help us out with a project we're working on?" Beth flashed her Newsworld ID, its cachet once again opening a door for them.

"Please, come inside, won't you? There's a real chill in the air today." She hurriedly closed the door behind them.

Beth admired the woman's stock in trade: unflagging poise and a welcoming smile that had faltered only for a moment when she saw the Newsworld logo.

"Newsworld? In Denville? Oh, my," she chuckled. "I am impressed. Why don't we chat a bit over tea. As it happens, your timing is excellent. I've just made a fresh pot."

She led them into a sunny kitchen with windows on all sides. Given the freezing weather, the room should have been cold and drafty, but a wood-burning stove was keeping everything warm and cozy. "Please, make yourselves at home, ladies."

Beth and Diana seated themselves at the big oak table and made small talk with their hostess for the few minutes it took her to set out tea and cookies. As soon as Mrs. Cudahy claimed her seat at the head of the table, Beth spun another tale about an imaginary article she was writing, this one on teenage suicides. The lies were coming so easily now that it almost worried her.

After an hour of tea, excellent home-made chocolate cookies, and long, drawn-out stories about local history, it turned out that there was nothing at all suspicious about the death of Lenore Trotter. Mrs. Cudahy, 'Mary' now that the three of them were on a first-name basis, had lived in Denville all her life and had known all the Trotters. She remembered Lenore as being an ordinary, decent girl whose death had nothing to do with drugs or depression. Peritonitis had killed her just two weeks before her seventeenth birthday. It was sad, even tragic, but definitely not at the hands of a sinister coven. Beth and Diana thanked Mary for her hospitality and left soon after.

Still, as they drove back toward Greeley, Diana duly noted Lenore Trotter's name below that of Lenore Mariczek's in her journal. She shook her head wonderingly. "I tell you, Beth, if this is the best we can come up with, God help us. It's like putting Snow White and Cinderella in a police line-up."

Beth started to laugh, but a wheeze was all that Diana heard. She reached a hand out to her sister's forehead. "You feel warm."

Beth hadn't been feeling very sharp for the past few days, but she thought it was only the effect of the cold weather and high altitude in the Rockies. The sudden wheeze told her otherwise. "It's probably just the start of a cold, but I'll see Doc Adams when we get back to New York tomorrow just to be sure." Her sister's immune system was too compromised to risk exposure to any germs, even a garden-variety cold. "Meanwhile, crack your window a little, Di, and try not to inhale from my direction."

The next morning, Beth was so ill that Diana wanted to cancel their flight, but Beth insisted that they go home on schedule. When she fell into bed as soon as they got to her apartment, Diana immediately called their family doctor. The Gresham billions ensured that house calls were still very much in vogue any time of the day or night, and Doctor Adams hurried right over. After diagnosing a severe respiratory infection that was rapidly sidestepping bronchitis in its hurry to settle into pneumonia, he ordered complete bed rest and called in prescriptions for the usual battery of drugs to be delivered stat.

Before leaving Beth's bedroom, he gave them both strict instructions. Pointing to Beth, he said, "Complete bed rest until I tell you otherwise, young lady." Turning to Diana, he said, "Just tell Paulina to keep her on a light diet for the next three days. Plenty of fluids, meds, and an immediate call to me if her condition worsens in any way."

Diana quickly explained that Paulina was away on the impromptu vacation Beth had given her while they were out of town. "But she'll be back in a few days. Meanwhile, I'm sure I'll be able to manage just fine."

"But…" Beth's objection was cut short by Dr. Adams who put a finger to his lips to silence her.

"I'm ordering private nursing to be here 24/7, at least until Paulina gets back. Non-negotiable, Diana. It's either that or the hospital and possible exposure to MRSA and God knows what else. Take your pick." Avoiding Diana's glance, he tucked his stethoscope into his medical bag, then began fitting little vials and syringes back into their proper sleeves, as he continued to speak. "Your own health is precarious enough as it is, and you know it, young lady, so don't give me a hard time on this one."

"Okay. Okay," said Diana, trying mightily to control her temper.

"I want you out of here as soon as the nurse arrives, Diana. Check in at a hotel, stay with a friend, whatever, but you're not to be in this apartment again until Beth is completely recovered." He took a package of facemasks out of his medical bag and handed it to her. "Meanwhile, wear one of these whenever you're in this room." The man spoke with the authority of someone who had brought her into the world and cried with her when she told him she was dying. Diana didn't argue. She opened the packet of facemasks he'd given her and put one on immediately.

As soon as Doc Adams left, she made tea and toast for her sister, then called Chad to tell him what had happened. His frantic reaction and promise to be there within the hour spoke volumes about the depth of his feelings for her sister. She just hoped they would somehow find a way around his pride. She hated to think of Beth being alone when she could no longer be with her.

Diana knew that Olivia would not be a great comfort to Beth after she was gone. Her aunt and her sister loved one another dearly, but they were on completely different wavelengths, always had been. Liv would eventually find solace with her host of friends and parties, but Beth would not be so easily distracted from her grief. She would have only her work and Chad, both so intertwined that losing one meant losing both. What if Chad didn't come to his senses? What if...? No, Diana reminded herself, don't borrow trouble. Beth is strong, she always has been. With or without Chad Martin, she'll be okay. Please God, let her be okay.

Chad's voice from the lobby intercom was a welcome interruption from her maudlin thoughts. She was waiting for him in the hall when he rushed off the elevator, and she briefed him on all that the doctor had said. He, in turn, suggested that she should heed the doctor's advice to distance herself from Beth, since he planned to be with her until the nurse arrived and kicked him out. She responded by rolling her eyes and handing him a facemask.

Diana was still debating what to do when they reached Beth's room, but the happiness in her sister's eyes the moment she saw Chad left no doubt in her mind that it was time to be on her way. Since she hadn't even had time to unpack from their trip yet, she immediately said her goodbyes. Ten minutes later, she was on the road and headed to the last small town on her list, Windham, New York.

It was a trip she'd made many times before, and she didn't need any GPS to get there. She had fallen in love with the quaint little town five years ago, during a hectic holiday social season in Manhattan that happened to coincide with some of the best ski conditions the Northeast had ever seen.

She and her sister were on everybody's must-invite holiday party list, and there was never enough time between events to get away to Vail or any of her other favorite haunts. Desperate to strap on her skis, she'd done a little internet search and sneaked off to the Catskills early one morning. It was only a two and a half hour drive, and she was determined to get in a few hours on the trails at Windham before driving back for another dinner party that night.

She had no hope for great skiing in the Catskill Mountains, Lilliputian compared the Alps and the Rockies, but she was delighted with what she found there. The area was beautiful, and the skiing far better than she'd expected. Before she returned to the city late that afternoon, she had already put a deposit down on a new A-frame adjoining the slopes.

After that, whenever she was in New York during the winter, she escaped to Windham as often as possible, usually alone, rarely with Beth, and never with anyone else. Olivia didn't do rustic at all. It was Diana's private refuge, always warm and welcoming, close enough for a quick day trip, and as much a home of her own as she'd ever known. She longed for its comforting solitude now. It was smaller than any other place she'd ever lived in, but it was all hers, only hers, and she loved it.

It was exhausting always trying to be brave about her illness, and she needed time alone for the inevitable crying jags that hit her when she least expected it. Most of all, she needed time alone to meditate, practice her yoga, and give her telekinetic powers a little breathing room. They were screaming for release.

Beth wouldn't recognize the changes in the condo since her last visit the year before. Crystals were everywhere now, bookcases overflowing with storehouses of esoteric knowledge, and candles of every shape, size and color were in each room. Under normal circumstances, Diana could count on Beth to take it all in stride, but nothing was normal in their lives any longer.

Diana checked in with Chad as soon as she arrived at the Windham condo and was relieved to hear that the nurse was already on duty and that Chad seemed satisfied with both her bedside manner and competence. More good news was that Paulina was coming back a day early and would be there in the morning. Beth was asleep, but he assured Diana that she was okay and that everything was under control.

From Windham, she checked in on Beth several times a day with either Chad, Paulina, the nurse, or Doc Adams. She couldn't help but feel guilty about causing her sister to be so rundown that full-blown pneumonia was threatening every day.

It was five gut-wrenching days before Doc Adams pronounced Beth officially out of danger. He called Diana with the good news and warned that she still had to keep away until the coughing had totally subsided, probably in another week. After their discussion, Diana breathed a sigh of relief, said a quick prayer of thanks, and celebrated with a glass of champagne. Now that she knew Beth would be okay, she could really begin her search for Lenore, this time using all her psychic gifts to find her. There were no more small towns on the list for her to check out. This one was her last hope.

Our High Priest says that his old nemesis has returned.

But what does that even mean? He explains nothing about it.

The coven's older majority never questions anything he says or does.

But our younger minority can only question all of it.

We were lured into the group by the promise of free drugs. We're hooked, but not stupid.

For now, we'll stay the course and reassess if and when he finally goes off the deep end.

Meanwhile, he's sworn us all to secrecy.

If the worst were to happen, if we were to be discovered and arrested, we are to admit nothing.

He promises that if we stand fast, Hecate and her Dark Lord will protect us.

I wish I could believe him.

Chapter Four

Dawn was just breaking over the murky waters of the East River when Beth pulled onto the FDR Drive. At this hour, traffic was so light that she made record time getting to the Deegan and the northbound Thruway, one of her favorite roads for putting the BMW through its paces. It had been two full weeks since Diana had left for Windham, and she was eager to get there.

Her car was a relatively nondescript black compact that she'd bought four years ago, when Chad's predecessor had assigned her to do a string of features on rising political stars in New York State. A disgraced governor had just been succeeded by an ineffectual one whose days were definitely numbered. Everyone, regardless of party affiliation, agreed that the leadership vacuum in Albany was sucking the life out of the State, and concern about the upcoming election had been at fever pitch.

Voter interest in her series kept it going for weeks, and Beth logged almost twenty thousand miles getting the job done, much of it on the road she was traveling now. She'd interviewed likely gubernatorial candidates in both major parties throughout the state, including the former attorney general who ultimately won the seat, and her BMW had handled all the miserable ice and snow so well that she'd decided to keep it.

It gave her a warm fuzzy to know that the car was truly her own, completely paid for with money she had earned writing for Newsworld. Most of her other possessions had either been inherited or charged to a very generous trust fund. Not that she was complaining. She'd been blessed with an ancestor who'd turned out to be a Wall Street superstar. He was super-savvy or just lucky enough to sell off all his holdings a few weeks before the 1929 crash, and he was wise enough to plow every penny of his financial windfall into real estate. He'd bought up everything from Long Island potato farms to Florida swampland, ultimately enriching the family coffers into the billions.

Beth smiled at the irony of her wonderfully flamboyant aunt Olivia being forced to serve at the helm of stodgy old Gresham Enterprises. Her snug designer suits and stiletto heels certainly brightened up the annual meetings. Fortunately for all the shareholders, under the slightly ditzy socialite facade there lurked a brilliant mind and a steadfastly entrepreneurial heart.

Olivia had put an excellent Board of Directors in place with enough checks and balances within the system to ensure that nobody was going to run the company into the ground. She teleconferenced with her CEO and CFO almost every day, and each of her key players were regularly vetted by Paul Dunsford. She'd hired top-notch outside auditors to keep everybody honest, including one another, all of which freed up enough time for her to lead the kind of life she loved. Beth could only dread what the news of Diana's illness would do to her.

She was so distracted with worry about Olivia that she almost missed her exit. Fortunately, she was in the right-hand lane with nobody close behind her, so she easily braked onto the exit ramp leading to Route 23 North. Within half an hour, she was at her sister's home, a futuristic three-tiered frame dwelling that commanded a choice view of Windham Mountain.

Because there were so many similar structures in the immediate area, Diana referred to it as her 'condo,' but it was, in fact, a totally detached building. Even Paul had approved of her choice. The house didn't stand out from the rest of the ski lodges in any way, and it was ideally situated for setting up any security perimeter that might be needed.

Beth backed the BMW into Diana's driveway and wasted no time hurrying to the front door. Her luggage could keep. Right now, she just needed to hug her baby sister. She didn't feel at all guilty about not giving Diana fair warning that she'd be arriving a day early. The element of surprise could only work in her favor, and she needed all the help she could get. Phone tag and cryptic messages had been maddening, and it was time Diana told her exactly what was really going on up here. Beth had no interest in hearing the sanitized version she was sure to get if she came on schedule the next day.

Paul had assured her that Diana was safe, under constant surveillance, and behaving normally, at least by Diana's standards, with the same level of quirkiness that they'd all come to expect of her over the years. Still, for the past week, Beth hadn't been able to shake the feeling that her sister was in some kind of trouble.

She rang the bell and listened for approaching footsteps, but all she heard was the cheery peal of chimes from inside. It was after nine o'clock and Diana should have returned from her early morning ski run by now. She rang the bell again, more insistently this time. Still no response. She had her own key to the house and, reluctant as she was to turn a surprise visit into a complete intrusion, she used it now.

She smelled smoke as soon as she opened the door. Shouting Diana's name, she followed the smoke to its source, her eyes scanning the kitchen as she ran past it, her mind registering no fire or other evident problem there. When she reached the living room, she froze, relief anesthetizing her from panic at what she saw.

Diana was seated in full lotus position in the middle of the living room floor, ankles resting on opposite thighs, back of her hands on her knees, palms upward, index finger and thumb of each hand forming a perfect circle. Her eyes were closed. She was wearing headphones, and she was surrounded by clusters of quartz crystals, burning candles, and a haze of incense. Beth's eyes teared and she coughed, her body protesting the insult to her still vulnerable lungs, but Diana remained oblivious to everything around her, including Beth's presence.

Beth felt like the worst kind of voyeur, but she couldn't stop staring at the look of almost beatific tranquility shining from Diana's face. The pale blonde hair cascading to her shoulders, the flawless skin, and the slender body comfortably encased in her favorite pale lavender warm-up suit were all recognizable as Diana, yet the woman before her could have been a stranger. Beth had never believed that auras were truly discernible to the naked human eye, but just then she wasn't so sure. Her sister was absolutely radiant.

Sensing a loving presence nearby, Diana's eyes suddenly flew open, closed again for a few moments, then opened once more, slowly this time, allowing her vision to gradually come into focus. In one lithe movement, she tore off her headphones, stood, and jumped across the ring of candles separating her from Beth. She gave her sister a hard hug.

"You startled me," she said, not a hint of embarrassment in her voice. "I wasn't expecting you until tomorrow. Is everything okay?" She hurried to cover the incense burner.

"Everything's fine." Trying desperately to appear calm and relaxed, Beth leaned casually against the back of the sofa. "Sorry to barge in on you like this, Di." She shrugged apologetically. "My cell ran out of juice, or I would have called you from the road." Her cell had been working just fine.

Diana's most recent call, just last night, had hinted at some real progress in the search for Lenore, but she hadn't wanted to discuss it over the phone. "Thought I'd come up early and see what the big mystery is."

"Glad you did, Beth. Just give me a sec'" She opened the sliding glass doors leading out to the patio and pulled the screen door in place to air out the room. She then deftly began wielding the candle snuffer with practiced speed. "Sorry about all this," she said, waving at tendrils of smoke that were threading their way through the screen door toward the patio. "Damn!" She raced across the room and flicked a switch on the far wall. The distinct sound of a powerful rising whirr could immediately be heard. "Great fan. Works like a charm when I remember to turn it on."

Beth had a sudden coughing fit. Diana winced and ran into the kitchen for a glass of water for her while Beth quickly dug out one of several tightly wrapped cough drops that had escaped their flimsy outer packaging during the trip and fallen to the bottom of her purse. Between that and the water, her coughing quickly subsided.

"Guess I went a little overboard with the aromatherapy today. Just what you needed, huh?

"Not to worry. Doc gave me a clean bill of health. I'm fine." Diana hovered just long enough to make sure she really was okay, then moved quickly about the room collecting the candles and crystals from the floor. She set the candles out on the dining room table to cool, then gently tucked the crystals away in a velvet-lined drawer of the china cabinet, right next to the silver.

When she was done, Beth glanced pointedly up at the smoke detector on the ceiling. "And that never made a peep through all this because…?"

Diana shrugged and gave a quick little grin. "Had to take the batteries out, or give up meditating and go completely nuts. No contest."

Beth bit her lower lip, bit it hard. It was either that or scream. "Okay… And the security alarm? Why was it off when I got here?"

Diana laughed. "Busted again. I plead the fifth." Scooping up a rainbow-hued afghan from a corner of the window seat, she draped it over Beth's shoulders. "Cold in here with the door open."

With the indoor temperature hovering close the outdoor chill of mid-March, Beth welcomed the added layer of warmth. "Thanks, Di. Feels good." She snuggled deeper into the afghan. "So good that I think I'll go outside and take a peek at the slopes." The cloying smell of incense kept tickling her throat, and she needed the escape. She stepped out onto the deck and did a double take when she saw the newest additions to the patio furniture. "Love the chairs."

Picking up on Beth's teasing tone, Diana laughed. "I know. I know. I always hated Adirondacks, until I actually sat in one a while back. Still think they're ugly as hell, but so comfortable. They're great!"

Keeping the afghan tightly wrapped around her, Beth settled back into one of the chairs and allowed the mountains to work their magic. The sun was warm on her face, and the steady stream of skiers weaving down the slopes mesmerizing. If she hadn't been so hungry, she probably would have dozed off. As soon as Diana called out an "all clear," she hurried inside to ask about breakfast.

"My blood sugar's tanked, Di. Why don't we go somewhere for breakfast?" She knew better than to check Diana's refrigerator for bacon and eggs.

"Great idea." Diana closed and locked the back door. "And I know just the place! Best muffins anywhere."

"Sounds perfect."

Diana adjusted a control on the thermostat. "Should be comfy in here by the time we get back." She put on her jacket and tossed an extra one from the closet to Beth. She gladly traded it for the afghan. Her jeans, sweater and quilted vest had been almost too warm in the city, but nowhere close to what she needed to keep warm up here.

Shouldering their purses, they headed out the front door, Diana in the lead. When she sailed right past the alarm without breaking stride, Beth grabbed her sleeve and tugged her back. "Aren't you forgetting something?" Diana shrugged, genuinely perplexed.

"The alarm," persisted Beth.

"Oh! Um…" Shifting her weight from one foot to the other, she sighed. "Jeez, Beth, we're in the country. It's not a big thing. Just pull the door good and tight behind you. It locks automatically." She was already almost at the driveway.

Beth wasn't really afraid of intruders. Paul's team would be watching the house, and they'd make sure no strangers ever had a chance to get inside. It just made her heartsick to see how careless or, worse, forgetful, Diana had become about routines that had been second-nature to them for so many years. Clearly, she used the code so seldom that she'd forgotten it. Beth made a mental note to buy batteries for the smoke detectors and ask Paul about the alarm code so she could key it in herself. She closed the door behind her and followed Diana.

They took Beth's car, since it was blocking the entrance to Diana's garage, but Diana drove, skillfully negotiating the intricate web of back roads to Eliza's Country Kitchen, a homey little restaurant ten minutes out of Windham.

Beth ordered juice, coffee and a toasted blueberry muffin, while Diana feasted on a full-course breakfast of ham and eggs over light with home fries and assorted mini-muffins. She had lost more weight since leaving the city, so Beth knew she wasn't eating this well on a regular basis, but it was wonderful to watch her enjoy a good meal. Their conversation was strictly amusing small-talk, until they were done eating.

When the waitress had finished clearing their plates and topping their coffee, Diana took a deep breath, folded her arms at the edge of the table, and gave her sister a long searching look. "As I told you last night, Beth, I think I've actually come up with something. Only one problem… I'm not quite sure what it is."

Pausing to gather her thoughts, she managed to take a few sips of coffee without burning her mouth from the brimming mug. "I didn't want to freak you out by dragging you into all this until I knew what I was dealing with. But, as long as you're here, you may as well help me sort through it."

"Sort through what exactly?"

Diana glanced around the room as she struggled to express her thoughts, and the young waitress whose overconfident body language broadcast that she was likely Eliza's teenage daughter or niece, took that as her cue to bring the check. She gave the girl a twenty dollar bill, twice the amount of the absurdly reasonable check, and told her to keep the change. The girl was apparently accustomed to Diana's generosity, for she showed no surprise, only gum-chewing blasé entitlement.

"It's not anything I can explain without… Well, you'll just have to see for yourself. Come on."

Beth hurried to follow her out the door. Diana waved the car keys in the air. "Country air really agrees with me, so no meds needed this morning. Mind if I drive again?"

"Be my guest." The road they'd taken to get to the coffee shop was little more than a glorified cowpath, so Beth was happy to be in the passenger seat.

As before, Diana navigated the back roads with a certainty born of familiarity. Beth was surprised. She hadn't thought her sister visited Windham often, but clearly she did. She couldn't have become this adept at finding her way in just the past few weeks. Again that uneasy feeling. She thought she knew Diana so well, yet here was another unexpected revelation.

After a few miles, they reached a fork in the road where the smooth pavement continued left and a rutted old road veered off to the right. Without hesitation, Diana took the dilapidated right fork, more stones and dirt than asphalt. They had gone only a few hundred feet, when she pulled off onto the shoulder and cut the engine.

"Where are we?" As far as Beth could tell, they were at the back of beyond.

"Little burg called Chaetestown," said Diana. "There's a cemetery on the other side of those trees." She nodded to a thick stand of pine trees.

They got out of the car and plodded along an uphill path strewn with small stones that kept skittering under their feet. The only thing cheering Beth on was her sister's stamina. Diana was breathing easily, despite the steep climb.

"We're almost there, Beth." Diana threw an encouraging smile over her shoulder. "You okay?"

"Fine. Just thinking about all the thirsty deer ticks we've been disturbing." She was a city girl born and bred, and she never apologized for it.

At the crest of the hill, invisible from the road because of its elevation and the curtain of pines surrounding it, was a small cemetery enclosed by a sturdy black wrought-iron fence. They walked around its perimeter until they reached a heavy gate that had long ago fallen off its rusty hinges, leaving a gap wide enough for them to pass through.

"Cemetery's been closed for forty or fifty years. This is pretty much the only way to get in now."

"How'd you ever find it?"

"Dumb luck. One of the Windham librarians who's been helping me with research happens to have some great-greats who were buried here way back when."

Near the gate was the oldest section of the cemetery. Decades of harsh weather had sabotaged the symmetry of the rows of tombstones, giving the landscape a curiously informal, less intimidating appearance. She could see and smell remnants of oregano plantings here too, but the herb hadn't run amok.

"Some of these graves actually go back to before the Revolutionary War," Diana said. Seeing the immediate spark of interest in her sister's eyes, she quickly added, "But that's not what I wanted to show you." She led the way toward another section of the cemetery, walking with a clear sense of direction now. She stopped at a simple granite marker.

Beth was unimpressed with the inscription: 'Margaret Mowbray - Died April 30, 1952 - Aged 79 Years'. She was about to move on to another more interesting little tombstone just beyond it, until she saw the enthralled expression on Diana's face. Beth scrutinized the grave marker more closely, but still couldn't see anything unusual about it. "What am I missing here, Di?"

Diana shook her head. "I'm not sure, Beth. It's certainly not the tombstone we've been looking for -- the name and dates are all wrong. Yet it happens every time."

"What happens?"

"I stand here, and I feel so, so strange. Not in a bad way. Not at all. Actually it's just the opposite. Kind of... I don't know how to explain it. Kind of all warm inside, I guess. Don't you feel anything?"

Beth hesitated, trying to get some sense of what Diana claimed to be feeling, but the grave marker was just an ordinary piece of granite with no special meaning at all for her. She shook her head and shrugged. "Nothing."

"I was afraid of that," sighed Diana. "Oh well... At least the landscape's right, if that means anything. There's a great view of a gorgeous little valley, just as pastoral as you please, right through those trees."

Beth followed the direction Diana had indicated and walked to a clearing in the pines at the edge of the cemetery. The scene below was exactly as Diana had described. She shook her head and returned to where her sister was waiting. "Picture perfect and made to order, Di. Have you checked the other tombstones?"

Diana nodded thoughtfully. "Checked every last one of them the first time I came here, but this is what we've been looking for, Beth. This is it. Whatever *it* is, it's right here. I just know it"

"But that doesn't make any sense. The name's all wrong, and the woman certainly didn't die young. She was seventy-nine, for God's sake. And she was born closer to the Civil War than World War II. Absolutely nothing fits."

"I know. Believe me, I know. I've been meditating day and night trying to make some sense out of it, but I still can't connect the dots. Thing is, no matter how worried or frightened I am, just being here makes me feel better, not so afraid somehow. It's beyond weird, but I always leave here feeling as if I can cope with anything."

Beth didn't even want to think about her sister seeking comfort at the grave of a stranger, but she had to know. "How often do you come here?"

Diana shrugged. "At least once a day, ever since I found it last week." Her face suddenly pink with embarrassment, she quickly added. "It's so close, Beth. Getting here's no big deal."

Beth didn't trust herself to say a word. Nodding, she concentrated again on the tombstone. Closing her eyes, she desperately tried to pick up some sense of what drew Diana to this place, but nothing out of the ordinary presented itself. She was thankful when Diana began walking back down the hill toward the car.

Beth followed a few steps behind her. "What about all the meditating you do, Di? Hasn't anything ever surfaced about that Mowbray woman while you've been under?"

Diana laughed. "You make meditation sound like anesthesia!" Periodically over the years, Diana had coached her sister in meditation techniques, never with any success. "A town hall fire destroyed most of Chaetestown's records years ago, Beth, but I figure there has to be a record of her somewhere. I'm hoping the private investigator I hired will..."

"What?" They had just reached the car, and Beth was hearing alarm bells loud and clear when she saw the guilty expression on Diana's face just before she ducked into the driver's seat. Clearly, she had let slip something she hadn't intended to say. "I'm presuming, Di – no, make that praying – that this investigator is on Paul's payroll. Yes?"

Diana blew out a heavy sigh and slowly shook her head. "Get real, Beth. Dearly as I love Paul, he's the last guy I'd call in on this."

I'm next in line to be High Priest.

If there's still a coven left to rule when my time comes.

At the rate the old fool is going, we'll all end up behind bars.

This week, he's thrown all caution to the winds with these insane nightly gatherings.

We have families, jobs and businesses. We're known in the community. We can't just keep going off the grid for hours on end without people asking questions! And we're all running out of excuses to give them.

It's only a matter of time before one of us is followed to the secret caverns.

Then what?

He says that we're under siege from a powerful enemy.

But how can that be? The woman he speaks of died before most of us were even born!

He's becoming paranoid in his dotage, and his mad obsession with Margaret Mowbray will destroy us all.

The dicey drugs he's always taken to keep his youthful vitality may have burned out more brain cells than his gray matter can spare.

Chapter Five

On the way home from the cemetery, Beth questioned Diana about the private investigator she'd hired, and the answers were anything but reassuring. "I can't believe you told him all that!"

"Chill, Beth. I promise you he's totally discreet."

"*Chill?* What are we, twelve?"

It was a long and silent drive back to Diana's. Whoever this Charlie Hobson was, he'd already been given enough information to make Diana's obsession with the occult a public laughingstock if he ever sold her out to the tabloid press. Beth wished that she'd known about him from day one. It would have made damage control a whole lot easier.

Not that their family had any kind of a holier-than-thou image to preserve and protect -- far from it. Olivia's penchant for notorious young rakes had kept gossip columnists on six continents salivating for as long as Beth could remember. But this was different. This time, the snickering and jeering would be at Diana's expense, and it would all come down on her during the roughest time of her life. Unfortunately, her illness was one of the few secrets that she hadn't confided in Hobson, so there would be no compassionate spin on any story that he might leak to the press.

Beth knew that Paul Dunsford, master of damage control, had to be brought on board with the whole story immediately. He was the most practical, pragmatic, sane and sensible man she'd ever known. If there was a solution, he would find it. He was like a second father to them, and she dreaded having to tell him about Diana's illness and the bizarre psychic journey it had triggered.

With each of them nursing their anger, the drive back to the condo seemed endless. Figuring that the tension in the car couldn't get any worse, Beth decided to go on record with something else that needed to be said, no matter how much Diana wouldn't want to hear it. "Obviously, I really need to meet this Charlie Hobson. As in yesterday, Di."

Tires squealing, Diana accelerated into a sharp turn that had Beth reaching for the dashboard as she roared onto Route 23. "Why, Beth? Why waste everybody's time when you've already made up your mind about him?"

Beth gritted her teeth and didn't say a word until she saw the digital readout on the speedometer top eighty. "Slow down, dammit!" She'd seldom yelled at Diana, especially lately, so her words had the desired effect. Diana immediately eased off the accelerator.

Lowering her hands from the dash to a death-grip on her knees, Beth waited until their speed had settled into a steady sixty before venturing to say another word. "You know as well as I do that Charlie Hobson has to be checked out." She suspected that Paul had already done his homework on the guy, but she'd long ago learned to presume nothing where her sister was concerned. "Paul can get the job done with a Louisville Slugger or I can do it with kid gloves over dinner tonight. Your call entirely."

"Some choice." After a few grumbling moments, Diana pulled her cellphone from the side pocket of the ever-present tote she'd left on the console between them. Beth watched her hit a speed dial number and had to bite back a groan. Great, she thought, this PI, whoever and whatever he might be, is already her BFF.

"Charlie, my sister's in town and wants a meet-and-greet. You free for dinner tonight?" He was, and they arranged to meet at an upscale Italian restaurant down the mountain at seven o'clock. Diana disconnected and tucked the phone back into the tote. She gave Beth a venomous glance. "Satisfied?"

"Actually, no. Far from it, in fact. I'll get back to you on it after I meet him." Neither of them said another word for the rest of the trip. When Diana pulled into her driveway, they dashed out of the car like escaping felons, each of them hurrying upstairs to the solitude and sanctuary of her own room.

Beth wasn't sure whether her sister intended to nap, meditate or just keep fuming the day away. Whatever the case, she decided it was as good a time as any to run some urgent errands before she phoned Paul. Partly because she was annoyed and partly because she wanted to alert her sister to her departure, she made a noisy exit, clumping down the stairs and slamming the front door behind her.

Windham wasn't exactly a metropolis, but she managed to find everything she needed in just over an hour. She returned to the condo with bags of fresh and frozen food, including the junk variety, wine, cheeses, and several batteries, all of which took three trips to transport from car to kitchen. After putting all the groceries away, she immediately tackled the smoke and CO alarms in each room, except Diana's. She'd take care of that later. Right now, she was in no mood to beard the lioness in her den.

Actually, she'd expected Diana to come storming out of her room at the sound of a piercing triple chirp after she'd switched batteries in the first alarm she tackled. She was pleased when that didn't happen but, when none of the battery chirping elicited any response from Diana as each alarm was activated, she had to worry that something might be wrong.

Risking her sister's wrath, she tiptoed to her door and put her ear up against it. Holding her breath and hearing nothing, she couldn't stop herself from turning the knob and peeking inside. Relief flooded through her when she saw Diana in full lotus position on the rug beside her bed. Earbuds in place, she was obviously okay and lost in a world of her own.

With little green lights now visible on every alarm unit she passed, Beth congratulated herself on a job well done. Looking to find a place to put the dead batteries clunking around in her pockets, she went back downstairs and into the garage. She almost laughed when she saw a pristine plastic container clearly marked "Used Batteries." It was of course empty until she filled it.

She was pretty sure this was the first time the alarm batteries had been changed since her sister bought the place. It was the kind of thing that had always been taken care of for Diana by a long line of household servants, but there weren't any trusty retainers up here. Apart from a weekly cleaning service, she was very much on her own, just as she'd said she wanted to be.

Beth washed the dust off her hands and nuked hot water for a cup of green tea to take upstairs with her. No more stalling. She needed to talk with Paul. Closing her bedroom door behind her, she made herself comfortable in a padded blue velvet armchair at a combination vanity table/desk under the window facing the slopes. She set her tea down to cool on the desktop, rummaged through her oversized purse for her cellphone, then dialed Paul's private line. When he answered on the first ring, tears sprang to her eyes at the sound of his voice and they kept right on falling until she'd finished telling him the whole story. Keeping Diana's secret had meant isolating herself from the two people she could never overtly lie to, Paul and Olivia. Until she heard Paul's voice, she hadn't fully realized the depth of the loneliness that had been gnawing at her soul for months.

He listened quietly until her tears subsided, then told her what she should never have even doubted. Paul had been fully aware of Diana's illness from the very beginning in St. Moritz. One of his many surveillance teams had immediately picked up on her sudden spate of doctor visits, and a little judicious hacking had filled in all the blanks. Now that medical records were almost always entered on a computer somewhere, there was very little that couldn't be discovered online. He had only one criticism of how they'd been handling all of it thus far.

"You have no right to keep Olivia out of all this, Beth."

"I know," she sighed. "Diana keeps promising to tell her. Just hasn't worked up the courage to do it. And, sadly, she absolutely forbids me to do it for her."

"Keep after her. It's well past time that she confided in Liv." The comment was ambiguous enough to have Beth wondering if Paul had already told their aunt what was happening. Paul and Olivia were so close that she had to figure he would have, but before she could press him on it, he quickly changed the subject, "So, what do you think of your sister's latest conquest?"

As she expected, he already knew about Charlie Hobson. As she hadn't expected, he gave the guy high marks. "Highly decorated cop. Twenty years on the Albany force. Worked his way up through the ranks to a detective's gold shield. Commendations all the way down the line." She could hear the tap of keyboarding as he scrolled through the information he had on file. "He's a widower. Wife died after a long bout with cancer. No kids." More tapping. "Retired from the force a few years after the wife died." More keyboarding.

"Absolutely nothing about him raises any flags, Beth. Obviously anybody this close to Diana bears watching, but that's my job, remember? Appreciate your due diligence on this one, but do me a favor and cross the guy off your worry list, okay?" He chuckled in that familiar way he had of always making her world seem a little less menacing. "As if, huh? Really, kiddo, trust me on this one. I'm all over it."

Paul had once told her that she and Diana were the children he'd never had, and he'd never given them any reason to doubt it. She knew that he shared her heartbreak about her sister's illness and the insane quest for Lenore, but he was very much the parental authority figure as he talked her through all of it. He spoke with so much love, compassion and reassurance that Beth had a hard time ending the conversation.

After they disconnected, she cried. And cried. There were tears of sadness for what Diana was going through and tears of gratitude for Paul Dunsford's always healing presence in their lives. Her tea had grown cold, but she drank it anyway before going into the bedroom's private bath and splashing cold water around her eyes until the redness faded. When she finally saw Diana again, she didn't want her seeing any telltale evidence of a crying jag.

Returning to the bedroom, she grabbed her laptop and took it with her to the bed. Propping her back against a mound of pillows piled against the headboard, she went to work on the article she'd promised Chad. Between deadlines and the horrendous subject matter, she knew she owed it to all those lost children to shelve her personal nightmare, at least for the next few hours.

She made good progress on the article and shut it down at six, just in time to get ready for show time at seven. Diana had been careful to park Beth's car on the side of the driveway that wouldn't block her own car, so this time she was driving the Porsche. During the ride to the restaurant, after only grunting monosyllables at one another all afternoon, it was a tossup about who was more anxious.

What little conversation they managed came to a grinding halt when Diana explained how she had come to select this particular P.I. The randomness of it left Beth speechless, and they drove the last few miles in total silence. By the time they entered the elegantly appointed lobby at La Stella, Beth's antennae were on high alert as the maitre d' escorted them to the table Diana had earlier reserved. It was in a primo corner spot overlooking Catskill Creek, and Charlie Hobson was already there waiting for them.

Tugging at the collar of his starched white shirt, he stood politely as they approached the table. Feeling hostility pinging off him like radar, he put on his warmest good guy smile and hoped for the best.

After Diana's quick introductions, the maitre d' made a great show of seating her while Charlie did a workmanlike job of seeing Beth comfortably into her chair. Nowadays, he just never knew what was PC and what wasn't, so he half-expected to be swatted away by a feminist hand. He was relieved when she rewarded his efforts with a small nod of thanks and an almost-smile, even though no hint of a smile was reflected in those wary green eyes.

The maitre d' had profited from Diana's largesse too often to ignore her now, and his fawning attention as he took their drink orders was starting to grate on Charlie's nerves. He managed to get the green-eyed monster back in its cage by the time their drinks arrived, and he actually enjoyed watching the uppity guy grovel.

This place was way above his pay grade, and he'd only ever been here once before. That was on a rare date, one of two blind dates he'd had that year courtesy of well-meaning friends who kept telling him he needed to get himself 'out there' again, whatever the hell that was supposed to mean. Back then, this same maitre d' had shown him and his date to a table for two at the back of the restaurant, a very, very small table near the entrance to the rest rooms.

He clearly remembered thinking that there might as well have been a table marker designating the table for 'Peons Only.' He knew it wasn't fair, just fact, that money not only talked but was fluent in every language on the planet. He consoled himself with loving every minute of all the kowtowing going on around him tonight. He just hoped he didn't make a complete fool of himself. It wasn't about which fork to use. He couldn't have cared less about that. It was all about being with the first woman who'd found her way into his heart since he lost the love of his life. Hard to be Mr. Cool when Diana made him feel like a klutzy teenager.

He wondered how many people ever guessed that these two women were sisters. Probably not many, he supposed, because of their dramatically different coloring. Still, after twenty years of looking at mug shots, he knew he would have had no difficulty immediately recognizing them as siblings. Their facial bone structure was identical: each a perfect oval with delicately contoured features, high-ridged cheekbones and wide-set eyes. They were both astonishingly lovely and, like every other guy in the room, he was having a hard time not staring at them.

About half-way through her first vodka martini, Beth felt a few of the knots inside beginning to unravel, and she started to breathe a little easier. As predisposed as she was to dislike and distrust Charlie Hobson, he was certainly not the shark she had feared. Evidently Paul's instincts about him were right on target once again.

Everything about Charlie was average -- his height, his weight, his medium-brown hair and eyes, his well-modulated baritone, even his name – and he had a smile so genuine that she couldn't cast him in the role of villain no matter how hard she tried.

He was the kind of guy everyone would describe as 'nice' if they could remember him at all, and she supposed that his ability to blend into the woodwork was probably his greatest professional asset, although hopefully not his only one. She envisioned him snooping virtually anywhere without arousing suspicion, an advantage not shared by the high-profile amateur sleuth who had hired him.

Diana sensed that her sister's attitude toward Charlie was beginning to thaw, but she doubted that Beth would ever forgive her for the way she'd chosen him. The Greshams and the Wendells networked. Always. Their empire was vast, and there was seldom a reason to look beyond it for their needs or wants. But, in choosing Charlie, Diana had completely ignored all the family's resources. Fanning through a dog-eared local yellow pages that she'd kept even after the directory went digital, she opened the book to the listing for investigators, took pencil in hand, closed her eyes, and speared the page.

The instant she opened her eyes and saw that a neat little graphite dot had made a donut of the first 'o' in Hobson's last name, she had never had any doubt about her selection. As she had explained to Beth's complete dismay in the car on the way over here, she knew Charlie had to be the right man for the job because she had allowed her higher self to choose him.

Beth hadn't bothered to challenge Diana's methodology. It would only have brought on a mind-numbing lecture about a benevolent universe, and the damage had already been done anyway. Besides, as it turned out, she had to admit that the situation could have been a great deal worse. Charlie Hobson actually seemed to be a lucky choice. The man Beth was now observing so carefully reminded her of nothing so much as a schoolboy with his first crush.

He became tongue-tied each time he looked at Diana, an awkward situation, since he couldn't seem to stop looking at her. Beth happily withstood the ordeal of trying to make small-talk with him, delighting in every moonstruck glance he cast at her sister, knowing that it would take the acting performance of a lifetime to hide any intent to betray behind those adoring brown eyes.

Diana was the picture of casual elegance in ivory cashmere slacks and matching cardigan. The teal silk blouse she wore with it highlighted the perfection of her skin and was unbuttoned just low enough to provide a flawlessly seductive background for a brilliant aquamarine necklace. It was the genuine article, worth more than two million dollars, but it was one of her favorite pieces, and she never had any qualms about wearing it.

Taking a page from Olivia's book, Diana had long ago let it be known that she only wore costume jewelry when she traveled. With all the good imitations on the market, she felt that nobody had reason to doubt the lie. Beth disagreed, but she never begrudged her sister the joy of having at least one of her treasured jewels always with her while its imitation rested in the vault.

Looking at her sister, Beth realized that Diana was right about her own wardrobe needing a major infusion of light and color. She felt positively dowdy in her black silk slacks and tunic top. Gold earrings and matching gold chains at her waist and around her neck were elegant accessories, but the outfit had absolutely no pizzazz. For months, Diana had been threatening to mastermind a complete makeover for her, and Beth decided it was time to let her do it. If she hated Diana's choices, so what? Her sister would have the time of her life playing Oprah.

After the waiter had served their second round of drinks, Diana crossed her arms on the table and leaned in toward Charlie. "So, let's hear it, guy. Find out anything new today?"

Charlie was not a man given to self-deception, and he had no illusions about why Diana had invited him to dinner tonight. His professional expertise was on display, pure and simple, his worth being judged by her sister, someone whose opinion clearly mattered a great deal to his favorite client.

He took a quick sip of his Dewar's, then retrieved a well-worn notebook from the depths of the inside breast pocket of his jacket. Beth was amused to see how quickly his beleaguered basset-hound expression morphed into alert Dobermann mode the moment he looked away from Diana and focused on his notebook.

"I finally got a line on Margaret Mowbray," he said.

"Really?" Diana's voice was shrill with excitement, her azure eyes bright with impatience. "Well? Go on!"

With a deadpan expression, he proceeded with the narrative that would already have been in progress if she hadn't interrupted to crack the whip, but he showed no trace of annoyance.

"Seems as if Margaret Mowbray had quite a reputation as a healer around here. Not a medical doctor. Kind of a faith healer. What they called a 'white witch' back in the day." Charlie smiled self-consciously, as if even he couldn't believe what he had just said. "Honest. That's exactly how they described her in the book I..."

"Book? You mean there's actually a book about her? Where is it?" Diana's tone made the question a regal reprimand, and Beth was embarrassed for her. The mood swings were often like this, quick lightning strikes that came out of nowhere. Beth was relieved to see Charlie riding out this particular storm with ease, nodding patiently as he waited to get a word in edgewise.

"It's at the Tri-County Historical Society in Chaetestown," he explained. "But it's not a book that can be bought or borrowed. If it were, it would already be in your hands, Diana." His tone was only mildly chastising. "In fact, I was lucky they even let me look at it. The regular archivist wasn't in, but I managed to con some sweet little old lady volunteer into letting me..."

"Okay, okay." Diana was making little hurrying gestures with both hands. "So what's in the book?" She was already at the edge of her seat, but she managed to lean even closer to Charlie.

"It's a history of folk medicine written by one of the locals," Charlie said, only a little flustered by the fact that, at that moment, he had Diana's complete and undivided attention. "Anyway," he said, clearing his throat, "it's been out of print for years. Only one copy and it's disintegrating, cover torn off, really a mess."

"I think we get the picture," said Diana, her tone threatening dire consequences if he didn't get to the point.

Beth couldn't help but feel another little twinge of sympathy for Charlie. Clearly he had something important to say, and he was trying to build up to his dramatic moment, but Diana wasn't having any of it.

"Right. Well. Thing is," he continued, "according to this book, Margaret Mowbray was one of the finest healers and exorcists in the Catskills, right up there along with old Dr. Brink. Of course, he was before her time, but..."

"Back up a little, will you, Charlie," said Beth, ignoring Diana's protracted sigh of impatience. "Who's Dr. Brink? Never heard of him."

"Me neither, until today," shrugged Charlie. "But then this is strictly local stuff."

"So what exactly was his claim to fame?" asked Beth.

"Mostly mumbo-jumbo, far as I can tell, but evidently he had quite a following. A child would get sick or a crop fail and people would think somebody had put a curse on them. They'd send for Dr. Brink and he'd come along and do his thing."

"Which was?" asked Beth.

"Spells, incantations, that kind of stuff." Charlie flipped a page in his notebook. "The mountain people called him 'the Old Doctor' or..." He squinted at his notes. "'Oom Jacob' -- that was his name in Dutch. Most of the early settlers were Dutch, you know, and the prevailing belief was that this Oom Jacob had great power to combat evil." Charlie shrugged his skepticism.

"You said he was before Margaret Mowbray's time. How much before?" asked Beth, her reporter's mind trying to pin down the exact timeline for what he was describing.

"Let's see..." Charlie consulted his notes and tried to ignore Diana's dramatic sigh of impatience. Index finger skimming a page, he found what he was looking for. "Old Oom Jacob died in 1843, thirty years before Margaret Mowbray was even born. Obviously, they never met but, whatever they were, they were evidently two of a kind."

Regretting the vain impulse to leave his reading glasses in the car, he looked up from his notes and used thumb and forefinger to massage the naked bridge of his nose. "Actually," he said, extemporizing in order to give his eyes a break, "I was amazed to learn that witchcraft has quite a history in this area...

"Legend has it that the devil appeared to early settlers all over the county, bargaining for souls and creating the worst kind of mischief and mayhem when he was refused. In fact, one of his favorite haunts was said to have been Stony Clove, a narrow mountain pass just a few miles from where we're sitting right now. Fascinating stuff. I had no idea that..."

Diana had heard enough about crop failures, mountain passes, and Oom-whatever-his-name-was. "Charlie, could we save the history channel for later? We were talking about Margaret Mowbray, remember?"

He flushed. "Yes, of course. Sorry."

"Really interesting stuff, Charlie," said Beth, her commiserating glance catching his eye.

"I thought so." He nodded, smiled his thanks, and burrowed his head back in his notebook. "Moving on to the grand finale... Drum roll, please..." He cleared his throat and added, "It seems that Margaret Mowbray actually lived in Acra, just a few miles south of here, and evidently she lived alone, except for her granddaughter." Suddenly he looked up, pausing for dramatic effect, savoring the moment. Diana held her breath. Beth did too. Locking his gaze with Diana's, he said, "Her granddaughter's name was Lenore."

Diana jumped up and startled the other restaurant patrons with a little happy dance before giving Charlie a huge hug. "I knew it! Didn't I tell you, Beth? We found her!" Urging Charlie to continue with his report, she returned to her chair and hung on his every word. Beth wanted to shout him down, to warn Diana not to listen to him, but the rapt expression on her sister's face told her that it would have been useless to try.

In a somber tone, Charlie finished his story. "Margaret Mowbray's son and daughter-in-law died in a car accident back in 1946, and Margaret took in their only child, a baby named Lenore. When Margaret died in 1952, presumably of natural causes, since she was seventy-nine when she passed, Lenore was taken in by another relative. Margaret had a younger sister, so I'm guessing that's who it was, but guardianship back then wasn't the big legal deal it is now, so the records are kind of sketchy. A friend at county archives is digging for me, but nothing yet." He took a quick sip of his scotch before winding it all down.

"I'll be going back to the historical society tomorrow to do more research," he continued. "They don't even have a fully computerized data base yet, so it's slow-going, but maybe I'll get lucky." He finished the last sip of his drink and closed his notebook. "That's about it, ladies."

"Charlie, you're fantastic!" Diana leaned over to hug him again, but her intention was thwarted by the arrival of their antipasto, bread and herbed dipping oil. Charlie longed to throttle the waiter's overmuscled young neck for looking like fitness personified while depriving him of another hug. Was he the only guy in the county who didn't pump iron? Desperate for comfort food, he tucked the notebook back into the breast pocket of his jacket and dove into the antipasto.

The food was excellent, but only Charlie was able to appreciate it. Diana was too excited to eat more than a few bites of each course, and Beth was so busy containing her panic that she couldn't taste a thing.

The fact that Diana had been inexplicably drawn to the grave of Lenore Mowbray's grandmother, before she even knew of their relationship, went well beyond the bounds of anything Beth could explain away by reason or coincidence. And what an idiot she'd been to think that Diana had insisted on their cross-country jaunt because she secretly wanted to say goodbye to places she loved. Clearly, a sentimental journey had been the furthest thing from her mind. Finding Lenore was all that had ever mattered to her.

Inevitably, the Mowbrays were the sole topic of conversation throughout dinner, as Diana and Charlie laid careful plans for a systematic assault on the historical society's records. Diana had already decided that she and Beth would be going there with him first thing in the morning, which was just fine with Beth. She had no intention of abandoning Diana to Charlie's obliging encouragement of her obsession with two dead women.

As they were leaving the restaurant, Beth caught a glimpse of Jeff Stratton sitting at the bar and she had to smile. When Paul said he was all over a situation, he meant every word. She would call him later tonight to fill him in on Charlie's report. First she had to survive the long drive back to the condo with her sister inevitably crowing I-told-you-sos all the way.

She was glad to see Diana routinely reactivate the alarm system when they came home. Clearly, she remembered the code, an encouraging sign. As Beth hung her jacket in the hall closet, she reminded her that all the smoke detectors were now fully operational. "So turn that super-duper ventilation system on and go easy with the incense, kiddo."

"Yes, mother." Diana tossed her jacket onto the club chair in the living room.

"Brat," smiled Beth. "I'm off to bed." She gave Diana a quick hug. "Sleep tight."

Beth showered and changed into her favorite old green plaid flannel pajamas, before settling into a comfortable position in bed with the handset of Diana's secure landline. Cell reception up here on the mountain was often dicey, and she had no bars on her phone right now, so she had to use the landline. Diana never even saw any of her utility bills – all of them went directly to Gresham's accounting office -- so she'd never know that Beth had contacted their guardian angel. She wasn't concerned about Diana interrupting the call. Beth calculated that she would be finished talking with Paul and sound asleep before Diana was done with meditating and entering the night's events in her journal. As a teenager, she'd become fairly manic about keeping a diary, and she still was. It was a habit she now called journaling, but it served exactly the same purpose.

Recently, because of concern for her sister's mental state, Beth had been sorely tempted to read the current little book that Diana kept in her bedside table drawer, but she just couldn't bring herself to do it. Once, when they were just kids, she'd sneaked a quick peek at Diana's first diary and been caught in the act. Since then, there'd been at least one new diary each year, but Beth had never again wanted to risk seeing that look of betrayal in her sister's eyes. Especially not at this point in her life.

After phoning Paul and updating him on all that she'd learned that night, she was exhausted. But her thoughts were so full of Chad that she knew she couldn't sleep. She'd grown accustomed to his daily visits while she was ill, and she missed him more than she would have ever thought possible. Even though it was late, she called him.

When he didn't answer after five rings, she resigned herself to the inevitable electronic beep, followed by his recorded monotone. Trying to hide her disappointment, she overcompensated with a ridiculously cheerful voice.

"Hey, Chad. It's Beth. No bars on my cell, so I'm calling from Diana's landline. Just use this number if you can't get through on mine. Later!" Cradling the handset, she felt her spirits plummet. Where was he?

He often worked late, and she told herself he must still be at the office. But what if he wasn't? What if he was spending the night with one of his old flames, maybe even a new one? It wasn't that she didn't trust him. She trusted him implicitly. They simply had no commitment to anything beyond caring as deeply for one another as their employer-employee relationship would allow, so he was free to do as he pleased. She decided not to try tracking him down at Newsworld. If he wasn't there, she didn't want to know it.

She had been so eager to pour her heart out to him about Diana that the desire to talk to another caring human being became a compulsion. It was after eleven o'clock, too late for a casual social call even if she had been in the mood for mindless chatter, which she wasn't.

So, who could she call? Certainly not Olivia. There were far too many off-limits subjects to worry about whenever she spoke with her aunt lately, and she was too tired to monitor every word she said. She did a quick mental scan of friends and acquaintances, rejecting them all, finally accepting the fact that there really was only one person besides Chad who could help her think this mess through right now.

Reaching for her purse on the floor beside the bed, she rummaged through it until she found her small, handwritten, blessedly-low-tech-and-always-reliable personal address book. She keyed in Ariana's unlisted private number quickly, not allowing herself time to think about the implications of what she was doing. Beth might not believe in Philip, and she didn't, but Ariana's extraordinary psychic gifts had been well-documented over the years, and she'd be a fool not to tap into whatever insight the woman could offer. Since she wasn't calling from her own phone, she was primed for yet another recorded greeting, but Ariana surprised her by answering on the second ring. Beth could only guess that the woman's psychic gift was a pretty effective screening tool.

"Hi, Ariana. It's Beth Wendell. I'm calling about my sister." She wanted to be sure Ariana immediately understood that this was personal, not anything to do with an interview. "I hope I didn't wake you."

"No, not at all, Beth. Is Diana all right?"

"As well as she can be, I guess, all things considered. It's just that... Well, something really strange is happening with her, and I'm not sure how to handle it. I was hoping you could give me some advice." She also hoped that Ariana would understand the motivation behind her call. She wasn't seeking apostleship in the psychic's esoteric world, but only the loan of a compass to help wend her way through it.

"Go on." prompted Ariana. "I suppose if I concentrated really hard I wouldn't have to ask, but it's late, so why don't you just take pity on a poor weary psychic and tell me all about it."

Beth heard the smile in Ariana's voice. Encouraged by it, she began her story, prefacing it with assurances that Diana had already confided in her about the session with Philip, and giving a concise summary of what she had been told so that Ariana would have fewer reservations about speaking candidly with her.

She explained Diana's total fixation on Lenore and their cross-country journey to find the town Philip had described. She also told her about Diana's obsession with Margaret Mowbray's gravesite in Chaetestown, and she finished with Charlie's account of Margaret Mowbray and her grandchild Lenore. At first, Beth felt foolish. It all sounded so bizarre, but Ariana gently probed for every detail.

"Wow, that's amazing," she said when Beth had finished her story.

The remark was so disingenuous that Beth had to laugh. "My sentiments exactly," she said. "The thing is, all of it can obviously be verified with some digging through historical records, so there'd be no reason for Charlie Hobson to lie about it. That's what scares me."

"Well, he probably didn't lie, Beth. But he might well have misinterpreted what he read and jumped to all the wrong conclusions. 'Occult,' you know, means 'hidden,' so occult terminology is often quite deliberately misleading and imprecise. Semantic camouflage, if you will. People often get confused by it."

"Somehow I don't think he misinterpreted anything, Ariana. He strikes me as the kind of guy who makes very sure he's got all his facts straight."

Ariana took a few moments before responding. "Okay… Then tell me, how did you react when you first heard his story?" Without allowing Beth time to answer, she added, "Instinct usually points the way to a truth that your unconscious or subconscious may be blocking from your conscious mind. When you heard Hobson's story, did you laugh or did you feel as if someone had just punched you in the gut?"

Beth well remembered the numbing chill she had experienced when Charlie had first mentioned Lenore's name.

"I sure didn't laugh. Frankly, I was terrified."

"And now?"

"I guess I'm more nervous and confused than frightened. Ever since I gave Diana a little unicorn pin about six weeks ago, it's been one freaky thing after another." She described the incident with the Tiffany unicorn to Ariana. "Thank God, I haven't seen her zoning out like that again, but…"

"Did you ever tell her what happened while her mind wandered off to wherever? Does she know she was thanking 'Gran' for the unicorn pin?"

"No. Didn't seem to be any point. She knows she's subject to mental lapses like that at any time. It's not as if there was any mystery about what might have caused it. Not then, anyway." Beth knew that, as she herself had done earlier, Ariana was now connecting the dots between Margaret Mowbray and the woman Diana had called 'Gran.'

Ariana took a very deep breath, exhaling slowly, willing away her fatigue, determined to stay calm and centered, for Beth's sake as well as her own. "Okay… So you were at first terrified, understandably so, I might add. But what was Diana's initial reaction when she heard that Margaret had a granddaughter named Lenore?"

Remembering how thrilled Diana had been, Beth said, "Like a kid on Christmas morning. I haven't seen her that happy in months."

"Not surprising," said Ariana. "Past-life quests tend to be very liberating experiences, Beth. Of course, Diana's not actually my patient and I have no way of accurately assessing her mental health, but right now it seems to me that you should be counting your blessings."

"How so?"

"From what you've just told me, your sister is thriving. Most days, she's able to function with minimal drug dosages or none at all. And, if I understood you correctly, even her nightmares have stopped."

"True. Definitely another one of those freaky things I mentioned. She hasn't had a single bad dream since she decided to go looking for this Lenore person."

"Well, that's great, isn't it?"

"But she's obsessed with two dead women!"

"Not unheard of in my line of work, Beth." Ariana chuckled, immediately regretting the impulse when she sensed the annoyance in Beth's silence. All business now, she said, "Okay, let's cut to the chase here. What is it that you're really so afraid of, Beth?" Her psychic persona already knew the answer, but Beth needed to acknowledge it for herself.

Beth didn't need any time to consider her answer. It was something she'd been grappling with ever since Diana had first told her about the session with Ariana and Philip. "Even though I suspect you already know the answer, I'll tell you. Now that we've learned that Lenore actually did exist, I'm terrified that we'll discover she really was the monster Philip described. I don't think Diana could deal with that."

"Nonsense! She's obviously already dealt with it. Why else would she still be forging full-steam ahead with her search? After listening to Philip, she can't have any illusions about her life as Lenore, and she must be okay with it, or she would have backed off by now."

Beth was amazed at how blithely people like Ariana and Diana always referred to reincarnation as fact rather than hopeful fiction. "Look," sighed Beth, "obviously I respect your instincts, or I wouldn't have called you. But, in this case... Well, let's just say that I can only hope and pray you're right."

"But you doubt it." Ariana let the silence play out for a few moments. "I guess we could use a tie-breaker here. Would you like me to touch bases with Philip?"

Beth swallowed hard and bit the bullet. "I don't suppose it could hurt."

"Why don't I then? I'll do it first thing in the morning. If he comes up with anything you should be worried about, I'll be in touch."

"Thanks. I'd really appreciate that."

"Glad to help," said Ariana. "Meanwhile, try to relax. Your sister told me that she's an old hand at past-life regressions. If that's true, I assure you she's not at all likely to be traumatized by anything that happened a lifetime ago."

The High Priest unlocked the strongbox and withdrew the black velvet pouch.

Untying it, he reached inside for the glittering little unicorn.

As always, it scorched his fingertips as soon as he touched it.

Wearing insulated gloves hadn't made any difference.

Margaret had long ago imbued the unicorn with a powerful spell against him.

She had given the shiny little bauble to Lenore and instructed her to wear it always.

But the child had been greedy for power.

He laughed at the memory of how easily he'd been able to persuade her not to wear it.

As if the Light could ever be more cunning than the Dark!

Chapter Six

Diana was so eager to get to the Tri-County Historical Society the next morning that she and Beth arrived fifteen minutes before its scheduled nine o'clock opening. Trying to get comfortable on an ornately carved black wrought-iron bench in front of the building, they were discussing possible strategies for gaining access to documents that might not be readily available to the general public. When Charlie's Taurus pulled into the parking lot, they scooted over to make room for him.

"Morning, ladies." He waved off their silent invitation to sit with them. "Thanks, but I'll just take the steps." He hated those little iron benches. Uncomfortable as hell, and you always ended up with little curlicues imprinted on your butt. No thanks.

Promptly at eight-fifty-five, a silver Honda CRV rolled into the parking lot space reserved for 'Senior Archivist.' When Diana saw a prim elderly woman emerge from the SUV, she called a cheery hello and gave a little wave, both of which were completely ignored. Head down, arms laden with books, the woman scooted around to the back entrance of the building.

"And top o' the mornin' to you too, me darlin'!" laughed Charlie. "I'm guessing it was really lucky for me that she wasn't around yesterday."

Expecting the door to be opened quickly, the three of them gathered on the top landing of the front steps, but the door remained steadfastly closed.

Beth slowly shook her head. "Want to bet she keeps us waiting until the exact appointed hour?"

"No takers," said Diana.

Alternately checking her watch and glancing at the door, Diana voiced a countdown of the seconds until precisely nine o'clock, when the door bolt was finally unlatched with a resounding thud.

"Won't you come in?" Holding the door open, the woman looked at them as if they were some alien species, her squinty-eyed frown reproaching their jeans and sweatshirts as they walked by her.

Diana immediately returned the insult. Removing her sunglasses, she arched one aristocratic brow and inspected the woman from head to toe, unhappily finding absolutely nothing to criticize from her gray-and-blue patterned Shetland sweater down to her calf-length gray skirt and gray suede heels. She decided that there must be an elderware catalog out there somewhere designed specifically for petite women with silver hair and ice-blue eyes. They all seemed to have that classic country chic look down to a science.

Before Diana could do any more damage to their cause, Beth quickly showed the woman her Newsworld ID. "We're here to research an article on the Catskills and its folklore," she explained, pleased that the story they'd earlier agreed upon actually sounded plausible. The woman took the ID and studied it carefully, checking Beth's face against the image on the card, then leveling a stern gaze at Diana and Charlie.

"These are my associates," Beth quickly said, deliberately omitting names. She wasn't about to give this peculiar little woman any more information than necessary, including the fact that they were particularly curious about Margaret Mowbray. Beth sensed that they would never be allowed inside if she even hinted at an interest in the paranormal.

Suddenly, with quick, jerky little motions, the woman returned Beth's ID and closed the front door behind them. "This way to the main reading room."

Said the spider to the fly, thought Charlie.

Mincing little footsteps led them down a short hallway to a room no bigger than an average-sized living room. There were six chairs neatly positioned around a rectangular table, a small desk and chair in the corner, and floor to ceiling bookshelves on each wall. As Diana and Charlie each claimed a chair, Beth approached the older woman.

"Obviously, you know my name is Beth Wendell. And yours would be..?"

"Ruth Nagle." She sniffed and tilted her chin even higher. 'Senior Archivist.'

Well aren't you just full of yourself, thought Beth. Aloud, she said, "Nice to meet you Ms. Nagle." Beth didn't even attempt a handshake, and this was not a woman who would welcome fist bump or elbow tap.

Pointedly clasping her hands at her trim waist, the archivist fairly hissed, "That would be *Mrs.* Nagle, if you don't mind."

"Uh, sorry. Yes, of course." Beth was annoyed with herself when she felt the flush of embarrassment on her face. She knew she had nothing at all to be embarrassed about, which was a whole lot more than she could say for this pretentious old harridan. "Pleased to meet you, *Mrs.* Nagle."

Knowing that the murderous gleam in Diana's eyes didn't bode well for their project, Beth gave her a warning look as she took a deep breath and quickly forged ahead with the keeper of the keys. "Well now." She cleared her throat. "When my associate stopped by here yesterday, he was told that you're the expert we needed to see. So here we are. I hope you have a few minutes to talk with us since, evidently, you are *the* regional authority on folkloric traditions in the Catskills." Beth was glad to see that the absurd flattery had found a home and softened the sharper edges of the woman's glacial expression.

"Well, I don't know that I'm *the* authority." She smiled immodestly. "But it's certainly true that I do know quite a bit about the area's history." She was speaking only to Beth now, completely ignoring Diana and Charlie. He was startled when she suddenly thumped his shoulder.

"If you would assist me, young man..." She waved a hand toward one of the bookcases and began pointing at items she wanted him to fetch. Reflexively, Charlie bristled, but quickly did her bidding. Suddenly he was back in grade school and in the principal's office, but he took consolation in the fact that she'd called him a 'young man.' Beth and Diana had to feign coughing fits to keep from laughing.

"That's nothing infectious, is it?" Mrs. Nagle's voice was full of unsympathetic concern. "One can't be too careful, you know."

"No Covid worries, I assure you. It's only TB," said Diana, smiling sweetly.

Seeing the sudden pallor of the archivist's face, Beth hurriedly said, "It's just allergies, Mrs. Nagle. My associate has a weird sense of humor."

The older woman shook her head as if to clear it of some vile thought, then she promptly resumed barking orders at Charlie. By the time he finished playing gofer, his breathing was a little strained, but it was Ruth Nagle who dusted off her hands and sighed heavily, as if she alone had just accomplished the actual work of stretching, bending, lifting, carrying, and stacking that only Charlie had done.

"There," she said, patting the pile of books nearest to her, "that ought to keep you going for a while." Standing just behind her, Charlie made a wickedly funny face before coming into her line of vision and taking a chair opposite Diana and Beth.

Directing her remarks only to Beth once again, she said, "It's a sad fact, Miss Wendell, that the rich folkloric heritage of the Catskills has been distorted by legends of the common folk, Rip Van Winkle to name the obvious. It would be wonderful if you could balance your article by mentioning some of our more distinguished citizens as well -- Van Buren, Schuyler, Livingston, the list is endless." Sensing the old quid pro quo, Charlie smiled at the subtext: "I'll find the really interesting documents for you, if you'll photograph us in our best Sunday clothes."

The archivist continued to make her elitist case. "I've taken the liberty of including some of the more notable biographies." She continued patting the same pile of books. "I think you would be most favorably impressed."

"I'm sure I would be," replied Beth. "But the regional aristocracy isn't the subject of this particular piece. And I do have a deadline to consider." Charlie and Diana thoroughly enjoyed watching Nagle's pinched little mouth revert to its already familiar stern line.

Ever the diplomat, Beth quickly added, "A follow-up piece is always a possibility, of course. But only if this one gets done in a timely and satisfactory manner." She gave a helpless little shrug and smiled apologetically. "You know how editors are."

"Indeed," sniffed Mrs. Nagle. For a moment she looked as if she might press the issue further, but something in Beth's eyes told her not to push her luck. "Well, if you're sure..." She sighed heavily. "Please," she said, gesturing toward the rest of the material she'd spread out randomly over the table. "Feel free to get on with your research." Clearly unhappy with the failure of her mission, she settled herself at the scarred old desk in the corner of the room and began cataloging cartons of books that were stacked on the floor beside her. The angle of her chair ensured that she could keep a watchful eye on her visitors.

For the next three hours, the only sounds in the room were the whispers of pages being turned and chairs being pushed back to allow trips to the water fountain or rest room. Beth, Diana and Charlie were each handling the books as reverently as anyone could have hoped, but clearly that wasn't enough to put Ruth Nagle's mind at ease. They felt her eyes boring through them each time a page was turned too quickly or a book laid carelessly on the table.

It was just after noon when Diana stretched, and yawned mightily. "Lunch anybody?"

"Good idea," said Beth. Without saying a word, Charlie immediately pushed away from the table and headed for the door, Diana right behind him. "If you don't mind, Mrs. Nagle," said Beth, "we'll leave all this as is and return to it after lunch." Mrs. Nagle absently nodded agreement and continued making meticulous notes in her ledger.

Shouldering her purse, Beth slid her chair so the backrest was flush with the table, then automatically did the same with Diana's and Charlie's. She had to smile at how the role of grown-up always seemed to be reserved for her. "We should be back here just after two. That okay with you?"

"That will be fine, Miss Wendell."

Beth suddenly remembered the name of the local book dealer that yesterday's infinitely more helpful library volunteer had given to Charlie. "Mrs. Nagle, do you by any chance know Henry Woodruff?"

"Ah, yes!" Ruth Nagle's eyes were suddenly alight with interest. "Dear Henry. Brilliant scholar, and quite the authority on Greene County. His bookshop is a wonder."

"If it's not too far, I thought we might check it out while we're on lunch break. Where is it exactly?" Beth was shocked when the woman actually smiled as she gave her precise directions. Charlie and Diana were waiting for her near their cars, Diana's bright red Porsche and Charlie's not-so-shiny-or-new green Taurus, each too precious to its owner to be left behind in a deserted parking lot. Beth hopped into the passenger seat of the Porsche and Diana took the lead, Charlie following them five miles down the road to the coffee shop Diana had suggested.

It was just the start of lunch hour and off-season at that, so they had their pick of tables. They chose a sunny corner booth with a pretty garden view of a gaily painted miniature windmill surrounded by the first greening shoots of early spring bulbs.

"This is really nice, Di," remarked Beth. "How's the food?"

"Pretty decent," said Diana. "They make a great tuna salad." When she saw the pained expression on Charlie's face, she quickly added, "And I hear the roast beef's fantastic." Charlie immediately closed his menu. He had just heard all he needed to hear.

The food was as Diana had promised, not the best, but better than average, and the coffee was good enough to warrant two rounds of refills. Diana was busily pushing food around her plate between occasional small bites, deftly rearranging and compacting the tuna salad around the lettuce to give the appearance of eating well, and fooling no one.

"It's so damn frustrating," said Diana. "This morning I learned more than I ever wanted to know about how to get rid of a wart. And if you ever need a demon expelled from a cornfield, just give me a ring! But not a single word about Lenore, other than what Charlie already found."

Beth and Diana had verified Charlie's earlier research, and it was just as he had said. Margaret Mowbray's granddaughter had been named Lenore. There was no possibility of misinterpreting the text, but she was never mentioned again anywhere.

"I don't get it," said Diana, drumming her fingers on the table. "Lineage was a big deal back then. Yet every reference to Margaret Mowbray is about her healing methods, nothing about her family. It just doesn't make any sense!" Eyes closed, she was rubbing her temples with her fingertips. When she reached into her purse for the small pillbox she always carried and swallowed what Beth recognized as one of her milder pain-killers, the reason for her lack of appetite was obvious. Beth marveled at the courage that sustained her little sister.

"Headache, Diana?" asked Charlie.

She opened her eyes. "Just a little." She quickly backed the conversation away from the state of her health. "So, Charlie, when do you expect to hear from the county clerk's office?" Resting her elbows on the table, she interlaced her fingers under her chin to support her aching head.

Charlie had just taken a big bite of his roast beef sandwich and could only nod and raise an index finger to acknowledge her question until he was able to speak. Diana smiled an apology for her poor timing, and waited while he swallowed and took a quick gulp of coffee before answering. "My friend who works there is still digging, but she hasn't..."

"Why don't you give her a call right now?" suggested Diana.

"Will do." Charlie took another quick bite of his sandwich and immediately went outside to make the call. He hadn't missed the 'no cell phones please' sign when they came through the front door, and he'd actually been glad to see it. Too many of his meals lately had been ruined by people cackling non-stop into the damn things.

He hadn't planned on bothering his contact at the county clerk's office. He knew she would call him as soon as she had anything to report. But he also knew an order when he heard one, no matter how prettily delivered, and he knew Diana wasn't accustomed to waiting for anything or anyone a minute longer than necessary.

He had no qualms about leaving the check behind for her to pay. He was working today, on expenses, and he wasn't about to pick up his rich employer's tab, no matter how blue her eyes were. Besides, she should have let him finish that last bite of the damn sandwich.

After settling the bill, Diana and Beth met him outside. He was leaning against the hood of his car, already pocketing his cell phone. "My contact's out to lunch," he explained. "I think I'll just drive over there now and see if I can catch her in person when she gets back." He was already opening his car door. "I can meet you back at the historical society later, if that suits."

"Works for me," said Diana.

Before she could have second thoughts, Charlie gunned the engine and drove off. He desperately needed a break from musty books and the snooty tartar who guarded them as if they were the crown jewels.

The two women hopped into the Porsche and strapped on seatbelts. Pulling out of the parking lot, Diana couldn't help but grin when Beth said, "I love it that your PI is too discreet to even name his contact at county." She decided to leave well enough alone and make no comment. It was enough to know that Beth really seemed okay with Charlie.

Following Ruth Nagle's instructions to Henry Woodruff's bookshop took them through some of the loveliest and most isolated areas of the county. They'd been driving just under ten minutes, when they saw the hand-painted 'Antiquarian Book Seller' sign on the right. Turning sharply onto a lightly graveled road, Diana cursed loudly when the Porsche bottomed out in a pothole. She hugged the grassy edge of the drive until they reached the front entrance where she parked directly in front of the porch steps.

Before cutting the engine, she leaned into the windshield for a closer look, bumping heads with Beth who was doing exactly the same thing. Paul had trained them well. They weren't about to get out of the car until they were sure that the driveway did, in fact, loop directly back onto the main road. It was a deserted spot, their research had them both spooked, and they weren't taking any chances.

"All clear," said Diana. She shut down the Porsche and checked her purse to make sure that the small handgun she always carried was readily accessible.

Beth wasn't so sure that she wanted to go inside. The weathered two-story frame building had to have been at least two hundred years old, and it looked as if it was falling apart. "Do you think the building can handle our weight?"

Diana laughed. "Not to worry, Beth. These old mountain houses go on forever." She stepped out of the car, Beth a reluctant step behind her. Seeing a tattered 'Open for Trade' sign propped in one of the windows, they went inside. As soon as they opened the door, a clanging wrought-iron bell suspended above the threshold heralded their arrival.

Floor-to-ceiling bookshelves lined the walls of what appeared to be a small waiting room, its only furniture a threadbare sofa, a scarred coffee table, and two ladderback chairs. Before they had a chance to explore any of the book titles, a solemn-faced elderly man bearing a stack of yellowed manila folders came to greet them. Tan slacks bagged about his tall frame, the style of his high-collared white shirt as unfashionable as the striped bow-tie that accentuated a still-taut and bony jawline.

"Henry Woodruff," he said, inclining his head somewhere between a nod and a bow. "How may I help you?" Beth began to relax when she heard his voice. It held all the warmth that was totally lacking in his expression.

"Beth Wendell," she said, displaying her Newsworld ID. I'm researching an article about regional folklore, and I understand that you're quite the expert on the subject." Beth was almost starting to believe the lie herself.

Woodruff glanced at her ID with minimal interest, then unceremoniously dumped the folders he was carrying onto one of the ladderback chairs so that he could shake the hand she offered. Post-Covid introductions could be tricky, but Beth correctly guessed that Henry Woodruff would expect the formality of a handshake. Diana introduced herself, and they shook hands as well.

The strong handshake and the intelligence behind his clear gray eyes had Beth re-thinking her strategy. This was no uppity matron with a low shock threshold and a personal axe to grind. This was a dispassionate scholar who could probably be enormously helpful to them if he knew the true object of their search.

"I hope this isn't an inconvenient time," said Beth, glancing at the pile of folders on the chair.

"Oh, no. Not at all." He gestured toward the threadbare sofa. "Please, have a seat."

Beth and Diana skirted the coffee table and gingerly eased themselves onto the dilapidated sofa, while Woodruff looked around as if he were trying to find a seat in a room he'd never seen before. Inevitably, he sat on the second ladderback chair, the only other seat available to him, short of squeezing onto the narrow cushion between Beth and Diana. Eager to escape from the protruding coil that was jabbing at her lower spine, Beth was leaning as far forward as she could without falling off the sofa, and Diana was having a difficult time keeping a straight face.

"You see, Mr. Woodruff," Beth began, "in the course of our research to date, my sister and I have unearthed some fascinating old legends about paranormal events in Greene County, specifically witchcraft." Easing a little further away from the menacing coil, Beth crossed her legs and draped a forearm over her knee, a posture that she hoped would come across as disarmingly casual. She had no intention of letting him know how important this search was to Diana. "We're particularly interested in a healer by the name of Margaret Mowbray. Have you ever heard of her?"

Without saying a word, Woodruff nodded absently, stood with surprising agility, then ducked under a beamed lintel into an adjoining room.

"I'm not complaining," whispered Diana, "but what happened to the subtle approach?"

"We need some answers, Di, and we're not going to get them from this man by beating around the bush."

"No argument there, kiddo." Diana shuddered at the sight of a large spider scurrying out from under the coffee table. "Dear God, what a dump. And what's with his clothes? He looks like an extra out of 'The Great Gatsby'."

Beth smiled and nodded quick agreement. "Maybe we've stepped through a time warp." She stood to examine some of the titles on the dusty books that lined the walls. "Most of these are collectibles that have been out of print for years." She shook her head wonderingly. "Amazing."

"Weird is more like it, Beth." Diana stood close beside her sister. "Maybe we should just leave before he comes back," she whispered. "Where the hell is he anyway? This is all just a little too..."

Woodruff suddenly reappeared in the doorway, a wave of his arm beckoning them to follow. In that instant, Beth considered grabbing Diana and making a run for the car, but then she reminded herself that a haughty librarian had just spoken glowingly of this man, so he wasn't likely to be an axe-murderer.

Diana hung back, waiting to take her cue from Beth, follow or flee. She wasn't pleased when Beth chose to follow the man, and she hurriedly transferred her cell phone and gun from purse to pocket as she trailed after them. Woodruff guided them into what appeared to be his office, then on through a rabbit warren of small rooms filled to overflowing with tottering piles of books and papers. Both women were clutching their cell phones by the time they reached their destination.

With considerable relief, they finally arrived at a large, airy and very unsinister room that was obviously a fairly recent addition to the back of the house. Here, order and technology had vanquished the chaotic and bizarre. Neatly labeled bookshelves lined three walls, and the fourth was an expanse of glass giving a beautifully tranquil view of the mountains. In the center of the room was an oversized partner's desk, a priceless antique, incongruously supporting what appeared to be a state-of-the art computer system.

While Beth and Diana quietly re-pocketed their cell phones, Henry Woodruff sat down at the computer, his surprisingly nimble fingers dancing over the keyboard. He soon began scrolling down the screen, scribbling numbers on a notepad beside the computer. Without saying a word, he tore off the top sheet of paper and left the room. Beth immediately hurried over to the computer and scanned the screen, while Diana checked to make sure that the sliding glass door was unlocked.

"God, this guy is strange." She tested the door to make sure it slid easily on its tracks.

Beth waved Diana to the computer. "Come take a look." There was a long list of titles arrayed on the screen, each of them relating to the subject of witchcraft in Greene County and its environs.

"Do you suppose they're all books?" asked Diana.

Beth shook her head. "I don't see how they could be. Very likely they're just subject headings cross-referenced to books."

"I hope you're right," said Diana. "If not, we'd have to hire somebody else just to scan through all this stuff."

"Don't even think about it, Di. The fewer people who know about this thing..."

"I know. I know." She reached out a hand to the keyboard, but Beth caught her wrist before she touched it. She convinced Diana to join her in examining the bookshelves instead.

After several minutes had passed without any sign of Woodruff returning, Diana said, "Maybe he forgot about us."

"Not likely. He's old, certainly a little strange, but he seems alert enough."

"Maybe we should give him a shout out," suggested Diana.

"Be my guest." Beth was absorbed in her newest discovery, a beautifully bound poetry anthology.

Diana began calling his name. When the decibel level began hurting her throat and there was still no response, she gave up. "What now?"

Beth closed the little poetry book and slid it gently back on the shelf. "Now we go find him, Di."

The building was a maze, but small enough so that they were able to advance somewhat methodically in their search. Ancient oriental carpeting muffled their footsteps over creaky floorboards as they moved from room to room calling his name and cautiously edging their way around the dusty piles of books, journals and notes that seemed to be everywhere.

Eventually they stumbled upon Woodruff's bedroom, its unique function discernible only because of the single neatly made bed wedged in amongst piles of books and papers. Beth instinctively averted her eyes and turned to leave, but Diana tugged at her elbow and drew her back into the room.

"Look at this, will you?" she said, her hands reverently caressing the vintage frame of an enormous landscape that covered the wall at the foot of the bed.

"Nice," said Beth. She was embarrassed to be in Woodruff's bedroom and in no mood for art appreciation.

"Nice?" Diana laughed. "I'll say. Check out the signature."

The space was so cramped that Beth had to edge around Diana. She squinted at the lower section of the canvas, but the light filtering in through the shabby cotton curtains was too dim. "It's so dark in here. I can't make it out."

Diana gaped admiringly at the canvas. "It's a Cole, Beth. A real honest-to-God original Thomas Cole."

"Cole? As in the Hudson River school of artists? That Cole?"

"None other," sighed Diana, nodding reverently, her eyes riveted to the canvas. "Around here, they even call him the father of American art."

"Really?"

"Really." Diana nodded slowly, her eyes still riveted on the painting. "In fact, there's a museum named after him right down in Catskill."

"So then the painting must be worth a small fortune, Di. Why would it be...?"

"In this firetrap? That's what I'd like to know." Diana began a careful examination of the framed documents and photographs that covered most of another wall. Beth ignored her conscience and gave in to her own curiosity, her eyes rapidly scanning for clues to the man's past.

"Well, at least we know it's not likely he stole the painting," said Beth.

"Why?" Diana tapped a finger at a frame holding a yellowed college diploma. "Just because he graduated magna cum laude from Harvard doesn't mean..."

"I didn't even notice that one, but look at this." Beth pointed to a black and white photograph of a woman smashing a bottle of champagne across the bow of a sleek schooner. Laughing beside her was a man whose resemblance to Henry Woodruff was unmistakable. Judging by the clothes they wore, she guessed that the picture had been taken in the twenties. "They must be his folks. And they must have been loaded. Poor boys don't own yachts with cutesy names like 'Woodie'."

Diana laughed. "Why would anybody ever name a boat or anything else 'Woodie?"

"Get your mind out of the gutter, brat. Their last name, remember? Back then, nobody would have thought of it in any other context."

"Maybe so, but still…" Diana shook her head and examined the picture more closely. "The parents look normal enough. What do you suppose happened to him?"

Suddenly they both remembered that they were supposed to be finding out the answer to that precise question. Diana cast one last yearning look at the Cole painting, then followed Beth along the corridor to the next room. When they had made a full circuit of the house and still not found Woodruff, they checked the front porch, again without success.

"He's probably wandered off into the woods somewhere, Beth. He might be gone for hours, and it's stupid to wait. Let's just go. This place really gives me the creeps."

Beth rummaged in her purse for paper and pen. "Let's at least leave him a note."

"Why, Beth? That demented old codger probably won't even…"

"Ah, there you are!" Woodruff was standing at the front door beckoning them back inside. Reluctantly, they complied. "Sorry to have kept you waiting so long," he said, gesturing for them to be seated. "The attic was in a sorrier state than I remembered, and it took me a while to find these." He gingerly placed the three books and two folders he was holding onto the coffee table.

"One of these books is of fairly recent vintage," he said, "two have been out of print for years, and the manuscripts in those folders have never been published at all. You're welcome to read them at your leisure. All I ask is that you treat them gently and return them to me when you're done with them."

Beth was deeply touched by the man's generosity. Before she could thank him, Diana blurted, "And what's the fee for all this largesse, Mr. Woodruff?"

Beth's embarrassment was nothing compared to the awful ache in her heart. Diana had never been cynical, crass or mistrustful, but her illness had changed all that. Here was yet another mood shift, as instantaneous and without warning as the last. This poor man was her latest unwitting victim, and there wasn't a thing Beth could say or do about it.

His gaze narrowed and the taut lines about his eyes went rigid. "There's no fee, Miss Wendell. Since you and your sister could likely buy and sell all of Greene County with your spare change, why wouldn't I entrust you with these few humble possessions?"

He obviously knew who they were, but how? 'Wendell' wasn't a particularly unusual name and he didn't look like the type to keep up with society news.

Easily reading the question in their eyes, he explained that Ruth Nagle had called to let him know they were on their way. He directed his remarks to Diana again, speaking quickly, weary of conversation, and eager to be rid of both of them. "Ruth was perplexed about Newsworld's sudden interest in our little corner of the world and, frankly, so was I, so I did a little research before you arrived. Don't you just love Google? Several hits on your sister, the only full name Ruth had, but helpful links led me to you as well. You take a lovely picture, I might add. But I'm sure you know that. In any event, Ruth very nearly fainted when I called her back and detailed your family's very excellent pedigree."

He handed the three books to Beth and the two manuscript folders to Diana. "I may be an old codger, Miss Wendell," he said, gazing down at Diana's suddenly stricken expression, "but I assure you that I am neither demented nor ungenerous. Good day to you both." He gave a half-bow to each of them, then retreated toward the sanctum of his books, leaving Beth and Diana to envy his dignity.

As they quietly closed the front door behind them, Beth couldn't bear to think about what Diana must be feeling. She focused her worry on Henry Woodruff instead. There was no sturdy lock on the door, not even a faithful hound to protect that old man and his priceless treasures. She hadn't even seen any smoke detectors in any of the rooms, and the house was an oversized tinder-box.

They walked quickly to the car, the air about them bristling with self-recrimination. As they settled into the Porsche and adjusted their seatbelts, Beth could only hope that Woodruff's words hadn't cut too deeply. Having time to make amends was no longer anything her sister could depend on.

Diana circled back to the main road, then slammed the shift stick into high gear and allowed the Porsche full throttle as she accelerated onto the highway. Her sister's driving told her that she wasn't in the market for any quick emotional fixes, so Beth didn't offer any. Besides, she reminded herself, what could she have said?

As they careened along the narrow mountain road back toward the historical society, Beth couldn't stop thinking about Henry Woodruff, and she was sure Diana was having the same problem. As sorry as she was about the hurtful words that had been so carelessly spoken, a bigger worry was his safety in that firetrap of a building that had no alarm system to protect him or the fortune in books, antiques and artwork that he owned. He seemed totally oblivious to everything but his old books and papers.

Obviously, he wasn't a complete recluse. After all, Ruth Nagle had felt comfortable enough to phone and alert him to their impending visit. Friends did that, not mere casual acquaintances. Beth smiled at the fanciful thought of crusty *Mrs.* Nagle carrying a torch for 'dear Henry' who had eyes only for his first editions.

"What's so damn funny?" Diana's bark jolted her out of her reverie.

"Just thinking about Mrs. Nagle," replied Beth, settling for a half-truth.

Neither of them pursued the offhand remark, and they drove the last few miles in renewed silence. Beth suspected that Diana was as relieved as she was to find Charlie's Taurus already in the parking lot, with Charlie himself dozing behind the wheel. The unmistakable roar of the Porsche engine alerted him to their approach, and he was instantly awake and out of his car before Diana had turned off the ignition.

"There you are!" he said in his most jovial tone. "I was beginning to think you'd deserted me." He held Diana's door open for her.

"Can it, Charlie." She stormed off toward the archives, leaving him to exchange questioning shrugs with Beth across the roof of the Porsche. Slamming Diana's car door shut, he shouted after her. "Hey, wait a minute! Don't you want to hear my news?"

Diana turned slowly on her heels, eyes ominously narrowed, instinctively wary of anything that threatened to lure her out of her black mood before she was ready to abandon it. "What's your big news, Charlie? Somebody's big old cow have a calf down the road apiece, or what?"

"Probably," said Charlie, deftly fielding the stinging sarcasm, "but that's not my news. Fact is, my friend at the county clerk's office has come up with a line on the Mowbrays. Seems that Margaret had two sisters, Eliza and Helen. Eliza's passed on, but Helen was the baby of the family. And guess what? She's still alive and a ward of the county at a rest home near Hudson."

Diana leaped at Charlie and gave him a great bear hug. "You don't know how much I needed some good news right now, my friend." She kissed his cheek. "Thank you!" Abruptly abandoning her hold on him, she turned to face her sister. "Beth! Did you hear that?"

"I heard, Di. I heard." Beth hated sounding like a mother trying to calm a hyperactive child, but that was exactly how she felt. When Diana and Charlie began working out their game plan for the trip to Hudson, she turned to go inside. "I'll just go tell Mrs. Nagle we're leaving."

"Wait up," said Diana, her hand hooking Beth's elbow. "Don't you think that at least one of us should keep going on the research here?"

Beth looked from Diana to Charlie, easily reading their expressions. "So, I'm elected for dusty archive duty, is that it?"

"Who better?" teased Diana. "This is your turf more than ours, so it just makes sense for Charlie and me to do the field work in Hudson while you do your thing here."

Charlie nodded solemnly, trying to hide his own glee at not being the one chosen to remain. "They probably wouldn't let all three of us in to visit the old gal anyway, Beth." He was already opening the passenger door of his car and waving Diana inside.

Diana hopped into the Taurus. As Charlie scurried around to the driver's seat, she lowered her window and gave Beth a roguish smile. "Take good care of my baby, will you, Sis?" She tossed Beth the keys to the Porsche. "See you home about six!"

Resigned to being deserted, Beth waved them off and trudged inside for another long siege in the archives. She almost laughed when Mrs. Nagle greeted her like a long-lost and much-loved relative. 'What's in a name?' Beth knew that the short answer for the Ruth Nagles of the world was 'everything.'

"I'll be on my own here this afternoon, Mrs. Nagle." Before the older woman had a chance to get nosy about Diana and Charlie, Beth commented, "Henry Woodruff is an interesting man, isn't he?" She settled herself in the same straight-backed chair that she had occupied earlier, the book she'd been researching still open on the table before her.

"Was he able to be of assistance?" She almost cooed the words, and Beth found herself struggling with a sudden bout of nausea.

"Absolutely"

"I'm so glad!" When Mrs. Nagle actually smiled, Beth decided that the harridan side of Ruth Nagle was a whole lot easier to take than the fawning one. "Such a fine man, and so knowledgeable," she enthused.

Beth felt uncomfortable with the subject of Henry Woodruff, but they were alone in the room, and with no distractions at hand, she was cornered. "Definitely a scholar and a gentleman," Beth assured her. "Extremely helpful too. Of course, I haven't had a chance yet to look at the material he gave us, but at a glance..."

"You mean he actually parted with some of his precious collection?" Her eyes were instantly wary.

"Well... yes," admitted Beth, wondering at her obvious distress. "What's the problem?"

Mrs. Nagle's color was high, her voice shrill with an emotion Beth couldn't fathom. "I can't believe that he actually gave you..."

"Whoa! Calm down. He didn't actually *give* us anything, Mrs. Nagle." Beth understood now. The woman suspected that the rich city slickers had somehow beguiled her friend into parting with some of his treasures. "It was just a loan of some reading material."

"Then he gave you nothing outright? Nothing at all?" she persisted.

"I repeat," said Beth, determined to hide her annoyance from the woman whose cooperation she still needed, "Mr. Woodruff gave generously of his time. Period. Beyond that, we were given nothing except the opportunity to borrow three books and a few manuscripts."

Mrs. Nagle sighed and belatedly remembered her manners. "I'm sorry, Miss Wendell. Forgive my badgering, please, and allow me to explain."

"Gladly," said Beth, too curious to pretend otherwise.

"For years," said Mrs. Nagle, "we've been begging Henry to gift the historical society some small part of his enormous collection, but he has consistently, adamantly refused. When I thought that he had given you... Well..."

"I see." Beth smiled her understanding. "Sorry if I gave you a start."

"Oh no, dear, it wasn't you. It's my enduring anxiety where Henry and his belongings are concerned. You see, his will leaves everything to our historical society, so we do have a legitimate vested interest in him and that old barn of a building he lives in." She closed her eyes and shook her head. "With the entire future of our organization at stake, well, we can't help but worry."

"With good reason," Beth acknowledged. "Even I was concerned when I saw how unprotected..."

"Precisely!" cried Mrs. Nagle. "We've begged him to let us install a complete alarm system, but he won't even consider it. Says if he wanted one he would have had it installed himself years ago. Doesn't want to be disturbed by sirens going off every time he gets up to use the bathroom during the night. Says if we keep after him about it, he'll revise his will." She shrugged helplessly. "Although Henry claims to have no family still living, we have to presume there must be a distant cousin or two alive somewhere, so we do have to tread cautiously at all times."

She began enumerating the highlights of Henry Woodruff's book collection, plus the antiques and paintings he had inherited from his family. "He even has an original Thomas Cole! It hangs on his bedroom wall in a dark room that... Oh Lord, Miss Wendell, it's a crime. Just a crime."

"It is a magnificent painting." Beth realized her gaffe too late, and there was no way to cover it.

"You saw it? Henry actually showed it to you?"

"Well, yes and no. I mean, yes, we saw it, but... But, no, he didn't show it to us."

"Oh?" The word was an indictment.

"Well it all happened quite by accident. You see, he left us in his workroom, then wandered off and didn't come back. When we went looking for him, we got kind of lost in a maze of small rooms and corridors. That's how we stumbled onto the Cole painting."

Beth was surprised to see an immediate easing of the tense lines about Ruth Nagle's eyes and mouth. She actually laughed. "To be perfectly honest," she confided, "I had a similar experience. Like you, I wandered from room to room, beyond curiosity, almost in a frenzy of discovery."

"Kind of like finding Aladdin's cave, isn't it?"

"Exactly! And when I saw that painting! Oh, Miss Wendell, it's as fine a Cole as I've ever seen. Easily the equal of his 'Oxbow', don't you think?"

"I honestly wouldn't know," admitted Beth.

"But surely you've seen 'The Oxbow'?"

"Not that I can recall, I'm afraid."

"What a pity," sighed the older woman. "It's at the Met, so I was sure you would have seen it. Definitely one of his best works." Beth listened with real interest as Mrs. Nagle began intoning a roll call of other local artists whose work was also on display at the Metropolitan Museum of Art in New York City. She hadn't realized there were so many. Finally, she heard a blessedly familiar name.

"Ah yes, of course," said Beth, "Frederic Church." She was careful to say the name with reverence. "I'm quite familiar with his work. In fact, my sister and I were given a private tour of his home some years ago. It was most impressive." Luckily, she'd been so intrigued by the eclectic architecture that she still remembered key points she'd learned about its Victorian, Persian and Moorish elements.

Glad for the opportunity to abandon the role of cultural half-wit, Beth enthusiastically recounted a few highlights about her visit to Olana, Church's wonderfully exotic mountaintop home, now a landmark building just across the Hudson River from the town of Catskill. She finished by saying, "You have every right to be enormously proud of your regional artists. Their landscapes are breathtaking."

Rearranging the folds of her skirt, Ruth Nagle sat a little taller in her chair. "We are indeed proud of our Hudson River School, Miss Wendell. I just wish that Henry's Cole could assume its rightful place with the best of them where it belongs. It's criminal the way he keeps it all to himself."

"Hasn't it ever been exhibited?"

"Not once," she said. "Oh, we've asked him many times, but he's never agreed to let us show it. Says it would be like extending every thief in the world a personal invitation to visit him. I promised to ensure his anonymity, of course, but Henry says we're a bunch of old tabbies who couldn't keep a secret if our lives depended on it."

Since she wasn't at all inclined to dispute Henry Woodruff's assessment of the situation, Beth said nothing.

"Oh he's not totally heartless," purred Mrs. Nagle. "Sometimes he does permit us to have a few small treasures for special exhibits. It's just that he flatly refuses to donate to our permanent collection. That's what galls me. He says we can have it all when he's gone, but not a minute sooner. Meanwhile, if we don't leave him alone, he promises to cut us out of his will entirely." She sighed. "Needless to say, we tend to give him a wide berth."

"I imagine so," said Beth, full of admiration for Henry Woodruff's canny solution to the problem of keeping the acquisitive Mrs. Nagle and her cronies at bay.

Damn Covid.

Too many people moving up here to get out of the cities.

My house has suddenly tripled in value.

Fat lot of good that will do me if I end up in jail.

Too many more eyes on us now.

At this very moment, three hikers are camping dangerously close to the underground portal.

And our fearless leader continues to be obsessed with a dead woman.

Chapter Seven

Beth was trying hard to concentrate on her research so she could finish the job and escape from Ruth Nagle, but the woman wouldn't give her a moment's peace. She was absolutely tenacious on the subject of Henry Woodruff and the items -- 'treasures,' as she insisted on calling them -- that he'd loaned to her and Diana. Beth knew there was only one way to shut her down, so she went out to the Porsche and retrieved the books and folders from Diana's car. Grasping little hands reached out for them at the front door the moment she returned.

Hurrying back to the reading room, Mrs. Nagle did a quick scan of the material, dismissing the three books immediately. "These are just standard reference texts," she said, unceremoniously dropping them on the table. She immediately turned her rapt attention to the two remaining items, faded and dog-eared folders that she reverently set on the table. "Now, let's see what we have here..."

Standing beside her, Beth winced when she saw the archivist's tongue darting across her lips when she opened the top folder and saw a small green leather-bound book nestled inside it. Ignoring the copious notes written on and within the folder, she immediately turned to the first page of the book. "Oh my," she sighed, "It's Eleanor Hathaway's diary. What a find!" Observing Beth's clueless expression, she said, "Eleanor Hathaway of *the* Clarence Hathaways." She paused only long enough to arch her brows and glare at Beth. "Surely you've heard of them."

Beth could only shake her head, shrug and smile apologetically. With her intellectual pride still smarting from the Cole episode, she braced herself for yet another cultural flogging and wasn't surprised when it erupted in a sputtering torrent.

"Oh my dear, Clarence Hathaway was quite famous back in the eighteen nineties. A true man among men." Beth struggled not to laugh when the woman launched into a long dissertation about the prosperous Greenville merchant who'd fathered at least twenty children with four wives, all but one dead in childbirth. "To this day, there are prominent Hathaways all over the county!"

A man among men indeed, thought Beth. Biting her lip to stifle a grin, she nodded solemnly. Clarence Hathaway, of *the* Clarence Hathaways, was no more than an oversexed guppy in a very muddy little pond. His unlucky wives were evidently even smaller fry, and there was no reason why anyone outside Greene County should ever have heard of any of them. Pride soothed. Case closed.

She watched quietly as Mrs. Nagle carefully set Eleanor Hathaway's diary aside and turned her attention to the second folder. The same hand, presumably Woodruff's, had written notes all over both folders and on loose leaf pages scattered within each one. The second folder also contained a small book, but this one was of far humbler origin. No fine leather here. Just a cloth cover with faded florals and a flimsy brass lock that had almost completely rusted away.

Already looking down her nose at it, Nagle opened the book and frowned when she couldn't find a name on the first page. Frown lines etching in even deeper, she riffled through the papers inside the folder trying to find a clue to its authorship. "Henry and his endless notes," she grumbled. After scanning through a few neatly scripted pages, she found what she'd been looking for. "Molly Beecham," she read. "Hmm. Never heard of her." Opening the little book, she began reading it.

After only a few pages, she wrinkled her nose and discarded the book back into its folder. "No wonder I never heard of her. Just a bunch of juvenile romantic ramblings. Obviously of no consequence at all." She once again reached for the Hathaway diary.

"Now this. This is truly a jewel." She hugged the Hathaway book to her meager bosom as she walked across the room to her desk, settled herself comfortably in her chair, and began to read.

Grateful for the sudden blessed silence, Beth took her seat again and closed the ledger on county land grants that she'd been skimming, pushing it aside to make room for the Beecham folder that Ruth Nagle had just discarded. Henry Woodruff had spent a great deal of time ferreting out musty old source material for them that afternoon, and she wanted to know why he thought this young girl's diary was important to their research. Determined to find out, if only out of respect for the man's efforts on their behalf, she began reading the voluminous notes that he'd written.

The diary's provenance was fully delineated in what the archivist had already identified as Woodruff's elegant script, and it included the fact that its author, one Molly Beecham, had died just six months after the last entry had been made. Molly, her two younger brothers, and both their parents had perished in a fire that had engulfed their home while they slept. The fire had been of suspicious origin but, since there was no will and no known living heirs, it was never investigated. Everything salvageable was sold at public auction, including an old metal trunk that had escaped the worst of the flames. A young Henry Woodruff had purchased it decades earlier and discovered the diary among its contents.

Finding nothing pertinent to her research in Woodruff's provenance notes, Beth settled in to read the diary. At first, she found it difficult to decipher Molly Beecham's script. But once her eyes grew accustomed to all the flamboyant loops and whorls, it was easy reading. The girl wrote of being an average student, which surprised Beth, since her grammar and spelling were absolute perfection. Clearly, she was reminded, educational standards had dramatically deteriorated over the years. As she'd written in a recent article for Newsworld, college was the new high school.

Momentous events were reshaping and restructuring the world in which Molly lived, but her perspective was that of a typically myopic teenager, as evidenced in her entry for May 7, 1945: "Daddy said that Germany surrendered today. I'm so happy that the war's almost over. Soon I can get my first pair of nylons!"

On August 15th of that same year, Japan's surrender was commemorated with this gleeful comment: "I can hardly wait for all those gorgeous men in uniform to start coming home!"

It wasn't until the second year of the diary, after the girl turned seventeen, that Beth caught a glimpse of the woman Molly might one day have become. Sandwiched in amidst all the teen egomania was an intrinsically kind and generous spirit. She was also showing some real spunk for a change, even playing hooky for the first time in her life.

She must have been plain. She saw herself that way, and the lack of any mention of flesh-and-blood suitors seemed to confirm it. She was a dreamer, endlessly fantasizing about an idyllic world full of handsome young men who adored her. Beth found herself liking the unsophisticated young girl, and she was deeply touched by what Ruth Nagle had disdained as 'juvenile romantic ramblings.'

Molly's father had been a land surveyor for the State, steady employment that had kept his family comfortable and well-fed until the Great Depression reduced their standard of living to virtual subsistence. Forced to give up their big house in Chaetestown, they moved down the mountain to a very modest rental in Purling.

Molly had written at great length about how devastated she was at having to leave her home and her classmates, one in particular, Matthew, a popular boy whom she'd adored from afar since seventh grade. "Thank God for Janet!" was a frequent refrain. Janet had been her best friend since they were toddlers. Her family had also been forced to sell their big house in Chaetestown and had moved to be near the Beechams. Misery might not always love company, Beth knew, but it was clear from what Molly had written that combining their limited resources and sharing the load had been a great comfort to both families.

One Friday night in February of her senior year in high school, Molly and Janet drove up the mountain to a party at an old friend's house in Chaetestown. There was snow on the mountain, as always at that time of year, but Route 23 was clear, as was the sky, and both girls were in high spirits as Janet's old Studebaker chugged up the road.

Molly had written tenderly of Matthew, her longing to see him again, and her fervent hope that he too had been invited. Beth's heart ached for the girl when she read that the boy had in fact been there, but that he hadn't even bothered to speak to her. Molly was so hurt that she convinced Janet to leave the party early.

It was just after ten o'clock, and they were half-way down the mountain when rain began to fall, just a drizzle, little more than a mist, but enough to glaze the road with a fine sheet of ice the minute it hit the frozen pavement. The little Studebaker went into a wild skid and spun into a ditch on the side of the road nearest the solid wall of mountain.

Molly knew they had been lucky. If they'd skidded off the other side of the road, they would both be dead now, their bodies at the bottom of the precipice beyond the narrow shoulder. She was sobbing with relief as she turned to Janet, her sobs immediately silenced by the sight of her friend slumped over the wheel, totally motionless. She screamed Janet's name, but there was no response, and her head was at such an awful angle! She couldn't allow herself to think of what that might mean.

The temperature was plummeting, and Molly knew she had to get help for Janet as quickly as possible. She covered her with a blanket from the back seat, took a flashlight from the glove compartment, climbed out of the ditch, and set off at a run back to Chaetestown. She raced along the gravel shoulder of the road, avoiding the treacherous glaze on the pavement, her breathing labored in the frigid air, her thin-soled flats affording little protection from the ribbon of rough stones she had to follow, her flimsy party clothes a poor substitute for the heavily insulated parka and ski pants she usually wore at night on the mountain.

The typically well-traveled highway was eerily quiet in the still night air, and Molly knew that the police must have just closed both ends of the mountain road until it could be salted. She had hoped to flag a passing car, but the salters would likely run her down without even seeing her and it could be an hour or two before the road was reopened. She knew Janet could not survive that long in the bitter cold.

She ran off into the woods along a familiar short-cut, an abandoned dirt track that had once been the primary access route for the long-abandoned Chaetestown quarry. Since the new highway had been completed, the old road had fallen into such a state of disrepair that it wasn't safe to drive across it any more. It had been free of cars for as long as Molly could remember, ideal for winter sledding, and a favorite shortcut for hunters and trappers headed to town for supplies or a drink at its only bar.

As a child, Molly and her American Flyer had won their fair share of races along that road, and cherished memories of all those wintry afternoons served her well now. She was able to run quickly along every familiar hill and turn in the old road, her flashlight bobbing so furiously that she was unable to keep a steady beam on the ground ahead.

About half-way to the center of town, she tripped and fell along a stretch of road that was littered with potholes. She was so numb with cold that she didn't realize she'd hurt her ankle until she tried to stand and couldn't. She lay there, sprawled face-down in the snow, crying silent tears of despair, praying for the strength to go on. Scudding clouds passing beneath the bright full moon cast a kaleidoscope of menacing shadows along the ground, and Molly felt more alone and frightened than she had ever been in her life.

It was then that she heard it, just a whisper of sound at first, its source unidentifiable. Defenseless in this desolate place, fearful of who or what might be coming her way, she quickly doused her flashlight and rolled over into a clump of bushes at the side of the road. Within moments, she saw two tall figures moving swiftly through the woods. From their size, she guessed they were men and, since they were headed from the direction of town and it was too late for the general store to be open, she figured they must have just come from the bar. She prayed they weren't too drunk to help.

She was about to emerge from her hiding place and call out to them, but the shout died in her throat when she suddenly saw them silhouetted in the amber light of an open doorway. They quickly went inside, leaving Molly to wonder if she was losing her mind. How could she have seen a lighted doorway in a place where no house existed? It was where the old Briggs tannery used to be, but that structure had been abandoned for years. Unless... She suddenly remembered overhearing her parents talk about one of the old buildings being renovated. They hadn't mentioned that it was the Briggs tannery, but it must be!

Her courage rekindled, Molly tucked the flashlight into her jacket pocket and limped along toward the tower, breathing through the pain shooting through her left leg, thinking only of Janet and the promise of help at the old tannery. She was within a few yards of the door when her ankle gave way beneath her once again. She began clawing her way forward and had just reached the sturdy pine that guarded the entrance when she was startled by the sound of rapid footsteps crunching across the icy turf behind her. Instinctively, she hid again, this time behind the sheltering boughs of the tree. What was going on? What were all these people doing in the woods on such a cold night? She watched and waited, desperately hoping that one of the new arrivals had a familiar face.

As the group drew nearer, she listened for voices, hoping to at least hear reassuringly normal and sober conversation, but no one was speaking. There were three of them, and they were trekking along in single file and in total silence. They were all of average height and build, and in their dark winter parkas and mufflers there was no way of telling if they were male or female. She was afraid to approach strange men in the woods at night, but she wouldn't fear three women or a mixed group. Listening carefully for a telltale voice, she squinted into the darkness and tried to see their faces as they approached the tannery door.

When one of them knocked softly in a strange staccato pattern, the door was immediately opened just wide enough to admit the group single file. Anyone standing directly in front of the door would not have been able to see inside, but from Molly's oblique angle of vision, the muted amber light gave her a clear view of a black-robed and hooded figure hidden behind the door. Her cry for help died on her lips.

The terrifying figure was just ten feet away from her, and she could hear him greeting the new arrivals as they entered, using words Molly had never heard before. They answered in the same odd gibberish as they passed by him and went inside. As soon as what seemed to be the last of the group had entered, the door was closed and Molly heard the sound of a heavy bolt hitting home.

Terror anesthetized her ankle and gave wing to her feet. She ran and fell and crawled the rest of the way into Chaetestown. When she finally reached old Dr. Masters' house, she fell into his arms as soon as he opened the door. It took a few moments to understand what Molly was saying between sobs, but then he immediately took matters into his own capable hands,

Dr. Masters called the police and gave them Molly's instructions about where to find her friend.

He then tended to Molly's ankle, splinting it until they could get it x-rayed at the hospital. His wife called Molly's home, helped the girl into warm, dry clothes, and gave her some hot tea. Later, when the police called him with a report on Janet, Dr. Masters gave Molly a sedative before telling her the sorrowful news. Janet was dead. Her neck had been broken when the car slammed into the ditch. She had died instantly.

Molly was inconsolable, blaming herself for Janet's death. If she hadn't insisted they leave the party early, they wouldn't have been on that treacherous stretch of mountain road just as the rain began to fall. If they had left even just a little later, the road would already have been closed and they would have been forced to wait until the salters had done their job. But no, a boy she cared about had ignored her, and she had salvaged the remnants of her wounded pride at the expense of her best friend's life.

Tears danced in Beth's eyes as she skimmed through the final pages of Molly's diary, the girl's pain and grief evident in every word she had written about that awful night on the Old Chaetestown Road. Nobody had believed her story about the figures she saw in the woods. It had been attributed to delirium brought on by shock and pain. "So be it," wrote a despairing Molly. "Janet's dead, so what does any of it matter anyway?"

Totally obsessed with guilt, Molly Beecham's last words had been chillingly prophetic: "Tomorrow I'll be eighteen, not very old, but already I feel as if I've lived too long. Oh Janet, I'm so sorry. Why couldn't it have been me and not you?" Six months later, according to Henry's notes, Molly was gone in the fire.

Beth closed the folder with a soft sigh, deeply touched by the girl's eloquently simple testament to the best that friendship can be. She was about to tell Ruth Nagle how wrong she had been about the diary, when she looked up and realized that she was very much alone in the room. She was surprised that she hadn't even heard the woman leave. Checking her watch, she saw that it was almost five o'clock. No wonder her muscles were so stiff! She had been in Molly's world for more than two hours without interruption. She stood and stretched, trying to ease some of the kinks out of her neck and back, as she thought about what had happened in the woods the night Janet died.

Barring a shock-induced hallucination, it was a fair bet that Molly had witnessed a coven gathering, and Beth dreaded the prospect of sharing the diary with Diana. Given the location and timing of events, she would be convinced that Molly had seen Lenore's coven, and her imagination would run wild filling in the blanks.

Beth considered not showing her the diary at all, but she knew that wouldn't work. Henry Woodruff had given them two folders, and Diana would be expecting to see both. Besides, Beth knew she didn't have the right to add 'censor' to her surrogate mom role. No. Diana had every right to read Molly's diary.

Anticipating Diana's reaction to what Molly had described in the diary, Beth was already trying to come up with alternative explanations to suggest to her sister. After all, Molly was in shock at the time, right? On top of being a hormonal teenager, she was half-frozen and running around on a broken ankle, so how reliable a witness could she have been? Any number of foreign languages would have been unidentifiable to her. A collar turned up on a dark bathrobe might have appeared to her as a black hooded robe in the shadowed amber light. "Yeah, right," she sighed. Any single rationale might be convincing. Cumulatively, not so much. Still, she had to try.

Rolling her shoulders to ease away the last vestiges of stiffness in her upper torso, she went to find Ruth Nagle. What was it that foolish woman had said? 'The romantic ramblings of a young girl. Obviously of no consequence.' Wouldn't she be surprised?

When she opened the door to the hallway, she saw a beehive of activity going on in what appeared to be a large meeting room at the rear of the building. The pocket door leading to it had been closed earlier, but it was wide open now and Beth felt as if she had once again stepped into a time warp. A trio of diminutive blue-haired ladies were setting out a magnificent silver tea service on a lace-covered table in the center of the room, while other women of less advanced years were scurrying around with ornately carved silver trays of finger sandwiches and pastries.

Beth had only been able to retreat a few steps when Ruth Nagle saw her. "Ah there you are, Miss Wendell!" Her grande-dame smile all in place, she hurried to greet Beth. "We're having our monthly meeting tonight. Perhaps you'd care to join us for tea beforehand. It's almost ready."

"Oh, no thank you, Mrs. Nagle. I'm afraid I'm not properly dressed for..."

"Nonsense, my dear. You look just fine," said the older woman, so convincingly that Beth almost believed her, except that she was wearing the same jeans and sweatshirt that had been so clearly objectionable to her that morning.

"You're very kind." Also one of the ten biggest phonies I've ever met, thought Beth. "But I really can't stay." She glanced at her watch. "My sister's expecting me home within the hour, and..."

"But our members have already begun to arrive. They'll be terribly disappointed if you leave without even so much as a cup of tea. They're so looking forward to meeting you."

"I'm flattered, truly I am, but I..."

"Oh, now, now, now, I am simply not going to take 'no' for an answer!"

With the woman's bony fingers already grasping her elbow and urging her forward, Beth honestly believed that she meant it. Rather than make a scene, she took another peek at her watch and relented. "I suppose Diana won't mind waiting a bit."

"Wonderful!" She was already waving to several women as they entered the meeting room. When she introduced Beth to everyone as 'Elizabeth Gresham-Wendell,' Beth stood a little taller. Her mother had been a Gresham, as was her Aunt Liv. Beth Wendell might slouch occasionally, but the great-granddaughter of George Gresham could never be seen with less than perfect posture. It was something that a string of nannies had drummed into her and Diana for as long as either of them could remember, and Beth now held her head a little higher, in deference to the ancestor whose financial savvy had enabled generations of Greshams to enjoy the good life.

"Now if you ladies will excuse me," said Mrs. Nagle. "I think it's time to begin pouring." The ornate Georgian tea service had been arranged at the head of the table, with a solitary chair before it. Ruth Nagle proudly seated herself at the position of honor and began pouring tea. It was a regal ceremony, each member proffering a delicate china cup for her to fill, and exchanging a brief pleasantry before moving on to claim a sandwich or pastry.

Beth was about to take her place in line when a cup of tea was brought to her by an attractive middle-aged woman of average height and weight, pleasant-faced, with fair skin and warm brown eyes. Her hair was the palest shade of ash-blonde, expertly cropped to give the appearance of casual chic, and she was wearing a beautifully tailored cream wool suit with a cherry-red silk blouse that exactly matched the shade of her lipstick. "Miss Wendell, I'm Martha Hastings. Welcome."

"Thank you," said Beth, accepting the tea with its slice of lemon.

"Sugar or cream?"

"No, thank you. This is fine."

They began making small-talk and were soon on a first-name basis, something Beth hadn't managed to achieve in an entire day with Ruth Nagle. She was listening with only half an ear to Martha Hastings' prideful account of her family, until she heard the woman speak of her son 'Billy.' Then she had Beth's complete attention.

"Billy?" asked Beth. "That wouldn't by any chance be Congressman Bill Hastings, would it?"

The sudden light in Martha Hastings' eyes made the words that followed unnecessary. "Yes, as a matter of fact," she acknowledged with a soft smile, "William... Billy is my son."

"You must be terribly proud of him," said Beth.

"Oh, yes. Indeed I am. He's a wonderful boy."

Beth smiled at the ingenuousness of the remark. "I've certainly heard nothing but great things about him. Except from Stanley Reed, of course." She was referring to the long-term incumbent who had lost his congressional seat to Bill Hastings in the last election. It had been a bitterly contested race, and Hastings' resounding victory had instantly catapulted him into the limelight as a major force to be reckoned with in New York politics. Beth had interviewed both men for a post-election piece, and Reed had been as close to apoplectic as anyone she'd ever met. Martha chuckled at the mention of Stanley Reed. "After all the rotten things he said about Billy, victory was oh so sweet, Beth. And that wonderful article you wrote was just the perfect icing on the cake." She quoted some of what Beth had written about her son.

"You have a prodigious memory, Martha." Beth smiled at the woman's unabashed pride in her 'Billy.'

Martha laughed. "Selectively so, I'm afraid. I bought out every issue of Newsworld I could find and sent copies to all our relatives and friends. Didn't you notice your circulation was up that week?"

"Is that what did it? We wondered." Beth was enjoying the comfortable repartee. "Seriously 'though, I was tremendously impressed with your son."

Martha Hastings smiled, her eyes glowing. "And he with you, Beth. I remember him saying that yours was one of the few interviews he'd ever actually enjoyed."

"You're very kind to tell me. Thank you."

They discussed Bill Hastings, his promising career, and his family, but only superficially, and Beth regretted that it wasn't the time or place to be delving into politics.

Martha seemed to be reading her thoughts. "I just had a marvelous idea," she said. "My son and his wife Jan will be visiting with the grandkids this weekend. Why don't you have dinner with us Saturday night so you can have a nice long chat with Billy. He'd love it, and so would I."

When Martha extended the invitation to include a plus one, Beth readily accepted for herself and Diana. It was obvious that Mama Bear was looking for a little impromptu media exposure for her son, but Beth had no problem with that. She too could profit from an interview with the charismatic young congressman who was always good copy.

Beth tugged at the hem of her sweatshirt. "And I promise to be far more presentably attired than I am at this moment."

Martha laughed. "Ruth wasn't about to let you escape without showing you off. If you'd been buck naked, I don't think she would have cared." They took a few moments to key in each other's contact information on their cellphones. Martha had just started giving Beth instructions on how to get to the Hastings farmhouse when Ruth Nagle appeared beside them with a cluster of her cronies in tow.

Touching a proprietary hand to Beth's forearm, Mrs. Nagle said, "Now Martha, you can't be monopolizing our guest of honor all evening, you know." Introducing Beth to the women she had dragged over to meet her, she orchestrated the entire conversation, parading Beth's lineage by invoking the name of George Gresham like a mantra whenever she could. Beth was reminded of the fairy tale about the emperor's new clothes. Everybody was acting as if there was absolutely nothing wrong with wearing old jeans and a sweatshirt to a tea party.

Martha Hastings managed a whispered "Call me for the rest of those directions," before maneuvering herself away from Beth and to the rear of the little group assembled around her, backing away until she could discreetly disappear. Beth longed to follow, but she had no opportunity to escape until ten minutes later when the business portion of their monthly meeting was finally called to order. At the first pound of the gavel, she ducked into the reading room to retrieve Molly's diary and Woodruff's other loaners. Then she bolted for the door, not quite at a run, but close.

Being a Satanist isn't a crime.

As an American citizen, I'm free to worship anyone or anything I damn well please.

Too bad that lovely Bill of Rights doesn't protect my role in what a Black Mass requires.

Far from it.

If it weren't for all the free drugs, I'd be out of here in a flash.

With all the new people in town, it's getting way to risky.

Added to that, our high and mighty leader really seems to be losing it.

He actually almost killed me over a stupid goat last week!

Even the healthiest animals aren't enough for him these days.

At least he allowed the three young campers to move on without incident yesterday.

There was safety in numbers for them.

A solitary camper would not have been so lucky.

But there will be others.

There always are.

Chapter Eight

Beth didn't need her key to open the front door. It was unlocked, but she was too tired to beat that particular dead horse right now. "Hey, Di!" She locked the deadbolt behind her but didn't bother arming the alarm system with the security code that Diana had given her that morning. Her sister's birthdate of course. What a surprise.

"Welcome back!"

Beth piled Woodruff's loaners on the hall chair. She didn't want to spring Molly's diary on her sister just yet. Shrugging out of her jacket, she tossed it over the pile of books and folders before going into the living room.

Diana was curled up in a corner of the sofa, one elbow hugging the armrest and supporting a huge magnifying glass aimed at her open right palm. The lamp on the end table was at maximum wattage, and Beth knew better than to ask about splinters. Reading her palms was a daily ritual for Diana.

"Here you go," Beth said, jingling the keys to the Porsche and dropping them on the coffee table. "Your baby's home, safe and sound." Kicking off her shoes, she slumped gratefully into the club chair opposite the sofa, toed off her shoes and propped her feet up on the coffee table. "How'd things go at the nursing home? Any luck?"

"Depressing as hell." Diana glanced up at Beth, shook her head and sighed. "Could we talk about it later?"

"Absolutely." Beth cringed at the thought of her sister spending the afternoon in a place devoted exclusively to end-of-life custodial care. She quickly switched gears to lighten the mood. "Wait 'til you hear why it took me so long to get back here." She had texted Diana earlier to tell her she'd be delayed, but hadn't explained why. "Ruth Nagle insisted, as in wouldn't take 'no' for an answer, that I stay for the historical society's monthly social. Dressed like this! Can you believe it?"

Diana laughed. "Was it really ghastly?" Hoping for some juicy details, she quickly set aside her magnifying glass, lowered the lamp wattage, and gave Beth her undivided attention.

"No, actually it wasn't all that bad," Beth shrugged. "Except for dragon lady, they were a nice enough bunch." Seeing Diana's disappointed expression, she quickly improvised and opted for farce.

Straightening her spine, sitting ramrod straight, she threw back her shoulders. Lowering her feet from the coffee table to the floor in one lithe movement, she crossed her ankles primly, pursed her lips, crinkled her nose, and tilted her chin toward the ceiling. She then proceeded with a fussy pantomime of Ruth Nagle pouring tea.

"I love it!" crowed Diana. "Just like Mrs. Peterson -- remember her?"

"How could I forget?" Beth sank back into the club chair and draped her legs over one of its deeply cushioned arms, laughing as she wiggled an extended pinky finger at Diana in memory of Isabel Peterson, one of many tutors their aunt had hired to get them through their pre-teen gawkiness. The woman's particular specialty had been etiquette and, after two months of having their manners polished by that estimable lady, each of them could pour tea as elegantly as any duchess.

"No comparison though," said Beth. "Peterson was one very classy lady. Nagle's just a pompous old windbag. She did a complete one-eighty once she found out who we were. Really sickening." Beth waved away the image of Nagle's toadying smile that had just invaded her mind's eye. "The woman had me on display like some prize pig at the county fair."

"Poor Beth!" When Diana grinned happily, Beth pulled the small throw pillow from her chair and tossed it across the coffee table at her. Diana quickly tossed it back.

Beth made an easy catch and tucked the pillow beside her, happy to see that Diana's reflexes and depth perception hadn't deserted her. Her aim had been right on target. "Actually, it wasn't a total loss." She told Diana about meeting Congressman Hastings' mother. "Okay with you if we take her up on her invitation for dinner Saturday?"

"With the historical society?" Diana's voice was shrill. "You can't be serious!"

"No, no," laughed Beth, "at the Hastings' home. Hope you don't mind, but I sort of accepted for us. Martha Hastings was very persuasive. Kept dangling the carrot of an interview with her son in front of my nose, so I couldn't resist. Chad would love the copy. You won't mind going, will you?"

"Why not?" shrugged Diana. "A good home-cooked meal would be great."

Beth shook her head and smiled. It never occurred to Diana that they might actually be able to provide such a treat for themselves. "Speaking of food, Di, pizza okay with you for tonight?" Beth was too tired to cook or go anywhere.

"Great idea. The works?" Diana was already hitting a speed dial on her cell.

"Sounds good," agreed Beth, immediately regretting her words when she heard what Diana was ordering. She was okay with the olives, onions, peppers, mushrooms, sausage, pepperoni and extra garlic, but she shouted "No way!" to the last item on Diana's wish list. "Absolutely no anchovies on my half!"

"Coward!" laughed Diana, relaying Beth's request over the phone.

Depending on the type and amount of medication that Diana was taking on any given day, her taste buds were either oversensitive or anesthetized. Not wanting to make her feel any more self-conscious about the vagaries of her appetite than she already was, Beth usually went along with her choices on shared orders, but she drew the line at salty little bearded swimmers. She didn't care how nutritious they were.

By the time the pizza arrived half an hour later, they were already drinking their chianti and enjoying the cheery warmth of the fireplace. After paying the delivery boy and handing him the ten-dollar tip that Diana insisted he be given, Beth carried the box to the glass-topped coffee table in the living room and sat beside her sister on the sofa. They wasted no time digging in.

Munching happily, Diana said, "Too bad it's just you and me, kid. That is one great-looking fire."

"Sure is." All Beth had done was flick a switch to turn on the gas, but the logs and embers looked amazingly real. A little balsam scent and an occasional hissing or crackling noise and the illusion would have been complete. As always, the moment she started to relax, she thought of Chad. He still hadn't returned her call. She knew all about his crazy busy schedule, but she also knew about all the single women at Newsworld who would happily have jumped into bed with him at a moment's notice.

Torturing herself with that line of thinking, mindlessly feeding her face, she welcomed Diana's sudden willingness to talk about what had happened that afternoon. Without any preamble, as if they'd been discussing it right along, she said, "Margaret Mowbray's baby sister has to be pushing a hundred, Beth. Poor woman has Alzheimer's. And I mean bigtime. When I asked her about Margaret and Lenore, she acted like she'd never even heard their names before."

"So you didn't find out anything?"

Diana sipped thoughtfully at her chianti. "Nothing. Nothing that made any sense anyway. It was really spooky. Her mind kept wandering. She was perfectly lucid one moment and totally bonkers the next. Honest to God, I don't know how families deal with it. Watching somebody they love..." She shook her head and topped off both their drinks.

"Anyway, she was sitting there quietly babbling about something or other, when all of a sudden she went ballistic over my pin." As Diana fluffed out the sapphire-blue silk scarf she was wearing in an intricate tie around her neck, the little unicorn pin emerged from within a deep fold of the scarf.

"What's wrong, Beth? You're white as a sheet."

"I'm okay. Just a little light-headed. Too much wine on an empty stomach, I guess." Beth took a deep breath, but it didn't help. "Or maybe I just OD'd on Ruth Nagle." Another incident involving a unicorn pin. Even her vivid imagination couldn't come up with any possibility that might make it a coincidence.

Diana put another piece of pizza on her sister's plate. "Eat!" She watched Beth carefully until she had forced down a few bites. "Thank heaven, you've got some color coming back. Don't scare me like that, Sis." Diana patted her sister's forearm and took a bite of her own pizza before going on with her story.

"Where was I?" she squinted. "Oh yeah, Charlie and I looked like such vagrants this afternoon, that we stopped off here to change before we went to the nursing home. Luckily, good little PI that he is, Charlie always keeps a change of clothes in his car, so we looked pretty respectable when we arrived. Not so luckily, we were both sweating bullets in no time. God, it was hot in there. Fifteen minutes in that sauna and I had to take off my jacket. I was just rearranging my scarf when poor old Helen noticed my little unicorn pin and just about had a meltdown."

Beth didn't trust herself to say a word. She wasn't even sure she could have if she wanted to.

"Anyway," continued Diana, "the pin had her so rattled that I took it off and stashed it away in my purse. Then she started yelling even louder for me to put it back on and never take it off again. She was carrying on so badly that the nurse had to ask us to leave. That poor soul. I felt so awful for her."

Beth was so crazed with worry that she stupidly spoke the first platitude that came to mind. "Tough to get old, Di."

Diana looked away. "Tougher not to," she said, dropping a half-eaten crust of pizza onto her plate and dusting off her hands. When she glanced up at Beth's stricken expression, she was instantly contrite. Leaning in toward her sister, she gave her a quick hug around the waist. "I'm so sorry, Beth. That really was a dumb and very cheap shot."

Beth hoped that her smile didn't look as shaky as it felt. "Forget it, hon. Dumb remarks all around tonight." Desperate to escape the emotional quicksand, she jumped to her feet and hurried into the hallway. Diana called after her. "What's up?"

"You'll see!" Moments later, she returned with Molly's diary and gently handed the tattered little book over to Diana. "It was in one of the folders Woodruff gave us today. Doesn't look like much, but I promise you won't be disappointed with what's inside."

Diana quickly opened to the first page, her expression clouding as she tried to decipher the words written there. "Is this supposed to be English?"

"Yes. And very good English at that. I had a problem with it too, at first. Just give your eyes a chance to adjust to the World War II era penmanship."

Beth began clearing the remnants of their pizza fest. By the time she returned from tidying up the kitchen, Diana was already so engrossed in Molly's world that she didn't even hear her say goodnight. Beth went to bed immediately, fully expecting the early reveille when it came, shortly after dawn the next morning.

"Up and at 'em sleepyhead!" Diana was pounding on her bedroom door. "Time to go tannery hunting!"

Twenty minutes later, with the Porsche already rumbling impatiently in the driveway, Beth raced out the front door, auburn hair still damp from her shower, not a bit of makeup on her face, clutching at a travel mug of coffee that her sister had left for her on the kitchen counter.

Ten minutes later, they were roaring along bumpy country roads and careening around hairpin turns, none of which was doing anything to improve Beth's mood. She desperately needed an infusion of caffeine, but the mouthpiece of the travel mug kept banging into her front teeth whenever she tried to use it. "Slow down, will you! What's the big hurry?"

"Sorry." She immediately downshifted the Porsche and eased off on the accelerator. "Guess I'm just a little over-eager."

"No kidding?" Taking advantage of the reprieve, Beth drank as much of the burning-hot coffee as her mouth and throat could handle.

"Pretty around here, huh?" said Diana.

Beth looked around at the dense forest of pine, birch and oak on both sides of the road. "Yeah, but where the hell are we?"

"Almost in Chaetestown. Keep an eye out for an old tannery, will you? I could have sworn I saw one somewhere along here a while back."

"And exactly what does an old tannery look like?" asked Beth. "Or a new one, for that matter."

"Well, there are no new ones in the area, just refurbished old ones or ruins. The building itself could be almost any size or shape, but look for a water tower. That's about the only thing that might be visible from the road anyway."

Beth was beginning to think they were on the wrong road entirely, when she finally saw a likely contender. "There!" She pointed to a tower rising from deep within the woods on her side of the road. "Could that be it?"

Diana slowed the car and glanced through Beth's window. "Yes!" She hit the brakes and pulled over to the side of road.

"I can't believe it was so easy to find," said Beth, amazed by their good fortune. She was already out of the car and hurrying toward the structure, Diana immediately behind her.

"I hate to disappoint you, Beth, but chances are slim that this one is *the one*. There are dozens of these old towers in the area."

"You're kidding."

"No, I'm not. Tanning used to be a big deal around here."

"Oh great," sighed Beth, slowing her pace now that she realized the odds were heavily against this being the one Molly Beecham had stumbled upon.

They were within fifty feet of the tower, when Diana hooked a hand around Beth's elbow and pulled her back a step. "No point going any further, Beth. This definitely is not Molly's tower."

"Why not? Looks eerie enough."

"That's only because it's old and falling apart, but this isn't the place." She shook her head with certainty. "Not a single negative vibe anywhere. We're wasting our time."

"You and your vibes!" Beth was laughing as she shook off Diana's hand. "Serve you right if there's a great big plaque saying 'Briggs Tannery' plastered to the front door."

"There won't be." Diana headed back to the car.

"Well, as long as we're here," Beth called over her shoulder, "I'll just check it out anyway.

Be right with you." Picking her way through knee-high brambles, she approached the deserted structure.

The stone base of the tower was dark with soot, the windows were boarded up, there was no sign of ownership or habitation, and definitely no hint of a name on what was left of the crumbling front door. She was tempted to take a peek at the back of the building, but the deep-throated rumble of the Porsche was broadcasting Diana's impatience loud and clear. She hurried back to the car, barely getting the door closed behind her before Diana gunned the engine and took off, tires screeching.

"Take it easy!" Beth was struggling with her seatbelt, while the car bumped along the rutted road at a speed that had her empty stomach skittering up to her throat. "What is your problem, little sister?"

"The problem is you, my pragmatic elder sibling! You and your pig-headed refusal to acknowledge that there's a whole wide wondrous world beyond that which you can see, smell, hear, taste or touch. I told you that wasn't the tannery we're looking for, but still you had to go check it out. Why can't you accept the fact that sometimes I just *know* things?"

"Okay, okay – I'm sorry!" Beth shifted in her seat so that she could see every nuance of expression that crossed her sister's face. Feeling as if she were about to defuse a time bomb, she started speaking again, slowly and calmly now, her tone as matter-of-fact as she could make it.

"I'm a reporter, Di. Checking and double-checking every fact, even from the most credible source, is what I've been trained to do, and I guess I've been doing it for so long that it's become instinctive. I'm sorry if you were offended, but I assure you that wasn't my intent."

Diana took a few deep breaths to rein in her temper. She had just come perilously close to blurting out the truth of how far she had come along her psychic journey, and she knew that Beth wasn't ready to hear it yet. Maybe she never would be. Tears threatening, she said, "Sorry, Beth. Seems as if you're always bearing the brunt of my God-awful mood swings."

"Hey, what's a big sister for?" Beth pulled a pack of gum from her purse and offered a piece to Diana.

"No thanks. Maybe later." Beth tucked the gum back into her purse.

"So… Tell me more about the tanneries, Di." She hoped the generic topic would be a totally non-confrontational one.

Diana settled both hands on the lower part of the wheel and relaxed her forearms on her thighs. "Well, for openers, the tanning industry originally started around here because of all the hickory trees, oddly enough. The whole area used to be loaded with them, and hickory bark was an essential part of the solution the tanners used on the hides."

"Interesting," said Beth. "Never knew that."

"Nice to be able to teach you something for a change, Beth. We kid sisters don't often get to do that."

"Enjoy the moment, kiddo," Beth teased.

Diana laughed, then continued with her mini-travelogue. "You might also be interested to know that this road we're on right now is actually part of what used to be the Mohican Trail. It goes straight up to Canada, so trappers all along the trail used to bring their pelts down to Chaetestown. It was an easy way for them to combine business with a little R&R."

"R&R? You're kidding." Beth was looking at the desolate landscape around them.

"No, I'm serious. The Catskills were a major resort area long before skiers put Windham and Hunter on the map. In fact, one of the most posh resorts in the country was just fifteen miles from here -- the 'Catskill Mountain House.' It burned down a long time ago, but back in the eighteen hundreds it attracted visitors from all over the world."

Beth was really impressed. "How do you know all this?"

Diana arched a brow and grinned. "I'm not a total intellectual dropout, you know. When something interests me, I have been known to crack a book on the subject now and then. And the history of this area has always fascinated me." And at long last, she thought, I'm beginning to understand why.

Beth insisted that they get something to eat before they did any more exploring, so they stopped in at Eliza's Country Kitchen. She pretended not to notice Diana rearranging the eggs on her plate to make it appear as if she had eaten more than a few bites.

During the course of their conversation with the always-chatty Eliza, Diana asked if she had ever heard of the Briggs Tannery, but she hadn't. When Eliza suggested that the historical society might be able to help, they thanked her and somehow managed to stifle their groans until they left the restaurant.

Without discussion or hesitation, Diana headed directly for the historical society. Her illness had taught her the wisdom of using her energy wisely, and she wasn't eager to spend the whole day driving all over hell and gone looking for old water towers. Spending more time with the obnoxious archivist would be a small price to pay if the woman could help narrow their search. It was worth a shot.

It was Diana's first exposure to the kinder, gentler Ruth Nagle, and she was as nauseated by all the fawning as she was delighted with the information that resulted from it. Not only did the woman know where the Briggs Tannery was, but she gave them precise directions to it, along with information about its current owner, an artist named John Devane, who had converted the upper reaches of the tower into his studio.

Fifteen minutes after leaving Mrs. Nagle, Beth and Diana arrived at their destination. "What do we do now?" asked Beth, as soon as Diana had parked along the shoulder of the Old Chaetestown Road. They could see the tannery about five hundred yards into the woods on their right, but there didn't seem to be any way to drive up to it. Beth lowered her window and craned her neck out for a better view. "There's a car up there behind the building. Has to be a driveway somewhere."

Diana surveyed the rutted terrain around them, and decided against risking any damage to the undercarriage of the low-slung Porsche. "Yeah, well I could lose an axle trying to find it. Let's walk. It's not that far." She edged the car in closer to the line of trees skirting the shoulder, but she didn't immediately cut the engine. Now that the moment of discovery was at hand, she found that she was more than a little reluctant to leave the safe confines of the Porsche.

Beth wasn't in any hurry either. The writer in her was trying to absorb the atmosphere of their surroundings, hoping to get some sense of the tower as Molly must have seen it the night her friend died, but there certainly wasn't anything at all sinister about its appearance now. Perky yellow crocuses danced along the blackened bricks at the base of the tower, and bright red semi-gloss paint on the shutters and front door had rejuvenated the old facade, giving it a quaint charm.

"It looks harmless enough," said Beth.

"Feels okay too," said Diana, disappointment tinged with relief in her voice. "Weird. Not a single bad vibe." She shook her head. "Doesn't make any sense. I should be picking up on something." She turned off the ignition and got out of the car.

Beth wasn't comfortable with the flimsy art-buying pretext they had devised to explain their visit, and she lagged a few steps behind Diana as they dodged and sidestepped their way along the rocky overgrown path leading up to the building.

"You'd think Picasso would pave this damn thing," said Diana. She pointed to the Land Rover parked beside the tower. "I should have guessed. Anything less and he'd be mired in mud every time it rained."

"Fed Ex must love this guy. What do you suppose he does about visitors and deliveries?" asked Beth.

"Who knows? From the looks of this place, I'm guessing he wouldn't welcome either one."

They reached the front door, the same door through which Molly Beecham claimed to have seen a hooded and robed figure, but there was nothing at all menacing about it in the morning sun. Annoyed by the obstacle course they'd just run, Diana ignored the gleaming brass knocker and pressed hard on the bell.

As they waited, Beth became increasingly uneasy about imposing on this man's privacy, something he clearly coveted. And from what Ruth Nagle had said, she didn't think he'd be greatly appeased to hear that they'd come to buy one of his paintings. Apparently John Devane was a well-established regional artist who was long-past the impoverished early years when he would have given any buyer the red-carpet treatment.

After a minute or so, Diana rang the bell again, even longer this time. Moments later, when the door was finally opened, it took every ounce of self-control either of them could muster to keep from laughing out loud. Before them stood an animated cartoon of an artist. Tall and thin, with baggy black trousers and a paint-spattered smock that must once have been white, he sported a trim Van Dyke beard and mustache, and a mane of black hair laced with silver. Poised on his lips was a stream of invective that died the moment he gazed into Diana's bright blue eyes. Suddenly he was all smiles.

She quickly explained who they were, including their full family name, and the fabrication about why they had come, all the while shamelessly batting her eyelashes at him. It had the desired effect, and Devane immediately invited them inside. It wasn't often that such incredible beauty and wealth arrived on his doorstep in a buying mood, and he planned to triple his prices for them, a special one-day sale.

"Excuse the mess," he said. Closing the door behind them, he immediately made the room even messier by shrugging out of his smock and tossing it on a chair, revealing a slim black turtle neck sweater that vastly improved his appearance. "The cleaning lady's due tomorrow, so I'm afraid you're seeing this old place at its worst."

Diana murmured all the requisite polite reassurances and monopolized Devane's rapt attention while Beth quietly observed every detail of their surroundings. With all the oddities of furniture placement imposed by the circular shape of the tower, the place looked like a stage-set for an off-Broadway theater-in-the-round production like the one Olivia's ex was currently starring in.

Dwarf trees and houseplants had been strategically placed to partition the living area from the smaller dining and kitchen zones of the first level. The foliage looked real, but Beth knew it must have been silk, for there simply wasn't enough light around them to sustain healthy green plants.

The first floor was dominated by a huge modular sofa angled around a fieldstone fireplace, the gray of the stone echoed in the rug, drapes and upholstery, its neutral tone allowing the artist to showcase his paintings to their best advantage. Beth was fairly certain that his work would never see a gavel at Sotheby's, but she could see that he was a talented craftsman.

They followed him up the spiral stairs that hugged the tower wall. When Beth saw that an ornate lacquered privacy screen had been cleverly angled to block all view of the second floor from the stairs, her imagination began making quantum leaps into Molly's world of terror, until Devane explained that the second level was his bedroom and private bath. Of course, she told herself. Get a grip, Beth!

"That privacy screen is a life-saver," he said. "Otherwise I'd have to make my bed every day!" They all laughed a little self-consciously and proceeded along to his third-floor studio.

The feeling that she had stumbled upon a stage set didn't really leave Beth until they entered the dazzling world of sunlit color at the top of the stairs. Devane may have looked like an overdressed actor playing the part of a pre-War Impressionist, but this was really a working studio.

The roof held an enormous skylight, and the southern wall had been squared off to accommodate a broad expanse of glass, with several smaller windows scattered across the circular planes of the room. There were three easels, each with a painting in progress, and canvases everywhere, some blank, some completed, all neatly stacked against the walls. Devane was no master, but both women were honestly able to praise the tremendous energy and skillful use of color in his work. Feigning anguished indecision about which ones to buy was a little more of an acting stretch.

In the end, they carried the charade through in grand style. Diana bought three small paintings, and Beth chose one of the larger pieces. She didn't want it for herself, but she had a feeling that the rolling hillside awash with bright spring flowers might make a pleasant enough addition to the wall of a middle-management office somewhere in Gresham's New York corporate headquarters building.

Their business transacted, Devane was six thousand dollars richer than he had been before their arrival and suddenly in the most hospitable of moods. He insisted that they stay for coffee. "I even have fresh croissants for us." Chatting comfortably about the paintings they'd chosen, he took a few minutes to tie them up into two well-padded bundles before leading the way back downstairs to his living area.

Gesturing to the sofa, he said, "Please, ladies, make yourselves comfortable." He leaned their purchases against the front door and scurried off to the kitchen area. Determined to hide their nervousness, Beth and Diana eased back into the plump cushions of the couch and made inane small-talk while their host made fussy noises with a tray he was prepping. It was ready in just a few minutes, and he set it down on the coffee table in front of them.

Beth gladly accepted the coffee he was pouring from a French press, but she refused the pastry. It was a decision she immediately regretted when she saw Diana's obvious enjoyment of the golden, flaky croissant that she'd lathered with butter and marmalade.

Beth was glad her sister had an appetite, but when she reached for a second croissant, it was clear that something else was going on here. Diana was never that hungry in the morning. She watched as her baby sister made a production of buttering the second pastry. When she licked her lips and gazed innocently up at their host, Beth could almost hear the guy panting. As she nibbled on the croissant, she plied a mesmerized Devane with questions worthy of a grand high inquisitor.

No, he didn't know the previous owners of the tannery. How long had he lived here? Eight years since he'd moved from Albany. Witchcraft? No, he had never heard anything about that, and certainly not in connection with the tannery. Oh, he'd heard some of the legends, of course. Just rumors started by a bunch of superstitious old Dutch settlers way back when. Certainly nothing he intended to lose sleep over. No, he wasn't being macho. He was comfortable here. But he wasn't crazy. If he ever started hearing things that go bump in the night, he'd be long gone before it ever happened again.

By the time they left the tannery, Diana was satisfied that John Devane was nothing more or less than he appeared to be, a moderately successful artist with the practiced eccentricities common to his breed.

Beth couldn't agree, nor could she fully understand her own misgivings. She'd done enough interviews to know that the man hadn't been entirely truthful in answering Diana's questions. But so what? Nothing unusual there. Everybody had something to hide. She could only guess that she had been preconditioned by Molly's diary. Expecting something ominous, she had felt it. She was glad when they returned to the familiar comfort of the Porsche.

'Hey, champ, you okay?' Diana gunned the engine.

"Sure. Why wouldn't I be?"

"That I couldn't say, but I know you're not fine. What gives?'

Beth shrugged. "I'm not sure. That place just kind of weirded me out.'

Diana laughed. "I'm supposed to be the psychic one here, remember?"

"I know. It's just..."

"Molly has your imagination running wild, Beth. I promise you, if there were anything at all evil about that tannery, I couldn't have gone near it."

Beth's uneasiness stayed with her long after they left the tower. When they arrived back home, Diana immediately went up to her room to lie down, taking Molly's diary with her, along with the other items Henry Woodruff had loaned them. She was hurting, and she knew she should take one of the pain-killers that always knocked her out for a few hours, but she was determined to return all the reading material to their owner the following day.

While Diana rested in her room, Beth busied herself with another trip to the supermarket to add to the staples she'd brought in the day before. When she returned, she organized the kitchen into some workable order as she put away the groceries. Then she made grilled ham and cheese sandwiches for a late lunch, and brought a tray up to her sister.

Diana was sitting at her desk studying Molly's diary and jotting down notes as she went along. She mumbled her thanks as Beth set the tray down on the corner of the desk, but she never took her eyes from the diary.

Beth returned to the kitchen to eat a quiet lunch and catch up on her Newsworld reading. The magazine had a great editorial staff, but even some of them seemed to have lost the ability to differentiate between fact and fiction, and it was almost impossible to figure out what was really happening in the world. When the house phone rang, she was glad for the interruption and picked it up immediately. It was Charlie Hobson calling for Diana. She shouted for her sister, hung up when she heard her on the line, and returned to the magazine. A few minutes later, Diana came bounding down the stairs.

"Damnedest thing, Beth. This woman just called Charlie and asked for me. Said she's a friend of that poor old lady we saw yesterday."

"How did she know...?"

"The nursing home. You have to leave a telephone number and address when you sign in to visit somebody like that."

Anticipating her sister's next question, Diana was already shaking her head. "I didn't leave any information about myself. Charlie signed us both in at his address and 'phone number. That's why he got the message. Anyway, this woman says she has to see me right away."

"Why?"

Diana shrugged. "I haven't the foggiest but I'm about to find out." She gave a little wave and turned to leave.

"Wait a minute! How do you know this isn't some kind of...?" Dread of kidnappers in every guise had been drilled into both of them from a very early age.

"Oh it's cool," Diana said. "Charlie already checked the caller out. She's harmless. Name's Katherine Vredenburgh. Retired now, but she used to have an antique shop in Acra. The shop's closed, but she still lives there. Kind of a recluse, but perfectly respectable. Can't wait to find out why she called!"

Beth scrambled to her feet and grabbed her purse. She could see Diana wasn't going to be dissuaded. "Okay. Let's go."

"Not so fast!" Diana waved off her sister's advance. "She wants to see me alone, Beth."

"Out of the question."

"Pulleeze! Charlie will be following me, not to mention one of Paul's goons." She patted the side pocket of her jacket. "And my trusty .22 is right here. I'll be fine."

Margaret's timing had always been impeccable.

The fertility festival of Ostara would soon be upon them.

And she knew what their offering to the Dark Lord would be.

At all costs, she must not be allowed to exact her revenge at their ritual.

Not when the ultimate prize is so close.

Chapter Nine

Acra was less than twenty miles down the mountain from trendy, thriving Windham, yet Diana felt as if she'd entered a parallel universe when she left the divided four-lane highway that Route 23 now was and turned onto the scenically meandering bypass that it used to be. The advent of the modern highway had clearly left the small town struggling to be remembered for its glory days.

Scanning the occasional street sign as she drove slowly past a scattering of houses, B&B's, and even a few small resort hotels, she soon found her destination. It was on a side road just off the main street, a dilapidated two-story frame house with the name 'Vredenburgh' in faded decals on its roadside mailbox.

Torn shingles that hadn't been white for decades, peeling green paint on the shutters, and the total absence of any sign of habitation gave the building a mournful air. Diana was glad to see Charlie's Taurus parked just down the street as he'd promised it would be, his car well-hidden from the house by a thick stand of pine trees that bordered the lot. Between Charlie and whichever Dunsford guy was tailing her today, not to mention the gun in her purse, she wasn't overly concerned about her safety. As she backed into the driveway, she was glad to find the perfect place to park, and she quickly tucked the Porsche behind an overgrown wall of shrubbery near the side door.

By now, she was sure that Paul had already heard from his field agent about the peculiarity of the location and the ramshackle appearance of the house, a report that would likely put an abrupt end to the grace period he'd given her for so many weeks. Before the day was out, he would want explanations that she wasn't yet prepared to give him, not until she had first told Olivia the whole story about her illness, the session with Philip, and all that had followed.

She owed Olivia the entire truth, and it was unthinkable that she might hear it from Paul, whose first loyalty had always been to her aunt. Keeping him at bay for a few more days would be tough, but then she had always enjoyed pushing the envelope with her favorite warden.

She was so close. She just knew it. Lily sensed it too. She just needed a little more time without interference from her watchdogs. The nightmares, Lenore, and her illness were all somehow linked together. She was sure of it because nothing else made any sense! She had to find the connection before time ran out on her, and no lead was too bizarre to follow up on, not even this one.

Before stepping out of the car, she pulled the .22 from her purse, checked the chamber to make sure it was loaded, then tucked it under the folds of the denim jacket that she draped casually over her right forearm. Her mother's family hadn't amassed the Gresham fortune without making dangerous enemies and, if this was a trap, Diana knew she could be dead before the cavalry arrived. She was adventuresome, but she wasn't stupid. With her left hand poised to knock at the side door, she was startled when it was opened on its safety chain.

A shadowy figure from inside whispered words she couldn't quite hear, but Diana could only imagine that she was being asked to identify herself. Feeling very exposed on the doorstep, she quickly gave her full name and mentioned Charlie's name for good measure. The safety chain instantly clattered off its track, and she was hurriedly waved inside by an elderly woman whose only greeting was a wary, tentative nod. Bolting the door behind them, she turned toward her young visitor as each of them took full measure of the other.

The older woman's skeletal frame and emaciated face spoke of chronic ill health. Her white hair was pulled into a neat tight knot atop her head, the obvious care she had taken to make it attractive a small vanity in someone who had probably once been very beautiful. She was tall, almost regal in her bearing, with vulnerable brown eyes and high cheekbones that accentuated the gray hollows beneath them. Diana knew she had passed muster when she saw the taut lines about the woman's mouth begin to ease. Nowhere near a smile, but definitely a more relaxed expression.

"I'm Katherine Vredenburgh. Thank you for coming so promptly, Miss Wendell."

"My pleasure, or at least I hope so," said Diana, still holding the gun under her jacket, counting on the fact that Covid had cured almost everyone of shaking hands. As she expected, they only exchanged stilted smiles and polite nods.

"I hope so too," sighed the woman. "Please, come inside. There's a fresh pot of tea waiting for us in the parlor."

For a split second Diana thought about the old poem that began 'Will you walk into my parlor?' said the spider to the fly, and she felt a chill creep along her spine. Shaking it off, she followed the older woman into a room that had long ago abandoned any pretense of catering to the demands and delights of the living. It was a world of chintz, lace, and lemon oil, where every gleaming mahogany surface reflected silent homage to the past.

Amidst the organized clutter were pewter and silver frames bearing the faded images of women in feathered hats, boas and white gloves, their men wearing bow ties and boaters, children in starched lace and high-button shoes, their smiles and frowns appraising this intruder from a world beyond their own.

A neat pile of logs were set on the hearth grate, and Diana hoped that this creaky old house would be a cheerier place at night with the wood ablaze and the dreary room suffused with a golden glow. That hope was short-lived, and she felt a small tug at her heart when she saw all the cobwebs in the hearth. Obviously tending a fire wasn't possible for this frail woman who surely would have welcomed its warmth.

In the center of the fireplace mantel was a sepia-toned photo of a dashing young soldier in full dress uniform. It was a formal portrait set in an oval of finely hammered silver, and it shared pride of place with a red-velvet-lined shadow box that showcased several medals and a letter bearing the presidential seal.

"My husband," offered the woman, following Diana's gaze. "He died in the Second World War." She reached out a gnarled hand to touch one of the medals. It was a five-pointed star with an eagle perched above it. "The Medal of Honor," she said, her sorrowful voice belying the proud tilt of her head.

"He must have been a fine man," said Diana, nodding solemnly and regretting that she couldn't think of anything more comforting or profound to offer. As Katherine pulled a white lace handkerchief from her skirt pocket and dabbed at her eyes, Diana deftly slipped the .22 into her own pocket. She felt only a little foolish for having it with her.

"Oh he was, Miss Wendell. He truly was." She touched trembling fingertips to the framed photo. "It's so hard to believe that he's been gone for most of my life." Tucking the handkerchief back in her pocket, she shook her head wonderingly, as if his death were a fact she still had not fully assimilated. She gestured toward the sofa. "Please, won't you sit down?"

"Yes, thank you." The two women sat at opposite ends of the faded blue sofa, each of them clearly needing the security of her own space. Whenever she was visiting anyone for the first time, Paul Dunsford's cautionary tales always prompted Diana to choose whatever seat was nearest an exit. In this case, the front door was only a few steps away, and the side door not much further. For such a large house, the 'parlor,' as her hostess referred to the living room, was almost claustrophobically small.

A beautiful old silver tea service was set out on the coffee table, and Katherine fussily rearranged the blue willow china cups and saucers so that they were shown to their best advantage against the backdrop of gleaming silver. A plate of Oreos looked wildly out of place amidst so much Victoriana, but mass-produced cookies were a welcome sight for Diana, tangible reassurance that she hadn't stumbled into yet another time warp.

Katherine could not have asked for a more appreciative audience while she poured their tea and began reminiscing about 'the old days' and what it had been like growing up in Greene County. Nobody was more surprised by that than Diana. She generally had a really low boredom threshold. Yet here she was hanging on every word the woman uttered, heart hammering, psychic receptors thrumming with anticipation.

"My parents had a small farm in Chaetestown," said Katherine. "Just enough to keep food on the table. Produce, chickens and pigs mostly. They were starting to turn a real profit by the time I was born." She paused for a breath. "Sad to say, I wasn't their lucky charm."

"Both my mother and I nearly died in childbirth. Almost certainly would have if Margaret Mowbray hadn't been there to help the midwife. The Mowbrays were good people. Always there when you needed them. We had no doctor in town back then, you see. When you got really sick, your family sent for Margaret. That's just the way it was."

For a few moments, Katherine sipped at her tea and stared off at a distant memory. If she guessed at the staggering effect of her words upon Diana, she gave no sign of it.

Hearing about Margaret Mowbray from someone who had actually known her had Diana's emotions on the brink of freefall. A hundred questions begged to be asked, but she couldn't trust her voice to phrase them in a way that wouldn't alarm Katherine. She could only pray that the woman would go on speaking about Margaret.

"Anyway," continued Katherine, "after I was born, Mother was never the same. She was too weak to help with the farm -- she had all to do just looking after me -- and Father couldn't afford to hire help. He nearly killed himself trying to do it all alone, but the rocks and weeds won out in the end." She paused to catch a strained breath.

"We had to give up the Chaetestown farm and move into this house with Mama's family. They had a small dairy farm here back then, and they welcomed Papa's help with it, but of course he hated being beholden to his in-laws. It was a bitter pill for his pride to swallow. But with Mama so ill and me just a toddler, he really had no choice."

Diana listened to the stream of personal remembrances, patiently waiting for some further mention of Margaret Mowbray, but it never came. Finally, when Katherine seemed to be noticeably tiring, Diana stopped being such a politely passive listener.

"I'll have to be going soon, you know, but you still haven't told me why..."

Katherine held up a restraining hand. "I know, dear. I know." She sighed. "I've delayed the inevitable long enough, haven't I? But you're right. It's time."

Reaching into a crewel-work sewing basket on the floor beside her corner of the sofa, Katherine retrieved a small brown leather book that she unceremoniously thrust onto the coffee table in front of Diana. "Helen wanted you to have this," she said, her voice suddenly hoarse with emotion. For a moment, only that, Katherine felt a pang of guilt about the photo she had removed from the book so many years before. Helen had probably intended that for Diana as well, but Katherine knew she could never part with it.

"Helen? You mean the woman I saw yesterday at the nursing home?"

Katherine nodded, her face sorrowful, the sheen of tears again misting her eyes.

Diana struggled to find a polite way to say what she was thinking. "I'm sorry, Mrs. Vredenburgh, but I'm really confused. Amazed really. It doesn't seem possible that she would remember me at all, much less want to give me anything." She shook her head and frowned. "Are you sure she meant me?"

"Quite sure." Eyes lowered, Katherine nodded slowly, sadly.

"But that just doesn't make any sense."

"I know." She raised her eyes and studied Diana's face as if seeing it for the first time. "I don't understand why either, Miss Wendell. I just know that Helen insisted that you have it." Katherine lowered her head and brushed an imaginary speck of lint from her pristine white sleeve. She hoped her visitor hadn't seen the lie in her eyes.

Margaret Mowbray and her sister Helen had been her two dearest friends, and Katherine knew a great deal more than she could ever share with this young woman. As she watched Diana pick up the book that she'd unwillingly guarded for so many years, Katherine was bewildered by her own feelings. After years of wishing she were rid of it, she actually resented seeing it in someone else's hands.

The moment Diana touched the book's scarred leather cover, she was stunned by the tactile familiarity of it. Closing her eyes, feeling the quick surge of energy that flowed into her hand, she suddenly understood. With a knowing smile, she opened her eyes and looked at Katherine. Her voice was strong and sure as she said, "This was Lenore's, wasn't it?"

Katherine's hand flew to the small gold cross she wore about her neck. Her gaze still held by Diana's, she could only nod slowly. She was too terrified to speak.

"I knew it!" cried Diana, her hands caressing the little book. Opening it, she felt a sudden flash of recognition when she saw the flourishing 'L' at the bottom of the first page. She fanned through several more pages, enough to confirm what she already knew. Lenore's diary had found its way back to her.

"How did Helen know…?"

"I… I have no idea," stammered Katherine. She was clutching her cross so tightly that her arthritic hand was starting to spasm. Releasing it, she clasped both hands on her lap to still their trembling. "According to the nurse who was with her when she passed…"

"Oh, no." Diana watched a single tear slowly etch a glistening path along Katherine's powdered cheek. "I'm so very sorry." She would have reached out a consoling hand, but she sensed that Katherine wouldn't have welcomed it.

Blinking her tears into submission, Katherine once again pulled the handkerchief from her pocket and brushed it across her cheek. "Helen was ill for a very long time, you know. Last night, her great and generous heart finally just gave out."

"When is the funeral? I'd like to go." Diana was shocked to hear herself saying those words. She loathed funerals.

"I'm afraid it's too late for that." Katherine was again fingering her cross. "We buried her early this morning."

"So quickly?" Inexplicably, Diana realized that she actually felt sorrow in her heart, not just empathy, but a real sense of loss. "Was she Jewish?" She knew that would mean the burial should occur within twenty-four hours after death.

"No. She was born Catholic, but she hadn't practiced any faith for as long as I can remember." She struggled for a deep breath that she took in slow stuttering stages before sighing it away. "She just hated viewings and funerals. Had it put in her will that she wanted to be buried the day after she died. Just as well, really. All the folks who might once have gone to pay their respects are already waiting for her on the other side. I'm about the only one left now."

Again, Diana had to reject the impulse to console with a touch of a hand or a hug. The woman was clearly struggling for composure, but her body language was still broadcasting a clear warning for her to keep her distance. Diana watched and listened quietly as Katherine spoke between ragged breaths.

"I tried to visit with her every Tuesday or Wednesday. Lighter traffic those days, you know. But these old bones just couldn't make the trip this week." Stalling for time, hoping to find the courage to go on, she took a few sips of her tea and returned the cup to its place on the tray. Fingering the handkerchief that had been in an out of her pocket so many times, she tucked it under the cuff of her blouse and she began fussing with her skirt, her fingers defining an already impeccably pressed center pleat in the blue wool.

"At least she wasn't alone at the end," said Katherine, continuing to worry the pleat of her skirt. "One of the nurses was with her. That's how I got the message about the book."

"Message?" Diana struggled to keep her voice even. She didn't want to jangle Katherine's nerves any further by revealing how critically important every word of this was to her. "What message?"

For a few long moments, Katherine quietly studied the parchment hands in her lap, despising the swollen knuckles and twisted fingers that she could never quite believe were her own. "Evidently," she sighed, "Helen was amazingly lucid at the end, Miss Wendell. The nurse said that often happens -- the mist clearing just long enough for them to make their peace." Another stuttered breath and sigh. Diana was getting seriously worried about the woman's health. All hint of color had suddenly vanished from her already pale cheeks.

"According to the nurse," continued Katherine, "at the very last, Helen insisted that I be given a message. It was so strange that the nurse wrote it down so she'd be sure to get it straight. It was: 'Give the book to the golden-haired girl with the unicorn'."

Katherine waved away Diana's obvious concern and took a few moments to catch her breath before continuing. "Helen died before she could explain what she meant, so the nurse didn't know what book she was talking about, but she certainly knew who the golden-haired girl was. Your little unicorn pin made quite a stir yesterday. She remembered it vividly."

Katherine bit lightly on her lower lip to stop its trembling. "As to the book, it's a diary that Helen gave me to keep for her years ago, when she first went into the nursing home. She didn't trust herself not to lose it, you see. Made me promise to keep it safe for her. Never once mentioned it again until yesterday."

Diana heard all the unspoken questions that Katherine was too proud, or too afraid, to ask, but she ignored them. The sooner she escaped, the sooner she could be alone to devour every word that Lenore had written. "I've taken enough of your time. I'd better go now and let you get some rest." As she stood, the weight of the gun at her hip startled her. She had completely forgotten about it being there.

Diana's polite smile froze when she saw Katherine's stoically erect posture begin to crumble against the back of the sofa. The woman's ghastly pallor made a death masque of her features. "What's wrong?" Diana hurried to her side.

"Nothing, dear. Nothing. This will pass." Katherine whispered, struggling for a breath, then exhaling slowly, repeating the process until she seemed calmer. Diana found her way into the kitchen and quickly returned with a glass of water, just in time to observe Katherine placing a small pill under her tongue.

"Do you want me to call a doctor?"

She shook her head and reached for the glass that Diana held out to her. "No. No, thank you. There's no need, I assure you." She took a small sip of water, then another, before handing the glass back to Diana. "You're very kind," she said, as Diana set the glass on the tray.

They sat quietly together for a few minutes while the medication worked its magic, finally normalizing her breathing and color. Still, her voice was shaky when she said, "I need to warn you about the diary, Miss Wendell. It could be very dangerous for you if the wrong people were to find out that you have it."

"The wrong people?" Diana couldn't help but wonder if the woman hadn't perhaps just suffered a mini-stroke.

Reading Diana's expression, Katherine's sharp eyes were full of rebuke. In a surprisingly strong voice, she said, "I assure you I'm still in total command of my faculties, Miss Wendell, and I beg you to heed my warning. You'll know why when you've read it. Until then, just keep quiet about having it, please." She paused for a few breaths, and Diana didn't dare say a word. Katherine's lash hadn't cut as deeply as Henry Woodruff's, but it had been enough to silence her.

"If I'd had my way," Katherine continued, "that wretched book would have been burned years ago, but Helen made me promise to keep it safe. She said it was meant for someone who would come for it one day and... well, here you are, aren't you?" She shrugged her fragile shoulders. "Somehow she knew it was meant for you. I don't know how or why." Pausing again to catch her breath, her eyes bored into Diana's. "I only know that you must guard Lenore's secrets as zealously as I have."

Diana could see that Katherine was getting dangerously agitated, so she quickly gave all the promises the woman needed to hear. "Now stop worrying and get some rest. I'll see myself out." At the risk of being rebuffed, she kissed Katherine's cheek. There was no resistance. Nor was there any response. Diana made one more suggestion that a doctor be called, but Katherine didn't even acknowledge her words with a refusal.

Leaving the house via the side door with Lenore's diary clutched against her heart, Diana hurried into the Porsche and tucked the little book into the glove compartment along with her gun.

Slowly engaging first gear to minimize the usual engine roar, she eased the car down the driveway and turned onto the narrow road.

As soon as Diana had gone, Katherine breathed a sigh of relief that the ordeal she had so dreaded was over. Leaning heavily on the armrest of the sofa, she hauled herself into an upright position and began the exhausting ritual of double-checking the locks on every window and door on the ground floor.

When she was done, her heart was again beating with an erratic and dangerous rhythm, but she refused to be intimidated by her body's familiar treachery. Clutching at the newel post, she took a few deep breaths, then grabbed onto the oak handrail to drag herself up the stairs to her room. Her heart had kept ticking on borrowed time for years. If she was going to die this day, she wanted the comfort of her own bed when it happened.

The staccato throbbing of her heart reached a frightening crescendo as she collapsed onto her bed. Several minutes later, when her breathing was a little easier, she stretched a frail hand out to her bedside table and picked up the ornate silver-framed photo that was one of her most treasured possessions. It was a picture of Margaret Mowbray cradling the infant Lenore in her arms.

Margaret had always shunned cameras, and Katherine knew that this was probably the only picture of her anywhere in existence. Collectors such as Henry Woodruff would pay handsomely for it, but it would be hers and hers alone for whatever little time she had left. Let the vultures fight over it when she was gone.

She'd already outlived two children and anyone else who might have cared about her or her belongings. Her only surviving child was a son in California, and he'd ignored her for years. Still, because he bore his father's name, she didn't have the heart to cut him out of her will completely. She'd long ago arranged to have her lawyer handle all the final arrangements and distribution of her estate, proceeds to be equally divided between various charities and her miserably self-involved son. The house and land weren't worth much, but the antiques would fetch a tidy sum at auction. In accordance with her wishes, there would be no funeral service, just a gravesite blessing from the parish priest when she was buried beside her beloved husband.

She stared at the picture of Margaret and Lenore until tears completely obliterated her vision, then she clutched it to her heart. No, it hadn't been wrong to keep it. Until today, she hadn't allowed herself to think about Lenore for a very long time. But Lenore, Margaret and Helen were very much in her thoughts now.

Lenore was only eighteen when she disappeared. She simply vanished one night, never to be seen again. There was never any sign of foul play, so the police had labeled it a runaway, just another kid tired of rural life with an elderly relative. But Helen and Katherine had known better. There was a strong bond of affection between Lenore and Helen, just as there had been between Lenore and Margaret, and the girl's devotion to both her aunts had gone far too deep for her to just run away without any explanation. It wasn't until she read the child's diary that Katherine understood what must have happened.

When Helen had handed the diary over to her for safekeeping, she had begged her friend never to read it, but of course Katherine had, much to her endless regret. The horror of it had silenced her all these years, and now, after honoring Helen's last wishes, she could only pray that Diana would allow her to take Lenore's secrets with her to a peaceful grave.

If it weren't for her family name and celebrity, she'd be dead by now.

But her disappearance would have the Feds descending upon us like locusts.

And we can't risk that.

Especially now.

Chapter Ten

Waiting at Diana's condo, alternately pacing the living room and trying to get some research done on her laptop, Beth hurried to the front door the moment she heard the Porsche roar into the driveway, Charlie's Taurus right behind it.

"Hey, you two! How'd it go?" Beth held the door open for them.

"Fine." Diana gave her a quick hug. "No problem." Without even pausing to take off her jacket, she rushed up the steps and shouted over her shoulder, "Tell you all about it later, okay?"

Charlie trudged into the hallway just in time to hear a door slamming on the second floor. "What's with her?" he muttered, closing the front door behind him. Shrugging off his jacket, he hung it on the coat tree.

"I was just about to ask you the same question," said Beth, her eyes flashing fire. He was the one who'd passed along the message that had sent Diana racing off to meet a total stranger under very peculiar circumstances, and the messenger wasn't about to escape unscathed. "Details, Charlie. What happened?"

"Damned if I know," he shrugged. "She was inside the Vredenburgh house for almost two hours. No sign of any problem at all. Suddenly she's racing out the door and hopping into her car. She creeps down the driveway, drives slowly down the street, then goes into warp speed as soon as she gets to the highway."

Clutching a hand to the back of his neck, he slowly shook his head. "I figured something important must have happened and she was in a big hurry to tell you all about it." He glanced toward the top of the steps. "Guess I figured wrong."

Beth had heard enough. "Make yourself comfortable, Charlie." She gestured toward the living room and hurried upstairs. She rapped hard on Diana's door. "Di? May I come in?"

"Can't it wait, Beth? I'm really beat."

After seeing her energetic bolt up the steps just a few minutes ago, the lie was transparent. Still, Beth couldn't bring herself to go barging into her sister's room. Diana had a right to privacy in her own home. She decided to back off for now and try again a little later. "You sure there's nothing wrong?"

"Positive. Just tired, that's all."

"Okay," sighed Beth. "Just give a yell if you need anything." Hoping to silence the alarm bells going off in her head, she went downstairs to talk with Charlie. She found him in the living room, sprawled in his favorite armchair, looking thoroughly exhausted.

"She's okay, Charlie, or so she says." Passing by his chair on her way to the liquor cabinet, she thumped his shoulder with a gentle fist. "Sorry I barked at you, guy. Can I buy you a drink?"

Charlie gave a weary nod. "Scotch would be great. Thanks."

"You got it."

"Neat, please." He'd sampled Diana's single-malt Glenfiddich a few days ago, and he wasn't about to repeat the mistake of diluting it over ice.

"A man after my own heart," she said, pouring two identical drinks. She handed Charlie his glass, then kicked off her shoes and tucked her feet under her as she burrowed into a corner of the sofa directly across from him.

For several moments, the silence in the room was absolute, each of them savoring the excellent scotch and mulling over possible explanations for Diana's odd behavior. Quickly finishing his drink, Charlie was happy to see his prayers answered, when Beth uncurled herself from the sofa and went to retrieve the bottle of Glenfiddich.

Alcohol dependency wasn't one of his problems, but right now he needed the crutch. Long before Beth arrived in Windham, Diana's behavior had started to become increasingly erratic, but what she planned to do tomorrow was flat-out crazy. She'd kept him on the phone half the night detailing her plan, and he still couldn't believe that he'd actually agreed to help her commit a felony. Not just agreed, but insisted on participating in the crime. What the hell was he thinking?

Somehow he had to make Beth realize how rapidly things were spinning out of control, without actually telling her about Diana's plan. He'd insisted on going with her in the morning to keep her safe, but why tell Beth about it and make her an accomplice too?

"Help yourself," Beth said, setting the bottle on the coffee table in front of him. He poured a generous amount of scotch into his glass while she fussed with the stereo remote and flicked on a CD. With no idea what selections Diana had stacked in the unit, half-expecting to hear a bunch of Johnny-one-note monks chanting, she was pleasantly surprised to hear the soft sounds of an early Norah Jones album.

Returning to her place on the sofa, she topped off her own drink, tucked her feet under her once again, and huddled against the cushioned armrest. Willing the Glenfiddich and Norah to soothe her frazzled nerves, she was almost beginning to relax when Charlie broke the comfortable silence that had been stretching languidly between them.

"You need to know something, Beth." His voice was so soft that she had to strain to hear him. "Diana jokes about it sometimes, but she really does have the sight."

"The sight?" She would have laughed, except for the utter solemnity of his expression. "Don't tell me you're buying into this whole woo-woo scene, Charlie. I was counting on you to have better sense."

"Don't kid yourself, Beth. She really is tuned in to something out there. Don't ask me what. I couldn't tell you." He took a deep breath and blew it out hard. "Thing is… Sometimes she sees things that really end up happening, and she can do things that…" He took a quick gulp of his drink. "Jeez, Beth, she has powers unlike anything I've ever seen."

"Powers?" Beth felt her heart skip a beat. Adrenaline shot her feet to the floor and had her sitting bolt upright, every instinct on high alert. "What the hell are you talking about, Charlie?"

He leaned forward in his chair, resting his forearms on his knees, drink cradled in his hands. He could see the fear in Beth's eyes, and he hated having to add to her worries, but she needed to know.

"I looked it up," he said. "What your sister does is something called 'telekinesis,' concentrating on something so hard that…"

"I know what it is, Charlie. But what does it have to do with my sister?" A memory stirred, but Beth dismissed it. Diana had abandoned her little flying trick a very long time ago.

"It has everything to do with her," he said. "She says it's no big deal, but she's so damn good at it that I have to believe it's absolutely one very big deal. She didn't want you to know. Said it would only freak you out. But I think maybe this is really something worth freaking out about."

"Don't tell me you've actually seen her…?"

"Hell, yes! Just last week, she dumped a whole glass of champagne over my head without ever even touching the damn thing."

"Oh come on, Charlie," scoffed Beth. "Just how much did you two have to drink?" Diana's childhood paper clips were light years away from what he was describing.

"We had a few," he admitted. "But not that much. And I know what I saw. And felt." Uncomfortable under the microscope of those penetrating green eyes, he lowered his gaze and took another quick gulp of scotch. Taking a deep breath, he looked across at Beth and challenged the censure he saw in her gaze.

"The two of us were sitting right there on the sofa where you are, Beth. We were talking. Diana was drinking champagne and I had my trusty scotch. She got a little tipsy and started telling me about this special 'talent' of hers, about how she can move objects around at will without ever touching them. Naturally, I thought it was a joke, so I teased her about it and laughed.

"Next thing I know, her eyes get like lasers, she puts her drink down on the table and stares at it for just a few seconds before the damn thing starts floating up from the table." Using gestures that emphasized *that* couch and *that* table, he pointed toward the ceiling and pantomimed everything that followed. "Her glass goes way above my head, tips, spills champagne all over me, then straightens up and floats back down to the table without so much as a clink when it lands. She sure made a believer out of me, I can tell you."

Beth was dumbfounded. Charlie would never make up such a crazy story, but how could it be true? And, if it were true, then what else was going on in her little sister's life that she didn't know about? She pressed him for every detail about that night, barely holding her panic at bay until he finished his drink and left to go home.

The moment he was out the door and the security system engaged, she hurried upstairs to confront Diana. Hammering at her sister's bedroom door, she went inside without waiting for an invitation. Privacy be damned.

Diana hoped she'd managed to slide Lenore's diary under the pillow before her sister saw it. She swung her legs to the floor and sat up, patting the mattress beside her. "Come sit. You look like you're ready to go off like a rocket. What's up?"

"You tell me, Di. No evasions. No half-truths. No lies." Anger wouldn't allow her to sit cozily beside her sister. Hands on hips, she stood towering over her. "Charlie tells me that your little flying trick has grown up with a vengeance. Was he putting me on, or...?"

Diana turned away, but not before Beth had read the answer in her eyes. "Dear God," she sighed. Taking a deep breath, she struggled to rein in her temper, knowing that ranting and raving at Diana would be worse than useless. It always was. "Why didn't you tell me?" Her hands fell from her hips and hung helplessly at her sides.

Diana shrugged. "There just never seemed to be a good time to bring it up, Beth. It's not exactly something you can casually work into a conversation, you know."

"You had no trouble cluing Charlie in."

"Only because I was drunk! And he promised to keep it a secret until I was able to tell you myself. Some friend he is."

"Probably a better friend than you deserve, so don't you dare give him a hard time about this" Not sure that her legs would be able to support her much longer, Beth sat on the bed beside Diana. She even managed to give her little sister an encouraging hug. "Go on. Let's hear it."

Diana nodded miserably. Eyes downcast, without preamble, she told Beth the truth that she'd withheld from everyone but Lily Verne for so long. By the time she finished detailing the psychic work she'd been doing with Lily for the past six years, Beth's elbows were resting on her thighs and she was cradling her head in her hands.

"At first, it was all pretty routine stuff," Diana continued. "Not much to crow about. Nothing at all like what I've been able to accomplish since I found Margaret's grave."

Beth lifted her head, holding back the threatening tears, praying for the wisdom to... To what? Where did she go from here? Fear and anger were all mixed up inside her, and she couldn't sort out any of it.

Diana's suddenly animated voice continued, her blue eyes sparkling now. "The moment I saw that headstone, it was like a psychic floodgate opening inside me, Beth. Instead of nightmares, I have visions now. Honest-to-God visions!"

Remembering the neurologist's predictions about how the end might come, Beth was suddenly having difficulty breathing, but she forced herself to maintain a calm and even tone that gave no clue to the panic welling inside. "Visions? What kind of visions?"

Diana shrugged. "Hard to describe. Past, present, future, you name it, all of it coming together. Sometimes a single isolated impression, sometimes a sequence like frames of a movie, sometimes a random collage of images, thoughts, sensations, that kind of thing. I start meditating, and there they are -- it's incredible."

"Do you... Do you hear sounds along with these visions?" Beth gave a helpless little shrug. "Voices?"

"Sometimes. Not usually 'though. It's kind of like cosmic e-mail, Beth. You click it on with meditation, and suddenly the images and messages are just there, sometimes with audio, most times not." Diana didn't need her psychic gifts to know what was going through Beth's mind. It was all right there in her eyes.

She tried for a reassuring smile, then hugged Beth close. "I'm not losing it, Sis. Truly I'm not. It's just that my meditations have suddenly become really intense."

Beth was too numb to argue and too worried to be comforted. She pulled away from Diana. "And what exactly does 'really intense' mean, Di?"

"You want an example?"

Beth nodded. "For starters, yeah. Please."

Diana shrugged. "Okay..." She took a deep breath and studied every nuance of her sister's expression as she began trying to explain. "Just a few hours ago, Devane popped into my head and I just about freaked out. Warning bells went off all over the place."

"Naked lust in a man's eyes can do that to a woman, Di. Devane couldn't take his eyes off you. Maybe that's what you picked up on."

"Maybe, but I don't think so. The vibes were really heavy and dark. I came out of trance feeling as if I needed a shower."

"But when we were at his studio..."

"I know. I know. That's what's so bizarre." Diana jabbed a well-manicured finger toward her sister. "Your reporter's instinct picked up on something being a little off, and I didn't get a single negative vibe." Diana slumped like a rag doll. "But now, only dark stuff is coming through on him and it's got me crazy. That's why Charlie and I are going to..." A sheepish little grin escaped. "Oops."

Beth shook her head wearily. "Let me guess. You're going to check out the tower again." She wasn't psychic. She just knew her little sister very well. When Diana glanced away, Beth had her confirmation. "May I ask why?"

Diana sighed. "I have to, Beth. I have to get a clearer reading on Devane before it drives me completely bonkers."

"And just how do you expect to accomplish all this? Another buying spree?"

Diana shook her head. "I had something a little more clandestine in mind."

"Such as?"

Diana took a deep breath, straightened her spine, and hurried on with her explanation. "Well, Charlie did some checking and found out that Devane jogs at the same time every morning. As soon as he takes off, we're going inside the tower. We'll be in and out long before he's done with his run."

"Are you...?" Words like 'crazy' and 'out of your mind' danced on the tip of Beth's tongue, and she practically choked swallowing them. "You could end up in jail! Or didn't Charlie bother mentioning that to you?"

"Of course he did, but I'll tell you exactly what I told him: I'm going, even if I have to go alone. Period. End of discussion."

"So that's it, huh?" Beth snapped her fingers. "Just like that."

"That's it." Smiling now, Diana snapped her own fingers. "Just like that." She jabbed a playful elbow into her sister's side. "Come on, Beth, don't be such a spoilsport! Where's your spirit of adventure?"

"Alive and well, Di." She stood, squared her shoulders and looked down at her sister. "So much so that I'll be going along with you tomorrow."

Inevitably, they argued, but Beth wouldn't yield. Charlie worked for Diana and had to follow her orders. If Diana did something really dangerous while she was playing supersleuth, he wouldn't be able to stop her. But Beth could. And would.

As soon as she returned to her room, Beth automatically reached for the landline to phone Paul, but had serious second thoughts and never even touched the handset. If everything went South tomorrow morning, why risk making him an accessory before the fact by bringing him on board now?

If she thought that he could somehow stop Diana from going ahead with her harebrained scheme, she would have no reservations about telling him tonight. But nobody was going to stop her sister, and she knew it just as surely as Charlie must have known it when he insisted on going with her, obviously to help keep her safe. Well, she'd be there too, and for the same reason. Between the two of them and Diana's usual protection detail, they should be able to keep her out of harm's way. Time enough to tell Paul all about it after the deed was done.

There was another call she didn't dare make tonight. As much as she longed to hear Chad's voice, she'd have to content herself with the knowledge that he'd at least tried to reach her a few times that day. Phone tag and voicemail would have to hold her until she could talk honestly to him about what was going on with Diana. She wouldn't lie to him, and he would be worried sick, not to mention livid, if he knew what they were planning. Better to stay incommunicado for a while longer.

The next morning, the trio of unlikely felons sat huddled behind an outcropping of rock in the woods across the road from John Devane's tower studio waiting for him to head out for his morning run. Beth and Charlie were flanking Diana.

When Devane appeared from somewhere at the back of the building and began jogging away along the Old Chaetestown Road, Diana was ready to make a run for the tower the moment he was out of sight. It was only Charlie's strong staying hand that kept her from bolting. "Sit tight, Diana. Town's the other way," he whispered in her ear, not daring to release his rigid grip on her arm.

From inquiries made yesterday, Charlie knew that Devane was a familiar figure jogging through Chaetestown at the same time every morning, but he was going in the opposite direction now. Why? There was nothing up that way except the old quarry near where Charlie had parked his Taurus an hour earlier. Had Devane heard the car? Not likely, but anything was possible. .

Charlie wished he'd done a better job of concealing the car, but who knew he'd be heading that way? Damn! The car was on the shoulder of the road about a hundred yards past the quarry and only partially screened by trees and shrubbery. If Devane decided to jog completely around the quarry, he couldn't miss it. Charlie could only hope that he was just stretching his distance with a loop up as far as the leading edge of the quarry and back before he headed for town. Maybe that was even part of his normal routine. He could only hope that it was.

With Devane now well out of hearing range, Charlie was able to raise his voice enough so that both women could hear him. Beth almost laughed when she saw that she and Charlie each had a lock on one of Diana's arms. "Patience, ladies. It shouldn't be long now."

For the next five minutes, Diana fussed and fumed about the time being wasted in the name of caution, but when she saw Devane coming in their direction again, she was instantly and totally silent and unmoving, the ultimate compliment to Charlie's good sense. Devane jogged past the tower without stopping, then continued on toward Chaetestown. Charlie watched him disappear beyond a bend in the road, then waited another two minutes before scrambling to his feet.

"You two stay here until I give you the all clear," he said, amazed at how calm he sounded. This whole escapade was insane, and he knew it, had known it the moment Diana told him what she intended to do. Problem was she had already decided to go, with or without him, and he couldn't let her go alone. There hadn't been time to discuss it, but he was sure Beth had signed on to the crazy scheme for all the same reasons.

Charlie was dressed, as the women were, in dark warm-up suits and sneakers. He had cautioned them to adopt the even stride of an exercise walker when they crossed the road so that, if they were seen, no one would think to question their presence. The Old Chaetestown Road was a favorite spot for joggers and walkers, and none of them would be suspicious of their own breed. Even the gloves they wore looked innocent enough, since it was just after eight in the morning and only slightly above freezing, chilly enough to warrant them.

Heeding his own advice, Charlie strode out from the copse of trees, arms swinging energetically at his sides as he crossed the road and vanished into the woods to the left of the tannery. Beth and Diana didn't see him again until a few minutes later when he peered out from the rear of the tower and waved the okay for them to follow. Mimicking his gait as they crossed the road, they traced his path to the back door. He was waiting for them, one hand resting on the knob of the open door, his burglar's tools already stowed in his pocket.

Beth could only imagine the frenzied thoughts now racing through the minds of the field agents assigned to them that day. She had recognized one of them in a nondescript silver Toyota parked down the street from Diana's house, and she had glanced out the rear window from time to time en route to the tower just to make sure they were still around. She knew they always were, but today she needed the extra reassurance of actually seeing them. By now, with a visible felony in progress, she guessed that one of them would be peering incredulously through binoculars, while the other was frantically dialing their supervisor.

"I disengaged the alarm," said Charlie. "You should have at least half an hour before he gets back." He waved Diana and Beth inside. "But give it ten minutes, no more."

Beth was eager to have it all over and done with, and she took a quick step forward, colliding with Diana who had suddenly stopped dead ahead of her. She was still as a statue.

"Jeez," groaned Charlie, "what a time for a trance! Snap out of it, Diana!"

Beth edged her way around her sister. Seeing Diana from Charlie's vantage point, she began to panic. Diana's eyes were glazed.

"Diana," whispered Beth. "Diana, look at me!" She shook her sister's shoulders. "Talk to me, damn it!" The urgency in Beth's voice finally broke through to her sister. Eyes wide with fright, she looked up at Beth.

"I can't. I can't do it. I can't go in there, Beth." Tears were streaming down her face, but her eyes were in clear focus, and she was speaking normally. Beth knew that this was no trance. It was garden-variety stage fright, pure and simple, and Beth was grateful for it. She would do the job herself and they would be out of there in no time at all. The crime had already been committed. They had broken into the man's home. They might as well go the whole nine yards.

"Give me the camera, Di." She extended her hand for the high-resolution Nikon digital her sister had slung over her shoulder. She knew that if they didn't check out the tower now, Diana would only insist on going back for another try, and Beth never wanted to see this place again.

"No!" Diana backed away, holding the camera just beyond Beth's reach. "You can't go in there, Beth!"

The fear in Diana's eyes was very real, but Beth refused to let it alter her decision. "Give me the camera, Di." She extended her hand, palm up. "We're just wasting precious time, you know. I'm going to do this right now, whether you like it or not. And if you don't give me the camera, I'll just use my cell. Either way, I'm not leaving here until the job is done."

With agonizing slowness, Diana unhitched the Nikon from her shoulder and handed it over. It was one of several that she owned, and Beth had never used it before. "Any tricks to this thing?" When Diana didn't respond, Beth quickly checked the camera. Satisfied that she wasn't likely to have any problem operating it, she edged past her sister. "Stay with her, Charlie," said Beth. "Get her out of here and wait for me back at the car. I won't be long."

With Charlie arguing that she shouldn't be going in alone and Diana pleading with her not to go in at all, Beth ducked inside. She wasn't sure what she was looking for, but she had an idea where it was most likely to be found. She wasted no time clambering up the spiral stairs to the second level bedroom area behind the ornate lacquered privacy screen, the only part of the tower that Devane hadn't allowed them to see.

She began taking rapid-fire photos immediately, not because there was anything suspicious about the room, but precisely because nothing out of the ordinary was apparent. Her heart was hammering in her ears, and she couldn't tell whether her perceptions were being heightened or incapacitated by her fright. She only knew that she wanted to be out of there as quickly as possible. Later, after the film had been downloaded, they could scrutinize it. For now, it was enough to let the camera record what her eyes might fail to register.

The king-size bed was not only unmade but thoroughly rumpled. John Devane was either a very restless sleeper or he had entertained a lively companion last night. Beth looked for signs of female occupancy, but there were none. Maybe he preferred male partners, but that wasn't her concern now. There was a book open on the bedside table, one of the new bestsellers, sex and spies, just the kind of thing half the literate population of America read all the time, certainly nothing sinister.

Running upstairs to the studio, she found that everything was just as innocuous as she remembered. She took a few photos of some newer canvasses she hadn't seen during her prior visit, then went back to the second floor one last time, hoping that she might see something she had missed a few minutes earlier. She checked his closet, even photographed its contents, determined to show Diana how thorough she had been so that she wouldn't be tempted to repeat this lunacy.

The medicine cabinet was interesting. Its shelves were crammed with drugs, both prescription and over-the-counter, everything from antacids to Prozac, all of it arranged with a compulsive neatness that surprised her, every label facing forward for quick identification. Beth took a few quick shots, closed the mirrored door, then bolted for the stairs. She almost cried with relief when she saw Charlie standing guard in the living room.

"Diana's safe," he said, anticipating her question. "Wouldn't go back to the car, but she's waiting for us where we were hiding earlier. You done?"

"All but this floor," said Beth, already panning the room and clicking away.

"I already checked this level out," said Charlie. "Take a look at this." He quickly moved toward the fireplace and threw back the hearth rug, revealing a trap door neatly set into the floorboards.

"It's locked," he said, "or at least I think it is. Couldn't get it to budge. Give me a hand with it, will you, Beth?" She knelt beside him and they both tugged mightily at the metal ring on the door, but still it wouldn't yield.

"Forget it," he said, helping Beth to her feet. Under the cool, calm façade, he could feel that her hands were trembling. He reached for the camera, and she gladly handed it over to him. Adjusting the lens, he stood in the center of the room, and pivoted his shots until every section of the circular wall had been covered, using the last frame on a close-up of the trap door. "Let's get the hell out of here, Beth."

Replacing the hearth rug, he scanned the room for any telltale signs of their presence, then used a special electronic tool to reset the alarm keypad near the front door. Tucking a strong hand under Beth's elbow, he hurried her outside, locking the door behind them, not daring to wave an all-clear signal to Diana. It would be just like her to come charging across the road, and he wanted her to stay safe, right where she was.

Ducking behind a thicket of pine trees behind the tower, they circled around to a spot where Charlie felt it was safe to cross the road at a power-walker's gait. Once safely across and into the woods opposite the tower, they made their way towards Diana, Charlie's heart giving a little lurch the moment he saw her. She was about two hundred feet away, crouched behind the rock formation where he had left her, her face an agony of worry for her sister and, he hoped, maybe even for him. She had clearly not seen them leaving the old tannery building.

He was about to give a low whistle to alert her to their presence when Beth's gloved fingers dug into his forearm. Instinctively, he froze, his eyes no longer focused on Diana, his antennae zeroing in on the danger Beth had seen, a running figure in red and black warmups just coming into view over the crest of the hill from Chaetestown. Charlie hissed a string of locker room curses. Devane was on his way back already, and Diana still didn't know that her sister was well out of harm's way.

When Charlie saw Diana's lips begin to move, his heart sank. Last night, as they were strategizing for today's contingencies, using a whippoorwill call as an emergency warning signal had seemed logical enough. They could both whistle, and it was the one birdsong they each knew. Now, with the woods ominously silent and Devane so close, he could only pray that Diana would keep silent. Not being much of a praying man, he was ready for the whippoorwill call when it rang out loud and clear, its trilling cadence borne on the wind.

Gun in hand, safety now disengaged, Charlie crouched motionless in the underbrush, watching as Devane slowed his stride and scanned the line of trees from which the sound had come. Charlie instinctively looked toward Beth, to make sure she was well-hidden, but she wasn't where she had been just a moment before. Where the hell did she go?

Devane was walking slowly now, sauntering along the road, the watchful tilt of his head belying the nonchalant pace. Charlie hoped he would finish the way he had begun, with a loop to the quarry and back. That would give him enough time to reach Diana without alerting Devane, but they weren't to be so fortunate. Devane turned directly toward the tower.

If only a car would come by, preferably a noisy diesel, something, anything to camouflage their presence, but Charlie knew there would be no such miracle along the deserted old road. He continued edging his way toward the place where he had left Diana, praying that she would stay hidden where she was, precisely as she had been told to do, all the while knowing how unlikely it was that she would ever obey his instructions. She was his boss, not the other way around, and she would do as she damn well pleased.

As Devane took his time about going into the tannery tower, Charlie found himself praying again, hoping that God might think He owed him one. Please, don't let her do anything stupid! Please, Diana, please, for once in your life listen to orders and stay put. His eyes never left Devane, and it seemed an eternity before the man finally went inside and slammed the tower door behind him.

Charlie glanced quickly around him, hoping to see some sign of Beth, but still there was none. Ducking and weaving through evergreens and underbrush, he hurried toward the rock outcropping where he had left Diana. He felt the weight of the world lift from his shoulders when he saw that Beth was already there with her.

"Charlie!" whispered Diana. "Thank God you're okay! I was so worried!" Seeing the happiness in her eyes as she reached out for his hand, he knew he was a lucky man. As he crouched down beside her, he almost laughed when he saw why she had been so docile since that first piercing birdcall. Beth had her sister's arm clutched to her side in an iron grip. He had no idea how she had managed to get there so quickly and quietly, but he was too relieved to feel embarrassed about not getting there first.

"Come on," he said. "Let's get out of here. Follow me, you two, and stay low."

Deeply shaken by their narrow escape, they did precisely as he told them every step of the way, following his lead through the maze of pines until they passed the quarry and reached the safety of the Taurus.

As they made their way in complete silence along the Old Chaetestown Road heading to the main highway, Charlie popped antacids and Beth quietly rubbed her temples to ward off the first stirrings of a migraine. It was Diana who broke the tension with a resounding whippoorwill call. With the shrill sound still ringing in their ears, she said, "I don't know about you guys, but I'm famished."

They all laughed. Once begun, the laughter spilled over into near-hysteria as they tried to decompress. Charlie didn't think anybody could eat a thing, but there was comfort in familiar routine, so he drove directly to Eliza's Country Kitchen without bothering to put it to a vote.

As soon as they were seated at their favorite window table, Diana ordered regular coffee. Charlie didn't even hesitate to countermand the order. He told the waitress to bring them all decafs. When she had gone, Diana growled her objections, but he wasn't impressed. "Look," he said, "we're all so close to the edge right now that caffeine's the last thing we need. Whether you realize it or not, we almost..."

"Of course I realize it," snarled Diana. "I tried to warn you, didn't I? But would you listen? Hell no."

"Now you're being ridiculous," argued Beth. "Going there was all your idea in the first place, remember?"

"It was also my idea to cut our losses and run before you ever set foot into that horrible place. Why couldn't you listen to me for once?"

The waitress arrived with their decafs and they all quickly scanned their menus, Rejecting breakfast, they each ordered banana cream pie instead. "Look," said Beth, once the waitress was out of earshot, "Not going in there today would only have been postponing the inevitable, and you know it. You'd go home, think about how close we'd come, and want to try the same dumb stunt tomorrow. I just wanted to have it over and done with!"

"Well the two of you almost made a real mess of things. I can't believe how close you cut it."

"That was my fault," said Charlie with more gallantry than truth. He told Diana about finding the trap door.

"So where do you suppose it leads?" Diana asked, her eyes alight with excitement. Before he could respond, the waitress served their pie. Each piece was about five inches high, rich with a sweet banana aroma, domed with whipped cream, and too tempting for any of them to resist. They attacked the pie. So much for his convoluted theory about the inhibiting effects of panic on appetite, thought Charlie. He wondered if he got the decaf thing right. The way doctors kept changing their minds, you just never knew any more.

Talking around his third bite of pie, Charlie gave Diana his best guess about the trap door. "Probably just an old root cellar that was boarded up a long time ago. Really no way of telling."

"Unless... How about we check it out tomorrow morning?" Diana laughed as Beth and Charlie both made little choking sounds. "Gotcha!" she grinned. Lingering over coffee, they began dissecting their morning adventure with an eye to humor, and they found it everywhere, always at their own expense.

"You know," Charlie said, his tone very much that of the old philosopher, "for a pair of rookies, you two weren't half bad out there."

"Thanks, chief," said Diana, giving him a smart little salute. "You weren't half bad yourself."

"I was just using skills I learned twenty years ago on the job. But you guys..." He shook his head. "What can I say? Well done!"

Diana started laughing. "What's so funny?" grumbled Charlie, running a napkin across his mouth just in case all that whipped cream had left him looking like a milk commercial.

"I'm sorry," said Diana, choking down a giggling fit. "It's just so funny hearing you praise my cool head under fire when I was actually behaving like a complete lunatic. I was all set to give another damn birdcall when Beth came out of nowhere and clamped her hand over my mouth."

Charlie's mouth dropped open. Snapping it shut, he rolled his eyes. "You've got to be kidding. How could you even think about doing it again?"

Diana gave a sheepish little grin. "I told you. I panicked."

Charlie pursed his lips and blew out a heavy sigh. Shaking his head, he looked gratefully over to Beth. "Thanks for saving the day, Beth. But I still can't figure our how you managed to get to her so fast. One minute you were…"

"Jeez, Charlie," smiled Diana. "Look at her. "She's slim, agile, and she moves like a gazelle. Beth's a runner. Very few people can beat her out in a sprint."

Seeing Charlie suck in his gut as he pushed away what was left of his pie, Beth's heart went out to his wounded pride and she was glad when Diana changed the subject.

"I don't know about you two, but I need a nap." She checked her watch. "How about you come by my place at four, Charlie, so we can all check out the pictures together. I know you both said there's nothing worth seeing, but we might as well run through them anyway."

"Sounds good to me," said Charlie. "I could use the time to catch up on some paperwork."

"Okay then. Let's do it!" said Diana, already on her feet and walking toward the cash register with the bill.

Charlie made no attempt to argue with her about who was going to pay the check, but he left a five-dollar tip on the table to soothe his pride, then sauntered outside to start the car. By the time Beth and Diana walked out of the restaurant, he had driven directly up to the door to wait for them. He wasn't really sure if guys were still supposed to do that kind of thing, but he figured it couldn't hurt.

Diana really was exhausted, but there was one very important stop she had to make that afternoon. They were tooling along Route 23, almost home, when she mentioned it. "After I catch a few zzz's, Beth, how about we go see Henry Woodruff?"

"Fine with me."

"Did I tell you I asked the gourmet shop to make up a basket of goodies for him?" asked Diana.

"No, but I'm glad you did," Beth was relieved to hear her sister speak about the man without getting upset.

"Kind of a peace offering," said Diana. "If it gets us through the door, maybe we can pick his brains about what Molly saw at the tower that night. It's worth a shot. I also want to ask him to check his database for info about that tunnel."

"What tunnel?" screeched Beth. "Didn't you hear Charlie? It's probably just an old root cellar."

"Maybe. But my gut instinct tells me otherwise." She wasn't about to tell her sister that it was more than just instinct. Lenore had written extensively about the tunnel.

Charlie wasn't in the mood to hear them argue. He cleared his throat, very loudly. "Why don't you let me look into it? I'll check with my buddy at the county courthouse and see what I can find out."

"Thanks, Charlie!" As Diana leaned over to kiss his cheek, the car immediately drifted off course. Beth lurched in her seat as he over-corrected before getting back to the center of his lane. She wondered if Diana even suspected how he felt about her.

"Just don't get your hopes up too much," he said in a very assertive tone that was clearly intended to cover up how flustered he'd been a few seconds earlier. "Even if it is what you think it is, who in their right mind would apply for a permit to build a secret passage?"

"Good point," acknowledged Diana. "But it's still worth a shot. Maybe we'll get lucky."

She's getting closer every day.

It's as if she has a death wish.

If only I could oblige.

Patience has never been my strong suit.

Chapter Eleven

Beth and Diana had steeled themselves for the worst, half-expecting the front door to be slammed in their faces the moment Henry Woodruff saw them standing there, but the dignified old gentleman surprised them. Clearly, he wasn't overjoyed by their unannounced visit, but his tentative expression wasn't overtly hostile, which Beth figured was the best they could hope for under the circumstances. She just hoped that he would accept Diana's gift as the peace offering it was meant to be.

The enormous wicker basket that they'd just picked up at a gourmet shop in Windham was wrapped in red cellophane, tied with a jaunty plaid ribbon, and piled high with enough cheer to keep his old bones warm for months. They'd set the basket down on a rickety porch table beside the door, but Diana continued to grasp the handle for fear that the weather-beaten old table would collapse under its weight. Henry's expression was equal parts shock and pleasure when he saw it. Saying nothing, he listened to Diana's softly spoken little speech. "Just a small token of our appreciation for all your help, Mr. Woodruff."

His injured pride dictated no more than a stern expression and a quick nod, but he was having a hard time suppressing a self-satisfied grin as he watched the two young women pick up the basket and struggle to support its weight between them. He was enjoying the show too much to lend a helping hand, but he was deeply moved by their obvious desire to make amends. Opening the door a little wider, he gestured with a sweeping hand for them to come inside.

Shifting the basket for better balance between them, walking sideways with the basket bumping into them at every step, they followed their host into the house, through the hallway, and into the dining room beyond it. Here, as in every other room they'd seen thus far, books and folders adorned every flat surface, from the oversized and ornately carved antique mahogany table to the matching sideboard.

"Just put it right here," said Woodruff, clearing a space on the cluttered table.

Muscles screaming, Beth and Diana struggled to lift the basket to table height. They almost dropped it, but a quick supporting hand from Woodruff saved the day. He'd enjoyed teaching them a lesson, but he wasn't about to stand idly by and watch all those goodies hit the floor. Beth had to suppress a smile. Bravo, Henry, she thought. Well-played.

"Please, sit down, ladies." Easier said than done, thought Beth. Following Woodruff's lead, she and Diana began helping him clear off the rest of the table and three of the chairs, transferring all the clutter to the sideboard and, as a last resort, onto the floor.

When the grunt work was done, Diana hurried outside to retrieve Henry's property from the Porsche. Returning to the dining room minutes later, she felt a sickening sense of déjà vu: Woodruff was nowhere to be seen. Her heart sank. Leaving the books and diaries near the basket on the table, she took a seat next to Beth, neither of them daring so much as a whisper.

Beth shrugged and grimaced a silent I-have-no-idea-where-he-went look, to which Diana replied with a mute oh-no-not-again shake of her head and roll of her eyes. Some minutes later, when he finally returned to the silent room, he found that he had to pinch his lips into a thin rigid line in order not to laugh out loud. How empowering to know that he hadn't lost the knack of intimidating young upstarts!

He was carrying a battered wooden tray laden with a thoroughly mismatched coffee service that he unceremoniously set down on the table. Beth guessed that the three earthenware mugs had probably been supermarket giveaways back in the fifties, along with the star-patterned glass sugar bowl that screamed five-and-dime. She was glad to see that the quart container of milk at least appeared to be of recent vintage, and she tried not to wince at the old percolator that reeked of leftover morning brew.

Tucked around the chipped crockery were a few elegant oddities: delicately lace-edged linen napkins yellowed with age, and teaspoons of finely wrought sterling engraved with a baroque 'W'. She wondered again about Woodruff's past and the privileged upbringing that had left him with such obvious disdain for the trappings of wealth.

He was firmly ensconced in his own eccentricities now, but she knew that there must have been years of conformance before he completely rejected his family's lifestyle. She remembered the diploma on his bedroom wall, magna cum laude from Harvard, so he had at least played the establishment game until he graduated from college. What had happened after that? Why had he traded the fast-track for a mountain hermitage?

Beth was touched by the way he was pouring coffee for them now, slowly and with tedious care, not chancing the waste of a single drop, an intrinsic frugality that she had often observed in older people who had lived through the privations of war rationing and depression. Studying his aristocratic features and clear gray eyes, she knew that he had to have been a prime catch in his day. Even now, despite his advanced age and crusty exterior, there was a certain charisma about the man and it had her writer's curiosity kicking into overdrive. Had he fallen in love with someone his family felt was unsuitable for him? Had the love of his life deserted him, maybe even died? Whatever had happened, Beth was sure a woman was involved. Unless...

No, she didn't think he was gay. The little twinkle in his eyes whenever he looked at Diana screamed hetero orientation. She guessed that he probably had an ongoing relationship with some sweet little old lady tucked away on the mountain somewhere. She found herself hoping that he did.

Her scrutiny of the man continued unobserved while he peeled the crisp cellophane back from the wicker basket, the delight in his eyes that of a child in a candy store. Clasping a hand to his chin, he surveyed his options, cheerfully undecided about what to sample first. He finally selected the box of imported petits fours.

Diana and Beth fibbed a little about not being hungry, correctly supposing that he had already developed a very proprietary attitude toward the contents of the basket. As he munched happily on one of the sweet little pastries, Diana wasted no time steering their conversation in the direction of the topic she most wanted to discuss.

"Molly Beecham's diary made for some pretty exciting reading, Mr. Woodruff. Kind of scary too. That part about the tower really gave me goosebumps." Woodruff nodded absently, quietly popping another petit four into his mouth. Undeterred, Diana persisted. "Do you think she really saw a satanic coven gathering in the woods that night?" Beth had expected her sister to be a bit more subtle in her approach, and she almost choked on her bitter coffee when she heard the question.

Swallowing the last bite of the latest petit four to strike his fancy, Henry made a loud harrumphing sound and commented, "A lady who never minces words." He gave a courtly nod of his head to Diana and she immediately broke eye contact with him, lowering her head in a vain attempt to hide the color flaming in her cheeks.

"The blush of modesty becomes you, Miss Wendell," he said.

They were all well aware that Diana's red face had nothing to do with modesty and everything to do with humiliation, but no one was inclined to argue the point. Nodding thoughtfully, Woodruff smiled. He knew he'd never forget how the lash of her tongue had wounded him the day before, but he was satisfied that they were even now. Watching him carefully, Beth felt her shoulders begin to relax for the first time since they'd arrived. There was no mistaking the quiet truce she saw in his eyes.

"To answer your question..." said Henry, "I believe Molly actually did witness a suspicious gathering of some kind that night in the woods. As to a satanic coven...?" Lips pursed, he tilted his head gently from side to side, carefully weighing the hypothesis. "It's possible of course, particularly given the date, but..."

"The date?" asked Beth.

He extracted the diary from its folder and carefully thumbed through it until he found the entry describing that fatal night on the mountain. "Here," he said, pointing to the date.

Diana was already on her feet, leaning over his shoulder to scrutinize the page. "February 5, 1945," she said, reading the date aloud and casting a questioning glance at her sister. Beth shrugged her response. It meant nothing to her either.

"February 5th just happened to be the date Molly wrote about the accident," said Woodruff, "but the tragedy itself occurred three days earlier, on the night of February 2nd.

"Of course!" exclaimed Diana. "Candlemas! That's why the coven was gathering."

"If, in fact, it was a coven gathering, Miss Wendell," he cautioned.

"Isn't Candlemas a Christian feast?" asked Beth, every instinct telling her to ground this conversation before it completely ventured off into lalaland.

"Was and is," answered Diana, nodding impatiently. "But the pagans celebrated it as a purification feast long before Christianity ever came on the scene, Beth. Witches refer to it as 'Imbolc,' and there's not a self-respecting coven anywhere that doesn't meet on that night."

Woodruff smiled and nodded approvingly, his expression that of an aged mentor listening to the surprisingly intelligent utterances of a pupil whom he had previously considered to be a complete dolt.

"Like both of you, like most people I suspect," he said, "I'm intrigued by the old legends about devil-worship in the Catskills. Witchcraft was certainly not confined to our Salem friends across the line in the Bay State, so it's certainly possible that Molly really did see a coven gathering."

Diana had a problem with the way Woodruff was using 'devil-worship' and 'witchcraft' interchangeably. Needing to clarify the issue, but not wanting to challenge him directly, she addressed her remarks to Beth.

"I know you don't believe in any of this, Beth, so it's got to be confusing for you."

"No, I..." Diana's semantic ploy was so transparent that Beth was almost embarrassed for her.

"But you see it's the 'black' witches who are the devil-worshippers. 'White' witches are the good guys, so to speak. Obviously none of this has anything to do with skin pigmentation, since both varieties come in every size, shape and color, but the white witches spend most of their time and energy undoing a lot of the mischief instigated by the black ones."

"I see," said Beth, playing along, pretending to be grateful for an explanation that she hadn't needed at all.

"Nor is the term 'witch' restricted to females," offered Woodruff, his ego clearly smarting. "Only a man can be classified as a 'wizard' or a 'warlock,' but witches can be male or female. Isn't that correct, Miss Wendell?"

Beth didn't attempt to be a player in the paranormal version of 'Can You Top This?' that ensued. She was way out of her depth with some of the technical terminology that was routinely being batted about by her two companions, and she didn't hesitate to excuse herself when she felt her cell vibrating in her hip pocket. With a quick apology, she hurried outside to take the call.

Unfortunately, it wasn't Chad, but at least the political robocall had given her a break from the claustrophobic confines of Henry's home, and she took her time about going back inside. The air was crisp and cold enough to be envigorating but, since she hadn't had time to put her jacket on before leaving the dining room, she was freezing. After only a few minutes, she went back inside.

Diana and Henry were still engaged in a lively exchange of information about the occult, clarifying definitions and fine-tuning reference points until each had a fairly precise assessment of the extent of the other's knowledge. If there was any wariness or resentment left over from yesterday's hurtful encounter, Beth could see no sign of it.

Interesting as their discussion was at first, after fifteen minutes of it, Beth found that she was having trouble stifling yawns. She decided it was time to refocus their concentration on the original purpose of their visit. "Look you two, as long as you're theorizing, let's get back to Molly for a minute. Just presume, for the sake of argument, that she really did see a coven gathering on Candlemas night. Black robes would mean a black coven, yes?" Knowing Diana's bias, she directed her question directly to Henry.

"Not necessarily, Beth," he said. By this time, they were all on a comfortable first-name basis. "Remember now, those were very lean years in Chaetestown, just as they were everywhere else in the country. People tended to make do with what they had, and dark robes were eminently practical. Everybody wore them on cold winter nights."

"With pointy hoods?" asked Diana, her tone drippng sarcasm.

Henry chuckled. "It's patently clear that it was a cult gathering of some sort, Diana. I don't dispute that for a minute. I'm only saying that even perfectly good little witches might have worn dark clothing with handmade hoods to match simply because they didn't have the wherewithal to deck themselves out in flowing white regalia."

"Then you're saying that the coven Molly saw, if in fact it really was a coven, could just as easily have been white as black?" said Beth.

Henry nodded thoughtfully, but said nothing.

"And if you had to hazard an educated guess, Henry, which would it be?" asked Diana.

"Well now..." With another loud harrumph, Henry folded his arms and studied the ceiling for a few moments. Lowering his gaze to eye-level, he looked first at Beth, then Diana. "Of course," he said, "you understand that there's no way of being absolutely certain." He took a deep breath and exhaled slowly, the labored sound of it audible in the hushed room. "However, if I had to venture an opinion, I would say black."

"Bingo!" said Diana, nodding her total agreement and clapping her hands. "You're outvoted, Beth. The blacks have it!"

"But why? I still don't get it," persisted Beth. "If the color of the robes is a non-issue, then what tilts the scales in favor of it being a black coven? What am I missing here?"

Henry shook his head, sighed eloquently, then went off on a scholarly tangent, even tracing the origin of the words 'coven' and 'convent' to their shared Latin root. Beth had to swallow another yawn before he finally came to the point.

"As we've already discussed," he said, "a coven isn't always an intrinsically evil thing. In fact, I'm quite sure there must be many more white covens than those of the black variety, though, as you can imagine, accurate polling would be a bit tricky." Henry took a sip of his cold coffee, seemingly unperturbed by its acrid taste. "In this instance, however," he said, "given the entire body of anecdotal evidence detailed in the material I gave you to read, I'd have to bet on Molly's coven being a black one."

Beth sighed and nodded unhappily. "And my gut reaction tells me you're right, Henry." With her listeners shocked into silence, she added, "I've been playing devil's advocate here, hoping that you two could give me some solid arguments against it being a black coven, but we're all on the same page with this, and that really bothers the daylights out of me."

Diana laughed. "My sister, the pragmatist. Likes everything tied up in neat little packages, Henry. Loose ends drive her crazy."

"Guilty as charged," said Beth, suddenly remembering a question she had meant to ask earlier. "And speaking of loose ends…" The loveliest green eyes Henry had ever seen leveled their shrewd gaze upon him. "Why did you give us the Hathaway diary, Henry?" She and Diana had already told him that they hadn't bothered to read it after hearing Ruth Nagle's fawning remarks about the Greenville society matron. "Whatever made you think we'd be interested in her?"

Henry chuckled. "If you hadn't allowed Ruth to con you out of reading her diary, you would already have the answer to that question." He set Molly's diary aside and extracted the Hathaway diary from its folder. He thumbed through it for a long minute before finding whatever it was that he was looking for. "Ah, here it is," he said, inserting a bookmark into the diary and handing it over to them. "Why don't you two just start reading that while I go make a fresh pot of coffee."

Beth and Diana narrowed the distance between their chairs and huddled over the book. At first, it was exactly what Ruth Nagle's accolades had led them to expect, a social artifact replete with mindless name-dropping and trivia. They had read only a few pages, however, when the narrative became riveting.

Eleanor and her husband had attended a party in Chaetestown where Clarence's roving eye had settled upon a young woman of great charm and beauty. Eleanor wrote that she knew who 'the vixen' was, but preferred not to soil her diary with her name. Whoever she was, the young woman had completely captivated Clarence, monopolizing his attention from the moment he walked in the door, forcing Eleanor to plead a migraine so they could leave early, her pride intact, but barely.

For weeks afterward, Clarence's dreamy infatuation with the mystery woman prompted him to sneak off to Chaetestown at every opportunity, and Eleanor became convinced that a spell had been cast upon him. Rumor had it that Clarence's mistress was 'skilled in the black arts,' and Eleanor had no cause to doubt it as she watched the slow disintegration of her marriage. Eventually, she sought the aid of her mother's cousin, Margaret Mowbray, 'a wise woman of many gifts, much feared by those who had chosen the dark side.' At this point in the narrative, Beth reached for Diana's hand and gave it a tight, shaky squeeze.

Coincidentally or by design, Clarence's affair ended just two days after Eleanor pleaded her case with Margaret. The diary was tantalizingly vague about the nature of Margaret's involvement, but it was evident that Clarence once again became addicted to home and hearth. Knowing that 'the temptress' was almost certain to seek revenge, Margaret had warned Eleanor never to look her in the eye if they ever chanced to meet and never to speak or write the woman's name. Eleanor never ignored a warning from Margaret. Throughout the diary, the woman was always referred to simply as 'X,' or 'the vixen,' or 'the temptress.'

Before "X" zeroed in on Clarence, as far as Beth and Diana could determine from the diary, Margaret's earliest intervention on Eleanor's behalf had to do with her first pregnancy. Eleanor had been terrified of dying in childbirth, and she'd begged Margaret to help her live through it. Clarence Hathaway was described as 'well over six feet tall and broad of stature.' His first three wives had died giving birth to children who were larger than their mothers' bodies could safely accommodate, and Eleanor wasn't about to be the fourth Mrs. Hathaway to lay down her life in the cause of producing a healthy male heir.

Thus far, only Clarence's female children had survived long enough to leave the nursery, but Eleanor's first child turned out to be a healthy boy of normal size. A year later, she presented her husband with another fine son, again a child of normal weight and length. She had hoped for a daughter, but she was thankful simply to be alive, a circumstance that she attributed entirely to Margaret's ministrations.

Having produced two sons to carry on her husband's name, Eleanor quietly resolved never again to endure the agonizing risks of childbirth. Somehow she actually managed to avoid another pregnancy, despite continuing marital relations with her randy husband. Clarence presumed that she had simply become barren, but Eleanor's diary told another tale. She wrote that Margaret and her magical pharmacopoeia were entirely responsible for her ability to avoid conceiving another child.

Long after Henry had returned with fresh coffee, Beth and Diana read on, skimming through the pages for each mention of Margaret's name. It was always easy to find, since Eleanor had written it with almost reverent care whenever it appeared, the swirling 'M' a tribute to her personal shaman, the only female contemporary for whom Eleanor seemed to have any real respect.

The vicious stroke of Eleanor Hathaway's pen never lashed out against Margaret, although Beth and Diana dearly wished that it had. She mercilessly dissected every other woman she wrote about in the diary, giving a vivid image of each victim. About Margaret, sadly, very little was revealed beyond vaguely descriptive phrases alluding to her 'kind face' or 'gentle eyes,' yet it was clear that Margaret was a dominating influence throughout Eleanor's life.

Up until the very end of the diary, Beth and Diana were certain that only self-interest had prompted Eleanor to care so much about Margaret, but the final entry seemed to indicate a far less egocentric motive.

"Margaret long ago warned me never to look 'X' in the eye, and today I understood why. This afternoon, while shopping in Chaetestown, I happened upon the vile creature for the first time since that awful night so many years ago when her beauty had left Clarence so besotted.

"*Remembering Margaret's warning, I immediately turned away from the crone, but not before our eyes met. The venom in her glance made me tremble, and the ugliness within her soul is now there for all to see. I may not be the beauty I once was, but I can still manage to turn a few heads, and I know she hated me even more for that.*

"*The woman is evil, beyond anything I could ever describe, and I'm told she has friends as hateful as she is, all of them ready to carry on her wicked deeds when she is gone. They assemble in secret to practice their dark magic, and they give my dear Margaret nothing but grief. Margaret is strong, far more powerful in her own good way than 'X,' but I fear mightily for her safety and that of her granddaughter.*"

When they finished reading, Beth and Diana sat quietly for a few moments, half-dazed from the implications of that final entry. Henry's voice, soft and raspy, scratchy in its lower decibels like a well-worn reed, intruded on their thoughts.

"Eleanor Hathaway died a few weeks later," he said, "supposedly from a bad heart."

Diana shook her head. "From what she wrote, she wasn't sick a day in her life! She didn't have heart trouble. She…"

"Calm down," said Beth, patting her sister's hand. "We're talking ancient history here, kiddo. Take it easy."

"Calm down? You've got to be kidding!" shrieked Diana. "Am I the only one blown away by that coven's staying power?" She looked from Beth to Henry and back to Beth again. "Look…" She edged even closer to her sister. "Molly and Eleanor each wrote about a Chaetestown coven, and their diaries span several decades. Do you really think that coven's not still around? And Eleanor Hathaway clearly indicated that it was a black coven. So, unless the woman was a complete flake…"

"Which she wasn't," interrupted Henry with a silently apologetic glance at Beth. "The Hathaway diary has proven itself to be historically accurate in all its verifiable content." When he looked at Diana, he didn't know what to make of her expression. It was positively bleak, which made no sense to him. This should have been a triumphant moment for her. Looking at her quizzically, in a voice husky with concern he asked, "Why the long face?"

Beth could have answered for her sister. She felt the same way. They were both suddenly very afraid of what might be waiting for them at the end of their search for Lenore. Before Beth could think of anything comforting to say, the moment had passed, and the pendulum of her sister's mood had swung back to euphoria. Leaping up from her chair, Diana gave Henry a great bear hug.

"Thank you, Henry! Thank you for Eleanor and Molly." She kissed his weathered cheek, and he flushed to the roots of his hair as she began jabbering excitedly about Chaetestown and her conviction that the black coven still existed.

When he was finally able to collect his wits about him once more, he ventured a suggestion. "Perhaps if you went back to the historical society…"

Beth and Diana groaned in unison. "Ruth Nagle hasn't exactly been very helpful to date," said

Beth. "Just the opposite, in fact. She made the Hathaway diary sound like a complete waste of our time."

"Yeah. Well, let's be fair here, Beth" said Diana. "We never exactly told her the truth about what we were researching."

Henry nodded thoughtfully. "But, you know, even if you had told her the truth, I'm quite sure that she still wouldn't have wanted you to read the Hathaway diary." He topped off all their coffees and added hefty doses of sugar and cream to his own.

Slowly stirring his muddy brew, he said, "Chalk it up to provincial snobbery, but Ruth wouldn't want the world knowing that one of the county's most distinguished matrons relied upon witchcraft as her preferred means of birth control." He chuckled. "Between that and all the nasty goings-on implied by having a black coven cavorting right in her back yard…" His lips twitched into a shadow of a smile and he tilted his head from side to side. "Not exactly the kind of thing she'd want a national newsmagazine reporter to write about."

"But she must have known we'd hear all about it from you," said Beth.

Gnawing fretfully at his lower lip, Henry was slow to respond. "Well…Maybe not…You see, when I spoke with Ruth late yesterday afternoon, let's just say that I left her with the distinct impression that the three of us would likely never be speaking again." He managed a smile, and his gray eyes couldn't resist a twinkle in their direction. "She would be apoplectic if she knew that we were talking at this very moment."

Beth couldn't help thinking that apoplexy just might be too good for her. "But getting back to the Mowbrays… Henry, do you have any other source material at all on them?"

"Nothing of any substance, I'm afraid, Beth. Of course, there are odd bits about Margaret in various books, but only in the context of her quasi-medical pursuits, nothing at all personal or having to do with witchcraft."

"And no mention of any family members?" asked Diana.

"Not to my knowledge," said Henry.

"What about anecdotal evidence?" asked Beth. "Anything at all you might have heard about her or her family?"

Pausing briefly, just long enough to consider how best to hedge the truth, he said, "I can't help you there either, I'm afraid."

"What about a census or social service records?" asked Beth.

Henry shrugged. "We're talking about something that occurred more than half a century ago. In rural areas back then, social services were handled by the clergy, not bureaucrats, and any census takers were as likely to be shot as given any information."

He began gathering cups and spoons onto the tray. "In any case, research is beyond problematic, since the town hall burned down in the late fifties. All of Chaetestown's official records are gone. There's nothing left except for the odd copies filed in county and state archives, some old books at the library, and whatever's been salvaged over the years by the historical society and private collectors such as myself."

Exhausted from all the drama and wanting to wind down the conversation, Beth began gathering the linen napkins and tucking them between the mugs on the tray. "How about school records? Maybe…?"

"Forget it, Beth! Leave it alone!" She didn't want her sister to do any more digging. Diana longed to confide in her about the diary, but she couldn't. Not until she knew it was the real deal. Maybe not even then. She still wasn't sure about that. No matter what, she needed to protect Beth. And right now that meant making sure she understood that they were in very real danger. Averting her eyes from the questions she knew she would see in Beth's eyes, she focused only on Henry when she spoke.

"I think we can presume that there's been a black coven in Chaetestown for a very long time, and I also think it's still meeting at the old Briggs Tannery where Devane lives. The evil in that place is paralyzing."

I don't buy all that mumbo-jumbo, but it's made me a very rich man.

The coven depends on me to get them through some of the grisly stuff.

And I've been doing a lot of business in Albany county too.

All it ever takes is a few free samples to create and own an addict.

Chaetestown's chief of police has been mine for years.

The coroner too.

Amazing how much loyalty a little white powder will buy.

And open borders have made it all so easy for supply to match demand.

Life is sweet indeed.

That fool of a High Priest could ruin everything.

I'm no psychic, but if he keeps on obsessing about a dead woman, I see an accidental overdose in his future.

Chapter Twelve

She hadn't forewarned Beth, but Diana had a private agenda for this visit, one that demanded she be completely honest with Henry. With a silent apology in her eyes, she glanced at her sister for only a moment before turning to Henry and beginning her story. Beth knew that short of clamping a hand over Diana's mouth there was no way to stop her from confiding in yet another virtual stranger.

On a long sigh, Beth stared off into middle distance and listened with dread as Diana told Henry the truth about why she had become so obsessed with Lenore. She didn't play for sympathy. Just the opposite. She made it very clear that any discussion of her illness would be strictly off-limits. When she was done speaking, long moments of painful silence followed before Henry reacted.

Shaking his head sadly, he sighed into his words. "Well now…" Again that familiar harrumphing sound. "I knew all of this couldn't just be idle curiosity," he admitted. "But of course I had no idea -- that is, who could have imagined…?" He glanced at Beth and ventured a tentative smile, but she only glared at him.

Observing their wordless confrontation, Diana said, "Don't take it personally, Henry." She patted Beth's forearm. "My sister's a worrier."

"No offense taken, I assure you," he said, and he meant it. His heart went out to Beth, even though her eyes were as glacial as any he'd ever seen. He supposed that there were some fools in this world who might take offense at her unwarranted hostility toward him, but he wasn't one of them. He wondered if Diana had always been so mercurial, or if it was a byproduct of her illness. Either way, she clearly needed looking after, and he didn't envy the job her sister had undertaken.

He could only imagine how emotionally, mentally and physically draining it must be to watch over this mischievous sprite day and night. Like Beth, he knew that Diana should never have entrusted such potentially damaging information to someone she scarcely knew. Unlike Beth, he knew he would never betray that trust. Neither woman had any reason to know how well he could keep secrets.

He wished there were some way to reassure them that he wouldn't be calling the police to report their illegal tannery search that morning. By his reckoning, no one had been hurt, nothing stolen or damaged and, with a death sentence hanging over Diana's head, well, no way could he condemn their behavior. Far from it. Besides, their escapades were providing him with the most fun he'd had in years, and keeping quiet about them wouldn't bother his conscience a bit.

He leaned across the table and spoke to Diana in a stage whisper intended for Beth's ears. "Don't worry, my dear. Whatever has been said here today will go no further. Las Vegas Greene County style. And please don't concern yourself about the tabloids hearing from me. Rest assured that I would happily go to my grave before I'd lift a finger to enhance the circulation of those despicable rags. You have my word on it."

"Thank you, Henry," said Diana, her eyes tearing and her smile warm with gratitude.

With a nod that said 'case closed.' Henry switched his focus from Diana to Beth. Again attempting an empathetic smile, he faced down the cynicism he saw so clearly in the depths of those lovely green eyes. Since all this high drama was way beyond his comfort zone, he decided it was time to move their discussion into problem-solving mode. Elbowing away some of the files in front of him, crossing his arms and resting his forearms on the table, he summoned his most professorial tone. "Perhaps you ladies would be kind enough to clarify a few details for me."

"Such as?" Beth had finally found her voice, and it was sharp enough to cut through steel. She was edging her upper body a little closer to Diana's, and Henry nodded knowingly at her instinctive protective gesture.

"Please understand..." He directed his appeal entirely to Beth. "I have no ulterior motive here. I know what you're thinking and..."

"You can't possibly begin to imagine what I'm thinking!" shouted Beth.

"Oh yes I can!" Both women were shocked to hear him outshouting Beth. "You're worried that I'll be digging for more juicy details to tell the police or the press. Maybe both, huh? Well you're mistaken. Nothing, absolutely nothing could be further from the truth!" He shook his head, took a deep breath, and gave a self-deprecating little shrug. When he spoke again, it was in his usual well-modulated voice.

"My apologies. I shouldn't have lost my temper." His gray eyes met Beth's, and neither of them looked away. "It's only that I lead a singularly uneventful life, you see, and I'm tremendously intrigued by all of this. I truly have no ulterior motives beyond that." They were still staring at one another.

"Oh really?" Beth's eyebrows arched on the words. "So tell me, Henry... Precisely which details would you like clarified?" The words were a gauntlet, but he pretended not to have noticed. He did, however, broaden his focus to include Diana in his next remarks.

"Well, to begin with," he said, "I don't quite understand all the conflicting reactions to Devane's place. On your first visit, as I understand it, you went inside the tower, bought some paintings and had a long talk over coffee, all of which presumably took some considerable amount of time. Yes?" As Beth nodded warily, Henry thought he saw the first hint of glacial thaw around her eyes. Encouraged, he went on hurriedly. "Yet this morning, Diana couldn't even bring herself to step over the threshold. Why? How do you explain it?"

When Beth only shook her head and shrugged, Diana replied. "A friend of mine back in

Switzerland knows a lot about all this stuff, Henry." She knew that Beth would realize she was talking about Lily Verne, but she didn't want to fan the fires of her sister's anger by mentioning yet another name that would give Henry more verifiable information. "When I asked her that same question earlier today, she explained how the presence of evil can easily be camouflaged by anyone skilled enough in the black arts. I can only guess that Devane is one of those people."

"But how?" he asked. "How would he have done it?"

"Spells, incantations, herbs, candles, that kind of thing." Warming to her topic, Diana mirrored Henry's body language and rested folded arms on the table. "Magic is real, you know." She narrowed her eyes in Beth's direction. "As much as some of us would prefer to deny its existence, it's been around for as long as we've been on the planet." Turning her gaze back to Henry, Diana's expression invited further discussion of the subject, but he wasn't about to be sidetracked, however much he might be tempted. He was a historian, and the devil really was all in the details.

"Be that as it may, Diana. Devane wasn't even expecting your first visit, was he?" asked Henry.

"No, he wasn't. We just kind of barged in on him."

"Then there couldn't have been any protective hocus-pocus before you got there, right?" he asked.

Diana nodded her head, a single fine vertical line appearing between her brows. "Right. Theoretically anyway. But damn it, Henry, there was something protecting that tower when we first went there, or I would have smelled the stench a mile away."

Beth remembered the inquiries they'd made about how to find the old Briggs tannery, first with Eliza at the Country Kitchen, then with Ruth Nagle at the historical society. Both women had known about their planned visit to the tower, and either of them might have contacted Devane before they got there. Had that given him enough time to camouflage...?

Beth couldn't believe the bizarre direction her thoughts had just taken her. For weeks now, she'd been making a conscious effort to acclimate herself to Diana's occult world, but it was a shock to realize that she'd evidently succeeded beyond all reason. Reminding herself that it wasn't unusual for 'townies' to be gossiping about nosey outsiders, she decided to keep her paranoid thoughts to herself.

Henry and Diana soon became engrossed in a detailed discussion of the paranormal, focusing on the sense of evil Diana had experienced that morning at the tannery. Beth stopped being a hostile audience and instead became an interested observer, mentally cataloging little facts and insights for future discussion with Diana, and fascinated by the evolving rapport she was witnessing between her vivacious younger sister and the old scholar who was hanging on her every word.

When almost half an hour had passed without either of them showing any sign of boredom with their topic, Beth decided it had gone on long enough. Touching a hand to Diana's forearm, she looked pointedly at her watch. "Charlie -- remember?"

"Jeez," said Diana. "Where'd the time go? He's probably at the house already." The words and facial expressions exuded dismay, but she made no move to leave.

Beth had no trouble reading the subtext. Diana didn't want to leave yet. "Look, Di, why don't you and Henry finish your talk? I'll run up to Windham and meet Charlie. Then he or I will come back to pick you up in an hour or so. How does that sound?" Since there were no secrets left to censor, Beth was eager to escape.

Diana nodded and smiled with quiet appreciation in her eyes. "Sounds perfect." She knew, just as Beth and Henry did, that a simple call to Charlie on his cell was all that was needed, but Beth's departure suited them all.

"Okay if I just hang here a while, Henry?" asked Diana. To no one's surprise, Henry said that it would be just fine with him.

Diana handed Beth the keys to her Porsche. "Take good care of my baby," she grinned.

Beth kissed her sister's cheek, gave a small wave to Henry, then hurried outdoors, grateful for the cool mountain air after the musty confines of the book shop. She was careful not to gun the engine, but still it came to life with a roar, and she took great pains to shift smoothly as she pulled onto the road, knowing how manic Diana was about her car.

Once beyond her sister's monitoring range, she allowed herself to relax and enjoy driving the Porsche, its handling and responsiveness always a thrill. Paul strongly objected to its flashiness -- a 'mugger magnet' he called it -- but Beth completely understood why Diana had insisted on having it. It wasn't just great to look at, It was also a helluva lot of fun to drive.

With Beth gone, Diana wasted no time getting on with her real agenda. She just wished that Beth had gotten bored sooner and left earlier. Without preamble, she opened her purse and withdrew the little book that was now her most precious possession. She held it out to Henry, but just beyond his reach. "One more secret, my friend, one that even Beth doesn't know about yet. And it has to stay that way for now. Absolutely not a word to her or another living soul about this. Can you handle that, Henry?"

Extending an arm, he was embarrassed by the slight tremor in his hand. "Of course, Diana." He smiled wearily, hoping that she wasn't about to give him the confessions of an axe murderer or something equally felonious. Being around Diana was like being infused with a constant flow of adrenaline. Invigorating, but ultimately, inevitably, debilitating. He could only marvel at Beth's stamina.

Diana reverently laid the book on his upraised palm. "It's the diary of Lenore Mowbray." He suddenly felt so light-headed that he was afraid he might actually faint. "So that's why…"

Diana nodded. "I'm usually a little more discreet than I was with you earlier, Henry. But I needed to give you as much background as possible before asking you to authenticate this."

"I see." He was already examining the little book, his eyes devouring it, intellectual curiosity bringing his mind back into clear focus.

"I don't have a single doubt about its authorship," said Diana, "but I need you to verify the accuracy of some of the details, Henry." She knew, just as surely as she'd ever known anything in her life, that Lenore had written the diary. The only question in her mind now was whether or not the diary was a truthful rendering of events that had actually occurred.

Diana had started keeping a diary when she was in her teens. She still did, though she called it a journal now. Almost every night, she made an entry, sometimes pages long, more often just a few sentences, before tucking it away in her bedside table drawer. When one book was filled, she simply tossed it into an old trunk she kept at the foot of her bed and started another.

Over the years, she had learned how foolish it was not to be completely honest with herself about what she wrote. Her earliest diaries were full of half-truths and embellishments, occasionally even outright lies. As a teenager, she had often reconstructed her life on paper into whatever she'd wanted it to be at the time. Those first diaries would be absolutely useless to any historian. Even she couldn't always recall where the lines between fact and fiction had been drawn, and she could only hope that Lenore hadn't made the same mistake.

Diana had brought the diary to Henry because she needed his read on it. Of course, she knew he would have no way of knowing with certainty if everything written there was a totally accurate rendering of events in Lenore's life, but he would easily be able to get a general sense of the diary's accuracy by evaluating its chronological and historical allusions in the context of his own vast knowledge of the area's history. More importantly, old manuscripts were his area of expertise, and his gut reactions would be telling.

Diana knew that she would be bitterly disappointed if Henry decided that the diary was more fiction than fact. Perversely, she also knew that she would be terrified if he decreed the opposite to be true. Lenore had written about a black coven in Chaetestown, a group that had been led for more than half a century by the same man, a powerful warlock whom she explicitly named as 'Richard Hastings.'

If she had written the truth, Diana knew that trying to find the coven would be dangerous for anyone involved in the search. She had no concerns for her own safety but she wouldn't put Beth and Charlie in jeopardy any more than she already had. And now there was also Henry to consider, not to mention Katherine Vredenburgh, who must know far more about Lenore than she had let on. Why else would she have been so frightened?

Since Diana's most urgent interest was in Richard Hastings, she first asked Henry to read the description of him that Lenore had written. After pointing out the two pertinent pages, she sat back and quietly waited for him to finish reading them. When he was done, he laughed, the last thing she had expected.

"My dear child, this is absurd. Richard Hastings? A mighty warlock?" More laughter. "Do you realize who he is?"

"I know who the internet says he is."

The sharpness of her tone brought an abrupt end to Henry's amused chuckle. Schooling his expression along more sober lines, he laid the flat of his hand on the open pages of the diary and spoke in as solemn a tone as he could muster. "The physical characteristics, background, and description of the farmhouse where he has lived all his life fit the Richard Hastings I know to a tee, but the rest is utter nonsense!"

"How do you know that? How can you be so sure?" Diana's voice was shrill. There was a great deal about Hastings' genial online persona that struck a discordant note with her. The images online ran the gamut of everything from tuxedoes at his son's wedding to Bibb overalls at harvest time, but none of them offered clear, full-face views. His face was always either turned away from the camera or just a dark blob under a Farmer Brown hat, and that really bothered her.

Henry cleared his throat, loudly. "Diana, you may remember that when Billy Hastings ran for congress, he and his whole family were all mercilessly scrutinized and thoroughly investigated by both the press and the opposition party. Rest assured that even the slightest hint of scandal would have been front-page news."

"Maybe, maybe not," she snapped. "In any case, I never would have expected an eminent scholar such as yourself to blithely accept other people's research as gospel."

He knew he was being manipulated, but vanity lured him to accept the bait. "Very well," he sighed. "Leave the diary with me overnight." He closed the little book and looked up at Diana with a knowing twinkle in his gray eyes. He wanted her to know that he was aware of being played. "I may need more time with it but, if all goes well, you could have this eminent scholar's assessment as early as tomorrow."

"I can't tell you how much this means to me, Henry." Mission accomplished, she gave him a grateful smile. "Just please guard it carefully. And remember, not a word to Beth or anyone else about it."

"You have my word. On both counts."

Glancing at her watch, she knew it was time to go. "I'll just wait outside for Beth, Henry. She'll be here any minute." Diana shrugged into the warm-up jacket she had draped over the back of her chair.

When the courtly old gentleman moved to push away from the table, she waved him back. "I'll see myself out, Henry." Standing, she hooked her purse strap over her shoulder and tucked her chair back under the table, then gave him a mischievous grin. "I know how eager you are to get on with your reading." On impulse, she kissed his cheek as she walked by him. "Fair warning, Henry: If you don't answer the phone in the morning, I'll be at your doorstep ten minutes later!" She laughed, but he knew she meant it.

The temperature was dropping rapidly, but it still felt good to get some fresh air while she waited on the porch. She hated the thought of parting with the diary even for one night, but she had no choice. She didn't have to wonder what Beth's reaction would be if she knew of the diary's existence or, worse, if she read it. Her calm, cool and collected sibling would definitely have a total freakout.

Lenore had written of the little golden unicorn that had once been Margaret Mowbray's gift to her. From its description, it was identical to the one that Beth had given her. Margaret Mowbray had threaded it onto a slim gold chain and placed it around the child's neck as a talisman to ward off evil, and Lenore had written that her grandmother sternly admonished her never to remove it. Diana knew that the incident with Helen at the nursing home hadn't been a coincidence. She no longer believed in coincidences anyway. For her, it was all about destiny.

She was meant to be wearing her unicorn pin that day she visited Helen Milligan, just as it was pre-ordained that Helen should see it and be reminded of her niece. She was sure of it. Alzheimer's might have eviscerated the poor woman's brain, but somehow that little golden unicorn had pierced the veil of oblivion and struck a long dormant chord in her memory. Diana shivered, not just from the cold, and she was glad to hear the rumble of the Porsche coming down Henry's drive moments later. It was a welcome intrusion on her thoughts

Beth knew that nobody, but nobody, ever drove Diana's car while she was in it. Seeing Diana waiting on the porch, she pulled up right alongside her and left the car idling in park. While she scurried around the back to hop into the passenger seat, Diana raced around the front of the car to get out of the cold and settle into the warm familiarity of the driver's seat. She lowered the volume on the Norah Jones CD Beth had been listening to and waited for the automatic seat and mirror adjustments to be finished before buckling her seatbelt. "Ready?" she asked Beth.

"All set." Beth clicked her seatbelt in place as they headed off toward Route 23.

Wanting to avoid any discussion about Henry, Diana immediately asked about Charlie. "He just called, Di. He's waiting for us in your driveway."

It was a quiet ride back to the condo. After a really long and eventful day, the silence was comfortable and it suited them both just fine. When she turned onto her street, Diana smiled at the sight of Charlie's green Taurus parked directly behind Beth's BMW. Opening the garage door remotely, she edged past both cars and parked in her usual place. By the time she unlocked the interior garage door that led into the kitchen, Charlie was right behind them. She closed the outside garage door and tried not to think about the sudden warm-all-over feeling she had just knowing Charlie was there.

She was eager to go over all the pictures, but after Henry's musty rooms, she needed fresh air and daylight. As she reset the alarm on the kitchen panel, she said, "Let's catch a few rays before the sun goes down, guys. "I'll just grab the prints from my computer and meet you out on the deck." She had downloaded her camera and activated the print program before going to Henry's, and she was glad to find it had all actually worked just as it was supposed to, a rare thing in her experience.

She tucked the photos into one of the manila envelopes she kept under the printer and took them out to the deck where Beth, Charlie, and three Coronas were waiting for her. The sunlight was warm, and sitting around the table was comfortable enough, but jackets remained buttoned and collars turned up while they examined the photos.

"They're clear," Charlie said, "but we'll have to use the computer to see if there's anything worth zooming in on for a closer look."

"Back in a sec," said Diana. She returned moments later with her laptop in one hand and a magnifying glass in the other.

They took turns examining all the shots, sometimes using the magnifying glass to check out the prints, most often using the computer's zoom function. Apart from the trap door, there was nothing even remotely suspicious in any of the photos. She tucked them back in the manila envelope and heaved a thoroughly dejected sigh.

Charlie knew he could no longer delay telling her what he'd learned that day. Beth would probably want to kill him, but Diana was the one paying him for information and he was obligated to give it to her. He couldn't think of any way to just ease into it, so he dove right in, dreading what he was sure their reactions would be.

Pulling his notebook from the same inside jacket pocket where he always kept it, he flipped it open to the rubber-banded marker. "As per your instructions, Diana, I ran a thorough check on Devane. Just got the final report this afternoon. The guy's a cokehead." Consulting his notes, he added, "Arrested twice for possession in Albany. No convictions. First time, was a juvy offense. Second time, he was old enough to need a high-priced lawyer to get him off. Family must be pretty well connected to afford that kind of mouthpiece. Even so, it was a close call. He almost didn't beat that last rap. Guess he got scared enough to leave town. Probably when he turned up here."

Diana was annoyed when Charlie interrupted his report to take a long sip of his Corona. "And...?" Her voice was shrill. "So the artist is a druggie. Occupational hazard, Charlie. Not exactly a big news flash."

"Give me a break, will you?" He took another quick sip of his beer, then continued speaking, more slowly now, prolonging the inevitable as best he could. "Anyway, going back to that first bust. It was a real weird one." Seeing the sparks flying from Diana's eyes, he immediately speeded up the pace of his narrative.

"They hauled in twelve other kids along with Devane, most of them fifteen, sixteen tops. One of the little smart-asses started howling about religious persecution. Claimed the arresting officers had interrupted some sacred ritual. All the yowling stopped pretty quick when the cops found the kids' coke stash, but not before the name of their would-be church had been duly noted by one of the arresting officers." He paused for effect, and his audience allowed him his moment, even though they had already guessed what was coming.

"John Devane and his friends," said Charlie, "were members of the Church of Satan and too damned stoned to keep their mouths shut about it. Of course, it was all hushed up because of the kids' ages, but a friend of mine at juvy managed to dig up the report."

When Diana didn't oblige him with the expected chorus of accolades, Charlie's features assumed the sagging contours of a beleaguered bloodhound. He had called in some long-standing markers to get this sealed information for her on such short notice, and he was completely baffled by her total lack of enthusiasm. Even Beth had no comment, and they were both studiously avoiding his gaze.

"What gives, ladies? Not that I was expecting a tickertape parade, but..."

"Ah Jeez, Charlie," sighed Diana, "I'm sorry. Please don't be offended. You did a great job, a really great job. It's just... It's just that..." She looked imploringly at Beth, but her sister clearly had no intention of rescuing her this time. Diana took a deep breath and forged ahead. "Damn it, Charlie, it's... it's like finding out that what you thought was only a bad case of dermatitis is really leprosy. Does that make any sense?"

He immediately understood exactly what she meant, but, if he'd learned anything at all after years of investigating and interrogating suspects and witnesses, it was the value of being patient and playing stupid. "I don't get it," he lied, convincingly, he hoped.

Charlie knew that Diana was stubborn beyond belief. Nothing he said would convince her that she was getting in way over head. She had to hear herself hollering 'uncle' before she'd believe it. He watched and waited, willing her to speak her thoughts as she stared blankly at the mountain.

Beth gave Charlie a quick nod and a knowing glance that told him she knew exactly what he was doing and approved of it. Taking her cue from him, she quietly sipped her beer and watched the skiers weaving their way down the last of the slopes that were still on snow machine life support.

Some moments later, Diana sighed into the silence. "Okay. Here goes." She leaned forward, elbows on knees, her eyes boring into Charlie's. "Listen up my friend: I'm scared shitless. Is that clear enough for you?"

Charlie shook his head and frowned, continuing the charade, as Diana moved out of her chair and perched on the top rail of the deck. Facing both Charlie and Beth, she said, "Don't you see? None of this is such a lark anymore! Instead of a wild-goose chase for a long-dead witch, I'm finding myself face-to-face with one very live warlock. And they don't usually travel solo, Charlie."

Charlie continued to bait her, "This morning could have just been an aberration, Diana. Maybe you picked up on something that wasn't even there. Maybe next time..."

"There won't be a next time, Charlie! I'll never go back to that tower again."

Charlie could only hope that her psychic abilities didn't allow her to hear the "Hallelujah!" resounding in his head.

Beth knew it was time to quit while they were ahead. "Look you two, it's getting cold out here, and I'm famished." She stood, did a shoulder roll to stretch out a sudden kink in her neck, then turned toward the patio door. "I'll throw some dinner together and give a yell when it's ready."

Grateful for the familiarity and ordinariness of the simple kitchen chore of preparing a meal, Beth put a pot of water on to boil for pasta and opened up a bottle of Bordeaux to sustain the chef.

The discussion out on the patio had rattled her more than she would ever let on to Diana, and she needed a little solo time to regroup.

Sipping her wine, she tossed a green salad, sliced some French bread, and heated up a few cans of red clam sauce while the linguini was cooking. When the food was all set out on the dining room table and she called Diana and Charlie in to dinner, she was glad to hear them both laughing as they came inside.

Canned sauce and all, the meal was delicious. After eating two heaping bowls of pasta, Charlie's eyelids were drooping, and it took half a pot of strong coffee before he was awake enough to drive home.

The moment he was out the door, Diana began preparing for her evening meditation, while Beth welcomed the chance to go upstairs and put through her long-enough-delayed telephone calls to Paul Dunsford. Since he hadn't arrived on their doorstep that afternoon to put them under house arrest and hadn't even reamed them out by telephone, she realized that he must already have doubled their protection detail, and she could only be grateful for that. Why else would he be cutting them so much slack?

Clearly, he still hadn't told Olivia about Diana. If she knew, nothing could have kept her away. Beth could only guess that, for once, he was allowing his emotions to overrule his professionalism. Paul was a cool customer, but she was sure that his feelings for her aunt ran more to love than friendship, and he simply didn't have the heart to deal Olivia such a crushing blow.

She longed for the comfort of Chad's voice and his instinctive grasp of problematic situations and solutions. Unfortunately, she knew that, if she called him, they would only end up having the same old argument, and no way was she leaving Diana now.

She washed up and put on her pajamas, but was still too wound up for sleep. She decided to bite the bullet and call Chad after all. Nesting her head into the mass of pillows piled against the headboard, she tucked herself under the blankets and was just reaching for the phone when it rang.

She was still fumbling with the handset when she heard, "Bonsoir, cherie! Ca va?"

"Aunt Liv!" Tears instantly welled up in Beth's eyes. "It's so wonderful to hear your voice. How are you?"

"As well as a broken heart will allow, my love. Jean-Pierre and I had a horrendous quarrel."

"Again?"

Olivia laughed. "Oui. Again. Only this time, I packed up and came home."

"Home? You mean you're calling from New York?"

"Oui, Cherie. My plane landed just an hour ago and I desperately need my bed, so listen carefully. You and Diana must be here tomorrow night at six. I'm having a dinner party, and it's a command performance for both of you. Whatever you're doing in that God-forsaken outback will have to keep. No excuses. D'accord?"

"Of course we'll be there, but what's the occasion?"

"No occasion, darling."

"Who else is coming? Anybody we know?"

"As a matter of fact, yes." When Olivia mentioned the names of the other guests, Beth was incredulous.

"You've got to be kidding, Aunt Liv. You've never even met any of them!"

"True, I haven't. Which is precisely the point of inviting them.

How I've always enjoyed the sad and lonely ones!

The Dark Lord has gifted me with the appearance of a man half my age and the stamina of a young stallion.

Well, maybe not quite. But close enough.

Certainly no one has ever complained.

Chapter Thirteen

Since Diana left, Henry had been completely engrossed in Lenore's diary. Relying on strong tea, brandy, and assorted snacks from the gift basket to keep his blood sugar from plummeting, he hadn't given a thought to his usual soup and sandwich supper. The diary had left him with no appetite for anything beyond mere sustenance.

He'd been reading it for almost three solid hours when his kidneys and old bones revolted against being abused any further. Knees and back screaming, he hauled himself up from the ladderback dining room chair and made his unsteady way to the bathroom just in time to spare his pride. After washing his hands, he took a minute to splash cold water on his face and was amazed, as always, to see a haggard old man looking back at him from the mirror above the sink.

As he patted his face dry with the flimsy hand towel he kept on a hook beside the mirror, he could only wonder where all the years had gone. In his mind and heart he was still young, and the reality of his reflection was always a rude awakening. He forced his spine into a more upright position and returned to the dining room to regroup.

Splashing a hefty dose of B&B into the Baccarat snifter that had been alternately consoling and cheering him for decades, he cradled the bowl of the glass in his left hand and used his free right hand to tuck the diary under his left arm before he switched off the overhead lights. Exhaustion, stress, low blood pressure, low blood sugar and, dammit, just plain old, very old age, often made balance a tricky thing these days, so he turned slowly into the corridor and took careful steps over the short distance from the dining room to the comfort of his study.

The moment he flicked on the soft lighting in his cozy book-lined sanctum, he could feel the tension beginning to ease from his shoulders. The modern addition at the back of the house had all the high-tech bells and whistles he needed for business purposes, but this was the place he most loved to be. The desk had a state-of-the-art task light for close work, but the room would otherwise have been totally recognizable to any Victorian.

He cleared the worst of the clutter from the desktop to make room for the diary and the brandy that had thus far likely prevented him from stroking out tonight. It had been one brutal shock after another, and he took a quick little sip before setting the glass down at a safe distance from the diary. He could still reach the anesthetizing liquid gold, but if his shaky hands caused any spillage, the book would be well out of harm's way. Sighing into his chair, he rested his head against its high back, closed his eyes and focused on his breathing.

As a young man fresh out of Harvard, his grand tour of the world had included a stay at a Buddhist monastery in Nepal, and the meditative techniques he'd learned there had been part of his daily routine ever since. Of course, he could no longer get his limbs into full lotus position and expect to get out of it unassisted, but at least his mind hadn't been similarly compromised. Wrinkles were everywhere, but the Good Lord had thankfully spared his cognitive powers.

Time had molded the chair's well-worn leather to fit every contour of his body, and its plush softness was always a great comfort to his sharply angular frame. Motionless, except for fingertips that slowly traced the companionable network of fine creases and cracks that the years had gouged out of the armrests, he explored every familiar little imperfection as he tried to clear his mind of the horrors recorded by Lenore. Breathing deeply, he visualized his faded bottle-green leather chair as it once had been back in the day when it had perfectly matched the rich marquetry inserts on the surface of his ornately carved mahogany partner's desk. Both pieces, desk and chair, had been left to him by his paternal great-grandfather, the only ancestor from whom he'd ever received unconditional love, and they were his most treasured possessions.

Unbidden, Ruth Nagle's gleefully avaricious face suddenly intruded upon his thoughts, her expression exactly what he knew it would be when his will was eventually read and she had official confirmation that his beloved desk was among the bequests to her precious historical society. The depressing image of her triumphant expression made him quietly resolve to outlive her. The historical society did wonderful work. Ruth not so much. He took great satisfaction in dispelling her image on a long, slow exhale.

He was so tired. If only he could relax into alpha state, even for just a few minutes! But clearly his mind was in too much turmoil to allow that to happen. The inner core of serenity he'd always relied upon to maintain objectivity in his research had deserted him tonight. Brandy was a poor substitute, and he'd already drunk way too much of it, but the numbness he'd sought still eluded him. Forcing his eyes open, he leaned forward and reached for a few more sips of his only solace. On a heavy sigh, he pushed the snifter back into its safe zone and turned on the task light before opening the diary once again.

Following the same procedure he always used when inspecting a new acquisition, he had earlier skimmed through the entire book, then gone back to focus on sections that had caught his interest at first glance. Usually, the excitement of discovery made subsequent readings a totally energizing experience. Not this time. He dreaded having to read through it again, but he had no choice.

Henry had lived long enough to know that no man can ever wholly comprehend all that is in the heart of another, but he couldn't believe that an entire town could have made such a gross error in judgment about the same man. Everyone liked and respected Richard Hastings. Yet, if Lenore Mowbray's words were to be believed, he was evil incarnate.

More than fifty years ago, Henry's wife had died giving birth to the little girl who would have been their first-born had she lived. Part of him had died with them that day, but the will to go on living had somehow survived. Like a flickering candle, it had sputtered and struggled for air, but the light inside him had never fully succumbed to the darkness. He'd owned a gun back then, had even held it to his temple during the desolate night after their funeral, but he was never able to pull the trigger. How he'd hated his own cowardice! The morning after the funeral, he escaped to his great-grandfather's old Chaetestown hunting retreat and buried himself alive in the mountain hermitage where he'd lived ever since.

With only his books for company, he'd seldom ventured out into the world. He'd been a trust-fund baby who had made enough savvy investments with that money to ensure he need never work a day in his life. Being a rare book dealer was certainly not the most lucrative of professions, and he knew how blessed he was to be able to make it his life's work. Since his trade was almost all mail order, he seldom had visitors.

Once each week, usually on a Wednesday and always in the same order, he went to the post office to send or receive books, the bank to deposit checks and withdraw cash, the library and historical society to browse, and the Hastings' general store to purchase milk, cheese, fresh eggs, butter, baked goods, jams, meats and produce. He prided himself on never needing to go near a supermarket, and he smiled at the thought of how little his routine had varied to this day.

Richard Hastings was a Chaetestown farmer, just as generations of his ancestors had been. Over the years, his marketing savvy had turned the seasonal farmstand he'd inherited into a year-round minimart of sorts. With plenty of paid help to work the fields and care for the livestock, Richard was usually at the store for at least part of each day, waiting on customers with a genial smile. He had the successful proprietor's knack for remembering his best customers' food preferences, and he had always made Henry feel as if the choicest apples or peaches had been reserved exclusively for him.

Over the years, as often as Henry had enjoyed chatting with Richard at the checkout counter, no actual friendship had ever developed between the two men. But not because of any fault or failing Henry had ever perceived in Hastings. Henry simply hadn't wanted any close relationships cluttering up his well-ordered life.

As affluent as Richard and Martha Hastings were by Chaetestown standards, Henry knew that few people outside of Greene County had ever heard of them until their son Billy entered the national political arena two years ago. Ever since then, the charismatic young congressman and his entire family had been under a media microscope, and Henry had never heard or read a hint of scandal concerning any of them.

How could they possibly be involved in black magic? How could any public figure keep a secret of such magnitude in this era of the internet, paparazzi and tabloid journalism? Granted, the press and social media always seemed to be vying for the role of kingmaker and they clearly adored Billy, but why wouldn't they? He was bright, hard-working, and the kind of man any parent would be proud to have as a son. Henry shook his head and sighed. Removing his wire-rimmed spectacles, he closed his eyes and gently massaged the tenderness at the bridge of his nose, willing his weary brain to refocus on the task at hand.

Henry shared Diana's conviction about the authorship of the diary. He didn't doubt for a minute that it had been written by Lenore Mowbray. Every reference to her family was completely borne out by what Henry already knew to be true about the Mowbrays. He just couldn't fathom the young woman's obsessive hatred of Richard Hastings. Thus far, he had found only one incident in the diary that even hinted at a possible motive.

On the day she was twelve, Lenore wrote about a 'woman-to-woman' talk initiated by her Aunt Helen the night before. In that day and age, Henry knew that it was remarkable for any facts-of-life conversation to have transpired at all, much less be initiated by a timid soul such as Helen. During their long discussion, Helen had confessed to once being in love with Richard Hastings. At the time, she had explained, Richard was shopping around for his second wife, and Helen had been a widow long enough to be interested. Laughing at her own foolishness, she told Lenore that she'd done everything short of hurling her body in front of his tractor, but he'd never even glanced her way.

Lenore's diary recorded every detail of the story, and it was clear that Helen had tried to make light of her spurned affection for Richard. If it hadn't been for the tears glistening in her aunt's eyes, Lenore wrote that she might even have been tempted to laugh along with her. As it was, that night's diary entry included a scathing denunciation of the man who had caused Helen so much heartache. If Lenore had obsessed about the episode in future entries, Henry would have been satisfied that he'd found his explanation for the dark fantasies she had subsequently woven about Richard. But the incident had never been mentioned again.

For the first time in more years than he could remember, Henry wished that he understood a little more about the inner workings of the human heart and that fine filament separating love from hate. Since losing his wife and child, he'd been a solitary, contemplative man with a singular aversion to emotional excess of any kind.

Not that he'd been celibate. Over the years, his sexual needs had been sensibly met by a series of mutually satisfactory long-term relationships with various women who either shared his fear of commitment or pretended that they did. Henry was never quite sure, and he really didn't want to know.

Apart from the wife he had adored, only one other woman had ever truly touched his heart, and that was Margaret Mowbray's younger sister, Helen Milligan, Lenore's aunt. His affair with Helen had lasted for a few years, right up until the day she'd sent him packing and set her cap for Richard. Helen was gone now, but he would honor her memory by continuing to keep their old relationship a secret, just as they had always done. He wasn't even remotely tempted to tell Diana about it.

Occasional loneliness was, for him, a small price to pay for the luxury of having sole dominion over the unruffled passage of his days and nights, especially when he recalled the quiet desperation of his own parents' marriage. They and their entire generation had crucified themselves on a cross of monogamy, leaving their children an emotional legacy that fed the Hydra of mental illness and enriched the coffers of psychiatrists everywhere.

Since moving to Chaetestown, Henry's solitude had become a familiar old friend, but tonight he regretted it. Parts of Lenore's diary read like a bad gothic novel, and he lacked the depth of interpersonal experience that might have enabled him to read between the lines more incisively.

He'd heard and read that all teenagers were notoriously self-centered, and that had certainly been his very limited experience with the breed. Why then would Lenore have become so psychotically empathic about her aunt being rejected by Hastings, an event that didn't involve the child at all? Determined to continue digging for an answer, he began reading those parts of her family history that he'd earlier flagged as being of secondary importance. Longing to catch Lenore in an error or an outright lie that would discredit all the horrors she'd detailed, his heart ached with the discovery that everything she had written about her family exactly jibed with what he knew to be true.

Orphaned as an infant when her parents drowned in a boating accident on the Hudson, Lenore was raised by her grandmother, Margaret Mowbray, until she was six years old. At that time, Margaret died, and her sister Helen became the girl's guardian. Helen was childless, a widow whose young husband had died of influenza in 1938, just a few years after their marriage, and Lenore was lovingly welcomed into her life as the child she'd never had.

Lenore's stories made it clear that the two sisters who had been the dominant maternal influences in her life were as different as any siblings could be. Margaret had a powerful persona that brooked no nonsense from her rebellious grandchild, but Helen was a total pushover, an artlessly gentle soul who was totally out of her depth with the spirited youngster. Uncertain of what to withhold, she had given Lenore everything she wanted.

Eventually, by the time Lenore was eight, she'd become so headstrong that even Helen realized it was past time to curb her indulgent parenting, and she finally drew a line in the sand. Lenore had always balked against the discipline of learning to play the piano, and Helen insisted that she begin taking private lessons with Richard Hastings' wife Norma, the music teacher at Chaetestown Central School. When Lenore flatly refused to go, Helen stood her ground, shocking her niece by sending her to bed without supper each night for an entire week until she agreed to take the lessons.

A small smile tugged at the corners of Henry's mouth as he read about the confrontation. It was a classic example of too little too late, but he applauded Helen's spunk just the same. It couldn't have been easy for her to stand up to that little tartar.

The diary spanned most of Lenore's brief life, and much of it was an open letter to Margaret, the grandmother whom she had clearly adored. The entries were sporadic, and there were frequent gaps in the chronology. Sometimes weeks, even months, would pass without a single notation, and Lenore never explained those curious omissions. She simply made blithe reference to the time that had passed, then continued on with her next entry.

Reading various passages in which Lenore had written about Helen, Henry began to feel a renewed sense of kinship with the woman he'd once actually thought about marrying. Like him, she was a meekly reclusive type whose tranquil and orderly life had been completely upended by a forceful young woman. Of course, if Diana were to be believed, he and Helen had both come up against separate incarnations of the same soul, but Henry didn't even want to think about the ramifications of that possibility.

He'd never actually met Lenore. He hadn't even known Helen until they literally plowed into one another outside the post office one day. Each of them had just picked up their mail and were thumbing through it when their elbows connected just hard enough to send envelopes flying to the pavement. As he bent to scoop them back up, Henry surprised himself by gallantly taking the blame for the incident and offering to buy her a cup of coffee by way of apology. When she readily accepted, they went to the lunch counter at the five and dime down the street and, since it was just past Noon, they ordered fried egg sandwiches to go along with their coffee. By the time they were done with their simple meal, each of them had found a new friend.

Fearing a scandal when they became lovers, Helen had always come to him for their trysts. His home was isolated enough so that her car wasn't likely to be noticed and, if someone did happen to see it parked there, his residence was also a bookshop, so it was a perfectly respectable place for her to be. Helen was almost twenty years older than he, and the possibility of a torrid affair between them never seemed to occur to anyone. He chuckled at the memory of all the good times they'd shared.

Their meetings were always brief, seldom more than an hour or two because she didn't want to be too long away from Lenore. The young girl tried her patience at every turn and Helen was at her wit's end dealing with her. She spoke of Lenore often, but she never asked for any advice about how to handle the little brat. If she had, he certainly would have cautioned against coddling her so much. He was no expert on child-rearing, but it was only common sense.

Then again, would it have made any difference? Given the kind of problems presented by a child like Lenore, who could possibly have given Helen sound advice? The Tommy Kramer episode she'd included in the diary, for instance. Stupid little bully. Henry would happily have booted the boy's rump if he'd been in the schoolyard that afternoon.

The very day after Margaret Mowbray's funeral, Tommy Kramer began harassing Lenore with little rhyming taunts. She had no mother or father, not even a grandparent any longer, just a guardian aunt and a house that was falling down around them, all of it fair game for Tommy's mean streak. Evidently the boy's cruelty was nothing new to any of his classmates, but he had chosen the wrong day to cast Lenore in the role of scapegoat. When he began mocking her grandmother's reputation, she lost control.

It had all been over in an instant: a baseball flying through the air straight at Tommy. No one saw Lenore throw it. Supposedly it appeared out of nowhere and sailed directly toward the boy, clouting him squarely on the head. He was lucky. There was no concussion, only a big goose egg at the back of his head; but it was enough.

The story of how Lenore had made a ball fly through the air to give Tommy what all their classmates felt he deserved was taken home by every youngster who had been in the schoolyard that afternoon. Reading between the lines, it was evident to Henry that most parents had been sensible enough not to believe it; but, because of who Lenore was, they couldn't help worrying. Margaret Mowbray had been a great psychic healer, loved and respected, but also feared for her inexplicable talents, and that fear had now attached itself to Lenore.

Within two weeks of the incident with Tommy Kramer, the good parents of Chaetestown had drawn up a petition to have Lenore expelled from the school, a request that was summarily denied by the Board of Education. Henry supposed that since Lenore had never touched the ball, no one could have seen her throw it, and the principal would never have wanted to publicly acknowledge that a supernatural event had occurred in his schoolyard. Lenore was officially exonerated of any culpability in the incident, but the gesture was meaningless. She had already been condemned by the community.

Henry turned once again to the section of the diary describing what had ostensibly been Lenore's first exposure to the black arts. Supposedly, it had all begun innocently enough after her weekly piano lesson at the Hastings' home. Late one afternoon, shortly before the child was scheduled to leave, a thunderous squall unleashed a torrent of rain, making it impossible for her to walk home. Her teacher, Norma Hastings, would have driven her, but Richard had taken the family car into town and hadn't yet returned. When Norma suggested hot cocoa and a board game while they waited for him, her stranded young pupil didn't object.

"What an exciting new game!" wrote Lenore in her diary that night. *"If only I could tell Aunt Helen about the magical board, but Mrs. Hastings says I can't. It has to stay our special secret. If I tell anybody, she'll never let me play with it again."*

After a lengthy description of that first session with what was clearly a Ouija board, Lenore went on to write at length about Norma, casting her now in the role of treasured friend rather than harsh taskmaster of the keyboard. Ostracized by her peers, Lenore's hunger for approval from someone other than her aunt echoed in every word she wrote, striking a responsive chord deep within Henry. Always bookish, never the young tycoon that his father had wanted and expected him to be, Henry well remembered the pain of his own solitary childhood. His parents had never hidden their regret that he was the last of the Woodruff line.

Feeling a sudden chill, he shrugged into the old tan sweater he kept draped over the back of his chair. The hand-knitted merino wool felt warm against his cold bones as he drew the sweater close about him. He took another comforting sip of brandy before reading on.

"Mrs. Hastings is so much fun," enthused Lenore, *"and she doesn't even mind that I'm different.*

The kids at school mind a whole lot. They still won't play with me. And all because once, just once, I lost my temper. The way they act, you'd think I killed somebody.

All I did was give that big fat bully a little bump on the head. Well, maybe a big bump, but he's a big bully and he asked for it. Gran always warned me never to show anybody my flying trick. Now I know why. Still, one bad thing shouldn't mean you're a bad person. It just isn't fair."

By now, Henry had a fairly clear image of Lenore as a miserably lonely and acutely fanciful child with a desperate need to wrap herself in the protective mantle of her dead grandmother's mystique. He had to believe that she had simply hurled a baseball at the little monster who'd been tormenting her, then fabricated the 'flying trick' version in her diary, molding the narration into a magical event. Not that he doubted telekinesis as a valid phenomenon. He'd seen it long ago in Nepal and knew that it was. He just couldn't believe that a self-absorbed child of six or eight would have been capable of the enormous level of concentration it required.

The diary went on to chronicle a chillingly systematic brainwashing supposedly engineered by Richard and Norma Hastings over the seven-year period leading up to Lenore's thirteenth birthday, at which time she claimed to have been formally initiated into their coven. Soon after this event, the diary began evidencing some real disenchantment with both her mentors, although her grudging respect for Richard's alleged position and power was never disavowed.

By the time she was sixteen, disenchantment had blossomed into abhorrence of many coven rituals that had once so delighted her. Still, she wrote of being an active member of the coven until her eighteenth year when, 'faced with being a party to murder,' she finally rebelled.

For Henry, it all read like pure fiction, and his intellect was poised to reject everything the girl had written. But a single persistently nagging question refused to be ignored, one that he couldn't rationalize away: How could Lenore have so graphically described some of the horrors written about in her diary if she hadn't personally witnessed them?

Lenore Mowbray was an unsophisticated young woman scarcely out of the schoolroom, yet she had managed to provide highly detailed and accurate descriptions of occult practices at a time when such information was not readily obtainable beyond the dark world. Who could have told her? Certainly not her aunt. Helen was such a good soul that she could never have been the source of Lenore's information. Of course, it was conceivable that her grandmother had described the rituals to her, but Henry couldn't imagine Margaret Mowbray poisoning a young child's mind with such obscenities.

As much as he didn't want to believe it, Henry had to accept the probability that Diana was right about Lenore belonging to a black coven that had existed in Chaetestown for many years, and probably still did. What he refused to believe, what he found impossible to credit, was that the leader of the coven was Richard Hastings.

But why then had Lenore painted Richard with such a villainous brush? Henry was just about to conclude that the girl had been totally and irrevocably insane, when the answer finally came to him, its stark simplicity a reminder of how tired he really was.

It wasn't empathy for Helen that had fired Lenore's hatred for Richard, although Henry guessed that was part of it. It was the fact that Richard's rebuff of her aunt had deprived Lenore of the strong and stable family unit that might have shielded her from the Tommy Kramers of the world. In not marrying her aunt Helen, Richard had unwittingly betrayed her as well, inflicting a wound that had obviously festered over the years, infecting the young woman's mind and spirit with a pathological hatred for the man. Henry decided that Lenore's disappearance when she was just eighteen years of age had probably been very providential for Richard's continuing good health.

Satisfied with his own psychological detective work, he closed the diary and struggled to his feet, head pounding with outrage on Richard's behalf, eyes aching with the constant effort of deciphering Lenore's florid script. Open-back slippers tapping lightly at his heels, he shuffled into the kitchen and splashed cold water on his face, then returned to his desk, reluctantly settling himself back in his chair to re-read the last few pages of the diary. He needed to reassure himself that he had missed nothing, that he was right and Diana terribly wrong, that the Richard Hastings he knew could never have been a part of the atrocities described by Lenore.

"They had William's consecration ceremony tonight. It was a full black mass, and the whole coven was there, murderers all, even me. How stupid I've been. All this time I thought Richard was excusing me from the sacrificial ceremonies because he knew how squeamish I was about killing the animals. But they haven't been killing animals. They've been killing children!

"Richard said I was old enough now to make a full commitment to the rest of the coven. I thought he meant I was going to have to butcher whatever animal they intended to sacrifice, and I agreed. He was right. I was old enough to accept that responsibility. But he didn't tell me! Oh Gran, he never told me that it would be a baby!

"The ceremony started with Richard holding little Billy up in his arms, kind of over his head, offering him to the goddess. It was all so beautiful that I cried. Then Richard put the baby on the altar. Billy gurgled and played with his toes, his naked little body all pink and white against the black cloth. Richard anointed him and said the words of consecration, while we all chanted.

"Suddenly I heard a child screaming. I looked at Billy, but he was still cooing happily where Richard had left him. Then I saw another baby being brought to the altar, also naked, also a boy child, his shrieks piercing the night air. He was placed on the altar next to Billy, but it took three of our coven to hold him steady. At first, when Richard held the athame above the children, I thought he was ordaining this child to be Billy's companion and protector. But it wasn't that. It wasn't that at all.

"I saw Richard's sword begin its descent toward the altar, and I screamed and lurched forward to stop him, but it was no use. The coven members on either side of me held me back while Richard murdered the child. Not Billy of course, but the other, the one who had been brought in as an offering to the goddess.

"When Richard was done with the awful deed, he filled the ceremonial goblet with the child's blood

and passed it to each of us to drink. I couldn't stop screaming. They had to pin me against the cavern wall and force the goblet to my lips. I bit the hand that held it, bit it hard, and the goblet fell to the ground.

"Richard was in a rage. A critical part of his son's consecration rite had been ruined, the worst kind of omen, and I knew he would never forgive me for it."

Days later, Lenore wrote, *"My days are numbered. I know that now. I only hope that I can destroy the coven before they kill any more innocent children. Richard Hastings has given Chaetestown a legacy of horror, Gran. He has to be stopped.*

"I can feel him trying to reach me even as I write this, trying to lure me back to the coven just one more time so he can eliminate me as a threat once and for all. So far, I've managed to hide out and keep him at bay. Oh Gran, can you ever forgive me? As God is my witness, I never meant to do evil things.

"Richard can't exile me from the coven. He knows I'll expose him if he does, so it's only a matter of time before he finds some other way to be rid of me."

Henry sipped at the dregs of his brandy and tried to sort fact from fiction, playing devil's advocate with his own convictions, disturbed by the seeds of doubt that the diary had sown. He thought about the dates. No way could Lenore have been referring to the current Hastings men. Every generation in that family had either a 'William' or 'Richard,' often both, so any such event would have involved the congressman's grandfather, maybe even great-grandfather. He even remembered occasionally seeing a 'III' or 'IV' suffix after the Congressman's name.

Henry could feel a migraine waiting in the wings. What was he thinking? What was wrong with him? How could any of this have happened at any time? His solitary lifestyle had kept him insulated from direct contact with most of the locals, but he was neither uninformed nor naive about what went on in Chaetestown. Discreet female companionship over the years had kept him up-to-date with gossip and events, and internet research had filled in the blanks. He'd never heard or read anything untoward about the Hastings family, but that gruesome passage about an obscene consecration rite had shaken him to the core.

There was no question in his mind about the authorship of the diary. Diana was right. It had clearly been written by Margaret Mowbray's granddaughter Lenore, but he knew that he could never in all conscience authenticate the veracity of the diary's contents. It was patently obvious to him that Lenore had been a deeply troubled young woman whose credibility could only be suspect, and he dreaded having to break that news to Diana.

In all fairness, he had to acknowledge that the death of Richard Hastings' first wife had in fact been suspicious. Norma was young, just over thirty, and had no prior history of any coronary problems when she'd had her fatal heart attack. However, the autopsy had failed to reveal the presence of any drugs that might have caused the coronary, and it had been ruled a natural death.

Not that Henry believed Lenore's accusation that Hastings had engineered Norma's fatal heart attack with some bizarre poison from his warlock's pharmacopoeia. Still, it had all worked out very conveniently for Richard when he married Martha Hilliard, the young widow of a Korean War fighter pilot. His first wife had been barren, but Martha produced his much-longed for son shortly before their first anniversary.

Suddenly overcome with weariness, he tucked the diary away in his desk drawer and went to bed.

Where did she go? And, more importantly, why?

Her flashy car hasn't been seen anywhere in the past twenty-four hours.

Nor has there been any sign of her sister or the bloodhounds who always follow them.

Something significant had to have happened, but what?

Even more disturbing is the Dark Lord's sudden silence.

Chapter Fourteen

After an hour of cocktails and hors d'oeuvres, everyone was smiling and relaxed as they took their seats around Olivia's dining room table. There was Chad Martin, Henry Woodruff, Charlie Hobson, and Ariana, along with Olivia, Diana and Beth, four women and three men, a ratio seldom seen at Olivia's parties. But then, Beth knew, this wasn't really a party. Tonight's gathering was an artfully contrived laboratory experiment, pure and simple, with each of them taking a turn under her aunt's high-powered microscope.

Settling back into her chair, Olivia closely observed the handsome young waiter who was adeptly pouring wine into each glass. Satisfied that no one, not even Diana, would guess that his real employer was Paul Dunsford and not the catering service she often used to help her regular staff on special occasions, she allowed her critical eye to roam.

It wasn't easy, but she managed not to grin when she saw the way Chad and Beth were looking at one another. Obviously, they were madly in love. But why hadn't Beth told her? Why hadn't she ever heard about him in any context beyond their working relationship? He seemed perfectly acceptable -- handsome, bright, and well-established in his career. Why all the secrecy? Olivia didn't like being left out of any loop where her nieces were concerned. She didn't like it one bit. And lately she'd had more than her fill of it.

Over the past few months, ever since Paul first brought her the unbearable news of Diana's illness, Olivia had been struggling with the aftershocks of a fluttering heartbeat and a hellish depression. It had taken Paul only a few days to ferret out the information about Diana's diagnosis, but by then she had already left for the States, running to Beth as she always had when there was trouble she couldn't handle. Olivia was okay with that, hurt, but okay, since it gave her time for the long round of therapy she needed to cope with the darkest days of her life.

Paul had urged her to confide in Beth about her own medical problems, but she had flatly refused to burden the child with more worry. It had been easier, certainly kinder, simply to pretend that her newest lover had been keeping her occupied in Switzerland. But she was well again now, no longer medicated into intermittent states of mind-numbing oblivion, and she was more than strong enough to take on her share of the heavy burden her girls had been carrying without her for far too long. She looked lovingly at Beth, thanking the powers above for the gift of that incredibly generous and caring spirit. Olivia had never been quite sure if anybody was really up there listening, but she was always a firm believer in the wisdom of hedging her bets.

As her gaze shifted to Diana, she felt tears threatening, but she willed them into submission. She had work to do here tonight, and she couldn't permit it to be sabotaged by her own her treacherous emotions. Taking a deep breath, she straightened her spine and allowed a radiant smile to camouflage her worst suspicions about a few of her guests. She knew all about Chad, and he was solidly in the good-guy column. But, despite Paul's reassurances, she wasn't convinced that Charlie, Henry and Ariana were as well-intentioned as his comprehensive dossiers on them had indicated. One-on-one, face-to-face, she needed to get a sense of who they really were. She could almost feel sorry for any of them who might have taken advantage of her cubs during her absence.

Olivia had personally telephoned each guest, blunting the sting of a last-minute invitation by arranging two nights of fully paid individual suites at the Plaza for them, along with chauffeured limousine service to ferry them from their homes to the city. The limos would also be available to take them to any touristy things they wanted to do in the city and to drive them back to their homes whenever they wanted to go. As long as they showed up on time for Olivia's dinner party, they were each free to do whatever they pleased for the next two days.

Pleading a Newsworld deadline, Chad was the only one who hadn't immediately accepted. Undeterred, Olivia sweetened the pot. She was sure that Chad shared her misgivings about three upstate strangers who had suddenly become so important to Beth and Diana, so she lured him in with a little name-dropping. As expected, once she shared the full guest list with him, he accepted immediately, only giving a thanks-but-no-thanks to the offer of hotel and limo, since he already lived in Manhattan.

Olivia was afraid that Diana was being victimized by some very clever conspiracy to bilk her out of her fortune. It wasn't unheard of, after all, the dying woman who leaves all her worldly goods to the peculiar sect or individual who had been holding her hand at the end of her life. Not that she cared about Diana's money for personal gain. Olivia had more in her own bank account than even she could manage to exhaust in ten profligate lifetimes. It was only concern for Diana's happiness that prompted her misgivings. She was determined that her baby, the child of her heart, would not be spending her last days as the dupe of false friends.

If only Paul hadn't declined her invitation to dinner tonight. How she missed him! Not only would he have evened out her table -- although she supposed that seven wasn't such a bad number -- but his strong right arm would have been a great comfort throughout the long evening ahead.

Of course, she knew he was right, as usual. His watchdog presence would only have unnerved Diana, putting her in a sullen, totally uncommunicative mood, irrevocably dooming the lighthearted, open ambience she needed for tonight's plan to succeed. It was a simple plan really. She would play the empty-headed socialite while she watched, listened, and hopefully learned how and why this odd assortment of people had managed to worm their way into her nieces' lives. Hoping to calm her jittery stomach, Olivia took a quick sip of wine, then another. It was an excellent Riesling, its effervescence just subtle enough to go down very smoothly. As she watched the soup course being served, she could only hope that everyone would appreciate the excellent madrilène and not think that they were being served canned broth. She was an inveterate snob, and she knew it, but she never made any apologies for it, not even to herself.

Olivia Gresham-Lazare was a celebrated international hostess whose lavish and well-publicized soirees were frequented by royalty, heads of state, entertainers, financiers, kingmakers and powerbrokers. She was a favorite of society columnists the world over, so she and Paul had taken every precaution to make certain that the media were never alerted to this particular gathering.

Even 'though she'd had to sneak off and leave her entire household staff behind in Davos, there were no loose-lipped outsiders working for her tonight. The food had been supplied by one of her favorite restaurants, but the cook, waiters, maids, and even the chauffeurs driving the limousines were all either from her personal New York office staff or on Paul's payroll.

It was Paul's responsibility to safeguard the three heiresses to the Gresham billions and, as the majority stockholder in Gresham Enterprises, Olivia made sure that he took that job very seriously. Several days ago, he had given her exhaustive dossiers on each of her guests. Ever since, he had been updating her at least twice-daily on the bizarre happenings at Windham.

Apart from Beth's evident involvement with Chad Martin, little of any importance went on in her nieces' lives that Olivia didn't know about very soon afterward, including a completely inexplicable breaking and entering episode in some little town upstate. That particular occurrence had her totally baffled. Diana was always up to mischief, but it was unthinkable for Beth to take the lead, as Paul insisted she had done. Whatever was going on, it was soon going to stop.

Chad was fascinated by Olivia's total mastery of all the social graces. Clearly, this was an inspection, and they all seemed to know it. Yet, somehow, the diminutive blue-eyed blonde whom Diana so closely resembled was able to make them feel more like the chosen ones rather than the lab rats they actually were. Only on Broadway had he ever witnessed a better performance. They were actually all having a wonderful time being thoroughly scrutinized. He certainly was. With Beth so close beside him, he really didn't much care what their charming hostess might have hidden up her classy silk sleeves.

Beth was amused to see her aunt's elitist radar immediately zero in on Henry Woodruff. He was seated to Olivia's right, with Diana opposite him on her left, and the courtly old gentleman's privileged upbringing was serving him well tonight. He seemed completely in his element. Henry had gone off to Harvard before Olivia had even been born, so they had never met during the glorious summers each had spent at Newport, but they were cheerfully comparing notes about three different generations of the families they had both known there.

Beth was presiding over the foot of the table, with Ariana to her right and Chad to her left.

Ariana didn't need her psychic gifts to see what was happening between them. She could feel their love for one another as if it were a tangible, palpable thing.

With the famous psychic sitting opposite him, Chad felt a little uneasy every time he stole a glance at Beth. If only the neckline of her jade green dress was a little higher. If only that jade pendant didn't keep drawing his eye to the hint of subtle cleavage beneath it. If only she was wearing her usual conservative power suit! Her appearance was so drastically different tonight that he was having a hard time not staring at her.

Charlie was seated between Diana and Ariana, but he was too nervous about the formality of the dinner to really enjoy their company. All the silverware! And how many different kinds of wine did you need with a meal anyway? One was way too many for him. He knew it all had to be prime vintage, but it was just making him perspire like crazy. What if it made him sick? That's all he needed. He sighed with relief when dinner was finally over without mishap.

When everyone had settled themselves comfortably over brandy and coffee in the living room, Olivia continued with her game plan, masking her intent with the kind of inane chatter that she hoped her guests had already come to expect of her. While she prattled on with seemingly idle questions, she was systematically ferreting out nuggets of information about everyone's likes, dislikes, family histories, jobs, hobbies, and favorite pastimes, pretending that they were each a completely blank slate to her. She kept hoping to catch someone in a lie or a telling evasion, but nobody fell into any of the traps that she set. Certainly not Ariana. What penetrating eyes that woman had! Olivia decided it was foolish to be offended by the mirth she saw sparkling in their indigo depths.

Against all odds, and certainly against her better judgment, Olivia actually found herself liking these people more and more as the evening progressed. Eventually, she became totally bored with her own sleuthing and decided to just kick back and enjoy her own party. Paul's security cameras would record it all anyway, so he'd pick up on anything she might have missed.

Relaxing more into the genial mood around her, she tuned in more closely to a high-spirited debate that was going on between Chad and Henry over the relative merits of urban and rural lifestyles. Chad was arguing in favor of the cultural and intellectual stimulation of cosmopolitan life, while Henry led the charge against him, quoting Emerson and Thoreau, and ardently extolling the more contemplative pleasures to be found at higher, less frenetic altitudes.

Beth and Ariana were taking the middle ground, finding merit in both lifestyles, while Diana and Charlie were having a wonderful time challenging arguments on all sides. The sound of Diana's laughter was music to Olivia's ears. She had been so worried about the child when she first saw her tonight. Even now, she looked bone tired, with fine lines etched around her mouth, and gray shadows under her eyes. But at least her laughter was unchanged, a small carillon of mirth that eased the tight knot of sadness within Olivia's heart.

During a rare lull in the great debate, Beth excused herself and Ariana. "We'll be back for round two in a minute, you guys. Just want to show Ariana the garden." She hurried Ariana away before anyone else could invite themselves along.

During cocktails before dinner, Ariana had begun a tantalizingly brief conversation that her aunt had interrupted, and Beth was eager to continue it. Opening the French doors leading from the living room to the walled garden, she waved Ariana ahead of her and quickly closed the glass door behind them.

Thanks to an elaborate heating system concealed within the garden walls and walkways, the air outside was warm and welcoming. Blissfully impractical white cushioned chairs surrounded a large glass oval patio table. Matching loveseats and chaise longues were nearby, with smaller glass oval tables strategically placed. Beth and Ariana sat on loveseats opposite one another, drawn there by proximity to a swathe of bright yellow daffodils and a softly burbling fountain in the midst of a small koi pond.

"Oh Beth -- this is magnificent!"

"Amazing, isn't it? Hard to believe we're in the middle of Manhattan."

Ariana nodded dreamily. "Just give me a moment to drink it all in, will you?" She breathed deeply of the hyacinth-scented air.

Taking her cue from Ariana, respecting the psychic's obvious need for a few tranquil moments in which to gather her thoughts, Beth said nothing. By the time Ariana finally spoke, Beth's heart was hammering so hard that she had to strain to hear her.

"Does the phrase 'Lenore's covenant' mean anything to you, Beth?"

"No. Should it?"

"Probably not, but it certainly meant something to Philip. He was very precise about it. Even insisted I write it down." She reached into her jacket pocket and withdrew a scrap of paper. "'Lenore's covenant, that covenant once forged in Hecate's town, must there be fulfilled'." Allowing Beth time to absorb the words, she read it slowly once more, then folded the note back into her pocket.

Feeling Beth's fear, she reached out with a commiserating touch and patted her hand. "It frightened me too, Beth. Still does."

Beth knew it was foolish for two grown women to be afraid of meaningless psychobabble, but she couldn't shake the feeling of dread that the words had engendered. She gave Ariana a quick update on the research she, Diana and Charlie had been doing.

Thinking aloud, Ariana said, "So… Given Philip's warnings and what you three have learned, witchcraft seems to have had a comfortable home in Chaetestown for a very long time. God knows what kind of holy or unholy covenants might have been forged along the way."

Beth looked searchingly at the psychic. "Is it possible that Philip might have been referring to hell when he said 'Hecate's town'? She was the goddess of the underworld, wasn't she?"

Ariana nodded. "I read up on my Greek mythology again after he mentioned her. On moonless nights, she supposedly roamed the earth with a pack of ghostly howling dogs. They haunted remote spots, particularly around crossroads, where they could prey on unsuspecting travelers. Legend also names her as consort of the horned god worshipped by satanic witches. Not a very nice lady at all, I'm afraid. But I don't think Philip was referring to hell. I think 'Hecate's town' is very much on this earth."

"But that doesn't make any sense," protested Beth. "Why would devil-worshippers want to tell the world where to find them? And who else in their right mind would want to name their hometown after the queen of all mayhem?"

Resting folded arms on knees, Ariana leaned forward and leveled her gaze at Beth. "Ever play anagrams when you were a kid?"

Beth wasn't sure she had heard correctly. "Anagrams?"

Ariana nodded. "Anagrams."

"Sure," shrugged Beth. "Why?"

"Well, it's a little convoluted, but just bear with me for a minute and I'll explain. When I was very young, my mom started me on the game as a way of enhancing my spelling and vocabulary. She made it so much fun! Of course, when I finally caught on to her ulterior motive, I refused to play anymore. But I apparently never lost my old fondness for the game.

"Years later, it started cropping up at odd times during meditation. I'd go into trance and suddenly see a bunch of random letters in my mind's eye. They would slowly begin to reshuffle into words, ideograms really, each one triggering an impression, sometimes even a clear vision of something or someone."

Ariana was aware of Beth's growing impatience, but she was careful not to hurry her words. "This morning, when I meditated on what Philip had told me, the old anagram gambit started up again, Beth, and there it was, clear as day. 'Hecate's town' is Chaetestown. And, if Philip is right, if Diana really is Lenore reincarnated, then that truly is where her destiny will be met."

In the protracted silence that followed, the sounds of the city intruded upon them. It was eleven-thirty, the theater crowd returning home or going to favorite restaurants for a late supper, impatient cabbies racing crosstown, dismayed tourists unused to their kamikaze tactics honking their horns in fear and frustration. It was a comfortingly familiar symphony to Beth, and a strident reminder to Ariana of all the reasons why she had left the city. Her psychic antennae were going into overload with all the frenzied activity beyond the garden walls, and everything that had been so clear to her at home this afternoon was suddenly a morass of confusion in her mind.

"What destiny?" Beth's voice was suddenly that of a small and very frightened child.

"Philip wouldn't say, Beth. But every instinct tells me that Diana is in very real physical danger every moment she's in Chaetestown." Ariana wished there were some way to sugar-coat what must be said, but there wasn't. "There are evil forces constantly at work there, forces that have already begun to conspire against her."

Anticipating some kind of response, Ariana paused, not speaking again until she heard Beth's unspoken question echo in her mind. "Honestly, Beth, I wish with all my heart that I could tell you precisely what Lenore did to incur such grievous karmic debt, but Philip won't say."

Objectively and intellectually, Beth rejected the psychic's words. Intuitively and illogically, however, she was terrified for her sister. "I don't know what to believe any more, Ariana. My head keeps telling me one thing, my gut another." She shook her head and sighed. "It's crazy, but Diana's convinced that there's been an active black coven in Chaetestown for a number of years, and she's just about got me convinced too. That's why I freaked when you told me about the anagram." Beth shook her head wonderingly. "I don't suppose the name John Devane means anything to you, does it?"

"No. Who is he?"

"An artist in Chaetestown. Dresses like a Monet wannabee and lives in an old tannery tower that used to belong to somebody named Briggs." Beth dropped the name casually, hoping to trigger some reaction from Ariana, but there was none. "Anyway, Diana's certain that the satanic coven meets there. And, since the tower's current resident happens to be John Devane, she's convinced he's some kind of powerful warlock. She..."

"She's convinced he's a warlock for some very good reasons." The sound of Diana's voice startled them. They had been so caught up in their discussion that they hadn't even heard the French door open into the garden.

As Diana approached, Beth was relieved to see Chad's steadying presence just behind her. Avoiding the empty cushions next to Ariana and Beth, Diana angled one of the patio table chairs so that she could observe both women equally. Beth instinctively reached for Chad's hand as he drew near, making room for him beside her, wanting the warmth of his touch, needing to feel his solid reassurance. Chad gave her hand a gentle squeeze as he sat by her side.

Diana finally broke the awkward silence. "I'm not imagining things, you know." She was speaking directly to Ariana. "John Devane's membership in the Church of Satan is a matter of police record. Or did my sister forget to tell you that little detail?" Beth was glad that Charlie wasn't around to hear how blithely Diana had just violated his confidence about the sealed juvenile record on Devane. When no one made any comment, Diana hurried on to describe their first meeting with Devane and the chain of events that had prompted them to search the tannery. "I still can't figure out how he managed to camouflage all the negative vibes the first time we were there. How could he do that?"

Beth knew why her sister was pointedly asking Ariana for an explanation that she already thought she knew. She wanted the psychic to confirm her theory.

Ariana sighed and nodded slowly. "A powerful warlock could easily have managed what you've described, Diana, and in very short order."

Seeing the inexplicably triumphant grin Diana directed at Beth, Chad decided he'd been a silent observer long enough. "Would someone please tell me what you're all talking about?"

At that precise moment, Charlie ambled out to the garden, his arrival providing a welcome reprieve for the three women, none of whom knew where to begin to answer Chad's question. Expecting to make an unobtrusive entrance, Charlie was embarrassed to find that all eyes were focused on him and, worse, that all conversation had ceased.

"Was it something I said?" he quipped. There were a few stilted smiles, but no laughter.

"Come sit, Charlie." Diana patted the cushion of the chair beside her. "Maybe you can explain things to Chad in a way that won't have him thinking we're all certifiable."

Charlie wasn't sure there were enough words in the English language to ensure that. "What exactly do you want me to explain, Diana?"

"Everything. Lenore. Devane. Chaetestown. The whole deal. Coming from you, maybe he'll believe it."

"You sure you want to...?"

"I'm sure, Charlie," she gave an exasperated little sigh. "Go for it."

Charlie's instinctive eagerness to please Diana won out over his natural aversion to being in the limelight, but he was clearly uncomfortable with center stage. With her continually prodding him along and filling in the blanks, he managed to stumble and stammer his way through a summary of all the bizarre events that had transpired since Diana had hired him, never realizing that his lack of polished delivery and his jaundiced view of the supernatural were exerting a far greater impact on his audience, particularly Chad, than any amount of practiced rhetoric could have achieved.

When Charlie Hobson spoke of witches and warlocks in the flat monotone of the cop on the beat that he once had been, Chad couldn't doubt the man's sincerity. He might not believe everything that was being said, but he knew that Charlie believed it, and that alone gave the words great credibility. Suspending his own disbelief, Chad listened attentively, making no comment until Charlie matter-of-factly alluded to Diana's telekinetic powers.

"I beg your pardon," interrupted Chad. "Surely you don't mean..."

Charlie silently cursed his own stupidity. He should have guessed that Diana's blanket go-ahead to tell all hadn't literally meant everything. He wouldn't blame her if she fired him on the spot.

He was struggling for words to get himself out of the hole he had just dug his way into when he suddenly felt the gentle touch of Diana's hand on his. The gesture encouraged him to lift his eyes from their ground-line focus, and his heart gave a little lurch as he looked up at the most beautiful smile he'd ever seen. "It's okay, Charlie," she said. "I'm sure my sister was planning to tell them anyway, weren't you, Beth?"

It was too dark for Beth to read Diana's eyes, but she heard the message in her voice and responded accordingly, glad for the opportunity to help salvage Charlie's pride.

"Diana knows me too well, Charlie. As a matter of fact, I was just about to tell Ariana about the flying champagne when Diana came out here."

"Flying champagne?" Ariana's voice exuded a schoolgirl's excitement. "What happened?"

Beth glanced at Diana, the tilt of her head a silent request for Diana's approval to tell the full story to Chad and Ariana. Beth knew how trustworthy they both were, so she had no qualms about confiding in them, but she didn't want to rescue Charlie at the expense of her sister's privacy. When Diana nodded and gave a small tentative smile, Beth went on to tell Chad and Ariana about the champagne bath Charlie had received in Diana's living room.

Chad's laughter punctuated the end of her story. "Good Lord, Beth, just how much champagne or whatever have you people been drinking up there?"

"Watch out, Chad," cautioned Charlie, a sheepish little smile tugging at the corners of his mouth. "You don't ever want to rile Diana on this one. Trust me."

Diana laughed. "Now look, Charlie, don't go giving me a bum rap here. I don't usually do things like that, and you know it."

"But this teleportation of objects is really something you can do at will?" interrupted Ariana, her innate good manners trumped by curiosity.

Diana smiled and shrugged. "I suppose so," she said, not at all pleased with having her psychokinetic abilities examined under the microscope of Ariana's probing questions. She couldn't explain her gift to anyone, not even to herself. It was just there, growing more frightening and wonderful by the day, and it somehow seemed almost blasphemous to be casually discussing it at a dinner party.

Diana looked about for some distraction, something, anything to put a stop to the questions, and when her eyes met Chad's, she knew she had found it. "Ah, we seem to have a non-believer in our midst," she said, her mischievous grin clearly visible in the moonlight. "Like Charlie said, better watch out, Chad."

She was teasing him, counting on his nimble mind to find a way to safer conversational ground, since he was obviously as uncomfortable with the topic as she was. Unfortunately, he didn't respond at all. No one did. There wasn't so much as a word, a laugh, or even a nervous chuckle to be heard, as all eyes were riveted upon her, dread on every face.

Diana was stunned by their reaction, hurt and humiliated to see that even Beth had interpreted her teasing remark as a real threat. She felt the hurt spill over into anger, and she didn't even try to contain it. Allowing it to feed off the current of anxiety crackling in the air about them, she decided that it would be a pity, after all, to disappoint her audience.

Without so much as the flicker of an eyelash to betray her intent, Diana focused all her concentration on Chad. Slowly, almost imperceptibly, the gray and red paisley handkerchief that had been tucked into the outside breast pocket of his jacket began moving upward, unfurling as it emerged into the air, its perfectly square outline now visible to everyone, even in the darkness.

For a fraction of a second, the handkerchief hovered just a few inches from Chad's face before the fabric began rippling inward upon itself to form a slim column of silk that slapped against his cheek in a whipping motion, as if guided by some unseen hand. Gently now, the handkerchief caressed the side of his face, then slowly fluttered downward on an unerring path back into his breast pocket. The point of the handkerchief was slightly askew after its journey but, apart from that, it was just as it had been before. Diana smiled. Beth moaned. Ariana gasped. Charlie crossed himself. And Chad froze. Olivia could not have chosen a worse moment to make her entrance with Henry Woodruff.

"Well now, isn't this a lively little group? Looks like we got here just in time, Henry." She adjusted a switch near the patio door as she spoke, her touch brightening the outside lights so that even the darkest reaches of the garden were now suffused with a soft silvery glow that allowed her to see everyone more clearly. A quick glance at the group made her wish that she and Henry had stayed inside.

Beth seized the opportunity to escape with Chad. She quickly stood, grasping Chad's hand firmly in hers. "Come sit here, Aunt Liv. You too Henry. Chad and I were just about to go inside and talk shop for a few minutes."

Under normal circumstances, Olivia would have protested about mixing business with pleasure, but Chad's stony expression prompted her to smooth over their departure rather than raise any stumbling blocks. "You high-powered publishing types never get a break, do you? Come on, Henry." Olivia forced a smile. "Let's liven up this party."

Beth hurried Chad inside to the living room. Without bothering to ask if he wanted a drink, she immediately went to the bar and poured them each a stiff shot of brandy. They took their drinks to the sofa, neither of them saying a word, Beth determined that it would be Chad who ultimately broke their silence. Remembering her own rocketing emotions when she first learned that Diana's childhood flying trick was all grown up now, she knew that any conversation between them would be pointless until he managed to get past the shock of what he'd just experienced.

Chad took a long drink before setting the snifter on the cocktail table. Turning toward the lamp on the table beside him, he removed the handkerchief from his pocket and held it up to the light for closer inspection, twisting and turning the patterned silk square. "Damn!" he muttered, tossing it onto the cocktail table.

There was no doubt about it being the same handkerchief he had bought at Brooks Brothers that afternoon, along with a matching tie. No doubt that it was the same silk square that he'd laboriously folded and tucked into his breast pocket earlier that evening. No doubt that it had been in his possession every moment since he arrived at Olivia's tonight. No possibility that anyone could have switched it for another. No strings had been attached to it. No possibility of some mechanism suspending it from the ceiling. It had all happened under a canopy of stars. No possibility that he'd imagined what happened. Everyone in that garden had witnessed it. Still, his mind refused to accept the empirical evidence before him. There had to be a trick. Oh he'd read about telekinesis, and he was sure there were some adepts in the world, but he was equally certain that Diana wasn't one of them. And yet...

The image of her face flashed before him, Diana as she had appeared while his handkerchief was doing cartwheels in the air. Never had he seen such single-minded determination, such focus, in anyone, much less someone generally regarded by most celebrity watchers as an intellectual lightweight. Reluctantly, he yielded to logic and admitted to himself that the evidence was too compelling to deny. Somehow she could move objects at will, and the implications of that were staggering. No wonder Beth refused to leave her alone.

He turned to face Beth, intending to apologize for giving her so much grief about baby-sitting Diana, but the quiet agony in her eyes completely obliterated the words he had meant to say. He simply took her in his arms. Nestling her head against his shoulder and holding her close, he whispered, "I've been such a selfish bastard. Can you ever forgive me?"

"There's nothing to forgive." Beth didn't trust her voice beyond those few words. She snuggled against his broad chest, content just to be in his arms. They sat quietly for a few minutes, each drawing strength and comfort from the other, their mood shattered when an enraged Olivia stormed through the French door, an ashen-faced Henry Woodruff trailing in her wake.

She stood before Beth like an avenging angel, not in the least repentant about having interrupted what was clearly a private moment. "Since when do the Greshams entertain their guests with sideshows?" she demanded. "How could you let her carry on like that, Beth?"

Henry assumed a neutral position a few paces behind Olivia, wishing he were miles away from Manhattan, and cursing himself for accepting Olivia's invitation. Vividly remembering the Tommy Kramer episode in Lenore's diary, the last thing in the world he'd needed or wanted to hear was that Diana was able to transport objects at will.

Chad stood, an automatic reflex at the sight of a woman and an older man standing in his presence. Olivia noted with satisfaction that he'd instinctively placed himself between her Beth, intuitively shielding her niece from the madwoman she'd become.

"Oh sit down, Chad. You too, Henry. Especially you, Henry. You look awful. Are you okay?"

"I'm fine, Olivia. And I will happily sit down, just as soon as you do."

Head held high, back ramrod straight, Olivia settled into a wingback chair opposite the sofa and primly crossed her ankles, the grande dame posture that Beth knew all too well. Her aunt would wait unflinchingly for as long as it took to hear a satisfactory explanation of what had just happened in her garden.

While Henry gratefully collapsed into a comfortable armchair, Beth was struggling for words to explain the impossible, when Chad came to her rescue. "No harm done," he said, sitting down again beside Beth, his hand reaching out to clasp hers.

Olivia's only response was a dismissive glance at him and a menacing glare at Beth. "I'm waiting," she said.

Chad knew he shouldn't get in the middle of things, but he couldn't sit idly by and watch Olivia browbeat Beth. He gave Beth's icy fingers a squeeze, then took on the dragon lady. He was neither impressed nor intimated by her bullying tactics. "Beth had nothing to do with what happened out there, Olivia. That was entirely a grudge match between Diana and me."

"Oh really?" replied Olivia, her tone glacial. Beth's young man had spunk, and she liked it, but she wasn't ready to back off yet. "I'll have you know that it's very unlike Diana to be vindictive."

"I didn't say that she was," said Chad, his tone even and totally unflustered. "She simply has a low tolerance level for non-believers."

"There's nothing simple about any of this," hissed Olivia.

Drawing upon years of experience with her aunt's tantrums, Beth tried a very different tack, one that she hoped would appeal to Olivia's finely tuned sense of the absurd. "Calm down, will you, Aunt Liv? You're blowing this way out of proportion. So what if Diana has this strange ability to make things go bump in the night? It's not as if we've just discovered that she's an axe-murderer."

Beth was relieved to see that her ridiculously flip remarks had their targeted effect. The stern set of Olivia's mouth began to ease, Henry nodded approvingly, and Chad's grim expression assumed a less apocalyptic aspect that, Beth supposed, was the best anyone had a right to expect of him under the circumstances.

Chad was beginning to think that he and Henry might just be the only sane people at Olivia's that night. During the awkward lull following Beth's inane remarks, he saw his chance to escape, and he took it. Scooping up his handkerchief from the cocktail table, he defiantly thrust it back into his breast pocket and murmured his excuses about needing to review Newsworld's cover layout for that week's edition before it went to press. He gave the impression that the presses were being held at a standstill pending his approval, but Beth knew better. He had at least twenty-four hours before that particular deadline, but his eyes asked for and received her tacit endorsement of the pretense.

She walked him to the front door. He looked at her, started to speak, then thought better of it. Brushing a tentative hand to her cheek, he made a half-hearted attempt at a smile, then was gone without a word.

She managed to have a pale semblance of a smile in place by the time she returned to the living room, but it was too meager to deceive anyone. Henry took his cue and promptly said a gallant farewell, then went out to the garden to say goodnight to the others. With a limo already waiting outside, Ariana and Charlie decided to go back to the Plaza with Henry, and they all said hurried good-byes.

Olivia dropped the masque of civility as soon as the door had been closed and locked behind her departing guests and the last of the hired help were gone from the house. A cardinal sin had been committed at her home tonight: a member of the Gresham family had humiliated one of her guests. Without preamble, she demanded a full explanation of everything that had happened and why. When it was unhesitatingly given to her, Diana's honesty only served to fuel her anger.

"How can you sit there and blithely..." began Olivia.

"Calm down, Aunt Liv," said Diana. "I'm not blithely doing anything. You asked me for an explanation and I gave it to you with a minimum of histrionics. I thought you'd prefer it that way."

Olivia raised her eyes to heaven. With no help evident from that quarter, she glanced hopefully at Beth. "Does any of this make even the smallest modicum of sense to you?"

Beth glared at Diana. "Only when I remind myself that my little sister has a tendency to behave like an infant when she's crossed. Then it makes eminently good sense, Aunt Liv."

The battle raged on until the three women were sick of it. In the end, as was usually the result of their arguments, there was no clear winner, but only a truce. Diana promised to apologize to Chad. She also swore that she would never again abuse her special gift. In return, Olivia and Beth agreed to lay the matter to rest. They sealed their bargain with a champagne toast, then talked into the wee hours, the kind of gab fest that they used to enjoy so much.

Olivia wondered if they would ever again be together like this. Her heart swelled with pride as she watched her girls, Diana sprawled on the Tabriz rug with her head propped up on a throw pillow, Beth with her feet dangling over the armrest of the club chair, talking and laughing as if they hadn't a care in the world.

What sustained them? If only she knew. If only she could tap into that magical wellspring of courage they both seemed to have found, then maybe she could find the strength to be brave for Diana's sake, to let her get on with what remained of her young life without tears and recriminations.

Diana still hadn't confided in her about her illness, and Olivia hated pretending she didn't know how sick her baby was, but her therapist had told her she needed to wait until Diana was ready to come to her. Meanwhile, the elephant in the room wasn't going anywhere. Of course, she hadn't told them about her meltdown either. Make that two elephants.

Her therapist, Dr. Girard, had said that Diana's reluctance to tell her spoke eloquently of the love they shared and the family dynamic that had always sustained her: Beth, the caring, dependable, responsible adult, and Olivia, the loving, laughing, high-spirited friend.

According to the doctor, right now Diana desperately needed the security of knowing that her aunt and her sister were still fulfilling the same roles in her life as they always had. In his opinion, stripping away that dynamic in the name of truth could only be emotionally catastrophic for Diana. Olivia wasn't sure she agreed, but she had gone along with it for lack of any better ideas. With luck, her resolve would get her through the morning when Diana planned to leave for Windham to spend a few days alone with Charlie Hobson. Olivia prayed for the strength to let her go without making a scene.

Seeing Diana again tonight, holding her in her arms, she could almost believe it was all a bad dream. But the gray shadows under those lovely eyes told their own story, and Olivia knew she had to accept the reality that each goodbye Diana said from now on could be a final farewell. As much as she wanted to spend every possible remaining minute with her baby girl, she had to let her get on with her own priorities. And if that included a romantic fling with Charlie Hobson, so be it.

Charlie was clearly besotted with Diana, and Olivia was thankful for it. She would come to no harm through him. Paul had assured her of that, and she had seen it with her own eyes tonight. Of course, had anything about Diana's life been normal at that point, a match with an older guy like Charlie Hobson would have been unthinkable. But, given the circumstances, her baby could indeed do worse.

Olivia managed to fall into an untroubled sleep that night, secure in the knowledge that Paul, Charlie, and even Henry would keep close watch over Diana while she was in Windham.

Beth could have told her how wrong she was about Diana's reasons for going back upstate so quickly, but it was kinder to let her aunt believe that Charlie really was Diana's lover.

She has returned.

But why?

He could feel Margaret's presence all the time now.

And, incomprehensibly, Lenore's as well.

What was happening?

Why was he suddenly being haunted by ghosts from his past?

I've warned the coven that we are under siege.

They all know what to do if we are discovered.

Offer no information and admit to nothing.

Deny! Deny! Deny all of it!

And leave it to the Dark Lord to protect us.

So mote it be.

Chapter Fifteen

When Beth's alarm went off at seven o'clock that morning, Olivia's house was eerily silent. Mrs. Meares, the live-in housekeeper and cook at the brownstone for as long as Beth could remember, had taken a week off to help care for an ailing cousin in Pennsylvania, and the rest of the household staff was still in Switzerland. Not that Olivia would be without help for whatever she might need during their absences. Her admin staff at Gresham's New York headquarters always took very good care of their generous employer.

Unless Olivia specifically requested the activation of indoor security cams and audio, as she had done for last night's party, all indoor surveillance feeds were routinely disengaged whenever she or one of her nieces was in the house. With his people watching the exterior of the brownstone twenty-four/seven, Paul saw no need to invade their privacy any further.

Without household staff or electronic spying eyes to critique her appearance, Beth relished the rare pleasure of padding through the venerable old Gresham townhouse clad only in a nightshirt as she slipped down the hall to Diana's bedroom. Not wanting to wake her sister if she were still asleep, she turned the knob quietly and peeked inside, disappointed but not at all shocked when she saw the empty bed. Nothing about her baby sister's behavior surprised her any more.

Diana had promised she'd be around for breakfast with their aunt before she left for Windham, but clearly she had reconsidered her options. The bedcovers were just as pristine as they'd been yesterday, definitely not slept in. Diana never made her bed. There were no toiletries or medications anywhere in the bedroom, and the bathroom countertops had been cleared. Beth figured she must have left as soon as she and Olivia had fallen asleep. The open closet was half-full, but that meant nothing. Diana always kept a good portion of her wardrobe at Olivia's anyway. Until she became so ill, the townhouse was party-central for her whenever she was in New York.

Beth trudged downstairs to see if she had at least thought to leave a note. As soon as she turned on the kitchen light Beth saw it, a scrap of paper propped against the sturdy Delft vase in the center of the table. The hastily scrawled *Gone to Windham. Love, Di'* revealed nothing that Beth didn't already know. More annoyed than she cared to admit, even to herself, she tossed the note back on the table and went to the fridge for some orange juice, needing a quick blood sugar fix before trying to work out the intricacies of Olivia's new high-tech coffeemaker. When she thought she had it right, she set the timer to start brewing in forty-five minutes, giving her enough time to shower, change, and make a quick run to the bakery.

Twenty minutes later, wearing jeans and sneakers, a comfortable old white cotton shirt and faded denim jacket, she was on her way out the door. It was only a few blocks crosstown to her aunt's favorite bakery, but she walked quickly, striding confidently and looking straight ahead, no jewelry, no flashy clothes, never making eye contact with oncoming pedestrians. It was the basic street-smart survival drill drummed into her by Paul when she was just a child. By now, it was an ingrained habit, despite the fact that a bodyguard was always trailing somewhere close behind her.

As soon as she entered the bakery, she took one long blissful breath, promptly forgetting everything that she'd ever learned about good nutrition. The bakery was already crowded, and she took her place in line, checking for messages on her cell while she waited. It was too early to return any calls, but the one message she was hoping to find wasn't there. Chad hadn't tried to reach her.

Fifteen minutes later, she was leaving the bakery with a shopping bag full of high-calorie fat-saturated brioches, croissants, scones and all the gourmet trimmings she could carry. This was definitely a morning for comfort foods. Just down the street, she stopped at a news kiosk and picked up two copies of the Wall Street Journal before hurrying back to Olivia's.

She'd timed it just right. The aroma of freshly brewed coffee greeted her as she opened the front door. After leaving her bakery treasures on the kitchen counter, she searched in vain for a coffee mug in cabinets that held only Minton and Sevres. Using an absurdly dainty cup, she poured herself a splash of what tasted like acrid mud to her, shuddering at her first and only sip, satisfying herself that it was strong and thick enough to swim happily in cream, Parisian-style, just the way Olivia liked it.

She draped her jacket over a chair, rolled up her sleeves, washed her hands, dug into the shopping bag, and started preparing a breakfast tray for her aunt. Olivia usually slept late, but since she was expecting to have breakfast with Diana this morning, she would probably have set an earlier alarm. Beth wanted to have the tray waiting on her bedside table whenever she awoke, if only as a peace offering on Diana's behalf.

When she was finished arranging the tray with all the elegant little niceties Olivia always expected, she stood back to admire her handiwork. The Sevres porcelain, Baccarat crystal, and Georgian silverware gleamed, and the mini assortment of breakfast pastries smelled wonderful. She double-checked to make sure that all the other essentials were there – coffee carafe, juice, cream, sugar, butter, and jam – before covering the food with a snowy linen napkin.

Plucking a delicate yellow rose from the floral arrangement on the hall table, she trimmed off a thorn that the gardener had missed, then, having no idea where to find a small vase, she draped the flower across the napkin. Olivia was a stickler for presentation, and Beth was fairly confident that the tray would meet her fussy expectations. With the Journal tucked under her arm, she carried the tray upstairs to her aunt's bedroom. Balancing the tray precariously between her hip and the door jamb, she tapped lightly at the door. Hearing no response, she let herself into the room, breathing a sigh of relief when she found Olivia snoring softly, totally oblivious to her presence. She wasn't at all eager to break the news about her sister's early vanishing act, and she was grateful for the reprieve. She set the tray on a bedside table, left the paper on the bed beside her, and tiptoed quietly out of the room.

Returning to the kitchen, she rinsed the dregs from her coffee cup and made herself some tea. Munching on breakfast goodies and sipping Olivia's custom darjeeling blend, she scanned her own copy of the Journal, all the while trying to decide what to do about Diana.

Unlike Olivia who thought Diana and Charlie were a hot item, Beth had no illusions about why her sister had hurried back upstate, and she felt entitled to hound Diana at will, particularly in view of all that Ariana had said to her in the garden last night. Whatever doubts Beth might harbor about Philip's existence as an emissary from the great beyond, she couldn't ignore an explicit warning from one of the world's most renowned psychics.

Trying to ease her anxiety, she did a quick mental inventory of every security measure already in place to protect her sister, a battery of precautions and procedures that Paul had implemented years ago in the aftermath of a kidnapping attempt on Beth and Diana when they were small children. As much as they all disliked being followed everywhere, twenty-four/ seven, they understood the reasons for it.

With pangs of guilt about how careless she and Diana had been lately, Beth reminded herself of the four cardinal rules Paul had insisted that they always follow: vary the timing of their daily activities to avoid any hint of routine; utilize the elaborate system of electronic alarms he had set up in their homes and cars; keep his office informed of their itineraries as far in advance as possible; and notify him the moment they perceived any threat to their individual or collective well-being.

Beth didn't envy Paul the task of keeping them safe in a world where rampant violence had become almost commonplace. Between partisan politics and the scourge of Covid, no wonder there were concurrent epidemics of mental illness and obesity. They didn't call it comfort food for nothing, and right now she desperately needed a little consolation. She lathered a brioche with butter and took a great big wonderful bite.

Varying her routine while trying to keep regular office hours had always been Beth's particular challenge, and Diana often forgot to reset alarms; but never before had they both so consistently and deliberately avoided keeping Paul informed about their plans. Not that he didn't know where they were every moment of the day and night. He had eyes and ears everywhere. They'd just given him a needlessly hard time by not holding up their end of a very fair bargain.

Beth knew that she had an obligation to tell Paul about Ariana's warning, bizarre as the circumstances were. But how was she supposed to tell that completely logical and pragmatic man about dire forebodings from the astral plane?

And what about Diana? Should she tell her what Ariana had said last night? Beth didn't even have to think about that one. No. Absolutely not. And not because she thought her sister would be frightened. Far from it. Ariana's words of warning would only feed Diana's obsession and likely drive her headlong into the midst of whatever danger might actually be lying in wait for her in Chaetestown.

Beth heard Olivia calling out to her. Tucking Diana's note into the pocket of her jeans, she immediately went upstairs to her aunt's room, taking her tea along with her. The house was so big and so solidly constructed that she hadn't heard a sound from Olivia until just a few moments ago, but clearly her aunt had been up and about for a while. Her bedroom door was wide open, and the lights were on in her adjoining study. She'd obviously gotten some work done and gone back to bed.

"How do you feel, Aunt Liv?" Beth kissed her cheek and smiled at her leisurely pose. Olivia was half-sitting, half-reclining against a cocoon of pillows, the Wall Street Journal folded open beside her. The brainless socialite façade that she often affected always amused Beth. Luckily for Gresham Enterprises, their major stockholder had a brilliant head for business.

"I'm feeling deliciously lazy, darling. Thank you for all this." She took a small sip of coffee, smiling her approval. "It's divine!"

"Glad you like it." Beth set her teacup down on the glass-topped dressing table near the window. "Ready to greet the day?" Her hand was already poised on the controls for the heavy yellow brocade window panels. At Olivia's nod, she opened the drapes, suffusing the room with pale sunlight that immediately brightened her mood and caused her aunt to wince.

Reclaiming her tea, Beth pulled the dressing table chair closer to the bed and sank onto its plump cushions. Toeing off her flats, she propped her feet on the edge of the mattress. She was about to tell her aunt that Diana had left, when Olivia spared her the trouble.

"Relax, darling. I already checked her room. My guess is she tiptoed out the door as soon as we both conked out, then headed for the damn hills." Olivia took another sip of coffee, her expression thoughtful. "Did she at least leave a note?"

Beth shrugged. "Sort of." Retrieving the scrap of paper from her pocket, she handed it to her aunt.

Olivia laughed as she read the meager note, tucking it carefully into the pocket of her pink silk bed jacket when she was done. "That's our girl!" she said, shaking her head and smiling.

Encouraged by her aunt's unexpectedly tranquil mood, Beth quickly broached the rest of the bad news. "I'm afraid our girl could be getting in way over her head up there, Aunt Liv."

"Oh? How so?"

Beth was totally perplexed by her aunt's composure. Her eyes were bright with curiosity, but she didn't seem at all worried, not even when Beth gave her a verbatim account of last night's discussion with Ariana. "Crazy as it all sounds, Aunt Liv, I think we should alert Paul, don't you?"

"Absolutely," said Olivia. "Just spoke to him, but I'll buzz him back asap and give him the information."

"Good." Beth knew she'd be getting a major lecture next time she talked with Paul, so she was more than glad to have Olivia make the call. "Did he have any news on Diana?"

"No. Nothing out of the ordinary. It was just our usual morning chat, Beth. Diana's fine."

"So, you two touch bases every day, huh?"

"At least once, usually more often." Olivia smiled, her finely arched brows rising like wings above blue eyes that sparkled with amusement. "You know, it amazes me that you and your sister still think you can deceive Paul. Ever." She laughed. "We've known everything, my dear -- Lenore, Margaret Mowbray, John Devane, Charlie, Henry, Ariana, whoever and whatever, almost as soon as you did."

As Olivia intended, Beth felt very foolish. "You must think we've both lost our minds."

"Quite." Olivia lowered her eyes and sipped quietly at her coffee.

For a moment, only that, Olivia thought that Beth was ready to unburden herself about Diana's illness, but evidently that was not to be. During their long conversation after the dinner party last night, Olivia had given them every opportunity to tell her, but Diana hadn't even hinted at so much as a mild headache, and she had clearly sworn her sister to secrecy. Olivia knew that Beth's loyalty to Diana had always been absolute, and she didn't even attempt to pry the information out of her now.

"At any rate," sighed Olivia, "don't worry about your sister. Paul has triple-teamed her bodyguards. She'll be fine."

"And what about Devane? Is he...?"

Olivia nodded. "He's been under surveillance, ever since your first visit to his studio. You know how thorough Paul is. He has bulging dossiers on everyone whose name has cropped up in this mad search of Diana's. He even has a tail on Charlie Hobson."

"Really?" Even 'though she knew it was wise not to trust anyone implicitly, Beth liked Charlie so much that she couldn't help feeling a little offended on his behalf.

Olivia's eyes were warm with understanding. "I like him too, Beth, and Paul tells me he checked out just fine. But we need to be sure he's all the good things he seems to be and that he doesn't owe any nasty favors to some kissing cousin. You know how some of those rural mountain areas are." She wrinkled her nose. "So much inbreeding over the years that everybody becomes everybody else's relative after a while, one nuttier than the other."

Beth laughed. "Your description of Windham is pretty funny, Aunt Liv." Thinking about the quaint little main street with its French Bistro and art galleries, she added. "It's *so* not a hick rural town."

"I'm not referring to Windham, Beth."

"Oh. Chaetestown then?"

Olivia pursed her lips and nodded slowly. "From what Paul tells me, it's one of those remote little burgs that somehow has managed to remain well out of the mainstream, just the kind of place where the old ways live on." She nibbled at the edge of a croissant. Beth knew her aunt well enough to wait silently for whatever else she had to say. Clearly, there was more, something she wasn't eager to mention. "Paul wanted me to give you a message, Beth. Though I'm sure you won't like hearing it."

"Oh? What?"

Olivia took a deep breath and exhaled on a long sigh. "As usual, he's being overly protective, but he's adamant about neither of us going anywhere near Windham or Chaetestown until he gets a better handle on what we're actually dealing with up there." Olivia reached out a hand to soften the stubborn tilt of Beth's chin. Brushing her fingertips along the taut jawline, she said, "It will only take a few more days to sort things out, darling."

Beth was in no mood to be cajoled. Angling her head away from Olivia's touch, she said, "That could be a few days too late, Aunt Liv."

"Be reasonable, Beth. Paul needs to concentrate on Diana. We'd only be diluting his efforts if..."

"So we're supposed to just sit here doing nothing while she runs wild up there?" Beth shook her head. "I don't think so."

"Well then, consider this: don't you think your sister deserves a little time alone with her guy?" Olivia smiled. "Which, incidentally, is something you might just want to consider for yourself, love."

Beth was always impressed by her aunt's ability to shift conversational gears so quickly and effortlessly. "After last night, I don't think Chad's even speaking to me, Aunt Liv."

"Nonsense. I saw the way that young man looks at you." Olivia's eyes gleamed with impishness. "A romantic getaway would be ideal! What about Bimini? Grandpa's old fishing hideaway is just sitting there on the beach beckoning, and it would do your relationship a world of good."

A sixth sense where Olivia was concerned brought a smile to Beth's lips. "If I didn't know better, Aunt Liv, I'd say you were trying to get rid of me."

"Moi?" Olivia's eyes widened in mock horror." She laughed. "You know me too well, love. Guilty as charged, I'm afraid. Jean-Pierre is flying in from St. Moritz tomorrow."

"You're kidding?" Feeling her mouth drop open, Beth promptly snapped it shut. She shook her head as if to clear it. "But I thought you two were history."

"A lover's quarrel, darling, nothing more." smiled Olivia. "We always have these little spats, but they never last long. The man has an insatiable hunger for the good life. He's always swiftly and charmingly penitent." She smiled, but only to hide the sorrow of a secret memory. Not wanting Jean-Pierre to see her while she was ill, it had been two months since they had been together. She was still on maintenance doses of medication, but only to calm her, no longer to render her virtually senseless. She was more than ready to take up where they had left off.

"But if he's such a parasite, why...?"

"Because he's utterly marvelous in bed, that's why." Olivia laughed. "I can't believe you're blushing! After all this time, after all the 'uncles' you and Diana have had over the years, why on earth should it shock you to hear me say that?"

Beth smiled. "Damned if I know."

"Look, darling, I know that some of my more scandalous escapades have caused you some... discomfort over the years. And for that I'm truly sorry. But I assure you I have no other regrets." She opened the carafe and topped off her coffee, liberally lacing it with sugar and cream.

"Marriage turned out to be a trap for me, Beth. It cost me millions to end it back in my twenties, but it was worth every penny." She took a few sips of coffee, finding comfort in its familiar strength and sweetness. "I couldn't bear monogamy then, and I don't think I'd be any better at it now. But you -- you, my love, are strictly a one-man woman."

"That boring, huh?"

Olivia reached out a hand to pat Beth's knee. "No, not boring, cherie. Committed. Both to the people you love and to the important work that you do. I may never understand your workaholic mindset, but that's your choice, and I respect it. More than that -- I'm tremendously proud of you and all that you've made of your life." Olivia was embarrassed to realize that she had probably never said those exact words to her niece before.

Beth swallowed hard. "Thanks, Aunt Liv. That means a lot to me."

Olivia's eyes were bright with tears, but she blinked them away. She couldn't go back to rewrite the past, and it was pointless to beat herself up over it now. "You've always needed more stability than I was ever able to give you, Beth, so you created it for yourself. Even when you were a little girl trekking all over hell and gone with me, a little framed picture of your parents was always the first thing you unpacked to put on a table next to your bed."

Beth's voice was a little unsteady when she replied. "But your picture was always there too, Aunt Liv, still is, right beside theirs. Don't go accusing me of playing favorites."

"And what about Chad?" Olivia smiled, adroitly moving to a lighter note. "No big eight-by-ten glossy of that handsome hunk next to all the old-timers?"

"Not even a three-by-five. He's camera-shy."

"Interesting man, Beth." Olivia smiled and nodded. "I really like him. And he seems somehow very right for you."

Beth laughed, but Olivia heard no joy in the sound. "If I were poor, Aunt Liv, maybe we'd have a good shot at happily ever after. As it is..." She shrugged and attempted a smile.

"I know what you mean, darling." Trying to tease her out of her suddenly bleak mood, Olivia added, "Why don't I ask Jean-Pierre to give him some lessons on how to become a happy parasite. That could work, don't you think?"

"What I think is that we'd better not let those two within a mile of each other." The words were said jokingly, but Olivia knew that Beth couldn't have been more serious.

"Wretched child," grinned Olivia. "Come sit beside me," she said, scooting her slim frame toward the center of the bed along with her tray to make room. She brushed away a wayward auburn curl from Beth's forehead, smiling when the stubborn lock returned to mar the perfection of that smooth brow.

"I worry about you, my love. You're always so giving. Learn to save a little for yourself some of the time, okay?" She cradled Beth's shoulders in a quick hug. "Now please, go on home, think about Bimini, and call that wonderful man who adores you. You tell me it's his pride that's getting in the way of a lasting relationship." She kissed Beth's temple. "Seems to me your pride might be an issue too. Don't let it be, darling. Pride is poor company on a cold night."

"I'll think about it," said Beth. "That's all I can promise." Beth kissed her aunt's cheek and said good-bye. She was headed to her own apartment, but agreed to return to Olivia's for dinner at six.

A mailbox stuffed with junk mail, a depressingly silent apartment, and no message from Chad on her land line had her seeking the comfort of her own bed within minutes of getting home. She slept away most of the afternoon.

Still feeling a little loggy from her long nap, she arrived at Olivia's townhouse promptly at six, looking forward to a few hours alone with her aunt. Olivia herself answered the door when she rang.

"Well don't you look smashing," said Beth, admiring her aunt's glossy good looks. "Great PJ's," she teased, referring to her turquoise designer lounging outfit. As always when with Olivia or Diana, Beth felt fashion-challenged. Her tan cashmere sweater and slacks looked positively drab next to what Olivia was wearing.

"Merci bien, cherie" laughed Olivia. After quickly locking the front door and resetting the alarm, she gave Beth a big hug and tucked an arm in hers as they made their way into the living room. "Our first course has already been delivered, and the rest of our dinner should be here in half an hour. Let's relax over some wine and cheese while we wait." Olivia gestured to a lavish display on the cocktail table. "I thought you might be hungry."

"And you were right." She was ravenous.

Olivia never cooked and seldom even boiled water for tea. When her staff wasn't around, the best caterers and restaurants in town obligingly delivered to her door. Beth hadn't eaten since breakfast, and the warm Brie was calling her name.

Olivia sat beside her on the sofa and poured their favorite Cristal champagne. Raising her glass, she toasted, "To our missing musketeer," her voice catching on the words. "God keep her safe."

Beth couldn't remember the last time she'd heard Olivia utter anything that even remotely resembled a prayer. Her aunt's words, that little catch in her voice, and the tears glistening in her eyes, told Beth that she knew everything. Paul had to have told her about Diana after all. "You suddenly getting religion, Aunt Liv?"

Olivia gave a sad little smile. "Just hedging my bets, darling." She took a few sips of Cristal and decided it was well past time to end the pretense, professional advice be damned. "You know, if I actually thought it would help Diana, I'd go to church, say novenas, wear a hairshirt, make a pilgrimage... whatever. Unfortunately, I suppose you have to believe in all those things before they work for you, and I just can't suspend my disbelief long enough to con God into thinking I'm one of the faithful."

Beth took a deep breath, holding it for a moment before sighing it out. "How long have you known, Aunt Liv?" The words were softly spoken, but Olivia felt the sting of the lash behind them.

"Pretty much since the beginning," she admitted. "Paul told me about it a few days after Diana was diagnosed." She took a long drink of champagne. "Oh, don't look at me like that, Beth. I wasn't here sooner because..."

"Because of Jean-Pierre." Beth didn't even try to hide her disgust.

Olivia shook her head sadly. "I suppose I had that one coming. But no. It wasn't because of Jean-Pierre. I just used him as an excuse."

"An excuse for what?" Under any other circumstances, Olivia would have been glad to hear the harshness in Beth's voice. She had always feared the child wasn't as tough as a Gresham needed to be. Clearly she was wrong.

"An excuse for going completely to pieces, love. It took the doctors all this time to put me and my fluttery little heart back together again. I was a basket case. In and out of the hospital, half the time drugged to the gills and totally unable to function for weeks." Beth was already in her arms, holding her tight, each of them in tears. "I came as soon as I could, dear heart." She went on to explain the course of her treatment, glossing over the worst of it, comforting Beth with reassurances that she was now completely recovered.

"But why all the secrecy? Why didn't you at least tell me?"

Olivia cradled Beth against her shoulder and pressed her cheek into the soft auburn curls. "You already had more than enough to deal with, love. I'm not totally self-indulgent, you know."

"Oh, Aunt Liv, I..."

"Hush. Hush, child. I know your heart as well as my own. There's no need to say another word about it."

When they had both exhausted their tears, Beth drew away from Olivia, studying her aunt's face as if she were really seeing it for the first time. "I love you so much."

"And I love you, Sweetheart." Placing her hands on Beth's shoulders, she backed away far enough to see clearly into those beautiful emerald eyes that had always seemed so much wiser than their years. "There'll be time enough for tears, and that time will come all too soon, Beth. Right now, tonight, let's just enjoy being together."

She kissed Beth's cheek and pulled away, managing a shaky but mischievous smile. "Not to mention this wonderful champagne," she added, topping off their glasses.

Beth gulped her drink, needing it, grateful for every anesthetizing drop. "It's been a nightmare trying to keep Diana's secret, but she insisted on telling you herself."

"I thought as much," she nodded. "And when do you suppose that might have happened?" Her smile was gentle, and full of sadness.

"Soon. Very soon," said Beth, knowing that neither of them really believed it. "Meanwhile,

I've been blundering my way along, grasping at straws. Once I even suggested that we start going to church. You should have heard her."

Olivia laughed. "I can just imagine."

"I never mentioned it again, I can tell you. Though I have stayed on her case about seeing a psychiatrist. No luck there either. She's been relying on psychics instead."

Liv shook her head, anger and sadness reflected in her eyes. "For years, psychics have been playing our vulnerable little Diana like a Stradivarius. Ariana 's just the latest in a long line of charlatans that began with Lily Verne."

"I don't think…" Beth was about to speak in Ariana's defense, but the front bell interrupted her.

"There's dinner. I'll get it." Olivia checked the peephole and disarmed the security system before opening the door to one of the Dunsford guards assigned to the brownstone. She stood aside while he ushered in two young busboys wheeling a serving cart, the VIP treatment accorded only to their restaurant's most preferred customers.

At Olivia's direction, they set the trays on the dining room sideboard, looked unabashedly pleased and surprised by the generosity of the tips she gave them, then clumsily bowed their way out the door. No doubt their employer had instructed them in this final act of deference, but had neglected to tell them that one bow would suffice. They almost fell over one another before they closed the door behind them. Even Dunsford's usually dour-faced agent couldn't help chuckling as he watched them drive off.

The food smelled wonderful, and Beth felt like a kid in a candy store as she uncovered each offering, delighted when she saw that Olivia had remembered some of her favorites: clams casino, pate en croute, lobster bisque, trout almondine, artichokes vinaigrette, tournedos rossini, and tarragon potatoes. Dessert was a sumptuous confection so layered with fluffy dollops of cream that there was no way of knowing what it was, but it looked amazing.

It was a festive meal and, by tacit agreement, all mention of Diana's illness was avoided. Olivia did most of the talking, an arrangement which suited both of them very well, since she had little appetite and Beth couldn't seem to eat fast enough. 'Remember when' rapidly became the most overused phrase at the table that night, and they each abused it shamelessly, as they shared fond memories of happier times.

They were pouring coffee and lustfully eyeing dessert at the dining room sideboard, when the telephone rang. Olivia went to answer it on the kitchen extension, presumably for privacy, while Beth assembled a dessert tray and brought it into the living room. She set it down on the coffee table in front of the sofa and immediately helped herself to a slice of the mysterious cake.

It tasted even better than it looked, and she finished a good-sized piece in record time.

Olivia laughed when she returned a few minutes later and saw the crumbs on her niece's dish. "That good, huh?"

"Wonderful." Beth topped off their coffee from the silver carafe on the tray. "You absolutely have to try this cake, Aunt Liv. It's incredible! And you've hardly eaten a thing all night." Beth was already cutting a piece for her, plus another for herself.

"Thanks, dear." Olivia took the heaping plate and the dessert fork Beth passed to her, and wasted no time sampling the cake, first a small nibble, then a real bite. "Oh my, that is good, isn't it?" After one more bite, she immediately put the plate back on the coffee table, pushing it away at arm's distance. Olivia worked hard to keep her tiny frame fit and trim, and she wasn't going to allow a treacherous palate to sabotage her efforts, especially not the night before Jean-Pierre's arrival.

Beth was curious about the lengthy phone call that had just transpired, but she didn't want to pry. If it concerned Diana, Olivia would have told her. If it didn't, it was none of her business.

A short time later, the telephone rang again, and once more Olivia took it in the kitchen. By the time she returned, several minutes had passed, completely annihilating Beth's polite resolve. The moment she returned, Beth asked, "Are you running a bookie joint here, or what?"

Olivia smiled. "I'm sorry, dear. Both calls were from Paul. And, yes, I did tell him about what Ariana said last night. I just didn't want to tell you half the story, and I needed that second call to fill in some of the blanks." She took a quick sip of her tepid coffee, then refilled her own cup and Beth's. The china was exquisite, the cup design elegant, but the coffee went cold so quickly in the dainty cups that even Olivia sometimes regretted the absence of a single mug in the house. As a matter of principle, she'd never allowed it, but she was starting to think she might need to revise those orders to her staff. She took a deep breath and began recapping what she'd just learned from Paul.

"A few years ago, the Chaetestown police actually had a complaint about a group of people seen cavorting naked in the woods. Apparently there was a bright full moon and they were spotted by some teenagers having a quiet little party of their own nearby. The kids went in for a closer look and started giggling so hard at what they described as 'a bunch of old wrinklies' that they scared the group off before any positive ID's could be made. Paul's second call confirmed that one of the descriptions they gave could easily have been Devane."

"What happened? Were they arrested?"

Olivia shook her head. "The kids had been drinking, so their testimony was suspect. And evidently Devane is a local celebrity of sorts. I suppose bringing him in for questioning would have really been awkward for everybody concerned, so the investigation never even got off the ground. They just filed the report and forgot about it."

"That's crazy! The guy's got a drug record, for God's sake. Why wouldn't they at least …?"

"Sealed records from juvy court don't count, Beth. Being a Satanist is no crime, and running buck naked through the woods isn't exactly a major felony."

"I just can't believe the Chaetestown police didn't even check into it."

"Well believe it. They didn't. But Paul did manage to turn up a very interesting fact: one of the kids actually counted how many of them he saw."

Knowing where this was headed, Beth shook her head miserably. "Let me guess, Aunt Liv. Thirteen, right?"

Olivia sighed and nodded her response.

Beth didn't intend to spoil her aunt's reunion with Jean-Pierre by telling her what she planned to do, but she knew she would be leaving for Windham first thing in the morning, no matter how vehemently Paul objected to it.

My entire life's work comes to fruition tonight.

The Light will yield to the Dark Lord's might.

Chapter Sixteen

By five o'clock the next morning, Beth was already on the New York State Thruway headed for Windham. She'd waited until she was on the road to leave voicemails for Olivia and Paul, avoiding their direct emergency lines for the same reason that she hadn't told Olivia about her decision the night before. She needed to be with Diana, and she simply didn't want any discussion or argument about it. She was glad that Martha Hastings had called a few days earlier to apologize for having to cancel their weekend dinner plans. Right now, Beth's entire focus had to be on Diana.

Hours later, when Olivia awoke and listened to her message, she immediately telephoned Paul. After comparing notes about the voicemails they'd each received, Paul told her to stay right where she was and not even think about going upstate. He made it clear that her presence in Windham would only create more problems by forcing him to assign staff to guard her, when their focus needed to be only on her nieces. When he promised to notify her the moment there was anything new to report, she stopped arguing with him.

Olivia was a born courtesan who had long ago happily resigned herself to the fact that sex was as vital to her well-being as the air she breathed. Right now, Paul had basically given her only one option: stay home! And what a lovely option it was right now! She would spend the day with Jean-Pierre until Paul gave her the okay to go up to Windham.

Checking the ormolu clock above the mantel in her bedroom, she saw that she had two hours to prepare for her young lover's arrival. She went into the bathroom to fill the Jacuzzi, tossed her nightgown in the hamper, then focused a critical eye on her reflection in the brutally honest floor-to-ceiling mirrors that lined the walls. The few nips and tucks she'd had done over the years had served her well, but the mileage was starting to show, and she knew it. Still, she had good reason to be satisfied with the three-sixty view, and she knew that too.

Taking a deep breath, she willed herself to relax and stop thinking about what might be happening with Beth and Diana. She firmly believed that worry was just asking for something bad to happen, and besides, the last thing she needed today was another worry line. Paul was like a second father to her girls, and he would keep them safe, just as he always had.

Paul Dunsford was as close to a soulmate as any man Olivia had ever known. He was attractive, intelligent, available, and eminently heterosexual, as she clearly remembered from all the teenage groping that went on during their summers at Newport, yet they'd never been lovers. Her track record with men was so abysmal that she'd never wanted to put their friendship at risk with a roll of the sexual dice. He was her anchor, always there to keep her and her babes safe in any storm, the only man she'd ever truly needed in her life.

When she had first hired Paul to track down an errant lover -- had it really been thirty years ago? -- he was a brash and angry young man, still licking his wounds after being forced out of the New York City Police Department. Technically, he knew he deserved it. Morally? Well, at least he had the satisfaction of knowing that, if he had it all to do over, he would do precisely the same thing.

As a detective on the homicide squad at Manhattan South, one of the youngest men ever to achieve that rank, he had been called in to investigate the murder of a child, a seven year-old girl whose fragile young body had been brutalized, raped and dismembered. Weeks later, when a suspect was found, Paul conducted the interrogation. It began routinely enough, with Paul's incisive questions eliciting no response from the sullen man before him, but he persisted, chipping away at the man's resistance long into the night until the dam of silence finally broke.

The suspect admitted his guilt, but he didn't stop there. He began to brag about his crime, boasting of how horrified the child had been when he showed her his penis and forced her to caress it, laughing at the memory of the look on the little girl's face when he jammed his engorged flesh into her.

The cretin had then begun describing the terrified child's screams, her futile attempts to escape the orgy of rape and sodomy, his frustration when she lost consciousness and couldn't struggle against him any longer. Without her screaming and writhing to feed his perverted arousal, he became infuriated by his own impotence and began hacking at the child with a butcher knife.

Paul Dunsford's face had been a mask of stone throughout the litany of horror, but when the confession had been recorded, when they had all the incriminating statements they needed and still the man continued to exult over how he had killed the child, insisting that she had deserved it 'for ending the party,' something deep within Paul snapped.

Remembering the frail and violated torso he'd found at the crime scene, the small decapitated head with its blood-matted hair, a mother's love unmistakable in every careful plait of the ribboned braids that had somehow remained intact throughout the horror of the little girl's agony, Paul lunged at the killer and slammed his fist into the leering and unrepentant smirk that he knew must have taunted the child until she drew her last terrified breath.

The murderer happened to be black, and Paul was white, as was the victim. The newspapers made a racial incident out of the coincidence, and charges of police brutality were brought against him. But it was an era that hadn't yet exalted murderer's rights to a sacrosanct level, and Paul was spared criminal prosecution.

At first, his buddies in the department were supportive, but they backed away in the glare of the sustained media blitz about the case. Paul soon found himself very much alone, without even a family to sustain him. He'd been married to his job and, except for occasional clandestine phone calls from his mother, all contact with his socially prominent Boston family had ceased the day he first entered the police academy.

To minimize his parents' embarrassment over his working-class aspirations, Paul had chosen to live and work in New York, rather than Boston; but even his own mother stopped calling when the national tabloids began sensationalizing his case. Reporters continued to dog his heels until he resigned from the police department, tried and convicted by the press. They were the darkest days of his life.

Olivia had known Paul since childhood. The Greshams and Dunsfords had shared adjoining stretches of beach at Newport each summer, and they'd been friends for as long as either of them could remember. When Paul was forced to leave the NYPD, it was Olivia who stood by him, encouraging him to use his skills to become a private investigator, loaning him the money to open his business, becoming his first customer, and touting his expertise amongst her friends, effectively establishing an instant and highly lucrative client base for him.

Whenever she needed him, Paul was there for her, and she never doubted that he always would be. With him watching over Beth and Diana, she knew it was foolish for her to worry. Even if dicey cell tower coverage in the mountains interfered with phone calls, Paul had a secure direct line to the senior agent on duty outside her brownstone. One way or another, he would get through to her in an emergency.

Stepping into the tub, letting the Jacuzzi work its magic, Olivia used familiar yoga breathing techniques to clear her mind of worry and focus only on her reunion with Jean-Pierre. Puckered skin was definitely not on the agenda for tonight, so she didn't linger in the Jacuzzi. After drying off, she applied scented moisturizer to her entire body, then dried and styled her hair in casual waves before sitting at her dressing table and carefully applying her makeup. As she glanced once more at the ormolu clock, a little shiver of anticipation danced along her spine. She had arranged for a chauffeured limousine service that wasn't part of the Gresham travel fleet to meet Jean-Pierre at Kennedy Airport, and he would be at her door within the hour.

Humming happily, she discarded the soft terrycloth robe she had huddled into after her bath and slipped into a pale blue satin lounging robe with a neckline that plunged almost to her waist. She usually wore a nightgown underneath it, but not today. Just two finishing touches, pale sapphire studs at her ears and high-heeled blue satin mules on her slender feet, and she was ready for a final critical inspection in front of the chevale mirror in her bedroom. Once she was reassured that she wasn't making a fool of herself and that she had achieved exactly the effect she was going for, she smiled knowingly at her reflection.

Everything about her appearance was an open invitation to swift and sure seduction, precisely what she intended it to be. Lingerie was what her attentive lover would expect her to be wearing at this hour of the day, and she didn't want him thinking that she was prepared to sacrifice any part of her routine for him. He knew she was in the habit of staying up half the night and sleeping until early afternoon. He also knew that there were no demure granny gowns in her wardrobe. With all that could be happening upstate right now, she actually would have preferred being fully dressed and ready to bolt out the door the moment Paul okayed it. But Jean-Pierre knew nothing of Diana's current situation, and she intended to keep it that way.

She was never quite sure how Jean-Pierre had become so skilled in the art of love. He was so young, not even thirty yet, and so deliciously insatiable that his patience was always a wonder to her. From their first time together, he had satisfied her in ways that she'd never experienced with any other man.

With long lingering caresses, he'd stoked little fires all over her body, his mouth setting them ablaze, gratifying her with blissful release until she was weak with pleasure. Only then had he considered his own need. He'd entered her gently at first, slowly, deeply, the enormity of his arousal titillating her every nerve ending, intensifying the tempo and power of his thrusts until a fierce climax consumed them both.

When it was over, he'd held her close in his arms, stroking her smooth shoulders with languid fingers as she lay spent beside him. She'd scarcely had time to catch her breath before the whole sequence was repeated, and not just once.

She had never expected to survive anything like it again in one happy lifetime; but she had underestimated Jean-Pierre's endurance, as well as her own. One magical night hadn't been enough for either of them and, almost a year later, they still hadn't quite had their fill of one another. Olivia smiled with anticipation. Because of her illness, it had been two long months since she'd been in his arms.

He had asked her to marry him the last time they were together, and he was still waiting for an answer. Playing the demure damsel, a role so alien to her that it had been nauseating to act the part, she had asked for a little time to consider her answer. Just a few days later, when Paul told her about Diana, she had collapsed and been rushed to the hospital, and she'd never confided in Jean-Pierre about any of it. Telling her young lover that she was falling apart simply wasn't going to happen. She'd told him she needed a separation of a few months to think over her answer, and left it at that. If he was foolish enough to force the issue now, she knew they would both regret it. She would honestly, sadly, have to tell him goodbye.

Fact was that she'd never had any intention of legalizing their arrangement. He was twenty-six, literally half her age, and the bedrock of their relationship thus far had been unbridled lust, nothing even remotely akin to love. When the time came to go their separate ways, Jean-Pierre was certain to make a dramatic exit, pretending that she had broken his heart, and she would try very hard not to hurt his feelings by laughing at his performance. She knew that he must already be scoping out her successor and probably had begun to do so the moment she had hesitated to accept his proposal.

Olivia shook off the image of Jean-Pierre in another woman's bed. With any luck, he wouldn't insist on an answer to his proposal while he was here in New York. If he did, his bad timing would deprive them both of a great deal of pleasure. They had today and tonight, if that, depending on what she might hear from Paul and when. She would be on her way upstate the moment he okayed it.

Hearing the merry chime of the doorbell, she drew aside the curtains of her bedroom window and gave a small shout of glee when she saw the silver limousine double-parked in front of her house. She had given Mrs. Meares two more days off with pay and, for the first time since returning to New York, she was glad that the rest of her household staff was still in Switzerland. She descended the stairs as swiftly as her high-heeled slippers would allow. Flinging wide the front door, she laughed with sheer happiness as she fell into Jean-Pierre's arms, all sensible resolve forgotten as they kissed.

For a few moments, the world beyond them ceased to exist, but practical considerations soon intruded in the form of a chauffeur waiting to carry the luggage inside. The lovers were squarely blocking the entrance, and there was no way around them. He coughed discreetly, and they jumped apart as if amazed and shocked to find another being in Paradise. After depositing the leather suitcase just inside the door, the driver received an inordinately generous tip from Jean-Pierre and went away a happy man, his mind already embellishing the story he'd soon be telling his buddies back at the garage. His wife would know what you call that flimsy thing the woman was wearing, but he wasn't about to ask her. 'Flimsy thing' would do for the guys.

Jean-Pierre closed and bolted the front door, leaving the alarm code to Olivia. Her hands were trembling so much that she had to reset it half-way through the process and begin keying in the sequence again, all of which gave him plenty of time to disconnect the phone at the hall extension. They'd long ago agreed to keep their cellphones muted whenever they were together, and he also wanted no interruptions from a landline today. As she turned to face him, he swept her into his arms and carried her upstairs, his unerring instinct for seduction and the telltale scent of her favorite fragrance guiding him directly to her bedroom.

He lowered her onto the bed and bent to kiss her again, then quickly pulled away, knowing that they could go no further until he'd complied with her absurdly fastidious ground rules. "Un moment, cherie," he whispered, quickly detouring to the bathroom to wash off the worst of the airport grime. As always, it amused him that such a shamelessly sexual creature as Olivia could be so scrupulous about basic hygiene.

Within minutes, he was leaning over her once again, his tongue warm in her mouth, his hands kneading her breasts through the creamy satin of her dressing gown. Knowing how it aroused her to watch him take off his clothes, he began to undress. He didn't do it theatrically, but slowly enough to entice, until he stood proudly naked before her.

As she reached out to touch him, he kissed her hand, pushed aside her dressing gown, and used his lips, hands and tongue to mark a searing a path along her body. Even when her soft moans told him that he needn't wait any longer, he continued pleasuring her. She had always been very obliging about oral sex, giving at least as passionately as she received, but this was a gift he would not expect her to return, not this time, not if he wanted her to agree to marry him.

Holding his own need fiercely in check, he slipped on the condom he'd left on her bedside table, straddled her slender hips, and moved deeply inside her, pacing his rhythm to suit hers. They were soon caught up in a familiar frenzy of desire, climaxing in a staggering moment of perfect bliss, as wondrous as it always was.

Afterward, as they lay together, their limbs entwined, neither of them with the strength or the will to move, Jean-Pierre marveled at the sexuality of the woman beside him. He had been involved with more than his share of young nymphets and women old enough to be their grandmothers before his affair with Olivia began, yet none had ever come close to satisfying him as thoroughly as she managed to do each and every time.

What was it about her that was so different? Her age? Not likely. He'd slept with enough women older than Olivia to know that the skill she brought to her lovemaking was uniquely hers, not just the product of her years. Why then was he so captivated by her? Her looks? Certainly that, but others had been as beautiful.

Was the determining factor really only her money? Possibly. Would he still feel as he did if she were penniless? Probably not, but then he reminded himself that the person he knew as Olivia could never have been nurtured in poverty. Wealth had shaped her entire lifestyle and character, and he could scarcely be blamed for failing to love an impoverished Olivia who would have nothing at all in common with the pampered playgirl he knew and loved. And yes, damn it, he did love her, and not because of her money, but for herself. Of course, it was lovely that she had several billion at her disposal, but that was only the icing on the cake, and a very lovely cake it was.

A few hours later, they made an attempt to bathe and dress, a process considerably delayed by the intoxicating scent of Olivia's bath oil. By the time they actually managed to find their way to the kitchen, it was almost six o'clock, and they were both ravenously hungry. Rather than dress to go out or wait for food to be delivered, they decided to stay home and make do with the remnants of the previous night's feast.

Olivia set out some fruit, cheese and crackers, while Jean-Pierre mixed their martinis. When the edge had been taken off their appetites, they emptied the refrigerator and allowed the microwave oven to serve as their chef for the evening. Jean-Pierre wasn't particularly enchanted with the idea of nuked leftovers, but having Olivia all to himself was more than fair compensation for the annoyance.

They were just about to sit down at the dining room table to enjoy their impromptu smorgasbord when the doorbell rang. Under normal circumstances, Olivia would have simply ignored it; but nothing in her life was normal right now. Dunsford's agent would have already intercepted any unwelcome intruder, so it had to be someone she knew.

Seeing Olivia move towards the door, Jean-Pierre reached for her hand, holding her back. "Let it ring, cherie." They'd been apart for two long months, and he had only begun to make up for lost time.

"Nothing would please me more, but I can't. I'll explain later." As she kissed his cheek, he reluctantly released her hand.

On her way to the door, she glanced in the hall mirror, an instinctive last-minute check for smudged lipstick after being with Jean-Pierre. When she saw her reflection, she laughed. There was no lipstick left to smudge, and she was half-naked, clad only in a flimsy peignoir that concealed very little. The same belated thought had evidently occurred to Jean-Pierre who had just raced out of the dining room to stop her.

"Perhaps I should see to the door, Olivia."

She didn't like the idea, but there didn't seem to be any reasonable alternative. His Lauren sweater, slacks and loafers at least made him presentable enough to be seen by company. She gave a quick nod. "Just stall whoever it is for two minutes. I'll be right back." She flew up the stairs.

Jean-Pierre was delighted that she was allowing him to answer her door. It meant that there was no other man in her life, or she never would have risked a meeting between them. His spirits soared, and he opened the door with a flourish, feeling as if all was suddenly right with his world.

A disinterested third-party observing the scene that followed would have been amused by the mirror-image of expressions playing across the handsome features of the two men who suddenly found themselves face-to-face at Olivia's front door. Surprise, shock and dismay quickly spilled over into overt suspicion and hostility as Jean-Pierre de Monsigny and Chad Martin stood glaring at one another with undisguised malice.

Chad had been at the office all day, and when Beth hadn't phoned by six o'clock, he'd called her cell. When he was kicked straight to voicemail, he left a brief message for her to call him, then tried her landline at home, only to be greeted by her answering machine. He'd left a message there too, then called Olivia's, but her line was busy. When it continued to be busy for more than an hour, he'd left the office and hailed a cab to her townhouse. He guessed that Beth and her sister were back upstate, but if there was any chance at all that Beth was still in the city, he needed to see her right away.

The last thing in the world he wanted to find at Olivia's door was an aristocratic-looking playboy, about his own age or younger, probably younger, definitely much better looking, someone who should have been in the movies and probably was, someone who didn't look at all pleased to see him. Well, buddy, he thought, the feeling's entirely mutual.

As he speculated about who the stranger might be, the cultured French accent did nothing to assuage his fears. He was far too young for Olivia, Chad decided, and, since Diana was only interested in long-dead people these days, it wasn't likely that he was here because of her. That left only Beth. If only he'd called her last night! How stupid could he be to expect her to call him and apologize for what Diana had done? Pretty-boy here sure hadn't wasted any time.

Jean-Pierre was also busily appraising the competition and finding no consolation in the ruggedly handsome face and lean-muscled frame before him. He also didn't like the way Chad's hands kept clenching and unclenching into formidable looking fists at his sides. He was certainly behaving like a jealous lover, but surely anyone acquainted with Olivia knew better than to attempt a surprise entrance.

"I'm Chad Martin, a friend of Beth's. Is she here?" Chad had no way of knowing why the countenance before him suddenly beamed, but the cessation of hostility was immediately apparent. Jean-Pierre grinned broadly, extended his hand, and introduced himself, ushering Chad inside.

"I hope you have not traveled far," said Jean-Pierre. "Beth is not here. If only you had telephoned..."

"I did," snapped Chad. "Several times. The phone's been busy."

"Bizarre," said Jean-Pierre, wrinkling his brow as he hurried to the telephone on the hall table. With his back to Chad to conceal what he was doing, he lifted the phone and reconnected it in one fluid motion. Holding the handset to his ear, he shrugged. "It seems fine."

Even from a few steps away, Chad could hear the dial tone loud and clear. "Glad it's working," he said.

Jean-Pierre gestured for Chad to follow him into the living room. "Olivia's upstairs," he explained, "but she'll be down soon. Let's have a drink while we wait, shall we?"

Chad could smell the food and, given the hour, he knew he was interrupting their dinner. Before he could decline Jean-Pierre's hospitality, however, Olivia came tripping down the stairs in beige slacks and matching cashmere sweater, a healthy glow to her complexion, looking years younger than the woman he had seen just two nights ago. Seeing the intimacy of the glance that passed between her and Jean-Pierre, Chad knew he couldn't get out of there fast enough to suit all of them.

"Sorry to barge in like this, Olivia, but I couldn't get through on your phone and I need to find Beth. She didn't answer her cell or landline, and I was hoping she might be here."

Olivia was already checking the hall phone. Hearing the crisp dial tone, she had a feeling that Jean-Pierre had been up to his old tricks, but she didn't want to make an issue of it now. "Beth's in Windham, Chad." Seeing his crestfallen expression, she quickly added what might have been the truth, although he guessed it was only a kind bit of fiction. "I know she tried to reach you before she left, obviously with no success."

Olivia took his arm and led him toward the dining room. "Jean-Pierre and I..." She stopped and whirled to face both men. "Forgive my manners. You two have introduced yourselves, haven't you?" They both assured her that they had. "Well, fine then," she said, once more taking Chad's arm. "We were just about to have dinner, and I insist that you join us."

"I think not, Olivia. Really, I..."

"But you must. It's only pot-luck, as you can see, but it's certainly a great deal more than

Jean-Pierre and I could ever eat. And besides, you couldn't deprive me of the opportunity to dine with two of the most handsome men in New York."

Chad looked at the groaning table, and smiled at Olivia's concept of 'pot-luck,' a smile she interpreted as one of acceptance.

"Good. It's settled then. Jean-Pierre, a drink for our guest. Bourbon on the rocks, isn't it, Chad?"

Chad was impressed by the woman's memory. Probably a little finishing school trick, he supposed, part of the curriculum in 'Quintessential Hostess 101.' Well, the peons had a few tricks up their bargain-store sleeves too. He hated warm bourbon, but tonight he'd drink it and love it.

"Neat, please." Seeing Jean-Pierre's questioning look, he added. "Bourbon, but no ice, if you don't mind."

Olivia acknowledged the correction with a tilting nod of her head, her smile and the twinkle in her eyes making it very clear to Chad that she had seen through his childish ploy. He felt like a fool when he nearly gagged on his first sip of the always excellent Maker's Mark, but Olivia truly was the perfect hostess. She covered his embarrassment with deft conversation, and he began to like the woman in spite of himself.

Chad made his excuses immediately after dinner, pleading yet another Newsworld deadline as his reason for declining coffee and dessert. In reality, their evident blissful cohabitation had depressed him mightily, and he was eager to escape their secret smiles and intimate glances. He had already learned all that Olivia was prepared to tell him about Beth, and there was no reason to linger on and be reminded of all the reasons why he and her niece could never have a future together.

Money talked loud and clear. It always had; it always would; and only a damned fool would believe otherwise. Olivia might defer to Jean-Pierre in small things, as she had occasionally done tonight, allowing him to take the lead when it suited her; but Chad could see that she ruled their relationship with an iron hand. The fact that it was encased in a dainty velvet glove made it only more lethal.

Not that he was sympathetic toward Jean-Pierre. Chad saw him as nothing more than a parasite living off whatever crumbs Olivia chose to throw his way. Overall, he guessed it was a very satisfactory arrangement for the guy, but Chad knew he could never endure anything like it. From certain references made during dinner, it was clear that Jean-Pierre was wealthy in his own right, at least by Chad's standards, and still the Gresham money made him nothing more than Olivia's lackey. His own case was completely hopeless. Chad walked the few blocks it took to hail a cab on Madison, then went home to drink himself into a mindless stupor.

Some of us are nervous about Sam roaming freely through the tunnels right now.

Not me.

He's a thoroughly trained attack dog, Cerberus incarnate.

Our used-to-be- fearless-and-sane leader is convinced that some dead woman will try to sabotage the Ostara ceremony tonight, so he's pulled out all the stops to defend against her.

Madness, of course.

He should be worried about the very real threat of discovery that grows each day.

All these damn nature lovers fleeing the cities and trekking through our woods!

They're cropping up like ants everywhere!

At least, thanks to Sam, we'll be safe tonight.

Whatever happens, only the coven will bear witness to it.

Any intruder who happens to stumble upon our ceremony will not live to tell tales.

Yay, Sam!

With our High Priest worried only about threats from the great beyond, the rest of us need all the help we can get.

Chapter Seventeen

While Chad was at home drowning his ego in bourbon, definitely on the rocks this time, Beth was struggling to keep warm in the woods across from the Briggs tannery, huddled with Diana and Charlie behind the same boulder that had concealed them from Devane three days earlier. They had been crouched there since nightfall, an old stadium blanket from Charlie's car trunk their only insulator from the rapidly freezing ground.

"I don't get it," whispered Diana, rubbing her hands together for warmth. "They should be here by now." No Nikon this time. Tonight, she'd be getting the job done with the cellphone she'd tucked into her jacket pocket. Its camera had everything technology could offer in a small package, and it was all set to zoom in for closeups of the coven as they arrived. Unfortunately, so far, there'd been no one to photograph.

Henry was convinced that Lenore had written a pack of lies about Richard Hastings in her diary, and Diana needed something, anything, to prove that it wasn't all smoke and mirrors. She still hadn't told Beth and Charlie that there even was a diary. Until Henry vouched for its authenticity, they would only fear even more for her sanity if she so much as hinted about some of the horrendous passages in it.

Charlie checked the luminous dial on his watch. "Eleven-fifteen. We'll give it one more hour, not a minute longer. Then we're out of here, ladies." Nobody gave him an argument. With an empty coffee thermos, a bag of doughnuts that had been reduced to crumbs, and no indication of anything at all suspicious going on at the old tannery tower, even Diana could think of no reason to continue their vigil beyond twelve-fifteen.

Beth saw her sister edge a little closer to Charlie's reassuring bulk, and she couldn't help but smile when she heard his contented little sigh. Charlie was in his element, an ex-cop on stakeout, seemingly impervious to frost, discomfort and boredom, his focus seldom wavering from the tower door. The fact that the woman who'd stolen his heart had just snuggled up against him was a bonus beyond anything ever promised him back in the days at the police academy.

Glancing at the two of them, Beth could only marvel at the wonders of random selection. The blind stab of a pencil point at a page in a telephone directory, and voila: enter Charlie Hobson. Maybe Diana was right. Maybe there were no coincidences. However it had come about, by accident or by some cosmic master plan, she could only be grateful that this wonderful guy had come into her sister's life, his solid common sense a steady counterweight to her increasingly unpredictable mood swings and memory lapses.

The decision to return to the tower, a place Diana had sworn never to revisit, had caught Beth and Charlie completely off guard. It had happened over coffee earlier that night after dinner at a comfortable little steakhouse in Windham. Beth and Charlie were trading sections of the Albany Times Union and USA Today, while Diana thumbed through an old witches' almanac she had just found at a second-hand bookstore in Catskill.

They had spent most of the afternoon exploring antiquarian bookseller shops in Albany, Hudson and Catskill, hoping to find more information about the Mowbrays, but they'd returned empty-handed, except for newspapers, a beautifully preserved Whittier first edition, and a tattered almanac. Beth had just begun to unwind after all the miles she'd logged that day, when her sister's excited voice suddenly shattered her relaxed mood.

"I can't believe I forgot what today is!" Balancing the almanac in the palm of her left hand, she turned it so that Beth and Charlie could read the ornate typeface that she was jabbing at with her right index finger. "Look!"

When they saw that it was a list of witches' festivals called 'sabbats,' Charlie rolled his eyes and groaned, while Beth rubbed the back of her neck and sighed. Diana was pointing to an entry identified as 'Ostara,' the vernal equinox, which was, in fact that day, March 20th.

"Come on, you guys," she cried, determined to rally the troops. "It's showtime!" Leaping up from her chair, Diana scooped up her jacket and purse. "Let's head back to my place right now so we can grab some stuff, Charlie. Move it, Beth!" She hurried out of the restaurant.

"What was that all about?" asked Charlie, his all-too familiar beleaguered basset-hound expression firmly in place.

"Go ask her," said Beth, waving him ahead. "I'll take care of the check." She had seen the look in Diana's eyes and knew that it could only mean one thing. She also knew how pointless it would be to try steering her out of the one-eighty she had just skidded into, but Charlie would need to find that out for himself.

The moment she stepped outside, she heard them arguing from across the parking lot. "This is the nuttiest stunt you've ever come up with," shouted Charlie. They'd gone together in Charlie's Taurus that afternoon, and he was literally going to be in the driver's seat momentarily. "You swore you were never going anywhere near that damn place again, remember, Diana? Have you completely lost your mind?" Beth cringed. He still knew nothing about Diana's illness, so he had no idea how close to the mark he had struck.

Diana's eyes were flashing fire. "Don't you dare use that high-and-mighty tone with me, Charlie Hobson! Just who the hell do you think you are?" Dismissing him with a scathing look, she turned and looked for support from her sister who was now standing right beside her. Silently refusing the bait, Beth reached out a hand to touch the rear door and gave Charlie the high sign of a jutted chin to unlock it. As soon as she heard the lock release, she opened the door and settled herself behind the front passenger seat, clicking on her seatbelt while Diana just stood where she was and quietly fumed.

Diana dearly wished that her Porsche was around so she could stalk away from both of them. As it was, she had no choice but to huff her way into the passenger seat after giving Charlie a final blistering gaze.

Before pulling out of the parking lot, Charlie tried one more plea for sanity. He and Diana argued, of course, and Beth stayed out of it. With every word, Diana was making it patently clear that nobody was going to stop her from photographing the coven in action tonight. She was sure there would be an Ostara gathering, and she was determined to document it.

Beth bit back any objections, partially because she knew she'd be wasting her breath, but mostly because Diana's tirade was revealing bits and pieces of things she hadn't known anything about until now. She would have continued her silence if she hadn't become concerned about Charlie having a coronary. When the color in his face turned from fuchsia to crimson, she knew it was time to intervene. For whatever reason, or maybe for no reason at all beyond brain cells run amok, getting pictures of John Devane in some sinister act had become critically important to her sister, and Beth knew that arguing about it was pointless.

"Give it up, will you, Charlie? We're not going to talk Diana out of going back there tonight. You know it. I know it. She knows it. So let's all just shut up and get the damn photo shoot from hell over with."

Hours later, as the temperature kept dropping, she could only be thankful that Diana had at least listened to Charlie about what to wear that night. Even with thermal underwear, wool slacks, heavy wool parkas, ski hats and gloves, she was really cold from complete inactivity.

A seasoned native, Charlie seemed untouched by the elements. Watching him look after her sister, anticipating her every need and want, Beth knew it had to be Diana's nearness that kept him warm. She just wished he hadn't been so maniacally overprotective about the cars that had been following them earlier.

On their way back to Diana's after dinner, even in the elusive shadows of twilight, Charlie had immediately picked up on the fact that two men in a blue compact were never far behind them. Beth had assured him that it was almost certainly routine Dunsford surveillance, but Diana managed to goad him into a game of cat and mouse. With her cheering him on, he easily lost the blue compact by detouring off on a series of back roads. Her "Yay, Charlie!" had been music to his ears.

An hour later, after grabbing some warm clothes from the stash of changes he always kept in his car trunk, the three of them had hurried into the Taurus and headed out for Devane's place. They were cruising along Route 23 toward the Old Chaetestown Road, when Charlie spotted yet another tail, this time a gray compact. Remembering what Olivia had said about Diana's surveillance being triple-teamed, Beth was virtually certain that these were also Paul's agents, but Ariana's warnings had been dire enough to warrant extra caution now. She immediately telephoned Paul's emergency line.

Unfortunately, Charlie had ducked off the main highway at the first opportunity, and her cellphone was no match for the dense canopy of tall trees along the winding mountain road he had found. She heard Paul's dispatcher answer the phone, but the connection cut in and out so often that it was impossible to tell how much of what she was saying was actually understood.

Hoping for the best, she spoke as loudly and clearly as she could. "I can't hear you, but if you can hear me, please get an immediate message to Paul that Beth and Diana are being followed by a gray compact somewhere between Route 23 and the Old Chaetestown Road near Windham. Before this, there was a blue compact tailing us. We're on our way to John Devane's place at the old Briggs tannery tower in Chaetestown. Please ask Paul to confirm that these are your people. Repeat. Ask Paul to confirm that your people are following us. We're..."

She gave up as the connection dissolved into a steady stream of static. She tried redialing when they came to a high point in the road, but it was useless. Even text messaging wouldn't go through. Nothing was penetrating the heavily forested mountains of shale that surrounded them.

As far as Charlie was concerned, with two of the richest women in the world riding in his car and no all-clear from Dunsford, he wasn't about to presume that their pursuers were harmless. They were really good, but he was better, and this was his home turf.

It took almost an hour of crisscrossing and backtracking, but he finally managed to lose the gray compact by ducking onto a narrow dirt road that appeared like a gift from the gods just beyond the curve of a particularly steep hill. It was the beginning of the approach to the Mohican Trail, a dangerous road full of sharp turns, hills and switchbacks that obscured all but immediate oncoming traffic. Watching their pursuers sail by them, Charlie smiled. "Okay to breathe again, ladies. By the time those jokers realize they've been had, they'll be in Massachusetts."

Diana stomped her feet and crowed, "That's my man – great job, Charlie!" As far as she was concerned, if they weren't Paul's guys, they certainly weren't friends, so losing them was all good. And, if they were working for Paul, it was even sweeter to beat them at their own game. Either way, Diana saw it as completely win-win. Beth didn't know whether to scream or cry.

They were doing precisely the posted twenty-five-mile-an-hour speed limit along the Old Chaetestown Road, as they passed the tower and continued on to the quarry. A loop of broken macadam encircled the old quarry like the hub of a battered bicycle wheel, its spokes a series of old hauling roads that had long since fallen into disrepair. Charlie decided to park further out than he had on their last trip to the tower, and he drove three-quarters of the way around the loop, before tucking the car behind a thicket of overgrown pines and shrubbery near what appeared to be the least dilapidated of the old hauling roads. As a possible escape route, it wasn't much, but it was all he had.

He had just stopped the car when Beth's phone began vibrating against her hip. The readout told her it was Paul, but again she could hear only static, and nothing was coming through as a text message. She shook her head in answer to Charlie's unspoken question, then disconnected and tucked the cellphone back into her pocket. Charlie and Diana both double-checked to make sure their own phones were silenced before they all exited the car. Following Charlie's lead, they backtracked through the woods, arriving at their observation post across the road from the tower shortly after dark.

For four hours now, they'd been watching for something to happen at the tower, and Beth had long since decided that the guys in the gray compact had gotten the better part of the bargain, by far. Cramped and cold behind the boulder, she looked up at the night sky for some distraction from her misery. It was a clear night, with a brilliant sky, ideal for picking out the constellations, if she could. Not for the first time in her life, she wondered if she had been born with some strange mental defect that always prevented her from seeing the figures the stars were supposed to represent. She could always find the North Star and the dippers, but nothing else, apart from an occasional brilliant Venus or Jupiter and reddish Mars.

It always seemed so simple when she looked at an astronomer's diagram with all the lines neatly drawn between the stars, but she'd never seen a crab or a bull actually glittering in the night sky. And as for Diana's Leo? No way. She was just tearing her gaze away from the reassuringly recognizable dippers, when she felt Diana's hand squeezing her forearm.

After hours of seeing no other human being apart from one another, it was a shock to actually distinguish the silhouette of a man, presumably John Devane, outlined in the lighted doorway of the tower. But he wasn't alone. Streaking by him and bounding across the lawn in their direction was an enormous dog. Before Diana and Beth could heed their instinct to bolt and run, Charlie grasped their elbows and held them perfectly still. When he was sure they would stay put, he released their arms, gesturing with the downturned palms of his hands for them to be completely motionless and quiet.

Belatedly realizing what Charlie had instantly observed, Beth was embarrassed by her own knee-jerk reaction. They were downwind of the animal and, as long as they didn't move and the wind didn't shift, they would be safe. The slightest sound, however, and the dog would be on them in an instant. It seemed an eternity before they heard the long low whistle that brought the dog loping back to the tower door. As soon as the hulking animal and its master had gone back inside, Charlie got to his feet, taking Beth and Diana with him.

"Let's get the hell out of here," he said. Nobody argued, not even Diana. She was prepared for witches and warlocks, not huge and hostile dogs, her greatest phobia, perhaps her only one. The dog was clearly well-trained and, given what they suspected of its owner, possibly trained to kill. Beth knew they all had to be wondering the same thing. Where had the animal been on their previous two visits to Devane's? Until tonight, blessedly, there had been no sign of it at all.

They were hurriedly gathering up the blanket and all other evidence of their stay when Charlie motioned for them to be very still. "Listen," he whispered. "Do you hear that?"

Beth heard nothing beyond the hammering of her heart and the wind murmuring through the trees, but Diana evidently had heard something more. "Damn straight, I hear it, Charlie."

"Can you make it out?"

Diana gave a small chuckle. "'Course I can. That's chanting, my friend. I knew it! I told you they'd be here tonight!" Diana's voice was a rising squeal of excitement. Regretting the keenness of his own hearing that had alerted her to the sound in the first place, Charlie touched a gentle hand to her mouth. "Not so loud!" he whispered.

"Where's it coming from?" asked Beth.

"The tower," Diana said, her voice considerably quieter than it had been moments ago. "The whole damn coven is probably in there right now."

"But we've been here all night and nobody went in. How…?"

"A tunnel!" Lenore's diary had been very explicit about a tunnel leading from the tannery tower to some remote spot in the woods. But, since Beth and Charlie didn't even know the diary existed, Diana had to pretend it was just a hunch. "That trap door in his living room has to lead somewhere, guys."

Charlie sighed wearily. "I told you before, Diana…"

Beth couldn't believe what she was hearing. "Who cares? Look you two, talk later, move now." She tugged at Diana's arm. "Let's just get out of here!"

"And pass up a chance to video a real-live coven in action? No way!"

"Stop jumping to conclusions," said Charlie, gathering up the last traces of their stay into the blanket. "We don't know there's a coven in there. It could just be Devane listening to some weird tape."

"Devane and his monster dog," said Beth, shamelessly using Diana's fear of the animal against her, anything that would get them all safely out of there.

"Well, we'll find out soon enough, won't we?" said Diana. She broke into a run for the tower.

Charlie would have stopped her, but she was much too quick for him, and calling her back simply wasn't an option. He dropped the blanket and started running, just as Beth sprinted ahead of him. He quickened his pace, and they both reached the tower moments behind Diana.

Charlie immediately began his pantomime for absolute silence, an arm-waving, hand-pumping series of gestures that had grown all too recognizable. The muted sound that Charlie had first heard was now easily recognizable as a chant, just as Diana had said it was, and it was clearly emanating from many voices.

Diana motioned for Charlie to give her a leg up to one of the narrow high windows at the side of the tower where the noise seemed to be concentrated. Charlie shook his head and thumbed a motion for them to leave, but Diana narrowed her eyes menacingly. Even in starlight, the message was clear. If Charlie didn't help her, she'd find an alternate solution. One way or another, she was going to photograph what was happening inside.

Beth could only guess that adrenaline had neutralized the paralyzing fear Diana had felt at the tower the last time they were there. After vowing never to go near the place again, here she was actually touching the building and demanding a boost to see inside. With a sinking heart, Beth wondered if her sister remembered anything at all about that earlier visit.

Charlie braced himself against the base of the tower and laced his hands as a perch for Diana's feet. She scrabbled up his body until she was standing on his shoulders, her ankles in his firm grasp, her hands balanced flat against the side of the tower, as she edged her eyes up over the sill. For a few moments, there was no sound beyond the dim atonal chant inside the walls. Then Charlie heard a soft moan above him.

Before she even had a chance to take the camera out of her jacket pocket, Diana was suddenly dead weight on his shoulders. He instinctively angled his body to break her fall, while Beth leaped between her sister and the brick base of the tower. Diana fell soundlessly, her body cushioned by Charlie and Beth, but the dog was already barking fiercely. His ears hadn't missed that single soft moan.

Charlie scooped Diana up in his arms and immediately broke into a dead run for the woods across the road. Beth was close on his heels, each of them with only one thought, knowing their only hope was to put as much distance as possible between them and the tower before the animal was let loose.

From the cover of the woods, Charlie knew it would be safe to shoot the hound, and he would do it without hesitation or compunction. No one would be the wiser about who had been trespassing on posted property, and they would have nothing to fear by way of reprisal from Devane. Shooting the dog in plain view of Devane, however, was not a scenario Charlie even wanted to consider.

Carrying Diana was slowing him down, but only a fraction. She was small and slight, scarcely more than a child's weight in his arms, and he was able to carry her with ease. He couldn't see Beth, but he knew he could trust her to stay close and not do anything stupid. She was a quick study. She'd take her cue from him and there'd be no unpleasant surprises, not from her at least.

They were almost into the safety of the woods when they heard the tower door open, the sound of the dog's bark now magnified tenfold, allowing Charlie to easily track the animal's path. It was headed straight for them. He tightened his hold on Diana and ran as fast as he could, gasping for breath, every muscle straining to keep his precious burden from falling, his mind feverishly trying to work out the logistics of aiming and firing a gun while carrying her on the run. He knew he couldn't risk it. He might misfire and hurt her. He called Beth's name, just once, and softly, but she was right there, her arms instinctively reaching out for her sister.

Charlie allowed her to shoulder Diana's full weight while he tore the gun from his holster, then quickly reached out his free hand to help support her, heaving a great sigh of relief when he saw Diana's eyelids begin to flutter.

"She's coming to," he said, handing over his car keys to Beth. "Get her out of here," he commanded, his gun already aimed in the direction of the barking dog. "If I'm not right behind you when you get to the car, go, just go, and don't stop until you get her home."

There was no time for noble argument, and Beth knew it. She drew Diana close to her side, encircled the slim waist with a steadying hand, and led her into the cover of the woods.

Charlie waited, gun in hand, while the dog approached. The barking had stopped. The hunter was close and instinctively silent as he narrowed the gap to his prey. Charlie strained to listen for the rustling of the underbrush that would pinpoint the dog's whereabouts, but he heard nothing. Then suddenly the animal appeared, its lunging stride covering the distance between them a split second before Charlie's senses had communicated their urgent message to his brain.

The dog hurled its body at Charlie and went right for his throat, the force of the attack knocking the gun from his hand as the animal wrestled him to the ground and pinned him there. Charlie could feel the fangs against his skin, the animal's hot saliva dripping along the pulsating flesh at the side of his neck. He could only pray that he was at the mercy of a thoroughly well-trained attack dog, a dog who would dutifully wait for one final command before killing his immobilized victim. If that command were given, or if the dog had flunked that particular aspect of his training, Charlie knew he was a dead man.

The dog's weight prevented him from moving, 'though that was the last thing he intended to do. He knew that any shift in position could cause those razor sharp fangs to pierce an artery, and Charlie was too fond of life to risk that. He lay quietly beneath the dog for what seemed a lifetime, but could only have been a few moments, when he was suddenly blinded by a bright light.

Someone, presumably Devane, had a high-beam flashlight focused squarely between his eyes. Charlie heard a brief unintelligible word and, in an instant, the dog had retreated to stand beside its master. Another strange word and the dog sat, a massive silhouette just beyond the beam of the flashlight.

"I'm sorry if my dog startled you," said the voice, "but this is private property and clearly posted to warn off trespassers. Who are you and what are you doing here?"

Startled me? If it weren't for the menace behind the civilized tone, Charlie might have laughed at the understatement. As it was, the guy held all the cards, and this was no time to be a wiseass. He could only be thankful that his gun was still hidden in the darkness just beyond the ring of the flashlight's beam. It was just out of his reach, and he didn't dare attempt to make a grandstand play for it. But there were other ways...

Willing a befuddled glaze into his eyes, he assumed the slouch and swagger of a drunk. He was suddenly very grateful for all those years working undercover in Albany.

"I'm waiting," said Devane. "So is my dog, 'though his patience is wearing a bit thin. I repeat: Who are you and what are you doing here?"

Unlike Beth and Diana, Charlie hadn't had time to go home and change after dinner, so he'd had to rely on some of the emergency clothes he always kept in the trunk of his car to keep him warm: thermals, plaid flannel shirt and old sheepskin vest, faded jeans and mud-spattered sneakers, all of it, he hoped, believable enough camouflage for the role he was about to play. Moaning softly, he rolled over on his side and palmed the gun, neatly slipping it into his pants pocket before wobbling slowly to his feet. He was careful not to make any sudden move that might antagonize man or dog.

"Name's Tom Sullivan," he said, slurring the last name into only two syllables as he stood tottering before Devane. "Didn' mean no harm," he added, belching loudly.

"My lady friend and me were out here havin' ourselves a real good time when some old 'coon came along." He gestured toward the boulder. The army blanket, thermos, and food remnants would still be there to lend some credence to his story if Devane decided to look. "She took off like a bat outta hell." He waved a shaky finger in the opposite direction of the route taken by Beth and Diana. "I was jus' goin' after her when your dog here…"

Charlie fell back a few steps, reeled, then planted his feet more firmly and belched again, suddenly thankful for those two greasy doughnuts he had eaten earlier. If Devane came too close, he'd soon realize that there was no liquor on his breath, and Charlie knew his survival might well depend on making himself as physically repulsive as possible so he'd keep his distance. "Look, sorry, man. Didn' mean no harm."

"But why here? Why in the middle of the woods, and on such a cold night?"

Charlie shrugged. "Her ol' man was home, so was my ol' lady. No money for a motel, an' keepin' warm's never been a problem for us." Charlie gave a sly laugh and hiccoughed. "Didn' mean to cause any trouble, mister. Look, you won't say nothin' about this to nobody, will you? My wife's a real pistol. I'd…"

"That's enough. Your marital problems aren't my concern." It was a command for silence, and Charlie took it as such. He hiccoughed again, reeled a little to one side, then fell to the ground in an ungainly heap. He rolled into a sitting position, forced another belch, struggled to his feet and began tottering off into the woods, praying as he had never prayed before.

"Ishtar, Anath, Kali…"

Our ceremonial chant will not be interrupted!

Sam heard something out there.

And I caught a glimpse of eyes watching us from the high window.

No question, the enemy is at our gate.

But nothing and no one will prevent the completion of tonight's ritual!

The appointed hour is upon us.

Get back here, John! Now!

All is in readiness.

But we cannot proceed with only twelve!

Chapter
Eighteen

Diana was fully conscious by the time she and Beth reached Charlie's Taurus, but she was still so shaky that Beth had to help her into the back seat and close the door for her. Without giving it a conscious thought, they were saving the front passenger seat for Charlie.

Trying not to make a sound that might alert Devane's dog, Beth leaned her hip into the door until she heard a soft click, then she hurried into the driver's seat, pulling her own door shut as quietly as she could. She immediately turned to face her sister. "You okay, Di?" They were both still breathing hard. Diana nodded wordlessly.

Beth's hands were trembling as she tugged the cell phone out of her pants pocket. Still no service. "Damn!" She did a quick scan of the area around them, but Charlie was nowhere to be seen. "Where are you, Charlie?" Tramping through the woods with Diana had been such slow-going that he should easily have caught up to them by now. The fact that he hadn't could only mean that he was in serious trouble. They had to get help.

Leaning forward, she reached for the ignition key, but jerked her hand back when Diana screamed, "Don't you dare! We're not going anywhere without Charlie!"

Beth was too worried to sound calm and reassuring. "Jeez, Di! The cell's useless up here. We have to go for help!" She turned the key.

"Cut the damn engine, or I'm out of here! I'm not kidding, Beth!" When Diana actually opened her door, Beth quickly turned off the ignition.

"Okay. Okay. We'll wait," she soothed, turning to face Diana. "Take it easy, kiddo."

Diana slowly closed the door, eyeing her sister suspiciously. Beth again tried to reason with her, but it was hopeless. Diana was staring straight through her, and she was completely unresponsive. Frantic with worry for Charlie and terrified that some critical linkage in Diana's brain had just snapped, Beth felt completely helpless.

Glancing at the dashboard clock, she saw that a full twenty minutes had already gone by since they'd left Charlie, surely long enough for him to reach the car, if he were able to get to it at all. She decided to give him another five minutes. If he wasn't back by then, she was activating the car's child-lock system and getting out of there, no matter what Diana threatened. That dog was so huge and sounded so vicious. Please God, she prayed, please let Charlie be okay.

Three minutes later, Beth saw a running figure approaching, Charlie's red plaid shirt and lumbering stride unmistakable in the bright moonlight. "It's Charlie! He made it, Di!" she cried, already gunning the engine and slamming the gearshift into drive.

She pulled up beside him, jamming on the brakes as he wrenched the door open and collapsed onto the front passenger seat, his chest heaving as he strained to catch his breath. Beth didn't need any instructions. No way was she driving past that tower again. Shifting into reverse, she backed up to where they'd been parked, made a quick K-turn, and headed out on the dark strip of broken macadam that had once been used to haul stone away from the quarry.

The old hauling road was dark, narrow, and littered with deep potholes and chunks of stone that forced her to lower her speed to a crawl. As they rounded a blind curve, she prayed that there wouldn't be a bottomless pit lying in wait for them ahead.

Knowing what she had to be thinking, Charlie rasped, "Been here before. You're okay." The lie came easily. They had to get out of there, and he didn't have a clue what was up ahead. She was already driving as slowly as she could without stalling out, and he didn't have the heart to tell her that this was a first for him too.

Several minutes later, Beth began breathing easier when the tires finally began thrumming along solid pavement. Charlie improvised directions as they went along, pausing to inhale deeply after every sentence, embarrassed by the evidence of how out of shape he was. He made a quiet resolution to join a health club in the morning. Well, maybe not exactly in the morning, but soon. He didn't allow himself to relax his guard until they were several comfortable miles away from Devane's place and cruising along Route 23.

A quick comforting bleep from Beth's cell announced that they finally had connected with a tower, but they were almost home now. She didn't want to risk an accident trying to drive and update Paul at the same time.

With no sign of anyone pursuing them, Charlie was finally able to turn his full attention to Diana. "You okay?" He could see that she was anything but okay. She was sitting motionless in the back seat directly behind Beth, staring off into the darkness beyond her side window. He stretched out an arm and gave a reassuring pat to her right knee, the only part of her anatomy within reach. He was hoping that she would turn toward him and reach for his hand, but she didn't do or say anything. Resisting the impulse to dig deeper for some response, he pulled his arm back and refocused his concentration on the rear view mirrors. Whatever was going on with Diana would have to wait until they could get her safely back home. That was the priority now.

Neither he nor Beth ever noticed the steady stream of Diana's silent tears.

After reading Lenore's diary, Diana had expected to see Richard Hastings leading his coven at the tower tonight. She had never met him, but even the few grainy, shadowy pictures she'd found online made him instantly recognizable when she looked in the tower window. She was thrilled that she would have photos to show Henry, but before she could even get her cellphone out of her pocket, Hastings looked up, seemingly right at her. The implacable gray eyes were unmistakable, as was his resonant voice as he led the chant. The nightmare that had plagued her for so long had suddenly become reality. Richard Hastings was the same murderous warlock who had for so long haunted her dreams.

Standing on either side of him, their faces clearly illuminated by the single black candle held in Hastings' hands, had been John Devane and Jim Forbes, Chaetestown's chief of police. She had seen Forbes' all-American good looks and affable smile on the front page of the local newspaper just last week.

Diana cursed her own conceit. What was wrong with her? Why had she ever thought she was clever enough to outwit an entire black coven that had survived for generations? Advanced age had clearly not diminished Hastings' psychic abilities. The dark power emanating from him had overwhelmed her, reaching out to touch her with its malevolence even through the tower walls, robbing her of breath and consciousness.

Her original plan had seemed so simple. From a safe distance, using her cellphone camera, she would take all the incriminating pictures she needed to convince Henry that Lenore's diary was the genuine article. She would then hand all the documentation over to Beth who would write a brilliant expose that would destroy the coven.

Unfortunately, she had passed out before taking a single shot. The cellphone had never even made it out of her jacket pocket. True, the dog had been an unexpected complication. Still, she could have taken photos from the tower window, if only she hadn't fainted like a complete coward the moment she realized that she was looking at the warlock from her nightmares.

She had no idea how Charlie had managed to escape, but she sensed the horror of the ordeal he must have endured. She had seen it in the pulsating red of his aura as he dove into the safety of his car, and she blamed herself for all of it. Her arrogance had very nearly gotten them all killed tonight. She wanted to beg Beth and Charlie to forgive her, to swear to them that she would never again put their lives at risk. But she was powerless to speak.

The shock of seeing the old warlock was wreaking havoc with the last slim threads of her hold on reality. With one glance, those steely gray eyes had irreparably breached the floodgates of her unconscious mind, inundating her consciousness with images from Lenore's life. She was no longer sure of where Lenore Mowbray ended and Diana Wendell began, but she now knew that her nightmares had been born of memory, not imagination run amok. It was Lenore's murder that her horrific dreams had relived so many times. They shared the same soul, a soul that was still fighting to be redeemed, and she made a silent vow to honor Lenore's life by destroying the warlock who had taken it.

She cringed as a searing pain shot through her side. The remission she had been blissfully experiencing for almost two months had come to a sudden and brutal halt the moment she touched Lenore's diary for the first time, and she'd been popping heavy-duty pills ever since.

It was as if Lenore was putting her on notice that the end was very near. As if she needed a reminder! Any more painkillers when she went to bed tonight, and she probably wouldn't wake up at all in the morning.

Time was so short. Wiping away her tears, she continued to stare out the window and plan her strategy, as the car sped along Route 23 toward Windham. She knew she had to act quickly, and it would have to be alone. No way would she ever again put Beth or Charlie at risk.

When they finally arrived at the condo, Beth parked the Taurus in the driveway behind her BMW to free up the side of the garage that housed the Porsche. Hating the constraints of constant surveillance, Diana was always manic about being able to come and go as she pleased.

They hurried inside, eager for the comfort and safety of solid walls and central heating. As Beth locked the door behind them, reset the alarm, and turned up the heat, Diana flew up the stairs to her room. Beth told Charlie to make himself comfortable, then matched Diana's record time on the stairs.

Switching on lights as he went, Charlie made a quick detour to the bathroom. The mirror reflected a man way too old to be rolling around in the dirt with a killer dog, but he didn't much care how he looked. Thank God, Diana and Beth were alive, and so was he. That was all that mattered right now. He splashed some cold water on his face, then made a beeline for the liquor cabinet in the living room.

Pouring himself a double Glenfiddich, he drank it greedily, then poured himself another double and collapsed onto the roomy club chair that was his particular favorite. Closing his eyes, he settled back to wait for someone to remember him, feeling more than a little sorry for himself after the ordeal he had just endured.

Just a few minutes later, when Beth appeared, she found him sprawled in his chair, head thrown back on the cushions, eyes closed, legs splayed out before him, an empty glass on the cocktail table. Still, he was instantly alert the moment he heard her soft voice.

"Sorry to desert you, guy, but I had to check on Diana and contact Paul asap. You okay?"

"Just resting my eyes." Struggling to stay awake, he sat a little straighter. "Diana okay?"

Beth shrugged. Since Charlie still didn't know about her sister's illness, she couldn't tell him the truth. Diana was anything but okay. "Seems to be. Just wish I knew what scared her so much when she looked in that window."

"Did you ask her?"

"Sure did. Same old same old answer. Too tired to talk about it now." Beth picked up Charlie's empty glass and carried it to the bar. "At least she said *something*, finally. Mind you, she's up there writing madly away in her journal as we speak, but she's too tired to tell me a damn thing." She topped off Charlie's drink and poured one for herself.

"She keeps a journal?"

"Religiously. Has since she was a kid."

"Never would have pegged her for the type." He took the fresh drink from Beth. "Thanks, kid."

Beth was chilled to the bone, equal parts fear and being outdoors for hours in plummeting temperatures. Correction, she thought. Mostly fear. Definitely fear. Sipping her scotch, she huddled against an arm of the sofa and began telling Charlie about the discussion she'd just had with Paul.

"Turns out his dispatcher was able to hear most of the message I left when we were on the road and, yes, both of those cars we ditched were his guys." Ignoring the muttered expletive from Charlie, she went right on speaking. "Paul sends his compliments to the eagle eye who spotted them."

Charlie shook his head and groaned. "Eagle eye almost got us all killed tonight, Beth. Thanks to me, the cavalry was off on a wild-goose chase miles away from the tower. We're just damn lucky we made it out of there."

"Let's not play the blame game here, Charlie. Plenty of that to go around. Anyway… Paul should be here in a few hours. Until then, we're to sit tight and not open the door to anyone, including the Chaetestown police." Beth shrugged. "He said he'd explain that one later."

Charlie nodded slowly. "Wouldn't surprise me if he found out that Forbes is running a dirty cop shop, Beth."

"Oh?" Beth hated the thought of adding more worries to the mix they already had, but she had to know. "How so?"

"Think about it," said Charlie. "If Devane really is dealing drugs in a place as small as Chaetestown, the cops have to be looking the other way."

"Good point," sighed Beth, "but, if it's all the same to you, Charlie, I'd rather not think about dirty cops right now."

"Yeah. Me neither."

An awkward silence fell between them for several moments, then Beth asked, "You ready to tell me what happened tonight?"

He took a quick gulp of scotch. "It's not exactly a bedtime story, Beth."

"And I'm not sleepy, so let's hear it. You weren't in this alone, you know."

He knew it only too well. The three of them had been seen traveling around in public everywhere together. If he had a target on his back, so did they.

Charlie wasn't quite sure about what Devane was protecting with his killer dog, but he knew it had to be something a whole lot more valuable than a bunch of chanting weirdos. Had to be a major drug ring. Given Devane's track record, he'd bet on it. He decided it was well past time for him to be talking face-to-face with Paul Dunsford.

After fortifying himself with a few more sips of scotch, he told Beth the whole story, modestly glossing over his encounter with the dog, pretending that his brave charade had been the most ordinary thing in the world.

"I staggered off into the woods mumbling and muttering like some old wino, praying to God that Devane wouldn't sic the devil pooch on me again. When I was finally out of earshot and well hidden by the trees, I bolted in the direction that my fictitious girlfriend was supposed to have gone, then made a wide arc and circled back to the car."

Deeply shaken by his story, Beth got up from the sofa, walked over to his chair, and gave him a big hug. "Thank God you're okay," she said. "Well done, my friend."

"Thanks, Beth."

"You must be exhausted, Charlie. Don't even think about driving home tonight." His eyes were rapidly developing a glaze. "There's a nice comfy bed with your name on it upstairs, last door on the right. Go crash for a few hours before Paul starts beating down our door."

"Sounds good to me," he said, the words muffled by a huge yawn. "Except for the part about the stairs. Okay with you if I just stay right here?" He rested his head back on the chair and closed his eyes, half asleep already.

"Suit yourself, champ."

Without even opening his eyes, he said, "Oh, and Beth, before I forget. Thanks for waiting."

Beth smiled. "Thank Diana, Charlie. She refused to leave without you."

For a moment, it was as if the sun, moon and stars were all shining on Charlie's world. He fell asleep with a smile of total contentment.

Beth dimmed the lights, draped an afghan over him, then hurried upstairs to telephone Paul again and to phone Chad and Olivia as well. Things were rapidly spinning out of control, and she needed all the help she could get. Before going to her room to make the calls, she looked in on Diana again, her heart sinking the moment she opened the door.

Our High Priest has completely lost his mind.

There can be no other possible explanation for it.

With the coven in danger of exposure at any moment,

Richard insists on having the fertility rite at his precious outdoor shrine.

The altar room in the caverns is totally secure.

But being at Hecate's crossroads puts us all at risk.

The yellow tape and orange cones that Jim has always used to divert intruders from the area will be useless tonight.

Those women and their friends are like bloodhounds.

Chapter Nineteen

"She's gone!"

The panic in Beth's voice instantly penetrated Charlie's alcoholic stupor. Bolting out of his chair, he sprinted up the stairs, almost colliding with her at the top landing.

"No sign of her anywhere up here, Charlie. I'll check the garage."

As Beth ran downstairs, Charlie began a quick scan of the entire second floor, breathing easier when he saw no hint of foul play. Diana had clearly escaped under her own steam. The central alarm system had been disabled from the auxiliary control panel beside her bed, the sliding glass door to the small deck off her bedroom had been unlocked from the inside, and the metal fire-escape ladder had been lowered from deck to ground level. A first-grader could have figured out what she had done and how she had done it. The only question was why?

Beth shouted up from the front hall, confirming what he already expected: Diana's car was gone. He trudged down the steps, cursing all the booze that had filled his legs with lead and his ears with cotton. Even if she had coasted down the driveway, how could he not have heard that damn car pulling away? The fact that Beth hadn't heard it either could only mean that it had happened while she was upstairs on the phone with Dunsford. The garage was on the opposite side of the house from the bedrooms, so Beth had an excuse for not hearing her leave, but he sure didn't.

By the time he reached the bottom landing, Beth had already pulled on her heavy jacket and fleece-lined leather boots. "Think you'll be warm enough, Charlie?" He was still wearing the clothes he'd had on all night, but the temperature had been steadily dropping.

"Are you kidding? With all the scotch I've just had?"

"Okay then, let's do it." She opened the front door and ran outside, calling to him over her shoulder. "I just hope we find her before she does something really stupid."

Charlie could think of only one really stupid thing Diana could do. Locking the door behind him, he hurried after Beth. "You don't think she'd actually go back...?"

"I sure as hell do, Charlie."

Their likely blood alcohol levels left no question about who was going to drive, so Beth fired up her BMW while Charlie hurried to get his Taurus out of her way. Jumping the curb and scraping his tires, he parked on the street. By the time he grabbed his flashlight and binoculars from his center console, the BMW was already right beside him. He jumped into Beth's car and fumbled with his key fob to lock the Taurus as Beth drove off. He hated the thought of being chauffeured around a second time tonight, but he was just sober enough to know that his reflexes were shot and nothing else made any sense.

Switching cars ate up a few precious seconds, but Beth couldn't risk being challenged once again by a car that wasn't as easily maneuverable and responsive as her own. Also, she knew with certainty that the BMW had a full tank of gas. She hoped that wouldn't matter, but the way things were going tonight, she couldn't count on it.

After three previous trips to Devane's place, Beth had no trouble remembering the short-cut to it, and they were there in less than ten minutes. She slowed to a crawl as they passed the tower and drove on to the secluded spot where they'd parked the Taurus earlier that night. There was no sign of Diana or her sleek red Porsche anywhere.

"Where could she be, Charlie? I thought sure..."

"Hey, take it easy, Beth." He patted the hand she had rested on the gear shift. "This is the one place we emphatically did not want to find her, remember?"

She acknowledged the point with a silent nod, then drove slowly back along the road past the tower. They headed for home, neither of them saying a word until they were well away from the Old Chaetestown Road and cruising along Route 23.

"No all-night diners around anywhere. Maybe she just went for a ride," suggested Charlie, not really believing it, but unable to resist grasping at straws.

"No way. If that's all it was, she would have told us."

"Then where the hell is she?" He slammed a fist on the dashboard.

Beth had been wracking her brain for an answer to that precise question. Given Diana's mood, where would she have gone if not to Devane's? Suddenly, she knew.

"Hang on, Charlie." With no other cars around to worry about, she braked into a screeching U-turn. "Bet you anything she's at Henry's."

As soon as she had the car back up to speed, Beth used her cell to put an emergency call through to Paul Dunsford. They were on the main highway now, and she had no trouble at all hearing him when he came on the line. She had put him on speakerphone so that Charlie could hear both ends of the conversation.

"Diana's missing, Paul. Please tell me you know where she is."

"Wish I could. What in hell is going on up there, Beth?" She gave Paul a quick run-down on all that had happened since they last spoke. "I'm hoping she went running to Henry Woodruff to crow about what she saw tonight. A few things she said in the middle of a rant earlier tonight made me realize Henry probably knows a whole lot more about what's going on than we do. So Charlie and I are headed there now."

"Fine. Just promise me you'll stay at Henry's until..."

Beth didn't want to make any more promises that she couldn't keep. "Sorry, Paul. You're breaking up." She quickly ended the call and tucked her cell back in her jacket pocket. "J e e z , Beth," said Charlie, "whatever your family pays that guy can't be enough. He has to have one of the worst jobs on the planet."

"No argument there, especially lately." She was squinting into the darkness ahead, searching for the reflectors that marked the entrance to Henry's driveway. Finally, there they were, three vertically aligned red discs on a rusted metal strip that decades of spring thaws had leveled to a position almost parallel to the ground. She turned into Henry's drive.

The Porsche was nowhere in sight, but Charlie's pulse started racing when he saw lights burning throughout Henry's house. "Either he's a real night owl, or something's happened to disturb his sleep," he said, racing out of the car a split second before it stopped.

The front door was opened just as he reached the top of the porch steps, a bedraggled and distraught-looking Henry Woodruff waving them both inside. He was wearing pajamas, robe and slippers, and had obviously been recently rousted from his bed.

"Come in, come in," he said, closing the door behind them. "I was just trying to find your phone number, Beth. Diana was here. You just missed her."

"Where did she go?" asked Beth.

Henry's mournful face and the stoop of his bony shoulders gave her little encouragement, as he wearily gestured for them to follow him into a cluttered little room that he used as an extra office when he was in the front part of the house. A large map, creased and yellowed with age, was spread across the ancient desk that dominated the cramped quarters.

"I pleaded with her, Beth. Begged her not to go. But of course she wouldn't listen. She's determined to get incriminating pictures of the coven she saw tonight." He shook his head in disbelief.

"But she wasn't at Devane's," said Beth. "We just came from there, and we sure didn't pass the Porsche on the way over here. We couldn't have missed seeing her."

"We didn't," said Charlie, his voice grim.

Henry shrugged. "There are so many little side roads through these hills. She could have taken any one of them, but never mind that now. Look, there's something here you need to see."

Charlie was too worried to be polite. "We really shouldn't be wasting time..."

Henry waved away his objection. "It's the fastest way to explain how you can find her." He smoothed the map before them with shaking hands. "This is a surveyor's map of Chaetestown that was done back in eighteen-sixty. You can see the Briggs Tannery right here," he said, jabbing at the map with the eraser-tip of a pencil.

"And look," he continued, his fingers tracing an amateurishly-drawn and faded black streak leading away from the tower. "This is where Diana went. It's clearly a tunnel of sorts, probably a natural limestone formation. Evidently it's still very much in use, or you would have seen all those people arriving above ground at Devane's tonight."

"Did Diana see this?" asked Beth.

Eyes solemn, Henry nodded. He didn't have to think twice about how much to tell Beth. He'd never forgive himself if something happened to Diana because he went on keeping her secrets. "She already knew all about the tunnel, Beth, from reading Lenore's diary."

Beth shook her head and blinked hard. She'd been up for almost twenty-four hours straight at this point, and she couldn't believe what she'd just heard. "Lenore's diary? What are you talking about?"

Henry's pallor became even more pronounced.

"There's no time to explain it all now," he said, "but Lenore wrote in great detail about the tannery tunnel. This morning, when I found this map, I called Diana and left her a voicemail about it. Next thing I know, she's storming in here tonight demanding to see it." Henry shrugged helplessly. "Said she was going to check out the tunnel entrance in the woods and needed all the information she could get."

"The location on this map is pretty vague, Henry. And it has to be well camouflaged. How does she expect to find it?" asked Charlie.

"Quite easily, actually." Henry sighed. "The diary indicated some fairly precise markers. Once I cross-referenced them with some of my own research about the area, I was pretty much able to zero in on the exact spot." He quickly detailed the directions he had given to Diana.

Charlie was halfway to the door when Henry shouted after him. "Wait! If she's not in the tunnel, she might be here." Adjusting his glasses higher on the slender bridge of his nose, he tilted his head back to peer down at the map through the thick lower lens of his bifocals. He jabbed a trembling finger to a point on the map where three narrow meandering lines met. Charlie retraced his steps to study the map again.

"These three old trappers' trails converge at what used to be a trading post," said Henry. All overgrown now, of course. But," he sighed, "according to that diary of Lenore's, the site of the old trading post was a favorite fair-weather meeting spot for the coven. Something to do with crossroads being sacred to their goddess Hecate. Winters they'd be in the tunnel, summers above-ground. The night of the vernal equinox..." Henry's shoulders slumped as he shook his head. "Who knows? They could be in either place."

Everything Henry had said was so much an echo of Ariana's warning that Beth had to fight sheer panic as she forced herself to focus on the map. It was too fragile and cumbersome to take along in the car, so they had to spend a few moments memorizing its key features. As Henry quickly summarized directions to both places, Charlie's careful clarifications reassured Beth that at least one of them would know where they were going. She sure didn't.

Charlie clapped a hand to Henry's shoulder. "Got it. Thanks, Henry." He turned to leave, Beth right behind him, but she took a moment to give the older man a quick hug. He looked so desolate that her heart went out to him. "We'll find her, Henry. I promise." She sprinted out to the car after Charlie, each of them keenly aware of the fact that Henry had given Diana the same detailed set of instructions they had just received. She had a good head start on them, and there wasn't a moment to lose.

Hating the infirmity of old age, Henry stood on the front porch and wished them a silent Godspeed as they drove off. He knew that his creaking limbs would only slow them down, but oh how he wished he could have gone with them! There was so much he wanted to tell them about the diary, so much that might be useful to them in finding Diana. He felt the hot sting of tears biting at his eyes as he shuffled inside, his heart full of love for the young woman whose destiny had somehow become so inexorably linked with his own.

Henry had seen the silent rebuke in Charlie's eyes tonight, though the younger man had no real reason to begrudge him the warmth of his little patch in the sunlight that radiated from Diana. Theirs was a purely platonic relationship, a fact of life that Henry had long since accepted with equal parts relief and regret.

He had never given much credence to Diana's peculiar brand of metaphysics, but he had begun seriously questioning his disbelief when he learned of her telekinetic ability, the same gift Lenore claimed to have had. There were just too many parallels in the two women's lives to be explained away as bizarre coincidence, everything from unicorns to doting aunts. Henry no longer knew what to believe, although Diana's esoteric philosophy certainly offered him the most comfort.

How lovely to think that he and his beloved Loretta might return as man and wife again in another lifetime, maybe even have a bunch of happy, healthy kids the next time around. Henry smiled at his own foolish musing, thought about some chamomile tea to soothe his shattered nerves, then realized he didn't need any after all. He was already dozing off in his chair.

Awakening with a start to the insistent ringing of his front doorbell, the stiffness in his back and limbs told him he had slept in a sitting position far longer than he should have. A glance at the clock on the mantel confirmed it. More than two hours had passed since Beth and Charlie's departure, and he was praying that Diana had come back. When he saw that it was actually Olivia and Chad at his front door, he was literally speechless. Olivia was not.

"About time, Henry Woodruff. Don't just stand there gawking, man. Where are they?" She pushed her way past him, followed closely by Chad and another man who stood quietly behind them. "This is Jack Lanier, Henry. He works for Paul Dunsford. Jack, this is Henry Woodruff."

As the two men nodded to one another, Chad said, "We've just left Diana's place, Henry. Nobody's there, and Beth's not answering her cell. Do you know...?"

"Yes, yes, of course," sputtered the older man, finally finding his voice as he closed the door behind them. "Please, come this way." He gave them a quick replay of all that he had said to Beth and Charlie.

"How long ago did they leave?" asked Chad.

Henry checked his watch. "Beth and Charlie left just over two hours ago, about ten or fifteen minutes behind Diana. I suppose..." Chad was already on his way out the door, Olivia right behind him, Jack Lanier at her side.

"Throw on some clothes and let's get moving, Henry!" shouted Olivia over her shoulder. "No time to memorize old maps or have the GPS crap out on us. You'll have to show us the way." Jack Lanier had been dispatched to meet Olivia on Windham mountain when her helicopter arrived there about thirty minutes ago, and his orders couldn't have been clearer. He was to serve as her chauffeur, bodyguard and shadow, keeping her safe at all costs, no matter what she said or did to prevent him from doing the job that Paul had sent him to do.

When Jack opened the front passenger door of the car for her, she ignored it and hurried into the back seat. "Easier for Henry to navigate if he sits up front," she said. "And pull up as close as you can to the porch, will you, Jack? He's had a really rough night already."

Jack edged his car right up to the bottom step, while Chad stood outside waiting for Henry. Scarcely more than a minute later, Henry came shuffling hurriedly out the door, struggling into a bulky jacket as he walked across the porch, clearly exhausted and looking every one of his venerable eighty-two years. Respecting Henry's pride, Chad resisted the impulse to reach out a supporting arm, but he stood close enough to lend a hand, if needed, as he watched Henry make his unsteady way down the steps, untied shoes flapping at his heels, the hem of a pajama bottom visible under one leg of his trousers.

"Hurry, Henry. Hurry!" shouted Olivia.

Chad held the front passenger door open for Henry, as he collapsed onto his seat and pulled the door closed behind him. Chad hopped into the back seat with Olivia, and Jack Lanier immediately gunned the engine. "Where to, sir?" he asked Henry.

The answering voice was a surprise, very different from the breathless wheeze Jack had expected to hear. It was hoarse and full of a sense of urgency, but strong and clear. "Just make a right at the end of the driveway, then a left at the first stop sign."

Jack waved a small salute and accelerated down the drive while Henry fussed with his shoes. When he finished knotting the laces, he sat back and put on his seatbelt.

"Good idea," said Jack. "From what you've said about these roads we'll be driving, it could be a rough ride."

Henry nodded, but didn't attempt any small talk. He was never a man to waste words, particularly when his heart was hammering so hard in his chest.

They were approaching the first stop sign. Jack quickly negotiated the left turn. "Now what, Henry?"

Henry's directions and Jack's responses were the only words spoken as the car sped through the dark night. Chad and Olivia were both movers and shakers, with very low tolerance levels for doing nothing and saying less while critical events were unfolding, but they were too smart not to know when to keep quiet. Struggling to cope with the awful waiting, Olivia was steadily slapping the palm of a hand on her knee with the precise timing of a metronome, and Chad had rubbed the knuckles of his fisted hand across his mouth so hard and so often that his lips were getting numb.

In desperation, just to feel as if he were accomplishing something constructive, Chad asked Jack for a flashlight. "I can't imagine we'll be able to find that tunnel entrance too easily without one," he said, thinking aloud, if only to break the awful silence.

Jack had two flashlights, one that he always kept in the center console beside him, and another in the glove compartment. He asked Henry to retrieve the one from the glove compartment. "New batteries," said Jack, as Henry passed the flashlight back to Chad who tested it anyway. The beam was reassuringly bright.

Jack put in a quick call to his boss to give him a status report, but he had only said a few words when Olivia suddenly pitched forward and unceremoniously grabbed the phone away from him. "Paul," she said, "I'm going to put you on with Henry Woodruff. He'll tell you exactly where we're going. With any luck, you're even closer to that tunnel than we are. Yes. Yes. Yes, Paul. I understand. I promise I won't. Here's Henry." Olivia passed the phone to Henry. "Sorry, Jack, but I..."

"No problem, Mrs. Lazare. I was about to do the same thing."

When Henry finished speaking, he handed the 'phone back to Olivia. When she waved it off, he gave it to Jack.

Quickly finishing his report to Paul, Jack signed off, the dark and narrow road needing all his concentration now. It seemed like an eternity before they found the cars.

"There! There they are!" cried Henry, jabbing a finger at his side window.

Lanier had spotted them too, a Porsche and a BMW on the shoulder of the road, visible only as he had come abreast of them. Hitting the brakes as hard as he dared, he edged back onto the grass in front of the Porsche. Before the car actually came to a stop, Chad leaped out the door. Jack could only envy him. After playing chauffeur all night, he was itching for a little action, but he knew that Paul would skin him alive if he left Olivia unguarded.

Watching Chad vault over the hedges and run off into the woods, Olivia fully expected Jack to follow his lead. When he didn't, when he reached for his cell instead, she leaned forward and began hammering his shoulder with an angry fist. "Are you crazy? This is no time for talk! Do something! For God's sake, you fool, go after him!"

Hearing the terror behind her angry words, Jack spoke softly, his voice as deliberately calm as hers had been hysterical. "Wish I could, ma'am, but I can't. Mr. Dunsford gave strict orders that..."

"To hell with your orders! Your employer works for me, dammit, and I'm telling you..." She caught a glimpse of Jack's impassive expression reflected in the rear-view mirror, and she knew she was wasting her breath. "Forget it!" she cried, flinging open her door. If he wouldn't go after her babes, she would.

Anticipating that he might have serious problems with Olivia, Jack had already moved out from behind the wheel. By the time her feet touched the ground, he was blocking her exit. He was a martial arts expert, trained to move with lightning speed, his easy-going manner adroitly camouflaging a very deadly head-to-toe weapon.

"Please don't leave the car, ma'am." Bracing himself against her flailing arms as she tried to push her way past him, he stood just inside the open door, the bulk and angle of his body effectively halting her forward momentum. "I can't let you leave," he said. "Please, get back inside."

"Damn you! My girls are out there! Who do you...?"

Suddenly a shot rang out. Panic seized Olivia, and she desperately tried kicking and clawing her way past Jack; but she was no match for his superior size and strength, and the effort quickly exhausted her. Abandoning the skirmish, reeling from the shock of hearing the sound of gunfire, she retreated into the car. Jack closed her door and locked both rear doors from the driver's control panel the moment he was back behind the wheel. He immediately picked up the phone and gave a grimly concise report to Paul, while Henry tried to comfort Olivia.

"It might only have been a car backfiring," he offered.

In a voice full of desperation, she cried, "That was gunfire, Henry. And you know it!" She struggled to open her door, then slid across the seat to try the other rear door. When she realized that Jack had locked her inside, there was no holding back the tears.

All those years of Sunday school her mother had insisted upon had poisoned her soul with the illusion of an all-knowing, all-powerful, all-loving God.

A God Who had never been there for her.

And why not?

She had always blamed herself, presuming some fault or failing within her for which she must be punished.

Until Richard Hastings and the rest of the coven had made her realize that she was blameless.

It was Richard who had sated the demands of her woman's body after her husband had died.

It was Richard who had loaned her the money when the final foreclosure notice came to her house.

It was Richard who gave her the drugs and healing potions that kept her mother from suffering unbearable pain when she was crippled with arthritis.

It was Richard who had always been there to rescue her from the havoc brought into her life in the name of a Christian deity.

She had long ago spurned the God of her childhood, but she still felt occasional pangs of doubt about the dark path she had chosen.

Particularly on nights like this when the little ones had to be sacrificed.

Chapter Twenty

Two hours before that single shot rang out in the forest, Beth and Charlie had finally located Diana's car on the desolate country road. Beth had parked close behind the Porsche, effectively wedging it between a big oak tree and her BMW. No way was her little sister getting away from them again tonight. Charlie hopped out to check the interior of the Porsche, strafing it with his flashlight, relieved to see no visible sign of any more trouble than they already had.

Following Henry's instructions, they'd set off into the woods and soon found a clearly defined path that climbed from the base of the hill. A chill crept along Beth's spine, and she quickly narrowed the distance between herself and Charlie. She knew they had to be sharing the same disturbing thought: only a steady stream of footfalls over a period of many years could have carved such a smooth track into the forest floor.

Based on Henry's calculations, the tunnel entrance was so close to the road that it should only have taken about two minutes walking uphill to get there. The problem was finding it, since the path didn't conveniently dead end anywhere. It continued on up the hill as far as they could see. Walking slowly, they used both their flashlights to probe the dense foliage on either side of them. After five minutes without seeing anything unnatural in the landscape, they'd had to retrace their steps even more painstakingly.

Desperately looking for the telltale reflection of a metal lock or hinge that would betray the location of the secret door to the tunnel, Beth was afraid her eyes were playing tricks on her when she finally saw it. There was a momentary flicker of light reflected from a dense patch of foliage clustered along the side of the path, then nothing. Tapping Charlie's arm, she aimed her flashlight where she thought she had seen it. When he focused the beam of his own flashlight on the same spot, they knew they had found the door.

The high wall of concealing foliage was impenetrable directly in front of the door, but they found a gap in the overgrown hedge several yards ahead. Ducking through it, they skirted behind the thick row of shrubs and found themselves on another well-traveled path, this one leading directly to the tunnel door. As soon as they reached it, they saw what had caused the telltale glint of light that had first caught Beth's eye. The door had two hinges, both of them painted a dull brownish-green color that blended perfectly with the moss-covered natural oak of the door itself, but specks of paint had flaked away from the movable parts of the bottom hinge, leaving just enough bare metal to cause a reflection.

The door to the tunnel was low to the ground, circular, and set neatly into the hillside behind the cluster of overgrown shrubs. Beth guessed that, even in daylight, it would be totally screened from the view of any locals or back-packers hiking the trail here. Except for that pinprick of exposed metal on the hinge, the camouflage was so flawless that even the high beams on their flashlights didn't reveal any point of entry.

Handing his flashlight over to Beth, Charlie began exploring the door with his fingertips, exerting gentle pressure along its surface as he searched for a hidden lock. Suddenly he felt a break in the rough grain of the wood, and his fingers traced the outline of a smooth little disc set into the rough-hewn lumber near the bottom of the door. He took a deep breath and pressed down on it. The door immediately yielded, opening just a fraction of an inch, but enough for him to get a handhold. He pulled it open, reclaimed his flashlight from Beth, and stepped inside. When she tried to follow, he waved her back, motioning for her to wait right where she was.

He had to presume that whoever had set up the elaborate camouflage they had just penetrated would be shrewd enough to have a second line of defense, and he was right. About twenty feet into the tunnel, he found a tripwire that he guessed would be hooked to an alarm somewhere near the old tannery tower. Examining it, seeing that it was intact, he began to breathe a little easier. At least Diana had managed to get this far without any problem.

Abruptly turning back toward the entrance to get Beth, he almost knocked her off her feet. She was right behind him. He shook his head and glowered at her for coming into the tunnel before he gave the all-clear, but it wasn't a very convincing display of anger. Ignoring his silent command had just saved them precious moments, and they both knew it. Following his lead, she stepped gingerly over the tripwire and into the blackness of the tunnel beyond, sick with the knowledge that Diana was somewhere ahead of them, alone and possibly unarmed. Beth could only hope that she had her .22 with her.

Expecting a musty old relic of a tunnel replete with spiders, mice and bats, Beth's heart sank when she saw no sign of abandonment. The limestone tunnel was clearly in regular use. It was narrow, and they had to walk single-file, but the ceiling was high enough so that they didn't have to stoop, and they were able to move quickly. They were descending at a noticeable incline with each step, and she was thankful when the ground finally leveled off.

Hurrying along behind Charlie, taking comfort in the stalwartness of his broad back, Beth was startled when he suddenly doused his flashlight and fell to his knees. She instinctively did the same, not understanding why until her eyes had completely adjusted to the blackness of the tunnel and she saw what Charlie had already glimpsed from his lead vantage point: a flickering light reflected against the cavern wall ahead of them.

They crept forward soundlessly, the light brightening with each step, the tunnel widening as they drew nearer to the light's source. Now there were voices too. Not the chanting they had heard coming from the tower, but shrill, angry voices, an argument, loud and divisive, a cacophony of unintelligible words echoing through the tunnel, a din so strident that Beth and Charlie never heard the soft padding of an animal's paws along the limestone floor of the cavern.

The bull mastiff attacked without warning. One moment Beth was just behind Charlie, hugging the wall of the cavern as they inched their way forward toward the light and sound. The next instant, she was flat on the ground, her left side pinned underneath Charlie as he struggled with the lunging, snarling animal in a savage replay of what had happened just a few hours ago. The dog recognized Charlie's scent as a prize that had already been denied him that night, and his fangs were instantly at Charlie's throat, every primal instinct railing against the discipline demanded by his master. The fangs dug in deeper.

Immobilized beneath the combined weight of Charlie and the dog atop him, Beth could feel the animal's hot breath against her own face, smell the acrid scent of the kill, and see the small hollows being dug into Charlie's neck by the pressure of those lethal fangs. Scarcely able to breathe, she moaned softly when she saw that the animal had actually drawn blood, a fine red rivulet that trickled along Charlie's neck and dripped onto her jacket. It wasn't the bright red gush of arterial bleeding, but with the dog's fangs digging into flesh so close to his carotid artery... She instinctively lashed out at the animal.

With her left side still hopelessly pinned between Charlie and the cavern floor, she used every ounce of her strength to flail out at the enormous animal with her right arm and leg, pummeling his flank with her right fist, and hammering kicks into his lower torso and leg. The mastiff completely ignored the assault until one well-placed kick found its mark solidly on bone, the metal-tipped toe of her boot drawing blood from the lower part of his leg. Suddenly, Beth was no longer a mere nuisance. She was now a threat, a second foe to be reckoned with, and the animal's training dictated a different game plan.

Without releasing his primary adversary, the dog eased the pressure of his fangs at Charlie's throat so that he could more effectively leverage his huge mass to keep both captives thoroughly immobilized. He then summoned his master with a rapid succession of deep-throated bellows that echoed through the limestone cavern, totally obliterating all other sound.

Beth could see nothing from her restricted vantage point, but Charlie caught a brief glimpse of several figures rushing out of the shadows, moments before he was blinded by a brilliant beam of light. For the second time that night, he heard the strange word that brought the dog to heel. The voice was the same as before, and he was sure that Beth would also have immediately recognized it as Devane's.

Even with the glaring light restricting his functional vision to ground-level, Charlie was able to see enough to confirm that the dog was injured. Blood was oozing from the lower part of his left hind leg as he hobbled to his master's side. Evidently that last kick of Beth's had done some real damage, a lucky hit to a vulnerable spot where the bone lay very close to the skin.

Devane turned the beam of his flashlight on the animal and stooped to do a quick damage assessment, giving Charlie a few unobserved moments to ease his weight off Beth, allowing her to free her left side from beneath him. She slowly inched away, careful not to draw any attention to herself with a sudden movement.

His eyes adjusting to the shadows, Charlie concentrated on the remaining cast of players, but none were recognizable, silhouetted as they were beyond the arc of light surrounding Devane and his dog. They wore dark robes, and their faces were heavily cloaked in hoods, their features totally indiscernible in the darkness, their voices a whispered chorus of fretful confusion.

If he could only be sure that Diana was somewhere safe, he would already have shot the dog and made a run for it with Beth. As it was, he could only play the cards he'd been dealt, and hope. He had managed to con Devane once tonight, but he dared not even attempt to explain away this second act of trespass. He just prayed that Devane's only sin was playing at witches and warlocks. If he were dealing drugs, as Charlie suspected, and if the stakes were high enough, he was apt to panic and kill them both.

The dog yelped when his master touched the wounded leg, and the sound was music to Charlie's ears. He loved dogs, but not this one, and he could only be thankful for any impairment of the animal's ability to execute the murderous maneuvers he'd been so diligently trained to perform. When the spotlight inevitably returned to him, moments later, Charlie could actually feel the mounting waves of raw hatred coming at him from Devane. He had no doubt about what his fate would have been at that moment, if his captor had been holding a revolver instead of a flashlight.

"What now?" Some brave soul had spoken from the shadows, posing the question on everyone's mind. It was a woman's voice, and Beth thought it sounded vaguely familiar, but those two short words hadn't been enough to match the sound with a face.

"Quiet," commanded Devane.

Charlie heard a whispered discussion, but couldn't make out the words. He felt Beth's hand reaching for his, and he clasped it with as much reassurance as he could muster, his heart heavy with guilt. He had led her into this trap, and now her fate was irrevocably linked with his own. Dear God, if anything happened to her, Diana would never forgive him. He'd never forgive himself.

Charlie's silence, his utter stillness, was a cue Beth did not miss. She lay motionless on the tunnel floor, alert to every sight and sound around her. Sound distortion in the tunnel made it difficult to eavesdrop on the sibilant chorus of whispering voices, and she couldn't see clearly enough to count the dancing shadows on the cavern walls; but she guessed there must be twelve plus Devane, the requisite thirteen for a coven, just as Diana had been saying right along. She could only hope that they'd all live long enough to listen to her crow about it.

Beth had no way of knowing whether her previous encounter with Devane would serve as an asset or a liability now. When she and Diana had bought his paintings, they'd had no reason to hide their identity, so he had to know who their family was. If so, he would also know that there would be an exhaustive investigation if either of them should suddenly disappear. Still...

She knew it would be a close call: the Gresham billions would either intimidate him into good behavior or frighten him into doing something they would all regret. She could only be thankful that the nature of Charlie's work demanded a low profile. If Devane even suspected that he was a private investigator, she knew that the scales weighing their fate would be irrevocably tipped against them.

Listening intently, her ears becoming attuned to the cavern's acoustics, piecing together random words and phrases as the angry coven assigned blame to one another, Beth began to understand why the dog hadn't immediately detected their presence in the tunnel. When they first opened the door, the dog had been at the end of the tunnel nearest the tower. With no wind in the cavern to carry their scent, and with the coven making enough noise to conceal whatever sound they made, the dog hadn't discovered them until he went on routine patrol of the entire length of the tunnel, end to end. Beth also understood why they hadn't seen any evidence of the dog on their first few visits to the tower. This was no house pet.

Beth guessed that Diana had avoided immediate detection for all the same reasons they had, but, with a two-hour head start, she would have been much further along into the tunnel than she and Charlie were. Had she found someplace to hide, or had the dog found her? Beth hoped that the dog had simply caught Charlie's scent and dashed headlong after him, ignoring all else along the way, focusing on the known enemy, rather than an unfamiliar scent. Whatever the reason, it seemed that Diana had somehow managed to stay hidden, and Beth prayed that she had already found her way to safety and gone for help.

The whispering voices suddenly grew silent, as four hooded figures bearing a tangle of ropes began to approach. Beth and Charlie were immediately blindfolded, then pulled to their feet and clumsily searched for weapons. Charlie was glad to hear a few audible gasps when the gun in his shoulder holster was found. The reaction was happy reassurance that there were at least a few rank amateurs in the group.

For a moment, only that, as they began tying his hands behind his back, he considered overpowering them. He knew he could have done it easily, using them as human shields to make good his and Beth's escape; but, again, with Diana still missing, he could see no percentage in anything but meek submission. He just hoped that all the scotch he'd consumed earlier wasn't impairing his judgment now.

With their hands tied behind their backs, he and Beth were herded along by their captors, Charlie bearing the brunt of their anger. He was prodded along with quick jabs to whatever part of his anatomy they chose to punch, adolescent tactics that did nothing to break his concentration on the number of steps and the direction they'd traveled since being blindfolded. For all he knew, there might be a labyrinth of small caves within the broader framework of the relatively straight line shown on Henry's map, and he wanted to be sure they could find their way out when the opportunity to escape came. And come it would. He would make sure of that. But first, he had to find Diana.

He logged three hundred and fifteen steps before he was pushed sharply to the left. He counted another twenty steps before a jab to his back turned him to the right. Twelve more steps and he was kicked to the ground. No one had uttered a word since their forced march had begun.

Beth felt herself being eased into a sitting position with some measure of care, but when she heard a grunt and thud beside her, she knew that Charlie hadn't fared as well. She took heart from the muffled curses she heard. If he was as angry as he sounded, then it was likely that he hadn't sustained any real damage.

They were being clumsily trussed with endless lengths of rope repeatedly coiled and knotted around their legs and feet. Beth told herself that they wouldn't be bothering with all this if they intended to kill them, but she didn't dare believe in her own logic until she heard the rustling murmur of retreating footsteps. Had they actually gone away?

After a few moments, she decided to test the waters. "You okay, Charlie?" She held her breath, hoping her words wouldn't be answered with a clout to the side of her head.

Charlie must have had the same worry. He didn't answer immediately, and when he did, it was with a heavy sigh of relief. "Yeah. I'm okay. How about you, kid?"

"So far so good," said Beth. She had never been so glad for the sound of another human voice.

They listened quietly for several moments, each of them straining to hear if anyone was nearby. Then Charlie decided to press their luck a little further. "Keep talking, Beth. I'll follow the sound of your voice." He began his painstakingly slow progress toward her, inching his butt along the ground, rocking from side to side as he dragged his bound legs behind him, all the while anticipating a sharp kick from some unseen observer. He couldn't believe they really would have left him and Beth alone. And where was the dog? Probably having his leg tended to, Charlie supposed, wishing he had some idea of the full extent of the dog's injury.

"Just how hard did you kick that hound, Beth?"

"Pretty hard. God knows I had a lot of incentive."

"Enough to break something?"

"Maybe, but I doubt it. I'm afraid he won't be out of commission any longer than it takes Devane to bandage the leg." She paused a moment to listen to the sound of his labored progress toward her, adjusting the angle of her head so that her voice projected more in his direction. "How's your neck, Charlie? It's not still bleeding, is it?"

"Just a little. No problem..." A soft wheeze told Beth he was very close. "Unless of course the mutt's rabid."

"Not likely," she said. "Mastiff's are a pricey breed. And Devane's obviously got a bundle of time and money invested in turning him killer. Had to have had him inoculated against every disease known to man or beast."

"Yeah, I guess you're right. Keep talking, kiddo. I'm almost there."

"What do you suppose they're going to do with us, Charlie?"

"I wouldn't worry about it, darlin'." He spoke with a great deal more bravado than he felt, carefully enunciating his words on the remote chance that they were being overheard. "There's really no reason in the world for them to worry about..."

"Right, Charlie. And I'll just bet you still believe in the tooth fairy." Charlie had never heard more beautiful words.

"Diana!"

"Quiet," whispered Diana. She tore off his blindfold. "Hang on, Beth. I'll be with you in a sec'." Nobody argued with her priorities. Each of them knew that the sooner Charlie was free, the safer they would all be.

He was shocked to see her wearing a dark robe and hood, but there was no time to ask for explanations now. "Quick, Diana," he said. "Get the army knife out of my right pants pocket." He angled his body so that she could reach into the pocket, amazed and embarrassed by his exhausted body's instantaneous response to the touch of her fingers as she felt for the knife.

"Got it." With one deft movement, she severed the rope at Charlie's wrists, then handed the knife over to him while she hurried to Beth, removing her blindfold and working to undo the ropes around her wrists.

Charlie began slicing through the tangle of rope around his ankles. The knots were clumsy, nothing that would have held over the long haul; but cutting through and unraveling the bizarre overlapping knots and crisscrossing ropes was an awkward process.

He welcomed the inept trussing as further proof that their captors weren't all a bunch of trained killers. Professionals would never have presumed that he was disarmed simply because they had taken the .38 special from his shoulder holster. They would have frisked him for other weapons and found the Swiss-army knife in his pants pocket, not to mention the snub-nosed .32 tucked inside the small holster at the base of his spine.

With his hands free at last, and with Diana at his side, Charlie's world was beginning to look a whole lot brighter. The two of them worked quickly to free Beth, Charlie concentrating first on the ropes binding her lower body. There was no way of knowing when the coven might return, and Beth had to have the mobility to flee, even if time ran out before they could free her hands. He was just cutting through the last rope around her ankles, when he looked up at the two women with a quick smile, his heart giving a little lurch at what he saw in that moment.

Diana was sitting on the ground beside her sister, quietly working to untangle the ropes that bound Beth's hands. The concealing black hood had fallen back onto her shoulders, releasing a halo of blonde hair that framed her face. He had never seen such beauty. It was soul-deep, radiating light, stunning him with its force. Shaking himself free of its spell, he hurried to cut through the last of the ropes still binding Beth's wrists. They had to get out of that tunnel, and fast. "Now look, you two," he whispered, "stay low, stay close, and follow me." With Diana and Beth right behind him, he pulled the snub-nosed .32 from his belt and began retracing the steps he had so carefully counted. As he was about to turn into the main shaft of the tunnel, Diana grabbed at his arm.

"Get Beth out of here, Charlie. I'll be right behind you. Just as soon as I get a few more pictures."

"Pictures? Are you crazy? This isn't a game, Diana!"

She touched a hand to his lips. "Not so loud," she sighed. "Look, the three of us know the coven exists, but we have to be able to prove it!" She knew that nobody would ever believe the truth about Congressman Hastings' father unless she was able to show them incriminating photos of him and his friends in full coven regalia. Escape was no longer a viable option for her. Beth and Charlie were in the coven's crosshairs now, and that changed everything. She wasn't leaving until she had every shred of evidence she could find to shut Richard Hastings down before he could hurt them.

Charlie whispered a clear command. "You and Beth get the hell out of here and call for help. Now! I'll take your damn pictures! Go!"

"Listen to me, Charlie," pleaded Diana, "if that coven sees you again, you're fido's dinner and you know it. At least I'm dressed for their party. They won't even notice me. And if they do, I've got a can of mace and a .22 in my pocket that says I'll get some respect. I'll be fine."

Seeing the grim set of Charlie's jaw and the totally intractable look in Beth's eyes, Diana knew this was an argument she would never win. Spinning on her heels, she hiked the skirt of her robe and raced off into the darkness. Beth instinctively followed, accelerating to match her sister's speed, all logic and reason completely sublimated to the protective instincts of a lifetime.

Charlie was dumfounded. He decided they were both insane, too much high-society inbreeding or something. This was beyond the eccentricity of the rich. It was sheer madness, and he knew it; but he also knew he couldn't allow them to go on without him. The dog could appear at any moment, and Diana's .22 wasn't going to be much help. He hurried after them, a surge of panic-driven adrenaline giving him a quick burst of speed that allowed him to catch up with Beth and overtake Diana.

He grabbed at Diana's shoulder, none too gently, and pulled her up short. "Where do they stash those robes?" he asked, the words a scarcely intelligible wheeze. There was no way he was leaving her, and he didn't want Beth and himself being the only two humans out of uniform in that tunnel tonight.

"The whole coven's here tonight, Charlie. There was only one extra," lied Diana, knowing that there were still several robes in the storage cabinet she'd rifled just a short while ago. "Now will you two please get out of here and go for help. Without robes you're..."

"We're not going anywhere without you, Di, and that's final."

Diana knew that her sister meant every word. She also knew that she couldn't allow Beth or

Charlie to get anywhere near the coven again. Darting ahead, she began running at a fast pace, her stride seemingly unaffected by the uphill gradient. Beth and Charlie both raced after her, but this time Beth quickly outdistanced him.

Charlie willed every ounce of speed and strength he could muster into his legs, but as soon as he lost sight of the two women racing around a bend in the tunnel, his adrenaline crashed and his spent muscles crumpled beneath him. He sat on the ice-cold ground, his chest heaving as he gasped for air, his body powerless to obey the urgent commands being transmitted by his brain.

Diana knew that he wouldn't be catching up with her a second time; but she also knew that she was too weak to outrun her sister over any distance. Sprinting along until a sharp series of curves completely concealed her from Beth's view, she dodged into one of the many small limestone caverns that branched off the main tunnel. Flicking off her flashlight, she waited with pounding heart until Beth ran past her, then she quickly backtracked to another side tunnel, the one where she had first seen the coven tonight.

After entering the tunnel a few hours earlier, she had followed the sound of voices to this cavern, inching her way along until she found a good place to hide. There was an outcropping of rock just twenty-five or thirty feet away from them, and she had crouched behind it, quietly watching and photographing as they prepared for their night's work. She counted twelve coven members, all of them robed and hooded. Their faces were in shadow, and she couldn't hear what they were saying, but she knew that Richard Hastings had not yet come amongst them. She would have felt his dark presence had he been there.

As the coven retrieved candles and other ritual paraphernalia from a storage area concealed in the wall, an argument began, shrill voices ringing throughout the cavern, words distorted by echoes. She had no idea what they were arguing about, but she took advantage of the distraction to edge her camera around the rock and take a few more quick shots, leaning back into her hiding place just in time to avoid being run down by the dog.

What was he doing here? Why would Devane risk having their ritual disrupted by a dog? She had been so sure that the animal would have been confined to the tower while the coven was gathering in the tunnel. Yet, here he was, appearing out of nowhere, running right past her, not even breaking stride as his powerful body came within inches of her own. She could only guess that the mingled scent of the nearby coven had camouflaged her presence.

After seeing the speed of the enormous animal in action, she had to marvel at her own idiocy in thinking she'd be safe with her .22 and a can of mace. The dog had come and gone before she'd even had a chance to reach for a weapon. Saying a silent prayer of thanks to her guardian angel, she tried to rethink her game plan. She was still struggling for inspiration when the dog began to bark.

One shadowy figure immediately raced toward the sound. Diana had to presume it was Devane, followed closely by the rest of the coven, their voices reaching a shrill crescendo as they swarmed past her hiding place. For a second time that night, the dog's presence instantly trumped her original game plan, morphing it into a simple blueprint for survival: grab one of the robes from the storage area, throw it over her head, follow the coven, sidle around them toward the exit, then run like hell.

She ran to the storage area where, as she had hoped, there was a plentiful supply of black hooded robes. She pulled out one of what appeared to be the smallest size and slipped it over her head. Transferring her gun, cellphone and can of mace from the pouches of her cargo jacket into the two deep pockets of the robe, she stuffed her gloves into one pocket and her ski hat into the other to muffle any sound that all the metal paraphernalia might make as she moved. Tossing her hood forward, she ran after the coven.

Dressed as she was, she was counting on the coven not even noticing her as she edged her way around them toward the exit while they were all involved with whatever had caused the animal to bark. She just hadn't counted on Charlie and her sister being the star performers in the drama that was about to unfold. Their arrival had changed everything, easily trumping her terror of the dog.

Hiding in the shadows, Diana had followed Beth and Charlie to their makeshift prison and waited until they were alone before making her move to free them. It had worked, better than she'd dared to hope, but now they were refusing to leave without her. The three of them were locked in a dangerous standoff, since Diana wasn't going anywhere without a full-face picture of Richard Hastings in full regalia, the final nail in his coven's coffin. Beth and Charlie had left her no choice but to hide until they gave up trying to chase her down.

From the deep shadows of a small secondary tunnel, Diana watched Beth run past her again, this time heading back toward Charlie. Following her sister from a safe distance, Diana couldn't believe what she was seeing when, instead of making a headlong dash for the exit, Beth and Charlie actually began pantomiming a fierce argument. Since they didn't dare raise their voices above a whisper, she couldn't hear what was being said; but Beth's frenetic arm waving and the stern set of Charlie's jaw told their own story. Each of them was clearly determined to be the one to stay in the cavern while the other went for help.

After five or ten seconds of angry charades, it was Beth who yielded, shaking her head and glowering at Charlie before setting off at a sprint toward the exit. At the rate of speed she was generating, Diana guessed she would be back with Paul's goon squad in fifteen minutes, maybe less, not much time for the rest of the pictures she needed, but hopefully enough. This was probably her last chance to catch Hastings in the act, and she was determined to finish the job.

The moment she saw that Beth was safely outside, Diana ran back to the cavern where she had first seen the coven gathering that night. It was eerily quiet now, and she knew they must have moved on to the altar room to begin their ritual. Not only did common sense dictate that the entrance to the altar room would be found here, but the layout of this particular cavern exactly matched the one described in Lenore's diary. Racing against time, she hurriedly strafed the walls with the high beam of her flashlight. Finding nothing, not a single unnatural seam or contour in the rock, she took a moment to get her bearings.

When she felt fairly certain about which wall was closest to the old tannery tower, she set her flashlight on the ground with its beam angled up toward it. Spreading her hands flat against its surface, she began sketching a zigzag pattern, giving her sense of touch free rein to detect what her eyes had failed to see, just as she had done with the door at the tunnel entrance a few hours earlier. On her second sweep of the wall, one well-manicured fingernail snagged on a thin crevice in the stone, sending her pulse hammering into overdrive as she traced the fault along a distinctly vertical line.

Confident that she had found the door, she looked for the spring lock that controlled it. The diary had indicated that the lock panel was just to the right of the door, and it took her only a few moments to find the telltale cleft in the rock. The panel was small, scarcely more than the size of her palm, and as well-camouflaged as the door it controlled. She had only to press it and the door would open, or so Lenore had written. But then what?

The diary had also included several references to a small anteroom just the other side of the door, but what if the anteroom wasn't there any more? Thus far, Lenore's descriptions of the tunnel had been accurate in every detail, but logic dictated that there had to have been some modifications made since the diary was written. What if the anteroom had been eliminated in favor of a single large chamber? If so, the door would now open directly into the altar room. What if she suddenly found herself face-to-face with the entire coven? And what about the dog?

The diary hadn't been clear about how the door would open once it was unlocked, so she had to presume it would slide into the wall. She couldn't see any hinges, nor could she imagine any that would be strong enough to support the tonnage of a swinging stone slab. With her right hand, she pulled the .22 from one of the deep pockets of the robe. Squaring her shoulders, she jabbed the heel of her left hand into the control panel, backed off a few paces, switched off her flashlight, and gave the door a wide berth.

A narrow column of light suddenly breached the darkness before her. Rigid with fear, she aimed the .22 at the widening band of brightness, as the massive stone door slid into the cavern wall, gliding soundlessly on its well-oiled track. When the door was fully opened, she felt weak with relief. The anteroom was still there, and it was empty.

Peering inside, she strained to hear what might be happening in the altar room beyond it, but all was silent. Puzzled, she stepped gingerly over the threshold and tiptoed towards the altar room, her path dimly lighted by candles burning in ornate wrought-iron wall sconces on either side of the cavern.

As soon as she saw the huge stone altar with its black candles, her breath caught in her throat, and she began feeling dizzy. Reflexively, she re-pocketed the gun, then braced her back against the cavern wall to keep from being swept away by the tide of horrific images that suddenly began coming at her in relentless waves.

There were faces, so many of them young children, even infants, their eyes wide with terror, their mouths agape with silent screams, their features contorted in an agony beyond human endurance, a kaleidoscope of ghastly visions that she was powerless to dispel. She wanted to escape, to put as much distance as possible between herself and the altar, but the walls held her captive. She collapsed, overcome by an onslaught of blinding vertigo. Her last conscious thought was a prayer that death had not chosen this evil place to claim her.

The old warlock felt it immediately.

The enemy that had been threatening for weeks was here now.

Lenore had returned.

And she wasn't alone.

Margaret and her precious Archangel Michael had returned with her.

Combined, their energy is formidable.

But the Dark Lord will prevail!

Chapter Twenty-One

As Diana slowly drifted back to consciousness, she sensed that she was no longer alone in the altar room. Had the coven returned? Listening intently, she heard no sound, not the soft tread of a cautious step nor the whisper of a breath. And suddenly she understood why. Whoever was here with her now was no mortal being.

Slowly opening her eyes, she felt the spirit draw nearer, filling the altar room with its unseen presence. Sighing with recognition and relief, she smiled as she felt its light and goodness envelop her. She didn't attempt verbal communication. There was no need. The same sense of well-being that she always felt at Margaret Mowbray's gravesite was with her now, amplified to infinity, clearing her mind, quieting her fears, and bolstering her courage. Laying down her psychic armor, Diana willed herself to become one with the spirit that had come to her.

For an instant, only that, she wondered if she was still unconscious, or maybe even awake but imagining things. The doctors had said there would likely be hallucinations at the end. But no. She was awake, and she was not imagining anything. This was as real as anything she had ever known in her life.

She shivered as the altar room suddenly grew cold and dark again. Margaret's spirit had clearly withdrawn from this vile place, and Diana had no time to speculate about why she'd gone as quickly as she had come. Losing consciousness had cost her precious minutes. She had to hurry.

Now free of the vertigo that had hit her the moment she entered the altar room, Diana stood and took a quick inventory of her belongings. The gun, cellphone and mace in her pockets had all survived the fall intact, but her flashlight was gone. She knew it must have rolled off somewhere into the shadows when she first lost consciousness, but there was no time to look for it now. She would have to rely on the candles burning in wall sconces throughout the caverns to light her way. Hopefully, they would go the distance for her.

Lenore's diary had mentioned two separate tunnel entrances from the woods, the one that had led her to where she was now, and the other that led from here to the crossroads above. The vacant altar room told Diana where the coven had to be now. Unless, of course, they had decided to disperse and go home after all the commotion Beth and Charlie had caused.

She decided that wasn't likely. Hastings and Devane had already taken too many chances to give up and run before they finished whatever ceremony they had planned for tonight. They must be at the crossroads. Nothing else made any sense. It was a powerful natural setting for their black rituals, especially under a waxing moon, and it was the last place she wanted to be.

She could think of only one reason why they would dare to venture above ground on a night when so much had already gone wrong for them: a major ritual must have been planned, one that could not be postponed, probably a full black mass requiring them to be at Hecate's sacred crossroads. She shuddered at the thought of the monstrous evil that might be unleashed within Hastings' circle this night.

"Diana!"

The same loving voice that had always been there to dispel her nightmares was calling out to her now. At first, Diana thought she must be imagining it; but when she heard her name shouted again, louder, closer this time, she knew that Beth had returned to the tunnel, probably just a few steps ahead of Charlie. Trusting that Paul's team would be right behind them, she knew they'd be safe, as long as she stopped them from reaching the tunnel that led to the crossroads. Locking them out would only force them above ground, but she hoped that finding their way through the woods to the crossroads would buy her the time she needed to deal with Hastings before they got there.

She frantically searched for the mechanism that would lock the altar room door behind her, but the walls adjacent to the door were smooth and solid. Looking about in despair, she felt like a fool when she saw it, a lever so large that it was a wonder she hadn't tripped over it. Of course, she realized, there would be no need for camouflage on this side of the door. Anyone who had ever gotten this far was either a member of the coven or a victim about to die. Until tonight, no one outside the coven had ever left the altar room alive, of that Diana was certain. No way was she going to allow Beth or Charlie to enter this evil place.

She tugged at the lever, and the stone door glided smoothly on its well-oiled track, closing quietly and efficiently, but not before Diana caught a glimpse of Beth's face as she turned into the narrow cavern and saw her baby sister being entombed in a wall of stone.

Forcing aside the memory of Beth's anguished expression, Diana fought back tears as she hurried out of the altar room and ran into the timber-shored passage that led away from it. Without her flashlight, she could only hope that the candles would continue to burn brightly in their wall sconces until she reached the portal to the world above that Lenore had described.

She knew she was headed for a direct confrontation with Richard Hastings tonight. Why else would Margaret have come to her? And yes. It had been Margaret. Diana was sure of it. And she'd come bearing the gift of courage. Diana knew she should be afraid to challenge a powerful warlock on his own depraved turf, but she wasn't. A strange calm was settling deep inside her. Tonight, she would do whatever it took to mark Lenore's karmic debt paid in full.

If only Beth and Olivia could understand why she had to do this! She'd tried to explain it all in her last journal entry before she sneaked out of the house earlier, but there had only been enough time to skim the surface. With time once again her enemy now, Diana ran even harder.

If the worst happened tonight, at least Beth knew where she kept her journal. She would read it, hopefully find some comfort within its pages, and maybe someday she would even realize that her baby sister hadn't been so crazy after all.

Diana came to a fork in the tunnel and unhesitatingly, almost instinctively, took the path veering off to the right. It was an unexpected bonus when candlelight abruptly gave way to state-of-the-art high-intensity amber lighting, and she increased her pace, running as fast as the terrain would allow.

Whatever happened, she had to reach the crossroads before Beth and Charlie. She knew that they had seen Henry's old map. How else would they have found the tunnel? And they could only have seen the map if they'd visited Henry, who almost certainly would have told them about the diary, or at least the parts of it that might help them to find her. Locking them out of the altar room had bought her a little time. Please God, let it be enough!

She sprinted through the cavern until it abruptly dead-ended at a stone stairway. The steps were profiled in muted amber lights that ascended to a circular door set into the ceiling of the cavern, and she didn't dare stop to think through any strategy. She would simply climb the steps and open the door. With luck, she would emerge unseen and have a few moments to assess the situation before having to decide what to do next. There was simply no time left for weighing probabilities now.

The Goddess and her Dark Prince have promised that the highest office in the land will one day belong to Billy.

But only if the requisite offerings are made.

William, as he must always be called after tonight, is a natural leader in a country of sheep.

The voters love him.

The stage is set for his ascendance.

So mote it be.

Chapter Twenty-Two

Lenore's diary hadn't mentioned any special security precautions at the coven's gateway to the crossroads above, but Diana knew that the intervening years had likely changed all that. Praying for luck, she hitched up the long skirt of her black robe and hurried up the steps, crouching low as she reached the top, hoping that she hadn't already somehow managed to trigger a silent alarm. The door was a ring of wide wood planking that had been sawed flat on one side to accommodate two sturdy metal hinges. On the side opposite the hinges, there was a massive deadbolt that had already been drawn back. She hadn't miscalculated after all. The coven had come this way.

Bracing her back against the cavern wall, she pushed her upraised palms against the door. It had the solid heft of oak, but it lifted easily on well-oiled hinges, emitting no sound that might announce her arrival to anyone outside. She raised the door only an inch or two at first, just enough to peer into the darkness beyond, not daring to breathe until she was sure that there was nothing human or canine guarding the immediate area above her. Stepping gingerly out of the tunnel, she gently lowered the door, then ducked behind the wall of overgrown shrubbery that surrounded the entrance.

Getting this far had been so easy that she had to wonder what trap might be lying in wait for her above-ground; but common sense told her that opening the hatch from the inside wasn't going to trigger any sirens or alarm bells outdoors. The coven would want to come and go swiftly and silently. Her only real concern now was the dog.

She wanted to believe that the animal had been too hurt to limp up the stone stairway; but, since he had obviously been trained to be meaner and tougher than most of his species, she knew that he could easily still be a threat. Forcing the paralyzing image of the huge mastiff from her mind, she took a deep breath and drew the hood close about her face. Edging away from her hiding place, she ventured only far enough to assess her surroundings.

It was a clear night, each star trying to outdo the other in a show of heavenly light. With a stand of pine trees obscuring her view, she could see no sign of the coven, but other senses quickly fueled her adrenaline as a sudden wind shift brought with it the acrid stench of burning herbs and the muted tones of a chant. They were close, very close.

There didn't appear to be any silent sentinels on guard, human or animal, but she carefully scanned the area once more before stealing away from her hiding place, gun in hand and ready to fire if the dog suddenly appeared and lunged at her. If only she knew where he was! Logic told her that he wasn't with the coven, or he would have already attacked. The wind hadn't shifted in her favor until several moments after she had emerged from the tunnel, giving the animal ample time to get her scent if he were nearby. Still, she wished she could be sure. It could make all the difference.

Inching her way along the line of trees to the last straggling pine, she gently nudged one of its spindly branches aside and peered through the narrow gap in the foliage. She froze, scarcely able to breathe. There, in a small clearing just beyond the row of pines, the nightmare that had plagued her for so long had become a living tableau under the stars. They were all there, thirteen hooded and robed figures, their silhouettes starkly etched by candlelight. The dog was nowhere to be seen, but there was a fourteenth among them, and not by choice.

A child was laid out on a black cloth that covered the primitive stone altar. The little girl couldn't have been more than five or six, flaxen hair fanned out about her head, her child's body naked and still.

Pale and lifeless, she made no sound, not a whisper of a cry or moan. Yet Diana knew she must still be alive, for there was no blood to be seen anywhere, and a black mass demanded the slaying of a living being. She knew they must have drugged her, as they probably had done with all the other victims slain at their above-ground rituals. In the tunnel, they could risk the screams of fully-conscious victims, but not here where the still night air would carry the terrible cries.

The coven continued their soft chant, a litany in praise of their goddess, an invitation for Hecate to join their circle, to bring with her the horned god who was her consort, and the fierce dogs who were her constant companions. Diana was trembling so violently that she knew the gun would be worse than useless in her hands now. She released her death-grip on the weapon and slid it back into her pocket. Her cellphone was in the same pocket, and there it would have to stay. All her energy had to be focused on the old warlock now. Anything less could be fatal to the child.

As she watched Richard Hastings presiding at the altar with his coven gathered closely around him, she felt his power being augmented with each profane word they all uttered. She saw Devane and Forbes on either side of Hastings, as she would have expected them to be, but she was shocked to see two of the others who were with them. They all still had their hoods on, but now they were turned towards her, their faces illuminated by candlelight from the altar. With a sickening rush of recognition, she identified Ruth Nagle and Eliza from the Country Kitchen.

Remembering all the long cozy chats she and Beth had enjoyed over endless cups of coffee at Eliza's homey little restaurant, Diana felt suddenly overwhelmed by the enormity of the task she had set for herself. If Richard Hastings was cunning enough to entice a seemingly decent, sensible, ordinary woman such as Eliza to join his murderous satanic cult, what chance did she have against them with her pathetically small arsenal: a small can of mace and a gun and cellphone that she was too shaky to use. Even if there were a few bars on her phone, there was no time to call for help. Besides, Beth had already taken care of that.

Feeling powerless against the dark forces being generated within Hastings' demonic circle, knowing that she alone had any chance of saving the child's life, she prayed harder than she had ever prayed before. In a voice that was only a whisper, her focus lasered on the child, she pleaded, "Dear God, please help me save her life. Archangel Michael, please protect us both with your mighty sword. And, Margaret Mowbray, please share your strength with me. Richard is so powerful! Please help me, Gran!" In her mind, at this desperate moment, Margaret was her grandmother. Diana could no longer tell where Lenore ended and she began.

"Ishtar, Anath, Kali," chanted Hastings, his voice a triumphant shout, his ceremonial sword, the richly jeweled athame, brandished high above the prostrate body of the child. The litany of the goddess' names had always immediately preceded the final sacrificial act in Diana's nightmares, and she knew there wasn't a moment to lose.

Stepping out from her hiding place, she focused all her mental energy on the athame. The entire coven was dancing about the altar, their faces grotesque with feverish anticipation. None of them had yet observed the slender black-robed figure standing quietly just beyond their circle.

Hastings stood poised for the thrust, his hands grasped firmly about the jeweled hilt, the long blade of the athame glinting in the moonlight. It was the moment of consummation, and the coven's muffled chant accelerated to a frenzied cadence. Diana shut out the sound of their voices, shut out every distraction from the power rising within her.

The old warlock sensed it immediately, a deadly energy that was rapidly gaining ascendance over the barriers of his own negative force field. The threat was very real, imminent, and all too familiar. He felt its power and knew with certainty that it emanated from the spirits of Margaret and Lenore, their combined energies growing stronger by the second. He had to hurry!

Hastings tensed the still-powerful muscles of his forearms and prepared to plunge the ceremonial sword into the child's breast. He took a deep breath and put all his weight into the thrust, relishing the moment, sparing nothing of himself in homage to his goddess. But the sword would not yield.

A cold sweat broke out across his brow as he strained with all his might to drive the athame home, but the sword only quivered in response to the trembling of his hands. No! This couldn't be happening! Not now. Not when he was so close to completing the work he was born to do.

Hastings' muscular forearms were taut with strain as he willed the athame to yield, but the double-edged sword still held fast. His whole body was shaking now, as he mustered every ounce of his strength for a final forward lunge. When it came, the thrust of his momentum brought his hands slicing across the length of the sword. As he fell forward upon the young girl, his blood streaming over her pale flesh, the sword dropped harmlessly to the ground beside the altar.

At the sight of their fallen leader, the coven immediately stopped their wild dancing and macabre chanting. Stunned, they watched in total confusion as Hastings struggled to regain his balance and composure, but the cuts in his hands were deep, and he was bleeding profusely.

Devane was at Hastings' side in an instant, as was a female member of the coven whose face was hidden by the folds of her hood, but whose proprietary body language told Diana that she must be Hastings' wife. Still unseen, Diana watched silently as the woman pulled a small dagger from her belt and cut the underskirt of her robe for makeshift bandages which she and Devane used to staunch the bleeding of the warlock's hands. Hastings was totally oblivious to their ministrations, for he had just seen Diana.

"Lenore," he whispered.

Hearing the name and remembering all that Richard had told her about his one-time nemesis, Martha Hastings glanced worriedly at Devane. "He must be going into shock," she said. They both increased the pressure on his hands.

"Lenore," whispered Hastings once again, his eyes transfixed by Diana. She was dressed, as they all were, in black hood and robe, her appearance indistinguishable from the others, her presence thus far noticed only by the old warlock.

"We can't just let him bleed to death, George! Do something!" cried Ruth Nagle. George Bond, Chaetestown's coroner, staggered forward, but was immediately pushed back by Martha. It was clear that the man was too high on drugs to be of any use to anyone still living, and she didn't want him anywhere near her husband. When she looked to Devane for help, he decided that now was as good a time as any to flex a little muscle. He immediately took charge.

Motioning to Jim Forbes, he ordered, "Quick, Jim, help me get him back inside."

With Martha attempting to hold the bandages in place, the two men flanked Hastings and locked arms behind his back. They were about to lock wrists at his knees to carry him off, when the old warlock pushed them away, his unexpected strength catching them all off guard.

"No!" shouted Hastings. "The sacrifice must be completed."

"It will be, Richard," soothed his wife, "just as soon as we get back to the altar room."

"No! There can be no more delay!" Hastings' eyes never left Diana.

Martha was too busy caring for her husband's wounds to notice where he was looking, but Devane followed Richard's gaze, the color draining from his face when he saw Diana. Until that moment, he had hoped to brazen it out with the two in the tunnel, rather than kill them. He didn't know who the man was, but he had recognized Beth Wendell immediately and knew it would have been suicidal to escalate the incident beyond the already dangerous stage it had reached.

In desperation, he'd come up with what he'd regarded as a brilliant solution to their dilemma. As soon as the coven had completed their ritual, disposed of all the evidence and gone home, he had intended to telephone the police to report the presence of armed intruders on his private property.

He would have been perfectly willing to admit to being a devil-worshipper -- no crime there, and it was already on his juvenile record anyway. He would have screamed loud and long about his constitutional right to worship as he damn well pleased, claiming that he and his entire coven might all have been harmed or even killed were it not for the vigilance of his guard dog.

Jim Forbes, Chaetestown's Chief of Police, had been a loyal member of the coven for almost twenty years. With him refereeing what was sure to be a resounding dialectic, lawyers for both parties would eventually have come to some grudging acknowledgment that serious errors in judgment had led to over-reactions on both sides. It would all have worked brilliantly! He was sure of it! Until this moment. Until he saw Diana standing among them.

She had seen the child on their altar and witnessed an integral part of their ritual. She would have to be silenced, permanently, along with her sister and the man with her. None of them could be allowed to live beyond this night.

John Devane had no illusions about the domino effect that Diana's presence in the clearing had already set in motion. The disappearance of the two Gresham heiresses would be an event of such towering proportions that the Feds would leave no stone unturned in their search of the entire area where they'd last been seen. He was sure to be questioned, since there was a paper trail of their payment for his paintings, and his property would be thoroughly searched.

He wasn't worried about them finding human remains, not after the acid baths and tannery furnace did their usual thorough job. Over time, he'd taken great pains to give the old tannery ovens the appearance of rusted-out antique artifacts that hadn't been fired up in a century. Once cooled, and the unusually cold weather would be his ally tonight, the illusion would be complete, and they were unlikely to be painstakingly swabbed for DNA evidence. At least not immediately.

By the time they got around to it, he planned to be long gone.

But he would hate to abandon the drugs. They were worth millions on the street! He'd hidden them in a side cavern that had the same secure locking mechanism as the altar room, so they were unlikely to be found, but still... He would no longer be able to count on Jim Forbes to cover for him, so no way could he continue supplying his dealers. But... First things first. Luckily, he'd kept the gun they had taken from the guy in the tunnel tonight, and he knew it could never be traced to him. At such close range, he also knew that he couldn't miss.

Reaching into the pocket of his robe, he drew out Charlie's gun, then turned toward Richard for some sign of approval before pulling the trigger. Even injured and half-crazed with pain, Richard Hastings was still supreme warlock of the coven, and Devane was afraid to take it upon himself to kill Diana. He had witnessed the power of Richard's wrath too often not to fear it.

Oblivious to Devane's questioning glance, Hastings motioned for him to retrieve the ceremonial sword from the ground beside the altar. Habit of obedience prompted Devane to do the old warlock's bidding without hesitation. Snatching up the hilt of the sword, he handed it over to Hastings, then watched in fascinated horror as the old man once again raised the athame above the little girl. Blood oozed from the rough bandages on his hands and coursed along his upraised forearms, red rivulets on parchment skin.

"You will not harm the child," shouted Diana, her voice a command, her entire being focused on Hastings and the athame that was still poised over the little girl. Unseen forces suddenly wrested the sword from Richard's trembling hands. The athame, its jeweled hilt sparkling in the candlelight, flew through the air and impaled itself in a carpet of pine needles at Diana's feet.

Diana's eyes were riveted upon Hastings, but she could feel the coven's rising panic. Their warlock was being challenged and bested by a woman of immense power. Still, they had every reason to fear Hastings more than any interloper, and they closed ranks around him at the altar.

Diana instantly felt the subtle shift in the mood of the coven as their panic and fear yielded to anger and aggresssion. Marshalling their communal power, each of them brandishing small daggers, those closest to Diana began moving toward her. She knew she had run out of time.

Throwing back her hood, she shouted, "It's over, Richard!"

"Is that so?" Richard's eyes blazed fire. "Stay where you are!" he ordered the advancing coven. "She's mine, and I alone will deal with her." He glanced at his arms and seemed surprised to see so much blood. "You will pay dearly for this, Lenore, or whatever it is you call yourself now. And yes, it is over. But it's your demise we'll be celebrating tonight, not mine." He laughed. "In case you hadn't noticed, you are singularly outnumbered."

Hastings spread his hands in a stately gesture that embraced his entire coven. His bandages were saturated now, and the theatrical sweep of his arms sent droplets of his own blood splashing upon the altar and the child still sleeping there.

Diana felt Richard's power reaching out to engulf her in seductive waves that stirred the sands of unconscious memory, but selectively so, reminding her of the spiritual intimacy Lenore Mowbray and Richard Hastings had once shared. She saw it all so clearly now: Lenore's crushing loneliness after her grandmother's death, the feeling that no one fully understood her gifts, no one except Richard Hastings. He had cleverly nurtured those gifts and eventually molded them to his own depraved purposes but, along the way, he and Lenore had shared many good times, the wonderful camaraderie of two eminently gifted souls with membership in a very exclusive club.

Hastings was now compelling Diana to remember only those happy times. She knew it, and she recognized it as a deadly ploy, but her fascination with Lenore's life held her captive in the past. How exciting it had been for Lenore to be with an adult who actually encouraged her to do the kinds of things her grandmother had never permitted her to do! Why not make objects fly through the air? Why not cast spells to punish mean people? Wouldn't the world be far better off without them?

A sudden sharp pain just beneath her left collarbone brought Diana abruptly back to the present. When her hand automatically flew to the site of the pain, she smiled. It was the unicorn pin that Beth had given her. She had worn it for good luck tonight, but the catch had evidently slipped open, and the pin was jabbing into her skin. Without ever averting her eyes from Hastings, she slid the miniature golden unicorn from her collar and held it in her hand, comforted by the feel of it.

The warlock laughed even louder than before. "You may have learned a few tricks, old friend, but you're still no match for me. Surely you know that."

He continued baiting her, trying to dilute her concentration with poignant reminiscences from the pages of Lenore's life. And he might have succeeded, had he not made the mistake of boasting about how cleverly he had engineered Lenore's downfall.

"Margaret had put a powerful spell on the unicorn charm she gave you, Lenore. She told you to keep it always about your neck, never removing it for any reason. Remember? You should have listened to her, you know. It just might have saved you. But you were always so headstrong, so eager to show off your telekinetic abilities. All I had to do was hint that the spell on the unicorn had been cast only to sabotage your little flying trick, and you couldn't discard the amulet fast enough. From the moment you took off that little unicorn and handed it over to me, you were mine. I still have a scar from the burn of that amulet when I first touched it, and all these years it's reminded me of the day you became mine. You're still mine, Lenore. Why waste any more time with these foolish games of yours? You know you can't win."

His admitted manipulation of the young Lenore angered Diana beyond all reason, but she fought the impulse to draw the gun from her pocket and obliterate the complacent smirk from his face. She could easily have killed him without fear or compunction, but she knew it would be useless in terms of saving the little girl. She couldn't murder the entire coven, and they were sure to kill her before she could escape with the child.

Diana concentrated all her thoughts upon the altar, forcing herself to ignore the lure of Hastings' voice and the murderous glances of the coven. She focused every fiber of her being upon the little girl.

Almost immediately, the small figure of the child began to rise from the altar and move towards Diana, a marionette being drawn off center stage by a master puppeteer. The coven had witnessed many marvels at Hastings' altar, but they were wonders that only their supreme warlock had been able to perform. Never had they imagined that anyone would ever dare to challenge his supremacy.

Hastings was enraged. He stretched out an arm toward the retreating form of the little girl and drew a circle in the air with a bloody hand. Immediately a ring of fire sprang up about the child.

The coven watched in awed silence, proud smiles lighting a few faces. Ruth Nagle felt as if she had just been reborn, the weight of an enormous burden of guilt lifted from her soul. Her master had outwitted the young usurper, beaten her at her own game, once more vindicating Ruth's decision to follow in his path. Tonight the powers of darkness had confronted the light and won.

Ruth shouted a gleeful chant of triumph that was quickly taken up by the rest of the coven, save one, John Devane. He knew he had no time to lose. The Wendell woman must be killed immediately, with or without Richard's approval. No matter how much of a threat her disappearance might pose, alive she was certain to destroy all of them. Soon Richard would be done with his theatrics. The fire would die down and he would be able to see Diana clearly enough to take aim. He disengaged the safety on Charlie's gun.

The figure of the child was still hovering in the air within the ring of fire. Diana was unable to draw the little girl closer without exposing her to the flames, and Richard Hastings knew it. He laughed yet again, sealing his fate.

"Enjoy your laughter, Richard. It's the last you'll ever know on this good earth." Diana's lips had formed the words, but the voice was that of a much older woman, and the shocked recognition on Hastings' face confirmed what Diana's heart already knew. Margaret's spirit hadn't deserted her after all.

The warlock's jeweled sword was suddenly uprooted from the earth at Diana's feet, an invisible hand guiding its trajectory as it shot through the ring of flame and found its mark in the warlock's breast. He collapsed at the altar, impaled upon his own sword, the ring of fire vanishing with his last breath.

The coven was too much in shock to react when the child first started drifting toward Diana as soundlessly as a leaf borne on the wind. For a moment, Diana was as stunned as the others. The coven thought that she was controlling the movement of the child, but she wasn't. By now, her concentration was shattered, and she could never have managed such a feat on her own. This was Margaret's power at work. Hers and her steadfast protector, the Archangel Michael. There could be no other explanation for what had just happened.

Diana quickly shook off the inertia imposed by her own sense of wonder. Bolting toward the child, she dropped the unicorn pin into a pocket of her robe and raised both hands to snatch the girl out of mid-air. Scarcely breaking stride, she made a headlong dash for the blessed obscurity of the woods. But John Devane had other plans. Using the gun he had taken from Charlie, he fired at her back.

Diana fell, cloaking the child with her own body. She thought she heard Beth calling her name as she lost consciousness, but she couldn't be sure. Other loving voices were calling too, voices she hadn't heard in a very long time.

Devane immediately checked to make certain that his aim had been true. It had been. The woman was dead. The child was alive, but she was still drugged and she would keep until he had dealt with more immediate problems.

Surveying the devastation around him, he quickly began barking orders to the coven. They were in shock, moving like automatons, and they obeyed him without hesitation. He glanced at the bloody altar, and he wanted to laugh at the sight of the pathetic old man who had once struck so much terror into all their hearts.

Martha had fainted beside her dead husband, and the heir apparent, John Devane, wasted no time commandeering the throne. The coven was all his now! And if Martha and her precious son knew what was good for them, they would take very good care of him in the future, very good care indeed.

"Get Richard into the altar room. Fast!" he shouted. "Her too!" Martha's inert form had just begun to stir, and he wanted her out of there before she had a chance to realize that he had seized command.

The only blight on his happiness at that moment concerned Sam. He had put a lot of time and effort into that dog, and he'd hate to have to start training another one at this stage. There had only been enough time to take him back to the tower and bandage his leg, but the dog needed stitches, and if he didn't get them soon, he would probably bleed to death. Maybe he already had.

While Richard and Martha were being carried back into the tunnel, Devane directed the rest of the coven in clearing the altar, dousing it with the strong acidic solution they always used, then covering the altar stone with the usual blanket of moss and branches that regularly camouflaged it. Ordinarily, the coven needed no prompting about any of these routine procedures, but tonight it had been their leader slain at the altar, not an animal or nameless child, and Devane used a firm hand in guiding them through their assigned tasks.

When the altar had been transformed back to its natural woodland state and all their ceremonial gear safely and securely stowed in the tunnel, Devane was able to turn his full attention to Diana and the child. All that remained now was to move them both to the subterranean altar room where they would finish the black mass, the mass that would establish his own supremacy as coven leader. Diana was dead, and her sister, their troublesome friend, and the child soon would be eliminated, just as soon as his mass was celebrated. Acid and the tannery furnace would do the rest.

As for Richard, a disappearing act wouldn't do much good for his son's career, and Devane wasn't about to risk the promising future of an influential politician who would always be in his debt. Far better to gain public sympathy for Billy by having the local coroner certify Richard's cause of death as a heart attack. Dr. Bond's insatiable cocaine habit would insure his cooperation, just as it always had. The Hastings family could issue a statement about wanting a private funeral, and Billy could handle any questions the media might have. Not that he expected many tough questions to be raised. The media loved the guy and tended to ignore anything that might reflect poorly on him with his adoring public.

Satisfied that damage control was well in hand, Devane ordered everyone to the altar room except for Jim Forbes and his cousin Evan, the two strong backs he needed to carry Diana and the child into the tunnel. When he told them to hurry up and get on with it, Evan cringed at the thought of touching the body of a woman who'd shown such magical powers, but his fear of Devane was even greater. With one hand on Diana's shoulder and another on her hip, he rolled her onto her back so that he could reach the child.

Grabbing the little girl under the arms, he struggled to wrench her free from Diana's grasp, but the slender arms locked about the little girl's waist refused to release their charge. It was as if rigor mortis had already set in, but Evan knew it couldn't be that, not so soon. Cold sweat glistened on his brow and he looked fearfully up at his cousin.

Moving in to take charge, Jim knelt at Diana's head, pinned her shoulders to the ground with both hands, then nodded for Evan to pull the child free. Evan repositioned his hands under the child's arms and tugged mightily, until Diana finally yielded up her precious burden. Remembering all that he had seen just a short while ago, Evan couldn't get away from her fast enough. With the child slung over his shoulder, he bolted for the open tunnel door.

Jim retreated a few steps away from Diana's body and watched his cousin's flight with mixed feelings of loathing and envy. Devane's expression reflected pure disgust. "Get her below, Jim. And hurry."

Jim knew he had no choice, but he couldn't help being reluctant to touch Diana again. Devane saw his hesitation and laughed. "Not you too. It's just another corpse, Jim. She sure as hell can't hurt us now." He kicked the side of Diana's head, kicked it hard. The serene little smile on her face might have belonged to a rag doll. "Convinced?"

Jim nodded, his face burning with humiliation as he turned toward Diana's body. Suddenly a shot rang out, pitching Devane backward and hurling him to the ground. Jim had seen enough men die to know that there was no reason to stay. He bolted for the tunnel entrance.

The tunnel door was wide open, so he jumped inside and closed it after him. But before he was able to drive the bolt home to secure the lock, other hands were tugging at the door from the outside with a force that his awkwardly upraised arms couldn't match. He ran down the steps and into the tunnel leading to the altar room, where he knew the coven would be waiting. He had to warn his friends.

The shout of alarm died on Jim's lips as he raced into the altar room and discovered that there was no one there to hear him, no one except a terrified little girl who was just regaining consciousness, eyes wide with horror at the sight of the grotesquely impaled body of the old warlock lying on the ground beside her. Dazed and whimpering, the child sat huddled against the cavern wall, shivering in her nakedness, her pale hair matted with the blood of the witch who had saved her life and the warlock who would have taken it.

Guessing that Evan and the rest of the coven must have heard the shot, panicked, and fled to the tower, Jim would quickly be following their lead. But first he had to seal off the altar room from the tunnel he'd just run through. He had no more than one or two minutes before his pursuers reached him, and it would take about thirty seconds to activate the closing mechanism, another thirty for it to be fully closed, but it was his only hope. Not daring to breathe until almost a minute later when the stone slab moved into lock position, he ran harder than he'd ever run before. Short of blasting powder, there was no way whoever was chasing him would get through that limestone wall, and he needed to warn the rest of the coven so they could all escape.

At a fork in the tunnel, he turned into a short cavern that led directly to the basement of the tannery tower. The door guarding the tower entrance was open. He ran inside and bolted it behind him. Hurrying up the basement stairs, he shouted a loud and urgent warning as he flung open the trap door and leaped into Devane's living room. By the time he realized his mistake, he could only be thankful that New York had abolished the death penalty years ago. The men surrounding him weren't wearing uniforms, but Jim knew they were cops, none he'd ever seen before, but cops just the same.

Sam was dead, lying in a pool of his own blood just inside the front door.

Maybe shot by the cops.

Maybe bled out from his leg wound.

Either way, Jim felt a keen sense of loss.

Not that he'd ever even liked the vicious hound; but, in the end, Sam had been his only friend.

The others must have fled to the four winds to save their own hides as soon as they reached the tower.

Only Sam had stayed the course and waited for the last three men to return.

Two never would.

Jim knew he was looking at some serious jail time.

Too late for him to play the innocent.

All he could do now was request an attorney and keep his mouth shut.

Chapter Twenty-Three

Hearing the second shot, Chad ran even harder, crashing through brambles and vaulting over fallen logs as he sprinted toward the sound of the gunfire. Ears ringing, heart frozen with fear, his mind refused to accept the possible significance of those two bullets. Beth and Diana were all right. They had to be!

The moment he bounded into the clearing, he saw them.

Beth was huddled over Diana, holding her close, rocking slowly, crooning softly. Diana was lying in a pool of blood, and clearly well beyond any help he might have been able to give her. Two men stood nearby, their guns leveled squarely at him, as they hovered over Beth. Another sprawled and bleeding figure lay on the ground beside them. Charlie? Dear God, not him too.

Chad was unarmed, but nothing could have stopped him from trying to reach Beth. He covered the distance between them at a run, only to be trapped in a human vise before he could get to her. Struggling to shake off his captors, he saw the butt end of a gun coming at his head when he heard a small voice scarcely recognizable as Beth's cry out, "Don't hurt him!"

The men instantly obeyed, and the sudden drop in Chad's adrenaline surge left him weak with relief. They were protecting Beth, not menacing her. Thank you, God.

As he moved closer, she glanced up at him, her eyes wide with shock and horror. Bowing her head, she began brushing wisps of pale blond hair away from Diana's forehead, in death, as in life, watching over her little sister.

Shrugging out of his parka, he draped it over Beth's trembling shoulders as he knelt beside her and held her close, angling his body to support hers. "Oh, Beth," he whispered, gently stroking her hair. "I'm so sorry." Several moments passed before her body seemed to relax a little against his, but the doleful crooning continued, and she gave no sign of easing her hold on Diana.

The older of the two armed men guarding her crouched down beside Chad and spoke in an urgent whisper. "Name's Tom Mathison. Dunsford Security. State Police are on their way, but we can't wait here. She's too vulnerable. We've begged her to leave, but she won't. See what you can do."

Glancing around the open clearing and the stand of pines surrounding it, Chad nodded his understanding. There was no way of knowing who might be hiding behind those trees. He tugged gently at Beth's shoulder. "We need to go now, love."

She said nothing, but he felt the muscles in her arms tense as she tightened her grip around

Diana. Grim-faced, he looked up at Mathison and shook his head. It was pretty much what Mathison expected. He and his partner closed ranks and, with Chad, formed a human shield around Beth. With Chad's chest firmly planted against her back, she was as safe as their situation would allow. Mathison called Paul Dunsford with an update on their predicament, while his younger partner played sentry, his eyes constantly strafing the perimeter of the clearing. Mathison had just finished talking with his boss and was relaying Paul's orders to his partner, when the Chaetestown police arrived.

Standing tall, both Dunsford agents faced down the approaching uniformed officers and ignored the order to drop their weapons. "Look, officer," said Mathison, addressing the only one in the group who wore official chevrons on his jacket. "My partner and I don't want any more trouble here tonight. And certainly not with the police." He was speaking quickly, lowering his gun just a fraction, trying to explain his dilemma before they all decided to shoot first and ask questions later. "Problem is we've got orders to keep everybody away from this lady at all costs, at least until the State Police arrive. And we intend to do just that."

The officer hesitated only a fraction of a second before signaling his men to advance.

Mathison quickly began speaking again, louder now, and with a clear sense of urgency. "Jim Forbes, your chief of police, was just arrested for his hand in two murders here tonight, so you'll forgive me if I seem a little paranoid."

Mathison could almost hear the adrenaline coursing through his veins as he aimed the business end of his gun squarely at the lead officer's ample stomach. Dunsford had just told him about the chief's arrest, and Mathison knew that he'd have to be somewhere between foolish and crazy to presume that this man was any cleaner than his boss.

Nothing in Sergeant Maxwell's long years on the force had prepared him for this. Comfortable with command, sure of his own abilities, he had always prided himself on being a good cop. And a good judge of character. Jim Forbes was one of the most honorable men he'd ever known!

Oh, there'd been some nasty talk about him a few years back when he'd put his mother into a fancy nursing home in Albany. Nobody could figure out where he ever got that kind of money. But the chief had explained all that. His mother got left a small fortune when her brother died. That's where the money came from. People were always yelling foul anytime they saw a cop with a buck to spare, but Jim wasn't dirty. He'd stake his life on it. Then again… He took a closer look at the steely-eyed glint in Tom Mathison's eyes and suddenly remembered that he had a wife and family who were expecting him home tonight.

With the mantra of the State Police invoked, and with a semi-automatic pointed squarely at his mid-section, Sergeant Maxwell immediately made the only executive decision possible: he kicked the ball upstairs. Ordering his men to stand down, embarrassed by their collective sigh of relief, he phoned headquarters and asked for the Chief. No way could he be under arrest! The dispatcher was just starting to explain that Forbes seemed to have gone off the grid, when the State Police swarmed into the clearing.

To the sergeant's horror, he and his men were immediately surrounded, disarmed, and herded out of the clearing in the direction of the old tannery tower. Sergeant Maxwell protested, sputtering his indignation at being treated like a common felon, but it was all just so much background noise to the trooper in charge. Lieutenant Jarvis had been given his orders, and he had no reason to question them. Like most cops, he hated the dirty ones.

After verifying the ID's on the men guarding Beth, Jarvis deployed the remainder of his force, ordering three troopers to secure the crime scene and three others to escort everybody else to safety. "There's no way we can get a vehicle in here," he said, addressing Beth directly, "and we've commandeered the tower for questioning, so the only way to get you to safety right now is through the woods leading out to the road. Our people are already there waiting to escort you to a secure location."

Hearing the crisp tone of command, Beth knew that there would be no more reprieves. It was time to say good-bye. Shrugging Chad's jacket off her shoulders, she removed her own jacket as well, rolling it up and easing it under Diana's head as she rested it on the ground close beside her. Adjusting the makeshift pillow with painstaking care, she then bent to kiss her little sister's brow, feeling the soft warmth that was Diana one last time.

Beth offered no resistance when Chad wrapped his jacket around her shoulders once more and gently lifted her to her feet. Leaning heavily against him, his arm encircling her waist, she blindly followed his lead as they stumbled along the trail back to the road, the two Dunsford agents and three state troopers a moving wall of protection around them.

They were halfway between the clearing and the road when Beth's brain suddenly began functioning again. "Charlie! He's still in the tunnel. We have to go back!"

One of the troopers assured her that the State Police were already combing every inch of the tunnels. "They'll find whoever's there, ma'am. You can count on it."

Chad still didn't know who the second body at the clearing was, but he was relieved to know that it clearly hadn't been Charlie.

Now that the awful dam of silence had been breached, Beth suddenly seemed unable to stop talking about the horror of all that had just happened. Chad listened to the fragmented litany of self-blame without interruption, his heart aching for her. If only she had been quicker to reach Diana; if only she hadn't gotten so hopelessly lost in the woods on the way to the crossroads; if only she had never arranged for Diana to meet Ariana in the first place; if only...

Tom Mathison kept assuring her that there was nothing she could have done but gotten herself killed along with Diana if she had gotten there any sooner, but Beth didn't believe him. There must have been something she could have done to save her sister! Still in shock, leaning heavily on Chad's arm, she staggered along toward the lights flashing from the road ahead.

The moment they emerged from the woods, Beth saw Olivia standing beside the nearest police car, and she flew into her aunt's waiting arms. There were no words. None were needed. Olivia already knew what had happened. Paul had come to be with her, to tell her the awful news in person, to hold her in his arms while she cried her heart out for the lost child whose laughter she would never hear again. And Beth's blood-stained clothing had told her the rest.

The two women clung to each other as Paul led them to his car, Chad right behind them, along with a phalanx of troopers. Paul, Jack Lanier, and the State Police had already coordinated transportation arrangements, and they were eager to get Beth and Olivia out of there. The BMW and Porsche would stay right where they were until the police crime scene investigation was completed.

Paul helped Olivia into the rear seat of his car. Beth was about to duck in beside her when she saw Henry approaching, a dazed, solitary figure silhouetted in the glare of headlights, his anguished face wet with tears. Beth went to him immediately, and they embraced, holding fast to one another in their grief. Feeling the tremor in his old bones, she knew that he too had loved Diana. Kissing his weathered cheek, she hugged him even closer, then hurried back to Olivia, leaving Jack Lanier to look after Henry.

With the troopers urging haste, everybody got into their cars. Beth, Olivia and Chad rode with Paul, while Henry rode with Jack Lanier. Flanked by state police cars front and back, the sorrowful cavalcade drove to the Windham lodge where Paul had set up temporary headquarters. He had rented the entire top floor, anticipating that Olivia and Beth would be staying there for the night. He was stunned when they reached the lodge and both women declined the arrangements he had made.

He appealed to Olivia. "I know it's not the kind of luxury you're used to." He waved the back of his hand at the two-story pseudo-Swiss chalet. "But it's clean, comfortable, secure, and there's plenty of room. There's even a doctor waiting to check Beth out."

"I don't need a doctor." Beth's voice was wooden, belying her words. "I just want to go to Diana's."

It was the last thing he had expected her to say. "You can't be serious, Beth." He looked to Olivia for help.

"She couldn't be more serious," answered Olivia. "Nor could I."

Paul had heard that tone often enough to know it was pointless to argue. Lowering his window, he conferred briefly with the trooper who was waiting to escort the two women inside. Moments later, they were all on their way to Diana's.

As they drove away from the small hotel, Beth tucked her arm into Olivia's and drew her a little nearer, comforted to know that they shared the same need to be as close to Diana as they could be right now, to see her room, to touch her belongings, and to breathe in the lingering scent of her before it was gone for good.

They each had a hidden private agenda, as well. Olivia intended to make certain that all was in order at Diana's home before the police started poking around with warrants. She was determined that her baby's obsession with the occult would never become the subject of public ridicule. And Beth needed to read Diana's journal. She had seen her sister writing something in it just before she disappeared from her condo, and she had to see what it was. She knew the journal would be waiting in the bedside table drawer where it was always kept, and she ached to hear the echo of her sister's words, something, anything to keep her close and help her understand what had happened tonight.

Five minutes later, when they arrived at Diana's, the two troopers from the lead car instructed everyone to sit tight until they had completed a thorough search of the house. Paul used his key and code to get them in the front door, then quickly returned to his car. When the troopers waved the all-clear, Paul and Chad escorted Olivia and Beth inside, while Jack Lanier waited in his car with Henry.

Standing at the front door, the older trooper tipped his hat. "We'll be leaving now, ladies, but two of our guys will be right outside watching the house tonight." With solemn nods to both women, he added, "Please accept our deepest condolences for your terrible loss."

Olivia couldn't help but wonder how many times he must have had to make that same sad little speech. "Thank you, officer. You're very kind." He and the other trooper left, closing the door softly behind them, but Olivia immediately opened it again and looked pleadingly at Paul and Chad.

Reading her silent message loud and clear, Paul shrugged unhappily and walked out the door, while Chad turned to Beth, a question in his eyes. When she nodded slowly, her eyes mirroring the plea in Olivia's, he left.

The two men waited until they heard the door being locked and bolted behind them. Paul walked toward his car then, his tall lean frame slightly bowed, his mane of light hair disheveled, dark brown eyes burning from lack of sleep. Chad was just a step behind him.

Catching a glimpse of a bleary-eyed Jack Lanier slumped behind the wheel of his car, Paul remembered that the guy had just pulled a straight double tour of the worst duty imaginable. Henry Woodruff, sitting patiently beside Jack, didn't look as if he'd last much longer either, but right now Jack had to come first.

"Jack here's been up almost forty hours straight, Henry. Why don't you ride with Chad and me so we can make sure you get home safely?" To Jack, he added, "And you, my friend, get on back to the hotel immediately. There's a nice warm bed there with your name on it."

Jack was too tired to argue. "Thanks, boss." He was on his way as soon as he'd helped Henry out of the car and said his good-byes.

Paul pretended not to notice how long it was taking Henry to follow him from Jack's car to his own. He started the engine for Henry's warmth, but he wasn't going anywhere just yet. Leaving Chad to help Henry settle into the front passenger seat of the Mercedes, Paul went to confer with the troopers who had just checked the house. They were both sitting in their car, and nobody was yet stationed at Diana's front door.

"What gives, fellas?" he asked, leaning into the driver's window that was being lowered at his approach. "I thought..."

"Next shift's on its way, Paul." It had been a long night, and they were all well-acquainted by now. The troopers didn't generally like working with PI's, but they had enormous respect for Paul Dunsford. He was a legend in New York law enforcement, the brilliant detective whose career had been destroyed by a rabid press, his experience a cautionary tale at every police academy in the state.

Paul nodded his thanks and returned to his car. Chad was sitting directly behind Henry, and both men already had their seatbelts on, eager to get going. "Their relief should be arriving any minute," Paul said. "We'll take off as soon as they get here."

In just a few minutes, another State Police car arrived. The four troopers conferred briefly, then the first car left, the driver acknowledging Paul with a single nod of his head and a hand motion somewhere between a wave and a salute as they pulled away. When one of the new arrivals took up his station at Diana's front door and the other began making his way to the rear of the house, Paul put his car in gear and drove off.

At a stop sign just a few minutes from Diana's, he stole a sidelong glance at Henry and decided that he'd never before seen any living person look quite that bad. Guessing that he didn't look much better himself, Paul decided to make a suggestion that could be the ideal solution for all of them.

"Henry, my friend, I have a little proposition for you: It's late, and we've all had a hellish time of it. Maybe it's not such a good idea for you to be alone tonight." They were just turning onto Route 23. "We're only a few minutes from the hotel. How about you stay there with us?"

Henry attempted a small smile. "You're most kind, Paul, and I thank you for the offer. But I'm afraid these old bones need the comfort of a familiar bed tonight. Unless it's..."

"No problem. I just thought... Well, if you're sure you won't be wanting company..."

"Quite sure. I've lived alone most of my life, you know. Solitude is an old and welcome friend."

Richard had promised, "As long as we admit to nothing, the Goddess and her Dark Lord will protect us."

Yeah, right.

I've never been a Satanist.

Just went along with all the mumbo-jumbo for my cut of the drug trade.

Devane and I split it fifty-fifty, so I'm already a millionaire many times over.

I should have cut and run while I had the chance.

I got greedy.

At least two witnesses saw me with Devane when he shot the Wendell woman.

So my arrest on accessory charges is a sure thing.

Beyond that, it will all come down to that little kid and forensics.

If she starts remembering things or they find DNA in the tannery furnace, we've all had it.

If the D.A. offers me a deal, I'm taking it.

The coven ran out on me.

I owe them nothing.

Chapter Twenty-Four

Paul and Chad were in silent agreement about seeing Henry safely to his bed before they left his house. The man was so deathly pale that Paul was afraid he could be on the verge of a stroke or coronary. Knowing Henry a little better, at least well enough to know that he was a whole lot tougher than he looked, Chad wasn't so alarmed about his condition. Still, he shared Paul's uneasiness about leaving him alone, especially since Henry had leaned so heavily on his arm when he was getting out of the car.

As they walked into the kitchen, Chad saw a bottle of B&B on the counter and went right to it, while Henry slumped into a chair that Paul had pulled out for him. Grabbing an ancient jelly glass from the drainboard next to the sink, Chad half-filled it with brandy and brought it to Henry. "Drink up, my friend."

Fond memories came to mind as he watched Henry's fingers ease comfortably around the little glass. It was almost identical to those his grandfather had always used, a comforting reminder of grandma's annual jam-making, small, familiar, sturdy glasses easily managed by aging, arthritic hands. As Henry quietly sipped his brandy, lost in his own thoughts, Chad and Paul were both relieved to see some color returning to his face.

Henry suddenly looked up at the other two men and blinked hard, as if he'd just realized that he wasn't alone. "Where are my manners? Join me, please." He tilted his head toward the bottle of B&B that was still on the counter. "It was a gift from Diana," he said, more to himself than anyone else, recalling the day she and Beth had walked through the door with that huge basket of cheer. His eyes misted at the memory of the tentative, apologetic smiles that had won his heart.

Chad took two jelly glasses from several he found in the cabinet above the sink and quickly poured healthy shots for Paul and himself. The moment they each had a glass in hand, Henry raised his in a toast. "To Diana... Godspeed." Chad and Paul echoed the words and touched glasses with Henry, each of them taking a quick gulp of their brandy for an immediate anesthetizing hit.

Letting Henry set the pace, the two younger men sipped quietly at their drinks for several moments until he broke the silence. He began by blaming himself for what had happened to Diana, and they let him talk it out as he clearly needed to do, much as Beth had done a little earlier. If only he'd believed what Lenore had written about Richard Hastings; if only he'd told Beth about the diary as soon as he'd read it; if only he hadn't shown Diana the map; if only... Chad and

Paul listened quietly, each of them murmuring platitudes, grateful when Henry began to tire of browbeating himself.

On a long sigh, he finally said, "I can see you two aren't going anywhere until I'm safely in my bed." He downed the last of his brandy. "So let's be done with it." He stood up, faltering only slightly before he found his balance and almost managed to straighten his spine. "Goodnight. And thank you both."

Chad watched him walk down the long hall to his room, waited five minutes, then followed. He knocked softly at the door. "You decent, Henry?"

"That I am. Come in."

Chad opened the door just enough to satisfy himself that Henry was okay. In the dim light of a small bedside lamp, he saw that the old gentleman was already in bed, fussily arranging a snug pile of yellowed quilts around his long legs.

"Need anything before we go, Henry?"

"No. No thanks, Chad. I'm fine."

Chad knew that he was anything but fine, but he also knew there was nothing more that he or anybody else could do for him right now. "Goodnight, then." He started walking away, then turned back. "Call if you need anything, anything at all. Okay?" Henry nodded absently. Chad was about to leave when he noticed there was no telephone on the bedside table. "I don't see a landline in here, Henry. Do you have a cellphone handy?"

Henry shook his head. "Don't own one. Hate phones. Bad enough when the one in the kitchen rings. Don't need one waking me up in here. Goodnight, my boy."

This wasn't the time for an update on modern technology and how easily ringers could be silenced, but Chad resolved to have that discussion with Henry sometime soon. "Then I'll leave the hotel number by the kitchen phone. Remember, call me if you need anything, anything at all, or even if you just want to talk. Good night, Henry."

Chad couldn't remember when he'd last seen a bedroom without any kind of telephone in it, unless it was in an old movie. Leaving Henry alone tonight was tough enough. Knowing how far he would have to walk to get help in an emergency only made it tougher. No keypad for an alarm system anywhere he could see, museum-quality artwork on the walls, and no way to call for help from his room. Henry's concessions to the current century were clearly few and far between. When he returned to the kitchen, Chad smiled when he saw the hotel number already posted next to the telephone. He and Paul had clearly been on the same wave-length.

"How much do you want to bet that the guy doesn't even own an ATM card?" Paul's voice was raspy with fatigue.

"Sucker bet. No thanks. My grandfather never had one either. He was convinced electronic banking was a communist plot to overthrow our economy."

They locked the door on their way out, and Chad made a mental note to talk with Henry about the flimsy button latch. It offered absolutely no security. Between that and the phone situation, the great old guy was a disaster waiting to happen.

On the way back to their hotel, with the night sky already beginning to fade to a pre-dawn haze, they traded fond memories of their grandparents, each of them finding solace from the unthinkable present in a gentler past.

A bleary-eyed desk clerk greeted them with a quiet nod and sad attempt at a smile when they walked into the lobby. With robotic efficiency, he provided Chad with the essential toiletries he requested. There hadn't been any time to pack before racing to meet Olivia at the heliport, and he literally had nothing with him except his wallet and what he was wearing.

After a dicey ride in a rickety old elevator, the two exhausted men went to their second-floor rooms, just two doors apart. They'd already agreed to meet for breakfast in the hotel restaurant at six o'clock, little more than half an hour away.

Chad scarcely had time to kick off his shoes and loosen his tie before Paul knocked at his door with a care package piled in his arms. "Here you go," he said, handing Chad a clean shirt, sox and boxers, even a pair of jeans. "We're about the same size, so these should do 'til you can get to a store. See you later." Paul waved away Chad's thanks, as he headed back to his room to do some serious damage control.

Both men were so tired that they were on automatic pilot with morning routines, showering, shaving, brushing teeth, combing hair, and longing for coffee that was still about twenty minutes away. The coffee pouches near the pot in each room had seen better days, and neither of them was tempted to try it.

While Chad took care of urgent business on his Droid, Paul worked his iphone. His first call was to Sean Murphy, the agent who had apprehended the Chaetestown chief of police as he tried to escape. Murphy answered immediately, explaining that he was still at the tower where he'd been when Jim Forbes made his grand entrance.

"At least they found the Hobson guy alive in the tunnels. Some kid too."

"What kid?"

"Little girl. Drugged or catatonic, not sure which. They took her right to the hospital. That's about all I know."

"What about Hobson? What kind of shape is he in?"

"A few bruises, and he looks like hell, but he seems okay. They're questioning him now."

"Stay with him, Murph. Soon as he's released, bring him back here. Just make sure the media doesn't get to him first. And see what you can find out about that kid."

Murphy had worked for Paul long enough to know the drill – the boss needed to brief Hobson, as quickly as possible, on just how much he was expected to say about Diana for public consumption.

"Will do, Paul. Might be a while before I can leave here 'though. The troopers haven't taken my formal statement yet."

Paul sighed into the phone, equal parts weariness and exasperation. "Just stick with Hobson and get him here as fast as you can. If they release him before they let you go, call Mathison to pick him up."

Paul broke the connection. There hadn't been any need to remind Murphy to keep him posted as things developed. Like Jack Lanier and Tom Mathison, Sean Murphy was an ex-cop and a complete pro. Sloppy surveillance on the part of a few junior field agents had ended in disaster tonight, but his senior crew had more than earned their stripes protecting Beth and Olivia.

Paul shuddered at the thought of what might have happened if Beth hadn't had the presence of mind to keep in touch with him while she was chasing after Diana. During a critical time frame, she had been his only source of reliable information. The younger agents on his Windham surveillance team had screwed up everything they touched. First, they'd lost Diana. Then they didn't tell him that they'd also lost Beth. Paul would see to it that they never worked security again, not for him or for anyone else. Not much in the way of retribution, and nowhere near what they deserved, but it was all he had. He was no stone-cold killer, so full payback wasn't an option.

Paul checked his watch. In just fifteen minutes, he had to meet Chad downstairs, not much time for what he still had to do. Pulling up one of his contact lists on the iphone, he started calling in some markers. They were high-ranking wheeler-dealers in the press, police, and government, and they all owed the Gresham family enough favors to guarantee that the paparazzi and mud-slingers would be held at bay for a few days. Olivia didn't control any media anchors, but among her impressive roster of friends were many of the people who paid their salaries. Chad's boss, Newsworld publisher Barney Craddock, was close to the top of the list, but Paul saved that call for last, still uncertain about the relative merits of a direct appeal to Chad, as opposed to asking Barney for a favor.

Paul had amassed a thick dossier on Chad when Beth was first hired to work for him at Newsworld, and he knew the guy wasn't for sale. Right now, he also knew that could only be a mixed blessing. While he had no worries about Chad going public with any privileged information he might have acquired because of his relationship with Beth, that same integrity made it unlikely that he would ever agree to muzzle his reporters.

Barney Craddock, on the other hand, had always been an extremely reasonable cog in Olivia's wheel of power brokers. By the time he reached the end of the list, Paul decided to leave Chad out of this one after all. His last call was to Barney's private line and when they were done speaking, Paul wished it had been his first. It would have spared him from cashing in a few big markers. Barney had already heard directly from an aide to Congressman Hastings who had asked that they avoid sensationalizing anything involving the Congressman's father.

According to Barney, he was told that Richard Hastings was suffering from Alzheimer's and the family asked that Newsworld avoid publicizing events associated with his increasingly erratic behavior. Since this wasn't Barney's first rodeo, he heard the threat loud and clear. He damn well better cooperate if Newsworld ever wanted an exclusive interview with the Congressman in the future. Barney had no doubt that every other major publisher had received a call with the same thinly-veiled warning.

After talking with Barney, Paul breathed a little easier. Clearly, the Congressman's party was as eager to keep a lid on things as he was. He'd been hoping for a two-day grace period for Diana's funeral to take place without the added nightmare of a full-blown media circus. Now, it was looking as if that grace period could stretch to several days. Or maybe even longer.

If the fates were kind for a change, events in Chaetestown might just turn out to be another one of those horrific now-you-see-them-now-you-don't scandals that simply disappear when the press ignores them long enough. And there was little incentive for them to dig deep on this one. Satanism was considered a religion, and investigating a religious group of any kind was always a dicey affair. He'd promised Olivia that Diana's death would be avenged without making a public spectacle of her obsession with the occult. And he would keep that promise or die trying.

Paul was only two minutes late for his breakfast date, but Chad had evidently been early. He was already comfortably ensconced at a corner booth, sipping coffee and so mesmerized by his own thoughts that he didn't even see Paul until he slid into the booth opposite him.

Their waitress couldn't remember when she'd had two such attractive men at one table. Patting the overteased blond fluff that billowed about her neck, she sucked in her midriff, hiked her skirt a little higher at the waistband, and scurried right over with a fresh pot of coffee. When she began touting the breakfast special, they both ordered it, not really caring what they ate just as long as the coffee that came with it was hot, strong and plentiful.

When their food arrived, Paul was still bringing Chad on board with the latest developments in Chaetestown. They took a few quick bites in silence, then talked through their western omelets, both men surprised by their own hunger.

"So who called in the State Police?" asked Chad.

"I did. Soon as my guys heard gunfire."

The waitress came by to top off their coffee, depressed when neither of them even glanced at her. As if she needed another reminder that losing her looks to middle age was hell on wheels.

"Everything hit the fan at once," continued Paul when the waitress was safely out of earshot. "At first, after Beth called, we were just scoping the place out looking for some sign of activity. Murph was watching the tower, and Tom and his partner were searching the woods, when that awful first shot was fired." Paul lowered his eyes and shook his head. "They were close, so close, but Diana was already gone when they got there."

Raising his eyes again to look at Chad, Paul's voice choked when he said, "First thing they saw was some bastard actually kicking her in the head. Can you believe that?" He closed his eyes, viciously rubbing at his eyelids with the heels of both hands. Chad easily recognized the gesture for what it was: a man's way of explaining away tears. Not for the first time, he wondered what neolithic idiot had first decreed that it was unmanly to cry.

Opening red-rimmed eyes, Paul waited a few moments before continuing, giving himself a little extra time to get his emotions back under control. "Tom had no way of knowing whether Diana was alive or dead and no time to check, so he shot the guy who'd just hurt her. Pretty much tore his guts out to see her get kicked like that." He took a deep ragged breath. "He'd been on Diana's detail for years. He was pretty fond of her. I don't think he'll ever get over seeing that son of a bitch…"

"So that was the second shot I heard?" asked Chad, eager to help Paul back to less emotional and more factual ground.

Paul nodded. "Tom shot him on the spot, just a split-second before Beth got there. Meanwhile, of course, all hell was breaking loose at Devane's place. Right about the time you found Beth, Murph and his crew saw a bunch of nut jobs in black robes come streaming out the front door of the tower. When they ran off into the woods, leaving the door wide open behind them, Murph went inside for a closer look. He practically fell over some monster dog lying dead on the floor, blood everywhere. Leg wound. Murph said it looked like he must've gashed an artery and bled to death."

"Anybody else in the building?"

"Nope. Murph had his crew search the whole place, top to bottom, but there wasn't another living soul around. That is, not until Chaetestown's illustrious chief of police joined the party." Chad was glad to see something approximating a smile tugging at the corners of Paul's mouth as he continued speaking.

"Now picture this," said Paul, inching his elbows in a little further on the table. "There they were, Murph and his team, just standing around in the living room trying to figure out what the hell to do next, when all of a sudden a trap door in the floor flies open, and up leaps Jim Forbes, the police chief, right into their open arms. Talk about a present." Paul shook his head wonderingly. "Murph held the guy in custody until the troopers arrived. His end of the operation was textbook. Always is."

"Should be. You trained him, didn't you?" Chad liked this man. It was painful to see him being eaten up with guilt.

Paul shrugged. "He got the same training everybody else gets. Unfortunately, not everybody pays as much attention to the routine stuff as he does. Surveillance was a total clusterfuck last night," he sighed. "If only…" Paul stopped in mid-sentence and shook his head. "Listen to me, will you? I'm starting to sound like Henry."

"Beth's having the same problem. Olivia too." Chad signaled the waitress for more coffee.

"Olivia? Why?" Paul knew that she'd had no idea about what Diana was up to until it was too late to matter. How could she possibly be blaming herself?

Chad shrugged, uncertain of what to say. How could Paul not know about the lover's tryst that had kept her incommunicado?

Understanding dawned. "Ah, Jean-Pierre," sighed Paul.

Chad guessed that Dunsford Security must have amassed piles of X-rated reports on Olivia over the years, so he was surprised by the sudden hangdog look in Paul's eyes. His reporter's nose told him that the man sitting opposite him had far more than a professional interest in Olivia Gresham-Lazare. He wondered if she knew it. He wondered if Paul even knew it.

"Actually, Jean-Pierre did us all a favor by keeping Olivia out of harm's way," said Paul dismissively.

Message received, thought Chad. The subject of Olivia's young lover was officially closed. He watched Paul suddenly become manic about tidying up the remaining tableware on his placemat, and decided to rescue him.

"I think you'll like Charlie Hobson," Chad said. Paul had already mentioned that Charlie would be brought to the hotel as soon as the police were done with him. "He's a really good guy."

"Also a real pro -- to my everlasting regret. He kept leaving my surveillance guys in his dust."

The waitress returned to top off their coffee, taking her time as she tried to engage them in small-talk. They obliged, but only half-heartedly. Acknowledging defeat, she dropped their check on the table and removed their soiled plates. Neither of them even noticed her parting sashay back to the kitchen.

"Charlie was crazy about Diana," said Chad, thinking aloud. "My guess is he'll be blaming himself for her death as long as he lives. Another charter member of the infamous 'if only' club. I just hope all of you decide to disband quickly." Chad took a final sip of coffee, then pushed his cup away. His nerves were thrumming with caffeine overload.

"Dream on, Chad." Paul's deep baritone voice caught on the words, descending to a raspy bass.

"Come on, guy. Give yourself a break. That damn coven is responsible for Diana's death. Nobody else."

Paul took a deep breath and sighed it out from the depths of his being. "But a few of my guys made it real easy for those bastards to get to her, didn't they?"

"Maybe. Maybe not. Personally, I don't think it mattered at all that Charlie ditched your surveillance team. Even if your people had managed to stay right behind them every mile of those back roads, I don't see how the end result would have been any different."

"Oh really? Just how much pixie dust did that waitress put in your coffee, my friend. I sure could use some."

Chad rested his forearms on the table and leaned in closer to Paul. "You're so emotionally involved in all this that you're not thinking clearly. Look, once Diana went underground, there was absolutely no stopping her. She was like a juggernaut. And she had to have been through those tunnels before. Beth said that she seemed to know every secret passage and blind alley down there. Beth's a runner, for God's sake, and she couldn't keep up with her. She was right next to her and she couldn't stop her. Charlie couldn't either. Nobody could have."

Seeing a little gleam of hope in the mournful brown eyes boring into his, Chad continued even more earnestly than before. "Look, fire the jerks who screwed up the surveillance. They have it coming, and then some. But don't for a minute think that their failure had any effect on the ultimate outcome of what happened in Chaetestown last night. With or without your people on the scene, Diana would have accomplished precisely what she set out to do."

"Look, I appreciate what you're trying to do, Chad, but you can't know..."

"But I do know! Think about it. Charlie Hobson was good enough to lose your guys, so he knows his stuff, right? You said so yourself. But even he couldn't stop Diana. And he was with her, for God's sake!"

Paul was smiling the saddest smile Chad had ever seen, but there was a glimmer of amusement in his eyes when he said, "I hadn't quite thought of it in those terms, but I see your point. Since my surveillance teams were a bunch of idiots to begin with, their being out of the loop at a critical time couldn't have mattered worth a hill of beans anyway. That is what you're saying, isn't it?"

Chad almost managed a smile. "Sort of. But it sounded a hell of a lot more polite when I said it."

They left the waitress a ten dollar tip and returned to their rooms. Chad immediately called the front desk to arrange for emergency whatever-it-costs laundry and dry cleaning for what he'd been wearing the day before. He left the laundry bag just outside his door, then stripped down to the boxers Paul had given him and collapsed into bed. Thankfully, all the caffeine didn't keep him awake any longer than it took for his head to hit the pillow. He slept until Beth called a few hours later.

"You and Olivia okay?" he asked, instantly alert.

"I guess so." The voice could have been that of a lost and lonely child.

"How about a little company?" She didn't respond. "Just say the word and I'm there."

"I know, Chad. And thanks. But Aunt Liv and I still have some things to sort out. I'll call you again later today. Just didn't want you to worry. Try to get some sleep."

He checked his e-mail and, seeing nothing that couldn't wait, he promptly heeded Beth's advice. When she called again, five hours later, their conversation was almost an exact replay of the one that had preceded it. Completely rested and eager to touch bases with Paul, he dressed in his borrowed shirt and jeans and went down the hall. Paul's door was open, and he was on the phone, but he waved Chad inside and pointed to the bar. One hand over the receiver, he said, "Help yourself. Be with you in a sec'."

Chad was glad to see a bottle of Wild Turkey next to the Dewars and Seagrams. He poured a hefty shot of bourbon into a glass with some ice, then settled himself on the loveseat against the wall. Moments later, Paul was done with his conversation. He freshened his scotch and went to sit in a pink wingback chair opposite the equally lurid pink loveseat.

The largest suite in the lodge happened to be the bridal suite, and Paul had commandeered it for himself. The two men couldn't help but be amused by the tawdrily romantic decor. Paul chuckled as he waved a heart-topped swizzle stick at Chad before stirring his own Dewars and soda.

"Cupid run amok," commented Chad.

"You should see the bedroom," said Paul. "Absolutely incredible." Paul took a quick sip of his drink. "So, did you manage to get some rest?"

"Nothing but. How about you?"

"Caught a shower and shave, plus a few winks on the couch. Thank God for adrenaline. I really don't feel tired. Heard anything from Beth?"

"Two calls. She sounded awful, but she won't let me get near enough to help."

Paul nodded his understanding. "I've been talking with Olivia. Same deal. They've been sparring all day."

"You're kidding? Why?" When Paul didn't immediately respond, Chad turned up the volume on his voice. "Beth didn't sound much up to a fight, Paul. What the hell's going on over there?"

Paul sighed. "They're arguing about how to... how to lay Diana to rest."

"You can't be serious." Chad had always presumed that old money had such rituals down to a science.

Paul fortified himself with a few swigs of his drink before answering. "Seems that Diana left strict instructions that she wanted to be buried like a pauper. Beth's determined to honor those wishes, and Olivia is equally adamant about totally ignoring them."

Chad suspected that a Gresham's version of a 'pauper's funeral' wouldn't quite fit his own definition. "What exactly did Diana want?" he asked.

"Cremation. Her ashes scattered over the grave of some local woman by the name of Margaret Mowbray -- evidently she's buried in Chaetestown. No public funeral of any kind."

Chad was surprised. "And Beth's willing to go along with that?"

"Insisting upon it, as a matter of fact," said Paul. "She and Olivia have been arguing all day."

Chad finished his drink in a gulp and walked toward the door. "I'm going over there to run a little interference. Care to join me?"

"Actually I would, surprisingly enough, glutton for punishment that I am. But I'm waiting for the coroner's report to come in, and I sure as hell wouldn't want to have to take that call while they're around."

They all knew how Diana had died, but because of her terminal illness the Albany D.A.s office had insisted on an autopsy to certify that the actual cause of death was a homicide. Beth and Olivia had protested, but to no avail. It was such a high profile case that the authorities were taking no chances with technicalities that might cause issues with court cases down the line.

Chad was pleased to find that the desk clerk had earned his outrageous tip. Clean laundry and his dry-cleaned suit were waiting in his room when he returned. Jeans just wouldn't do it for the visit he was about to make.

Within half an hour, he was standing on Diana's doorstep, his ID being scrutinized by the state policeman on duty. The trooper was just checking his driver's license photo against the genuine article before him, when Beth opened the front door.

"It's all right officer. Come in, Chad." As they walked into the living room, she explained that she'd heard the taxi pulling into the driveway. "Figured I'd better come out and rescue you. The State Police have been very, very cautious about who they let in here."

The easy flow of her words might have put his mind at ease, if it hadn't been for the deathly pallor of her skin and the emptiness in her eyes. When they entered the living room, she avoided the sofa and sat in the club chair, effectively distancing him. Refusing to be put off, he went to her, crouched down in front of the chair, and took her hands in his. It would sound ridiculous, he knew, but he couldn't think of anything else to say. "Are you okay?"

She laughed, but it could as easily have been a sob. "Just great, Chad. Never better. Diana's gone, and Aunt Liv and I haven't said a civil word to one another all day. Doesn't get much better than that now, does it?" Her voice broke on a torrent of tears, as Chad pulled her into his arms and cradled her head against his chest.

"Cry, love. Go ahead and cry. No one has more of a right." He'd almost lost her. If she'd reached Diana just a few seconds sooner, she wouldn't be in his arms right now. She and her sister would both be dead. He held her even closer, knowing what an arrogant fool he'd been to think he could ever let her go. Swallowing hard, he kissed the silky auburn curls nestled beneath his chin.

Several minutes later, Olivia entered the room. By then, Chad and a much calmer Beth were talking quietly on the sofa, but Beth's swollen eyes and Chad's protective arm around her shoulders told their own tale. Olivia approached Beth and brushed a wayward auburn lock from her forehead. "Why don't you run upstairs and lie down for a bit, love. You've been awake virtually non-stop since you left the city yesterday morning. You need to rest."

"I'm not tired, Aunt Liv."

Olivia sighed. "Sure could have fooled me."

Beth knew her aunt well enough to guess that she was hoping for a chance to speak privately with Chad, probably to enlist his help in persuading her against the funeral arrangements Diana wanted. She also knew that Olivia wouldn't stop contriving little subterfuges until she'd managed to have some time alone with him, so she decided to get it over with and make it easier on all of them.

"Now that I think of it 'though, I do have some 'phone calls to make. Do you mind, Chad? I won't be long. You'll wait, won't you?"

"Of course I will."

He had intended to stay only a brief while, just long enough to help calm the troubled waters between Beth and her aunt, but he wasn't about to leave as long as Beth wanted him to stay.

"I'm glad you came," said Olivia. She settled next to him on the sofa as soon as she heard Beth close her bedroom door. "We've been trying to decide what to do about... about the arrangements.

I'd welcome your advice, my friend." She went on to explain the details of what Paul had already told him.

"Diana's journal is quite explicit about what she wants, Chad. I just can't believe she was in her right mind when she wrote it." She lifted a small cloth-bound book from the end table beside the sofa. "Has Beth shown this to you?"

Chad shook his head, "No. Is it her journal?"

Olivia nodded, and gave him the book. "I've read and re-read her instructions until I just can't bear to read them again, Chad. They're at the end of the journal."

Diana had reserved the last few pages for her final instructions, and several blank pages preceded it. He had no difficulty finding the section Olivia wanted him to read.

'When death comes for me,' Diana had written, *'I'll be ready for it. My earthly house is in order and, as long as I succeed in destroying the coven, my spiritual house will be in order as well.*

'Too many innocents have been sacrificed at that black altar. Not Chaetestown children. No, Richard Hastings has always been too clever for that. The kidnappings usually occur in the cities: Albany, Rochester, Syracuse, even New York. How do I know, Beth? (And yes, I know you'll be the first one to read this, and I can already imagine that little frown line between your brows as you do.) I just know things. Little bits and pieces come to me while I'm meditating. Don't ask me how. I couldn't explain it. It just happens.

'Since you're reading this, I know that I must already have begun the next and most exciting stage of my journey. Whatever happens, know that I love you, Beth, and you my darling Aunt Liv. Please don't mourn for me when I move on. Just be happy and know that we truly will see one another again. I promise."

A detailed list of instructions for her funeral followed, her final wishes itemized with no more emotion than she might have expended in writing a shopping list.

Chad shook his head and handed the little book back to Olivia. "Tough call."

Olivia set the notebook gently on her lap. Her fingers immediately began tracing nervous patterns across its surface. "This morning, when I read those last few pages over the phone to Paul, he was as dumbfounded as I was. Clearly the cancer had ravaged Diana's brain by the time she wrote that... that rubbish. Why can't Beth see that?"

He agreed with Olivia, but he couldn't stop the knee-jerk reaction of defending Beth. "On some level, I suppose she does, but..." He wasn't at all sure where he was going with what he'd started to say, and he was glad to be interrupted by a knock at the door. "I'll get it," he said.   Opening the front door, he saw Paul standing beside the trooper on duty. In answer to the unspoken question in Chad's eyes, Paul said, "The call just came in. Wish me luck, buddy. This ain't gonna be easy."

Chad gave him an encouraging pat on the shoulder as he closed the door. "Olivia's in there," he said, pointing to the living room and gesturing for Paul to lead the way.

"Hello, Liv." Paul bent to kiss her cheek.

She waved him to a seat in the club chair opposite her. "They called?"

Paul nodded soberly. He had hoped to lead into it gently, but he should have known Olivia wouldn't allow him to mince words. "Just ten minutes ago."

"And?"

"Where's Beth?" he asked, ignoring her question.

"Upstairs making some calls. What did they...?"

At that moment, Beth returned. "Heard your car drive up," she said, bending to kiss Paul's cheek. Seeing the rigid lines around his mouth, she knew that he must have received the coroner's report. She moved toward the bar. "How about a drink, Paul? You look like you could use one."

"I think we all could," said Chad, "but I'll take care of it, Beth." He was already standing beside her.

"I'll just get some ice," said Beth, starting in the direction of the kitchen.

Paul intercepted her. Beth was moving like an automaton, and he was afraid she was about to collapse. "I'll get the ice. You just sit down with Olivia and let us handle the drinks."

A few minutes later, when they each had a drink in hand, brandy for Beth, bourbon for Chad, and scotch for Paul and Olivia, all eyes turned to Paul.

"Oh, before I forget," he said, "you should all know about a statement just issued by Congressman Hastings." He was trying to give them a few minutes to get some alcohol into their systems before he broached the coroner's report. "It was kind of an amorphous mea culpa on behalf of his father who supposedly had been suffering from Alzheimer's and behaving erratically for years. Probably a big lie, but guaranteed to tug at voters' heartstrings. I only mention it now because of the way the party bigwigs are likely to spin what happened in Chaetestown. They're moving mountains to hush things up, so at least we won't have to worry about any inflammatory publicity from that quarter."

Before he could think of another delaying tactic, Olivia spoke up. "Enough! Not another word about that evil man until you can tell me that his entire coven has been obliterated from the face of this earth. Now stop stalling!"

Paul took a deep breath and sighed it out as he looked first at Beth, then focused on Olivia. "Cause of death was no surprise, Liv. As we all know, it was a bullet." He wasn't about to tell them that the bullet had been fired from Charlie Hobson's gun. "What might be of some small comfort to you though, is the medical examiner's certainty that death was instantaneous."

Paul chose not to add that the bullet had entered her back and lodged in her heart. He also said nothing about the injury to the side of her head from the kick that bastard gave her, an image that would haunt Tom Mathison for the rest of his life. He took another quick sip of his drink. "I know this will sound odd, ladies, but I'm afraid I need a little clarification here about Diana's illness. Was there ever any question about how sick she was?"

"Clarification? You've got to be kidding. She was dying of inoperable brain cancer," said Beth, amazed at how easily the awful words came to her lips. Now that Diana was gone, she was able to call the beast by its name. "But you knew that. We all did."

Paul leveled his gaze at her, a wealth of compassion in his soft brown eyes. "Thing is…" He cleared his throat. "The autopsy showed no sign of cancer anywhere in your sister's body, Beth. The coroner's report indicated no pathology whatsoever."

"You mean it was in remission?" asked Olivia.

"No. I mean that there was positively no evidence that it had ever existed at all."

"But that's impossible! Her diagnosis was confirmed by the best doctors on two continents! You saw their reports yourself, Paul!" Olivia's voice was shrill with anger, confusion, and fear. "Just because some jerkwater…"

"The Chaetestown jurisdiction was totally bypassed, Liv, for all the obvious reasons. This was the Albany coroner's finding, and he had all the lab work triple-checked. Either a dozen different doctors and technicians on two continents screwed up royally on diagnosis and pathology, or she was suddenly and miraculously cured. Take your pick."

Poor me, the clueless weepy widow who had no idea where her husband was on that awful night.

I invented a sad story about Richard suffering from Alzheimer's, cultivating friendships with odd people like Devane, and generally behaving in ways that had lately grown increasingly secretive and bizarre.

And the police believe me. Why wouldn't they? We all know that Alzheimer's plays no favorites.

My son has found me an excellent lawyer who is confident that I won't be charged with any crime. My feigned stupidity is thankfully not a felony.

Jim Forbes is still a wild card. I know he'd love to see us all suffer for running out on him.

But he's a smart guy. He knows that if he takes us down, he goes down even harder. So we should be okay.

We all continue to honor the oath of silence that we swore to Richard.

Hecate and her Dark Lord have not failed us. Forensics has turned up nothing. And the child seems to have lost both memory and speech.

For now, our strategy is really quite simple.

I will continue to play the innocent grieving widow.

And the Dark Lord will protect his Chosen One, my son William.

Barring new forensic evidence, we should be home free.

In due time, the coven will be reorganized.

We will meet again.

And I will rule as Hecate's High Priestess.

So mote it be.

Chapter
Twenty-Five

"It was a beautiful service, Livvy." Olivia couldn't even remember the woman's name, but she instinctively accepted the proffered hug. "If there's anything you need, anything at all, please don't hesitate to ask."

Olivia murmured her thanks, then edged a little closer to Beth when she saw who was next in line. Marianne Dupres was an old schoolmate of Diana's, but Olivia could feel no gratitude for her condolence call. Under the guise of friendship, Marianne had been jealously trying to sabotage Diana's happiness for years, and she despised the woman.

Knowing how her aunt felt, but unable to keep Marianne away from her without creating a scene, Beth immediately looked to Chad for deliverance. He was standing just a few feet away, speaking with Jack Lanier while they both kept watchful eyes on Beth and Olivia. The advantage of his height gave Chad an unobstructed view of the two women and the group of mourners clustered about them in the living room of Olivia's Manhattan townhouse. Beth had only to glance in his direction, and he was at her side in an instant.

Marianne was in the midst of a poignantly fictitious reminiscence of her last encounter with Diana in St. Moritz when Chad approached. He had seen Olivia cringe when she first saw the woman advancing toward her, and he had no doubt about the reason for Beth's distress signal.

"Pardon the interruption," he said, a hand already at Olivia's elbow. "There's someone waiting to speak with you in the library, Olivia."

Marianne devoured Chad with her eyes as Olivia made her excuses and took his arm. He led her across the room to the library, neither of them saying a word until they had made good their escape. As he closed the door behind them, Olivia saw that they were alone, and she smiled her gratitude.

"Beth thought you could use a little break," he explained. "Hope you don't mind the subterfuge."

Olivia kissed his cheek. She didn't need to ask how he and Beth had communicated. Over the past few days, she'd often observed them exchanging silent messages, keeping in intimate contact, even in a crowd.

"Bless you, my friend," she sighed. She crumpled into a corner of the sofa, leaned back against the soft white leather, and closed her eyes. Chad quietly eased himself into a comfortable position beside her, within easy reach if she needed a broad shoulder to cry on, but not so close as to intrude on her grief.

The autopsy results and the bizarre circumstances surrounding Diana's death had finally convinced Olivia to go along with the pauper's funeral her niece wanted. Even she couldn't deny that supernatural forces had been at work the night Diana was killed. And she was just superstitious enough to be genuinely afraid to defy her niece's last wishes.

Chad would never forget the sight of Beth sprinkling Diana's ashes over Margaret Mowbray's grave at first light of dawn that morning. Apart from himself and Olivia, the only others present to witness the quiet dignity of the little ceremony had been Paul Dunsford, Henry Woodruff, Charlie Hobson, and one of Charlie's cousins who happened to be a clergyman.

Recalling the rapid-fire events that followed after they hurried away from the Chaetestown cemetery, Chad shook his head in silent awe of the woman resting beside him now. He'd been there to see all of it, but he still couldn't comprehend the level of sheer chutzpah Olivia had displayed throughout the day.

With Beth still reeling from the horror of her sister's murder, Olivia had immediately activated her own agenda for a private memorial service at the family mausoleum near Hyde Park, followed by a funeral luncheon at her Manhattan townhouse. Yesterday she'd given Paul explicit instructions for the execution of her plan, and he had spent yet another long and sleepless night arranging every detail to her satisfaction. Olivia refused to allow her baby to pass unheralded from this earth. She had Paul leak the inurnment time and place to the press, and she instructed her secretary at Gresham Enterprises to email invites to the funeral luncheon to her Manhattan "A" list. Unfortunately, that included a few busybody socialites like Marianne Dupree.

Paul had arranged helicopter transport down the mountain from Windham to a private helipad just outside Hyde Park. From there, a stretch limousine took Olivia, Beth, Chad and himself to the cemetery that housed the imposing Gresham mausoleum. Henry and Charlie had both declined Olivia's invitation to go with them to Hyde Park and Manhattan. As Henry gently explained to her, they'd already said their final goodbyes at the Chaetestown gravesite. What he didn't say was that they planned on spending the afternoon drowning their sorrows at Charlie's favorite Windham watering hole.

Olivia was gratified to see a sizable group of mourners, reporters and photographers waiting for them when they pulled up alongside the family mausoleum. Beth's arguments against the awful charade had been useless, and she'd finally agreed to go along with it only because her failure to put in an appearance would have incited the scandal-mongers into a feeding frenzy at Diana's expense. She had stood tall, straight and serene beside Chad as the photographers made the most of their photo-ops, but Chad knew she had to be screaming inside as she watched a tearful Olivia carry a beautifully carved urn into the family crypt. Only those who had been present for the little ceremony at Margaret Mowbray's grave that morning knew what that urn actually contained. There were no ashes inside. There was only a little unicorn pin nestled in the folds of Diana's favorite Hermes scarf.

Paul Dunsford continued to manipulate the press like a skilled concertmaster. Along with the information about where the memorial service would be held, he'd leaked a few details about Diana's terminal illness, and the media had drawn the logical conclusion about her untimely death.

Later on, if some enterprising reporter started sniffing at the edges of the true story, Paul had another well-placed leak ready to emerge from his media bag of tricks. This one would reveal that Diana had been helping her sister research an article about missing children, when she stumbled upon a black mass in progress and had been killed while saving the child who was about to be sacrificed. Police forensics and hospital records supported that version of events, since it was well-documented that Diana's blood had been found on the little girl's back when she was admitted to the hospital. Any reporter would be hard pressed to challenge Paul's version of the truth, especially when Beth's article showed up in Newsworld's next edition.

Olivia was determined to keep Diana's mad obsession with the occult a private affair, but no way was she going to allow that coven to survive. She'd already instructed Paul to organize a team for the sole purpose of destroying the whole monstrous group. She left it entirely up to him to decide how that could best be done without alerting the media or breaking the law, but she vowed that her baby's murder would not go unavenged.

Just yesterday, Paul had assigned Tom Mathieson to get the job done, and his team was already in place. Immediately on board were Sean Murphy and Jack Lanier whose investigative skill levels were as top-notch as Mathieson's. He also asked Henry Woodruff and Charlie Hobson to join them, knowing that their wealth of local knowledge and regional contacts would be invaluable assets. They each jumped at the opportunity to bring Diana's killers to justice. Mathieson had no illusions about how long it would take his team to get the job done, but he promised Paul that the murdering coven would be obliterated.

Through Charlie, Mathieson was able to round out the team with a bright young attorney, Amanda Ellis. She was Charlie's niece, and she came through Paul's overnight vetting process with flying colors. They would be relying on her sharp legal mind to keep them all out of jail. Because of possible liability issues, Olivia couldn't allow anyone from the long list of Gresham corporate attorneys to be involved at all in what Mathieson was doing. She chaired the board of directors and, as much as she wanted to pull out all the stops and wreak swift and sure vengeance on the coven, she had no choice but to protect the conglomerate that generations of her family had worked so hard to create.

Watching Olivia, presuming she had just dozed off from sheer exhaustion, Chad's thoughts were inevitably drawn back to Beth. He knew he had to stop kidding himself about their relationship. He was hopelessly in love with her, and those feelings weren't going anywhere. Proof positive, if he'd needed it, was the fact that he'd had no compunction whatsoever about withholding information from his Newsworld staff in order to protect her and her family. For him, it was an inconceivable breach of ethics, but he hadn't even had to think twice about it.

His pride would just have to take a hike. He never thought much of pre-Nups, but he would ask his attorney to draw one up that deprived him of any claim to Beth's money. Odd as his request might strike any sane person, he would push hard for it. He needed to be very sure she understood how much he loved her in spite of her money, not because of it. His pride may have left the building, but it was still demanding to be remembered with respect.

Olivia's soft voice startled him. "Do you think we fooled them?" Her eyes were still resolutely shut, and he saw a small tear meander its way over the high ridge of her cheekbone.

"Sure looks that way. The tabloids didn't stand a chance, not with Paul around." Now that he didn't have to worry about disturbing her, he sat forward on the sofa, stretched his spine, and rested his elbows on his knees. "Where is he, by the way?" Chad remembered seeing him when they first arrived at the townhouse, but not since.

"I sent him home to sleep."

"Glad to hear it, but I'm surprised he agreed to go." Paul had told him he wasn't leaving until the last guest was out the door. "How'd you persuade him?"

"I didn't persuade him so much as embarrass him, Chad. I actually found him passed out right here on this couch. When I reminded him about all the undercover people he had on duty here this afternoon, he left without too much fuss. Poor love. I'm worried sick about him. I just don't know that he'll ever stop blaming himself for... for what happened."

"Give it time, Olivia. He'll be okay."

Chad wished he could believe his own reassurances, but he doubted that those who'd loved Diana would ever stop feeling somehow responsible for her death: Paul for the failure of those he had hired to protect her, Henry for ignoring her warnings about Richard Hastings, Charlie for outmaneuvering Paul's surveillance team, Beth for bringing Ariana into her life, and Olivia for being so involved with her young lover that she'd given very little thought to Beth or Diana while he was with her. Those who really were responsible, the entire Chaetestown coven, had left Diana's family and friends a legacy of guilt and horror that would probably plague them for as long as they lived.

"You know..." Olivia's voice was scarcely more than a whisper. "In my head I know that nobody could have kept Diana away from that coven once she'd made up her mind to confront Hastings. Nobody. Not me. Not Beth. Not Paul. Not anybody." She blinked back her tears. "Problem is, there's this great yawning gap between my heart and my head right now, and I'm not quite sure how to deal with it."

"You'll find a way. Just be a little patient with yourself, Liv." In spite of all the added grief she'd given Beth over the past few days, he couldn't help but like her and admire her spunk. He stood and bent to kiss her cheek. "You're quite a lady, you know."

At that, she smiled. "There are those who might disagree," she said, the merest hint of a twinkle amidst the tears. "But I thank you for the compliment, kind sir. It's one I don't often hear." She reached into her pocket for a handkerchief and dabbed at her eyes.

"Shall we go rescue, Beth?" Chad held out a hand to her.

Olivia nodded, then placed her hand in his. She was too tired to be embarrassed about how heavily she had to lean on his support in getting to her feet. The couch was comfortable, but its leather cushions tended to be possessive, and right now she simply didn't have the strength to battle them alone.

Dusting off an imaginary speck of lint from the flawlessly immaculate skirt of her black silk suit, she glanced up at him. "The truth, please: Am I presentable enough to go back out there?"

"You look fine. Just fine." He smiled down at her and gave an encouraging nod as he walked the few steps to the door and opened it. She patted his forearm and took a deep breath as she stood beside him in the open doorway for a few moments while she put on her game face.

Dear Chad, she thought, the only blameless character in the cast of villains she'd been drawing up in her half-crazed mind since that awful night. She'd grown very fond of him, and she knew she couldn't wish for a kinder, more compassionate friend. Beth had chosen well.

Most of the mourners had gone by the time they returned to the living room, except for Paul's staff and the inevitable few hangers-on who seemed in no hurry to leave. Clustered near Beth and clucking their sympathy, they were comfortably sipping their drinks and munching on canapes, showing no sign at all of intending to go home anytime soon. Olivia wasn't up to facing all of them just yet, so she waved Chad ahead. He needed no prompting. Leaving Olivia at the library door, he hurried to Beth's side.

"You look exhausted, Beth." He ran a gentle hand along her back and glanced pointedly at those surrounding her. "She needs to rest, folks." It was rude, of course, and he knew it, but he didn't care. They were the supposedly well-bred "A" list socialites, and they should have had sense enough to leave by now.

Olivia edged a little closer to the living room and ducked behind a leafy ficus so she could watch the scene unobserved. What she saw made her want to laugh for the first time in days. Chad gave Beth a quick hug before moving to the front door and opening it wide, his eyes strafing the visitors who had too long overstayed their welcome. Olivia's blue-nosed acquaintances finally got the message. Heads held high, noses in the air, they bade stiff little good-byes to Beth and shot daggers at Chad as they walked out. Totally unperturbed, Chad stood quietly at the door, resolutely holding it ajar until the last of the stragglers had gone, followed closely by the four women and three men who worked for Paul.

Olivia shamelessly continued to watch as Chad closed the door and turned to Beth, enfolding her in his arms, holding her close to his heart. The sight of them together breathed renewed life into the darkest reaches of her soul. She blew them a silent kiss, then tiptoed upstairs to use the telephone in her room. Hopefully, Paul wouldn't mind too much if her call awakened him. She was amazed to realize that she was suddenly thinking about him in ways that she'd never before even imagined.

- THE END -

Printed in the United States
by Baker & Taylor Publisher Services